A.D.
ANNO DOMINI

KIRK
MITCHELL

BERKLEY BOOKS, NEW YORK

A.D.
ANNO DOMINI

A Berkley Book/published by arrangement with
International Film Productions, Inc. and
Procter & Gamble Productions, Inc.

PRINTING HISTORY
Berkley edition/March 1985

ISBN: 0-425-07782-9

Book One

"THE LIGHT"

I

How the hooded figure intruded on their company, the two men could not later agree.

Cleopas believed that one instant they had been two and the next they were three, the sudden presence dropped down between them like lightning. Before, the air had been completely still; sparrows huddled in the ruts of the road to Emmaus, unwilling to take to the sky.

Zachaeus insisted that they had been gazing back at Jerusalem. The crosses on the hillock called Golgotha were being dismantled by Roman soldiers, and the remaining uprights were throwing long shadows that made the golden walls look as if they had been raked by claws. Then a breeze rattled the fronds of a nearby palm, and Zachaeus turned at the approach of footsteps. The stranger had come to them with a crown of clouds piled up behind his head.

Both men agreed about one thing: the light that had attended his features. It was like the glinting of the sun on the sea— not quite blinding, but always seeming to shimmer precisely where the eye tried to focus.

"What is this misfortune that you have been discussing among yourselves?" the figure had asked.

"Are you the only pilgrim to Jerusalem who doesn't know what things have happened there?" Cleopas looked dumbfounded.

"What things?"

"Concerning Jesus of Nazareth—the prophet. The High Priest Caiaphas and the Sanhedrin delivered him up to the Romans for crucifixion. We'd hoped this Nazarene would be the one to redeem Israel—"

"But that was three days ago," Zachaeus interrupted. "Since then, amazing things have happened. Some women went to his tomb early in the morning—and did not find his body.

They said they were visited by glowing creatures who told them he was alive. Our friends then hurried to the tomb and found it just as the women had said. But he was not there."

The clouds began pressing low on the countryside. Swatches of mist scudded through the olive groves and across the fields. The day had grown dim, but the light had not left the stranger's face. "My foolish men," he sighed, his breath visible—not unlike the scurrying fog. "So slow of heart to believe all that the prophets have spoken. This was foretold. You praise the scriptures but are heedless of them. Listen to what was prophesied . . ."

And then, with evening coming in waves of cool vapor, the stranger recited to them every promise for deliverance made to man. Cleopas and Zachaeus traded uncertain glances behind his back. Later, they would confess to each other that, during this hour of plodding along the road, they had shared the same peculiar sensation: Their hearts felt as if they had been chafed by some gentle fire and were dispatching warmth to the tips of their fingers and toes.

The stranger fell silent for several minutes, then asked, "Why are you going to Emmaus?"

"We were told some of the twelve are in hiding there," Cleopas said.

"And you seek the comfort of their companionship?"

"Yes."

A stripe of sunset was showing rose-colored between the overcast and the hills in the west as the three approached the inn. Slapping the dust out of his robe, Cleopas said, "This day is spent."

"Indeed." Zachaeus turned to the stranger: "Will you stay the night here with us? We find peace in the things you say."

The hood dipped once, then the figure strode toward an open door from which amber light spilled out across the flagstones.

Cleopas' eyes glistened in the guttering flame of the lamp when bread, olives, fish and wine were set on the table by a servant girl, who then brought out a basin in which the two men washed their hands. The stranger declined the bowl, and the girl turned to withdraw—but was so distracted by a glimpse of his face that she overturned a cup of wine. "Forgive me."

"It is no matter."

Cleopas looked into the spilled wine for the reflection of the stranger's features. There was none.

"It was the Lord's plan to fill him with grief," the figure said quietly. "But he will live again and make many to be counted righteous before the Lord, for he will bear away their sins." He reached out for the loaf of bread. "Do you see how all that has happened was announced long ago by Isaiah, Ezekiel, Daniel, Hosea, Micah and Zechariah? It will soon become apparent that this is the new beginning. So trust the Lord's word. *Believe*."

Cleopas' eyes narrowed. "But there's nothing in the scriptures to tell us how to deal with the Emperor Tiberius. What are we to do against the might of Rome? Not even the Nazarene could stand up to it."

"Well, I think it's finished," Zachaeus said bitterly, pouring himself a cup of wine.

The stranger raised the loaf off the table and prayed: "Blessed art Thou, O Lord our God, Ruler of the Universe, who brings forth bread from the earth."

A small gasp escaped Cleopas.

Zachaeus followed his friend's stare to the yet poised hands of the stranger. They had been wounded in a singular way: pierced through the backside to the center of the wrist. Cleopas had collapsed to his knees, and Zachaeus now did the same.

"The eleven men you seek are yet in Jerusalem," the stranger said. "Go now and you will find them. Tell them what you have seen—and that soon I will stand among them. Tell them that I will not leave the world desolate. All of you will abide in my love."

"You have risen indeed!" Zachaeus blurted.

"Yes, I have risen."

And then he vanished from their sight.

II

CALEB had set out from Jerusalem alone.

He felt that his solitary campaign against Caesar's forces made it safer for his mother and two sisters, although the foremost Zealots in Judea had repeatedly invited him to join his arms to theirs. He declined with good reason: The families of these well-known rebels invariably wound up in cells of the Fortress of Antonia, the Roman citadel that had grown on the wall of the Temple like a canker. One day, the Antonia would be reduced to rubble and the Jews would be one nation, free of the likes of Pontius Pilate—these were his dreams.

Caleb took the hill at a run, the limestone ground passing before his eyes in a blur. The first grass had already been beaten back by the hot spring sun; but a new growth, triggered by the tempestuous rains of a month ago, blazed green among the stones. It was a good afternoon for an ambush; plans were already filling his head.

He had stripped down to his loincloth and carried his linen mantle in his hand. Concealed inside the folds of the cloth was an object he wanted no one to see until he was ready to use it.

Reaching the crest of the hill, he hunkered over with his hands braced against his knees. He surveyed the country laid out before him. In the far distance, a road ran down a ridge. Nearer, a tan smudge showed against the blue-gray of the mountains. Caleb smiled: This was the dust kicked up by massed *caligae*, the ponderous, boot-like sandal worn by Roman legionaries. It had been a long march from Syria, and the soldiers were no longer snappily picking up their feet as they approached Jerusalem. Tired men made excellent victims.

Caleb checked over his bare shoulder. From this vantage, he could espy the roof of the Temple of Herod, but the towers of the Fortress of Antonia were not visible. This reassured him that his flight following the attack could not be observed by any sharp praetorian eyes posted on the uppermost battlements. These elite troops of the Emperor's own guard had been loaned to the procurator for any special needs the governor might have—such as keeping watch on the activities inside the court-yards of the Temple.

Taking his sling from his mantle, Caleb began hunting for a pebble. He would not waste one of his smooth stones with a hole bored in its center. These he reserved for the Romans. These would taste blood.

Satisfied with a small rock, he fitted it against the looped thong. His eyes glided across the arid woodland and eventually settled on a gall dangling off the limb of an oak. Twirling the sling, the muscles of his right arm taking definition from the strain, he let fly the missile with a snap of his wrist. It sang through the air, and the gall splattered into shards of pith.

He now felt prepared to take on Tiberius' legions.

Favoring the ravines and clumps of wild olive, he worked his way down to the brink of a pallisade that overlooked the road, then hid himself. The descending sun was warm on his back—but it would blind the eyes of the legionaries who would be desperate for a glimpse of their assailant.

A breath snagged in his throat: A red flag had shown briefly at a bend in the road before vanishing again.

Caleb laid out his special stones.

Within minutes, he could see the standard-bearer hoisting a *vexillum* that proclaimed his to be the Seventh Cohort of the Twelfth Legion. It was audacious of the Romans not to have yet covered their idolatrous eagle this close to the city, for Pilate had made such an agreement with Jerusalem's Sanhedrin, the supreme Jewish council. Behind the crimson banner marched six infantry centuries of eighty to one hundred men each. Caleb could see no cavalry contingent, which had been his biggest worry. A few of the high-ranking officers were mounted, but he would wait for them to pass out of sight. He had no intention of being chased down like a brown bear and nailed to the ground by a dozen lances.

Cradling his chin between his knees, he studied the faces in the column. These soldiers had good reason to look ex-hausted. Each man had lugged from his garrison in Antioch a spade, an ax, a coil of rope and a half bushel of wheat. Then there were his javelin, short sword, cuirass, shield and brass helmet. As Caleb had hoped, the legionaries had taken comfort over caution and slung their helmets across their breastplates for the extended march. Their heads were naked.

"As you steadied David's hand . . ." Caleb whispered. Then he stood up and whirled the sling around his ears. The stone whistled down into the midst of the century forming the rear guard. A soldier pitched backward, his armor clattering as he hit the paving stones. His comrades huddled around him, gaping stupidly at the smear of blood in his hair until a centurion bawled, "Raise your shields, you fools! Hold them athwart that hillside there!"

Caleb's next shot thudded against the stiffened leather of the centurion's shield. The officer squinted around its edge to scan the heights. When a few of his men flung their *pili*, seemingly at the sun, he shouted, "What in the name of Mars are you hurling at?!"

No legionary had an answer.

Caleb sifted back through the stunted olive trees and began running, his strides long but not panicky. He leaped over clumps of rock and wind-torn branches with grace until he had put a Roman mile between the road and himself, then he wriggled into a copse of briar and waited. Perhaps fearing further treachery, the legionaries did not pursue him; their commander was not about to be lured into a fiercer ambush.

At nightfall, Caleb reentered Jerusalem screened by a throng of pilgrims from Samaria. He got past the Syrian auxiliaries manning the Garden Gate without being challenged. Heretofore, the procurator had considered these inferior troops sufficient to cow the people of Judea. This assessment had evidently changed, and it was a compliment to the effectiveness of the Zealots that Pilate had been compelled to call in a cohort from the Twelfth Legion. Caleb smiled to himself as he hurried up the lanes that were not torchlit, proud that he had been the Jew to welcome the soldiers of Roman blood to the Golden City.

He knocked on a stout cedar door, and an old woman answered. "Ah, Caleb." She patted his head as if he were still a boy and turned toward a flight of stairs. "Samuel?"

"What is it?" a tense voice asked from the loft.

"Your brother-in-law-to—be arrives!"

"You mean Caleb?"

"Who else?" She smiled back at the young man. "Go to him. He's terribly nervous."

Caleb bolted up the steps three at a time.

Samuel met him at the top. "What would your sister think if we were late? Where have you been?"

Caleb became aware of his mantle: It was sweat-soaked and flecked with burrs. "I've been out in the hills . . . running. There is news."

Samuel's eyes darted toward his mother. "Come inside." He shut the door and motioned for Caleb to step closer to the wan flame of the oil lamp. "Tell me everything."

"I attacked them."

"How many were there?"

"Nearly six hundred—the Seventh Cohort of the Twelfth Legion."

"The *Thundering* Twelfth—they're the right fist of the Syrian proconsul." Samuel frowned. "So it's true. Pontius Pilate has been reinforced."

"Why the sour face? It means only that we have been doing our job." Caleb noticed the betrothal gifts Samuel had arrayed on his sleeping pallet: a sash, veil and two silver hair combs.

"Do you think Ruth will like them?" Samuel asked.

Caleb nodded absently. "Nice . . ."

"The handles of the combs were inlaid with onyx cameos of Roman goddesses. I pried them out at the shop and replaced them with these disks of gray-banded agate."

"Yes, it reminds me of a *tallith*," Caleb said, likening the bands to the stripes woven into a prayer shawl. "Where is the ring?"

Samuel was dumbfounded for a moment. "I almost forgot!" Then he rushed to the wall and used his knife to fish a thin gold ring out of a crack in the plaster. He inspected the workmanship, then grinned. "My first. I mean, my uncle gave suggestions, but my hands did the labor."

"You will make a fine goldsmith."

There was brash knocking downstairs, not one or two raps on the outer door, but a flurry of them as if a squad of legionaries was demanding entry.

The two young men crept down the steps. Samuel wiped his hands on his mantle and approached the peephole. Sliding the iron cover aside, he peered out onto the lane. A spot of torchlight danced on his cheek. Then he sighed. "What company for a man on the night of his betrothal!"

"Who is it?" Caleb whispered.

"Most everyone from *Rabban* Gamaliel's school." Turning back toward Caleb, Samuel hiked a nostril at him. "You're a sight—wash, quickly. I've hung your fresh things on the rafter."

Caleb bounded up the steps as Samuel threw open the door and was greeted by a cacophony of cymbals, flute, harp, drum—and, above it all, the excited voices of young men.

In his friend's room, Caleb splashed his face with water from a basin and, with a faint smile, listened to the teasing Samuel was enduring below. He donned the garments he had brought here from his own house earlier in the day as part of the precautions he took to keep his family from discovering how he spent these absences from them. Sometimes—quite evilly, he realized, he wished that he had no ties. Then he could loose his vengeance on Rome with sweet abandon.

"Caleb!" Samuel cried from the growing tumult. "You keep us!"

"He stalls, hoping a better brother-in-law will come along!" a wag said.

Caleb rushed down the stairs. "I could have none better than Samuel."

Most of the youths chortled, but one lithe young man could not prevent his eyes from glistening. "Well said, Caleb," he blurted with a slight Alexandrian accent, pleased by the show of affection.

"Thank you, Stephen. And now, my younger sister waits . . ."

Music reverberated in the room again. Under the happy gaze of Samuel's mother, the revelers filed out the threshold into the darkened streets of Jerusalem, calling for others to join them.

By the time the procession wound into the courtyard of his house, Caleb was feeling in such high and mischievous spirits he decided to give his sisters a fright. Slipping away from the rest of the company, he scaled the twisted trunk of a grapevine his great-grandfather had planted. Muscling up onto the flat roof of the first story, Caleb sneaked across the shadows to a window that, like most in Jerusalem, lacked glazing. He could glimpse his mother inside Ruth's bedchamber: The old woman was using the backs of her frail hands to carry the betrothal gown. This, as she had explained to the household a hundred times, was so that the more abundant oils of the palms and fingertips would not stain the pure linen. Smiling, she fluffed the dress over Ruth's pallet and gave it a final inspection. Then she joined Sarah across the room in the last minute arranging of Ruth's light brown hair.

"You look so beautiful, my daughter," Leah said.

Ruth wrapped her arms around her mother's waist and, with a nervous shudder, hugged her. "Do I really?"

"Of course you do," Sarah answered for Leah, enfolding her mother and her younger sister in her grasp. She leaned her cheek against the top of Ruth's head, and her gaze became thoughtful without seeming starry-eyed. Ruth, as the baby of the house, had always been Caleb's favorite, yet he had no doubt that of the two his elder sister had the stronger will. And now that he could compare them in the same amber lamplight, Caleb realized that Sarah was prettier as well.

Treading painstakingly across the roof so his camel-hide sandals would not creak, he neared the edge of the window. He was preparing to startle them with a shout when Ruth said to Sarah, "I would rather it was your night."

"You mean you don't want Samuel?"

"No—not that!"

Sarah's laugh fluttered out into the night. "Then what?"

"It's just that you're two years older . . . and so much better looking."

"I am not."

"I want you to have the happiness I feel."

"But I do."

By the rustling of garments, Caleb knew that the girls had embraced.

"We must be friends like this—always," Ruth said more brightly, as if she had relieved herself of some burden she had been bearing for weeks. "No matter what happens, we must keep this feeling."

Stifling a sob, his mother could be heard leaving the chamber. Caleb shrugged, then stole back down the vine into the gathering.

"What have you been doing?" Samuel demanded irritably.

"Calm yourself, friend. This is just the betrothal ceremony—not the wedding night."

The young men chuckled, their first growths of beard glinting copper and russett in the light of the torches. Then they jostled Samuel before a white-haired man wearing a *tallith*, who despite his solemn demeanor could not help but to smile at the suitor's discomfort. "Show a glad heart, Samuel," he whispered, "for I know you love my niece."

"I do, Matthias. It is just that I have never done this before."

"Ah. My family gives thanks for that." The old man rested his hands on Samuel's head in blessing, then spread his arms to embrace him. "You must not be unsettled. Innocence always fidgets as its time draws to a close."

Samuel nodded, then sighed. He crossed his arms over his chest, then let them hang at his sides for only an instant before clasping his hands together behind his back.

Finally, a flourish of pipes and a roll of drums announced the appearance of Ruth, whose steps were timid until she caught sight of Samuel. Then she hurried toward him, nearly losing the crown of myrtle leaves and flowers Sarah had just set upon her hair. Leah handed Caleb a similar yet less floral garland, and he in turn adorned Samuel's head with it.

"She's lovely," Samuel said in a hush, as if seeing Ruth for the first time.

Matthias motioned for Ruth and Samuel to join him in the center of the courtyard. They clasped hands under his smile.

"*Ruth*," Matthias said in a loud voice so some of the celebrants on the fringe of the crowd would quiet down. Then more benignly: "Ruth, as your uncle and head of your family after the death of your father, I have the right and duty to choose your husband for you . . . and have done so. Now I must ask you: Do you, Ruth, of your own free will and consent accept your betrothed, the man I have chosen for you? If your answer is yes, you will say: 'This is the man I love.'"

Her eyes darted to Samuel's face. "This is the man I love."

Matthias nodded in satisfaction. "Samuel, you may present your gifts."

Samuel took the sash, veil and combs from Stephen, who had been holding them for him, and offered them to Ruth. Tenderly, she admired each article before passing it on to Sarah.

"Now the ring," Matthias prompted.

Samuel offered it in the palm of his hand. "I made it myself." A glimmer of pride sounded from the depths of his shyness. "My mother gave me her earrings . . . for the gold."

Matthias guided Samuel's hand to slip the ring onto Ruth's finger. He caught the young man's eye and firmly held it. "Repeat after me: 'Behold: Thou art consecrated unto me by this ring, according to the law of Moses and Israel.'"

Samuel said the words so earnestly Caleb had to hide a smile behind his hand.

A cheer arose, and Leah hugged her daughter. "That your father could be here this night..."

"Let us recite the Psalm of joy!" Matthias cried. "'Shout with joy before the Lord, O earth! Obey him gladly!' Try to understand what this means: The Lord is God. He made us. We are his people, the sheep of his pasture. Go through his open gates with great thanksgiving. Give thanks to him and bless his name. For the Lord is always good, and his faithfulness goes on and on to each generation!"

Joining hands, the young women had formed a circle. The tentative strumming of a harp gave voice to their impatience.

"Yes, yes," Matthias said with a chortle. "I had much more to say—a wondrous new message. But, all right, be at your merriment."

Leah poked Caleb in the ribs with a fist that seemed as delicate as a sparrow. "Where were you this afternoon? Ruth and Sarah were beside themselves with worry."

"I wasn't late, Mother, was I?"

"No, but—"

"Look how my friends regard her."

"Who?" Leah asked, bemused.

"Sarah, of course. She's quite handsome, isn't she?"

"You'd never noticed before?"

"Noticed what?"

"Caleb, where is your mind these days?"

At first, he thought that one of the guests had grown boisterous, but then Caleb realized that the drunken caterwauling he heard was in an alien tongue. An imperial soldier had stumbled into the courtyard and was now reeling in a space that he had flailed clear with his fists. Caleb recognized him as a Spanish auxiliary of the Sixth Scipio, a cohort notorious for its street-brawling and effronteries to the women of Jerusalem. A quick look reassured Caleb that the Spaniard bore only his short sword—and was probably too far along in his cups to use it well.

His head bobbing, the man sputtered something unintelligible. When no one acted on his words, he growled and switched to broken Latin. He wanted more wine—and not just any wine: a vintage from Jura. His eyes skittered from face to face until they lit on Sarah's. He wetted his teeth with his tongue, and his feet hurled him toward the young woman.

She held her ground and glowered at him.

Caleb and Samuel were pushing their way through the crowd to intercept him when a second auxiliary and then a third pursued their comrade and seized him by the arms. The intruder exclaimed joyously as if he had not seen them in some long time, then reviled them as they began pulling him out of the courtyard. They released him only once—to allow him to vomit into a pot that collected rainwater off the roof.

Shaking off Samuel's restraining hand, Caleb followed the soldiers out into the lane. He was on the verge of wresting a sword from one of them when two Roman officers on horseback emerged from a passageway, preceded at a trot by a torch-bearing slave. The first rider was well known in the city: the prefect of the Sixth Scipio, a centurion of Roman blood who had been put over the barbarian troops. He was accompanied by a colonel of the newly arrived cohort from Syria. This Twelfth Legion officer did not appear to be pleased after his tour of Jerusalem—and seemed even less so when he noticed the young Judean glaring up at him.

Refusing to lower his eyes, Caleb waited for the colonel to shout, "There! This is the slinger who attacked us today!" Instead, the Roman gave an imperious shrug and peered over the top of Caleb's head into the courtyard, where the betrothal party stood hushed, awaiting Caleb's safe return.

"What's going on here?" the prefect asked his auxiliaries.

The three men remained silent.

"I asked what is going on!"

"Nothing, sir," a soldier finally muttered. "Returning to garrison."

The Spaniard who had invaded the courtyard began rambling incoherently—without asking for permission to speak.

"Deliver this man to the guard room," the prefect ordered. "Ten draughts of the vine-stock will sober him up."

Caleb smiled: the auxiliary would be thrashed with a cudgel of twisted vine twigs.

"What's the matter with this fellow?" the colonel asked the prefect.

Caleb realized that they were staring at him.

"Who are you?" the prefect asked.

"Caleb . . . of this house."

"Go back to your people—and stop trying to burn holes in us with your eyes, young Caleb." The officer turned to the slave. "Proceed."

"The Fortress of Antonia now, sir?"

"Where else are we welcome in this overgrown village?" the Roman said wearily.

III

<hr/>

It was not usual for a legionary to attend the person of the Emperor—that was properly left to the praetorian guard. But Tiberius Claudius Nero was an unusual Caesar, and in the midst of his reign he had withdrawn from Rome to the isle of Capri, exiling himself without relinquishing any of his powers.

This, the young signifer, or standard-bearer, reminded himself as he donned his cuirass in the Capri praetorium, had presented special problems to the praetorian prefect: He had to maintain a strong force around Tiberius on the island without weakening the presence of the guard in Rome. The prefect had begged the Emperor to increase the number of praetorian cohorts, but Tiberius—who was increasingly suspicious of everyone—had refused.

There had remained only one solution.

The call had gone out to a trustworthy legion commander to supply the Emperor with a cohort to safeguard him on Capri. It was requested that the man selected for this special force be as tall as guardsmen and that their "countenances be pleasing to the eye." The Third Legion Augusta was designated to draft this Capri Cohort because it was based in North Africa—and the legionaries chosen would not have pallid complexions, which the Emperor found offensive.

It was for this reason that the signifer, Julius Valerius Licinius, had been assigned to the imperial retinue. He had departed from Africa with keen expectations. "I cannot express my delight at being handpicked for this honor," he had written his father, a centurion with the Seventh Legion in Gaul. "I only hope that I will prove worthy of our Emperor."

Yet now, less than two months on Capri, Valerius was no longer sure that this assignment was an honor. In truth, he had begun to despise it and was trying to think of some means by which he could be transferred back to his old cohort without raising the ire of his colonel. During his long hours of sentry duty, he rehearsed the speech he would give the officer: "Sir, I was brought up in an *insula . . .*" He was referring to one of Rome's shabby tenements: This would instantly mark him as a member of the plebeian class. Previously, he had glossed over his humble origins, but now he hoped they would help serve his plan. "I'm just not used to rubbing elbows with the nobility. I'd never even met a patrician until I joined the legion." He reminded himself not to add: "And I thank the gods! These are the most perverse and debased people in the Empire!"

"Valerius Licinius!" a voice jarred him out of his musings.

"Good morning, colonel. Hail Tiberius!"

The officer rested his hand on Valerius' shoulder. "You are looking quite smart today. I want you to *shadow.*"

Valerius almost groaned. He had hoped to be posted on a rampart of the Villa Jovis or, if not the imperial mansion, one of the paths skirting the top of the cliffs. But he was being ordered to keep track of the Emperor without making his presence felt—*shadowing.* "Very well, sir."

"You have the quietest footfalls in the cohort," the colonel said with a smile.

Valerius resolved to tramp around Capri like an elephant from now on. "Where may I find the Emperor?"

"In his *piscina.*"

Arriving at the handsome pool, Valerius was immediately alarmed to find Tiberius nowhere in sight, although the surface of the water was dotted with children—all nude, of course. Then he glimpsed a form streaking across the green depths. It was Tiberius, submerged. The small pink bodies flashed away from him like minnows. He grasped the slowest of them by the ankle and, bursting up into the air on a loud chortle, gathered the child to his chest. "I have got you!" the master of the Empire cried, spanking the tiny buttocks.

The others, screeching in mock terror, churned for the far side of the *piscina* and clambered up onto a parapet to giggle and goad the old man into chasing them anew. But, unexpectedly, Tiberius released his small captive and allowed her to swim free. He was staring up into the deep green of a pine tree as if he had spied something unpleasant there.

Valerius looked up but saw nothing but spiky foliage.

Over seventy years old, Tiberius' body was yet strong and muscular. Spinning around, he glared eastward into the haze that concealed the Italian mainland. Then he motioned for a servant to meet him at the edge of the pool with his tunic. As he sloshed through the shallow waters, he became more stooped with each step. His face, so exuberant a few moments before, grew dour. Assisted out of the pool, he said, "Rome robs me of my light."

"Emperor?" the servant asked, drying Tiberius' tanned skin.

"Don't call me that." Tiberius eased onto a marble bench and exhaled wearily as his tunic was dropped over his head. "I never asked to be that." Then, sighing even more heavily, he stood and held his arms out to the sides so he could be fitted with his toga. "The throne was forced on me, was it not?"

"It was," the man echoed absently.

Tiberius had fixed his gaze on a boy of ten years, who was warming his naked body on the sun-baked flagstones. Valerius sank deeper into the shrub that concealed him. "Not now— please," he whispered to himself.

But the Emperor had put aside his lust and crawled back into his growing funk. "I would've been happier left a soldier," he groused.

Valerius nodded silently in agreement, recalling what Augustus had written of his adoptive son: ". . . dearest and bravest and the most conscientious general alive." This was the Tiberius whom Valerius' own father had called "the toughest but fairest Roman to ever take up the purple." Yet, so far, the signifer had observed only Tiberius the Lecher, an elderly satyr who wiled away his days in endless debaucheries, pining over insults both real and imagined.

Sandals slapped the walkway in approach, and Valerius peered through the flowery boughs at the intruder: It was Curtius Atticus, who had on his toga the broad stripe reserved for a senator.

"What are you doing on Capri?" Tiberius sternly asked him, although Atticus was one of his few friends.

"We landed last night, Caesar."

"*We?*"

"Yes, a delegation from Rome to consult our Emperor." The senator indicated a group of men standing off by themselves in a forest glade of a garden. They forced smiles as a host of boys and girls, some quite lewdly dressed as divinities or nymphs, dashed around their legs. Paling, Atticus averted his eyes from the scene. "And now, Caesar, we have been invigorated by our night's rest, so there is the business of the Empire at hand—"

"Are you truly?" Tiberius asked in a dire tone of voice.

"Caesar?"

"Invigorated?"

"Why, yes—of course."

"I so seldom enjoy that feeling anymore. And if I do, it's brief...a glimmer." Tiberius fortified himself with a deep breath. "Well, let's face Rome."

Atticus brightened. "Does Caesar intend to return to the city, then?"

"No, no," Tiberius snapped. "I mean face those who bring Rome's poisonous tidings."

The men began strolling away, and Valerius had to rush down between tall rosebushes, the branches clawing at his red military cloak. He settled into another hiding place from which to view his imperial charge.

As Tiberius waded into the midst of the patricians, nodding sullenly, Atticus hurriedly briefed him as if afraid Caesar might suddenly change his mind and refuse to hear anything about the Senate's difficulties. "You should know that Sejanus came on the same boat with us last night."

"Good."

Atticus hesitated. "And there is news of a revolt in Pannonia."

"Pannonia?!"

"We're not sure of its extent."

"I humbled Pannonia when I was a general!"

A corpulent man sidled up to them. "Do not trouble Tiberius Caesar with rumors, Curtius Atticus," he said in a honeyed voice. "Wait for Sejanus to clear up these matters."

"The praetorian prefect is more apt to cloud an issue than clarify it." Atticus then gave his back to Lucius Marinus, who shrugged off the insult.

Valerius chuckled at the sight the nobleman offered. Tiberius' chief whoremaster, Marinus had donned a *synthesis* dyed a gaudy shade of amethystine. This gown was never properly worn outdoors except during the riotous festival of the Saturnalia.

"Children!" Marinus clapped his pudgy hands over his head. "Come!"

Valerius was startled as boys and girls began streaming past

him through the shrubbery, trampling the flower beds as they
ran up to Tiberius.

"Your own Olympus, Caesar!" Marinus proudly declared.
"May I present the gods and goddesses!"

"Hail, Tiberius!" the children cried in listless singsong.

"Oh, my." Instantly, the Emperor's face became lively. The
roundness of his shoulders disappeared as his eyes leaped from
child to child. "Well done, Lucius!"

"Your joy is mine, Caesar." Then the portly man pointed
out each divinity: "Mars—supple-looking, yes?"

"Oh, for certain." A silly giggle escaped Tiberius' lips.

". . . and Diana . . ."

"Who is she?" Tiberius whispered.

"The daughter of Praetor Medullus here."

"Medullus, the gods have been good to your daughter!"

"Thank you, Tiberius Caesar," the magistrate said with a
sickened grin.

Marinus continued escorting the Emperor down the line.
"Mercury, Jupiter in the flesh, Aphrodite—"

"Ah!" Tiberius gasped. Wistfully, he studied the girl, his
tongue protruding slightly from his teeth. "How old?" he asked
Marinus.

"Fourteen or fifteen, I believe."

"A bit advanced—but lovely nevertheless. We should call
her Venus, not Aphrodite. Her beauty is somewhat haughty.
Therefore, it is more Hellenic than Sabine. I want to see more . . ."

"You are too clothed," Marinus barked at the girl. "We
know Venus when we see her, don't we, Caesar? This marvel
should not be concealed from reverent gazes."

The girl took a step backward from the line. Reflexively,
her hands flew to her upper breast. The color left her face,
then returned in an angry blush. She spun on a middle-aged
senator, whose blue eyes were only a pale forgery of her own.
"Father!"

"Corinna!" The senator gaped at her and then at Tiberius.
He appeared to be on the verge of fainting. "I ask you to forgive
her, Caesar!"

The girl's lips were thinned by hatred as she watched her
father beseech the Emperor with upturned palms.

Tiberius chuckled after a grim silence. "What? A mortal
forgive a goddess? Come now, Fabianus, her reluctance must

spring from divine purposes." He gave Corinna an avuncular smile. "There, my little Venus, take your exalted place in the pantheon again. Youth, innocence—I trust them, celebrate them on this isle. They are not the fountainhead of betrayal. That is—" Tiberius froze halfway through an oratorical sweep of his arm and squinted down the length of the walkway at a white-bearded man who was sauntering through the fruit orchard, hands clasped behind him. "Come with me, Curtius Atticus." Then the Emperor stormed off toward the distant figure. "I should have let this Greek kiss the stones on Rhodes!"

Valerius bolted after them, grasping the hilt of his short sword to keep it from rattling in its scabbard, mumbling apologies to the patricians as he darted through them to another hidden path that traversed the shadows of the immense garden. The signifer knew exactly what Tiberius had meant when he spoke of kissing stones—a centurion had told him all about it on a long night watch:

Prior to his becoming Emperor, Tiberius had voluntarily exiled himself to Rhodes, an island off the coast of Asia Minor. His allies claimed that he had done this to put to rest any suspicion that he wanted to supplant either Gaius or Lucius, Augustus' grandchildren and adoptive sons, as heirs to the throne. His detractors noted that he was an insular man who felt comfortable enjoying his perversions only when cloaked on all sides by water. Valerius thought there was probably truth in both opinions.

On Rhodes, perhaps to relieve his habitual anxiety, Tiberius had decided to find a reliable soothsayer. He had a husky freedman escort the prospective diviner up a precipitous footpath to his house. If the prophesies failed to please Tiberius, the ex-slave hurled the astrologer to his death on the return trip down the cliff. Only one man had been able to save his own life and win the oracular post—Thrasyllus, the bewhiskered man now enjoying the imperial orchard. After puffing up the slope behind the freedman, this specialist in Chaldaean studies had made a number of interesting forecasts, including Tiberius' ascension to Augustus' throne. But then the young noble demanded that Thrasyllus foretell his own future. With meticulous care, the man cast a personal horoscope. All at once, the blood drained out of his face: "I face mortal peril this very day!"

Tiberius guffawed. "You did, my friend—until now."

Valerius slipped behind a bronze statue of the Emperor, then peeked between the gleaming forelegs in time to catch Tiberius accosting the aged Greek.

"Tell this ridiculous fraud your news!" the Emperor ordered Atticus.

"Well . . . there has been a revolt in Pannonia."

Thrasyllus blinked innocently. "Yes?"

"'Yes?' he says!" Tiberius exploded. "Why wasn't this fore-told?"

"As Petosiris, the Egyptian teacher, proclaimed, any up-heaval is forewarned by a commotion of celestial bodies . . . by blood on the moon. I saw no sign in the heavens. No blood. No tumult." The Greek folded his hands together to keep them from shaking, and finally achieved an outwardness of calm. "So it cannot be much of a revolt, Caesar."

Tiberius considered this in silence for several seconds.

The soothsayer appeared to be swallowing a peach stone.

"Yes," Tiberius said at last, "that must be it." Then he frowned at Atticus. "Well, have you any more gloom with which to douse me?"

"Caesar, it was not my wish to darken—"

"Everything about you is gloomy—your face, your com-pany, your wisdom."

"The aim of stoic philosophy is to find an alternative to despair."

Tiberius gestured toward a youth dressed as Pan who was pursuing a nude girl down a colonnade, the paleness of her body flickering between the columns. *"There* is the alternative, my dear Curtius."

"The senses fail a man, Caesar. At our age—"

"Our age? Speak for yourself."

"I am simply suggesting," Atticus continued, "that Rome would be better off if its people appreciated virtue for its own sake."

"Do not address me as if I were a child. When have you been put to the test?"

"I'm not sure that I have been."

"Yes," Tiberius said with a cross smile. "Nor have you seen your own son dying in pain."

"You were not there to see it either."

The Emperor glared at the senator. "I see it every night. He screams, begging me to punish his murderer."

"But so many were executed on suspicion. Why such a wanton revenge if the guilty one was never really known?"

"It will take many lives to repay me for the loss of my Drusus. And it's not revenge. It's policy—that of preserving the empire. They killed my son. That can only means they plot my death as well." With a palsied hand, Tiberius accepted a cup of wine from a servant. His teeth clicked against the silver as he gulped.

"Be calm, Caesar, and vanquish these agitations you feel."

"I try, Curtius . . . how vigorously I try."

"Take a calm mind with you to Rome. Restore justice to the city. Rome has become an immoral shambles in your absence. It needs its Emperor in his household on the Palatine Hill."

"Then tell me the truth about this—is this a common toast at dinner parties in the city: 'To the Tiber with Tiberius!'?"

Atticus pressed his lips together and said nothing.

"I thought so. Well, I will not go back to Rome." Tiberius saw that the patrician delegation had crept back up to the edge of his presence. "Do you fools hear me?!"

The senators and knights did not answer.

Then Tiberius vented a loud sigh, and Valerius tracked the Emperor's gaze to the reason for his relief.

"I thank the fair wind that returns you to Capri, Aelius Sejanus!" Tiberius cried.

The prefect of the praetorian guard advanced toward the Emperor with such a conquering stride the rotund senator at his flank had to half trot to keep pace. Sejanus filled the garden with intimidation in the way a thunderstorm makes the air snap and buzz. He was smiling as if his dearest ambitions were on the verge of being realized, although his expression grew modest as he regarded Tiberius. On his fingers was the gold ring of a Roman knight. Although born into the equestrian class—a step below the senatorial order—Lucius Aelius Sejanus had become the first citizen of Rome in everything but title. It was said he now wanted that as well.

Even before the prefect had reached him, Tiberius complained to Sejanus, "Atticus here has been ranting about some revolt in Pannonia."

"A false rumor, Caesar, spread by enemies to your peace. King Vannius continues to rule Pannonia as your faithful client."

"I knew it." Tiberius stared down his forefinger at Atticus.

"When I subjugate a people, they stay subjugated!"

Gasping for breath, the senator who had accompanied Sejanus embraced Tiberius with what appeared to be genuine affection. Cocceius Nerva, Valerius recalled, was perhaps the Emperor's fondest ally in an otherwise peevish Senate. "And when Caesar befriends a people, they remain his friends."

"Ah, if only that were true in all cases, Cocceius, as it is in yours." Tiberius gave him a squeeze on the shoulder. "I've been explaining to Curtius here that I won't return to Rome. I will die here on Capri. And I hope to die in my bed."

"You will live," Sejanus said, "for the glory of Rome. The mighty arm of your justice—"

"*Your* arm, Sejanus," Nerva said evenly, "and increasingly *your* idea of justice."

The prefect stared at the senator. He grinned, although his eyes remained mirthless. "—the arm of Caesar's justice shall crush anyone who intends him harm . . . whether the assassin lurks in the mob of the forum, or is wrapped inside a senator's toga or even within the nest of his own family."

"My own family?" Tiberius looked indignant. "Whenever has my own flesh and blood turned against me?"

Nerva and Atticus traded uneasy glances. "Caesar, don't you recall?" the latter finally asked.

"Recall?"

"Your niece, Agrippina the Elder—exiled to the island of Pandateria."

"You gave the order yourself, my Emperor," Sejanus said with exaggerated plainness, as if to a dotard.

"I did? My memory fails me at times."

"Agrippina conspired to have you deposed in favor of one of her two sons. It was proven."

"Beyond the slightest doubt?" Tiberius asked weakly.

"Yes."

Thrasyllus peered around Sejanus' broad back. "It was in the stars, woven in their dance."

"But what of her two sons?" the Emperor asked.

Sejanus patted his arm. "Safely guarded on the isle of Pontia."

"But Agrippina bore *three* sons, didn't she?"

"Yes, one remains at liberty—Gaius. He adores hanging around the camps and garrisons of your legions. The soldiers gave him his nickname."

"Yes," Tiberius mumbled, "'Little Boots' . . . *Caligula*."

"A good lad," Sejanus went on. "Quite unlike his brothers. He told me he's actually ashamed of his mother—said he despises her."

"So young Caligula is spared for the time being," Nerva said. "Until the mighty arm of Sejanus—"

"Which I would not hesitate to sever had I any suspicion it could betray our Emperor!" Sejanus looked seaward, striking a smarted pose that was lost on Tiberius, who was wallowing in his own thoughts.

"I like Caligula," the Emperor said quietly. "And his mother I have always loved and respected. Lady Antonia would never fail me. I was delighted when my Drusus married her daughter, the fair Livilla..." Then Tiberius fell silent: He was scrutinizing the face of his praetorian prefect. Standing taller, he perched his fists on his hips.

Valerius watched in fascination. Here, at long last, was a man with the lucidity and forcefulness to have beaten down the Illyrian Revolt, the most ruthless campaign since the sacking of Carthage. Tiberius' brain-fog seemed to have lifted, and he was prying something out of Sejanus' eyes that clearly displeased him.

A rumor was scampering through the praetorium that Sejanus had recently asked the Emperor if he might take Livilla as his wife. Tiberius had refused, claiming that Antonia would never allow it. Now the prefect was trying to wheedle his way into the old woman's affections through her grandson, Caligula.

Then the incisive moment passed, and Tiberius looked befuddled once again.

"Caesar," Nerva pled, "the Senate is on the brink of declaring Rome an orphan."

"What is that supposed to mean?"

"Your loyal senators demand that you return to the city to rule."

"How often must I declare this? I will not go back to Rome!"

"The praetorian guard concurs with the Emperor that Rome is not the place for him to be—it is treacherous," Sejanus said.

Nerva was opening his mouth to argue with the prefect when cries of alarm rose from the direction of the sea cliff. Drawing his short sword, Valerius raced toward the disturbance.

Along the marble balustrade that overlooked the choppy waves, two legionaries were holding a man to the ground with the points of their javelins. "Please do not kill me!" he begged.

"Be still or be dead," one of the soldiers said. "Ah, here's the signifer now."

"What is it?" Valerius asked.

"We caught this one climbing over the rail. He must've scrabbled all the way up from the beach."

The man in the frayed tunic had slung a fishnet over his shoulder; in it was a large mullet, still squirming with life.

"Are you a *retiarius*, my friend?" Valerius was referring to the gladiator who fought with a trident and net.

"No, noble centurion—I'm a fisherman! The net is to hold the fish I bring Tiberius Caesar."

"I'm a long ways from becoming a centurion." Valerius inspected the man's catch. "What is it?"

"A mullet, sir. Fresh from Neptune this very hour—an offering for the divine Tiberius."

"Not so divine if mortal men can climb his Olympus," a voice said from behind.

Valerius turned and saw, with a sinking heart, that the speaker was Tiberius. The signifer jolted to attention as the praetorian prefect strode up to him.

"Your name?" Sejanus insisted.

"Julius Valerius Licinius, sir."

"Are these your legionaries?"

"Yes, sir."

"And who is this?"

"A fisherman, who bears a gift for—"

"Throw him back over the side."

"He climbed up only with the intention of presenting this mullet to the Emperor, sir."

"He goes over the side," Sejanus said firmly. "And you three report back to the praetorium for discipline. I will speak to your colonel."

"Wait, Sejanus," Tiberius said. "A gift from Neptune for me, he says?"

"That fish might well conceal a dagger in its belly," the prefect warned.

The notion hit Tiberius like a slap. He extended a trembling hand. "Give it to me!"

A legionary hooked his thumb in the mullet's gill and carried the fish to Tiberius, who grasped it by the tailfin. "If Neptune has something for me, he should deliver it personally!" Then he swung the creature as if it were a club, striking the prostrate man across the cheek. Astonished, the fisherman touched his fingers to his face and felt how the sharp scales had cut him. Tiberius clouted him again and again. "What do you say now, my nimble messenger from Neptune?"

"I only thank the gods I did not bring the big crab I also caught!" the man moaned.

Tiberius' eyes widened. "Excellent! Send for the crab, Sejanus, and have him thrashed with it as well."

"An inspired thought, Caesar."

Tiberius enfolded the prefect under his arm. "You are right as always, my friend. If fishermen can surmount my defenses, so can assassins."

"And if this can happen on a natural fortress like Capri, imagine the impossibility of safeguarding your person in Rome!" Gently, Sejanus freed himself from Tiberius' embrace. "I will now see to replacing these inept legionaries with my more vigilant praetorians—if Caesar will grant my leave."

"Of course."

Tiberius plodded toward the Villa Jovis, and Sejanus made sure the Emperor was well on his way before speaking to Valerius again. "Toss him over the side—*now.*"

The fisherman began weeping miserably. "It was love that made me brave the cliff!"

"Prefect," Valerius said, "Caesar ordered no more than a thrashing with a large crab. Shall I signal the marines stationed on the shore below to seek out the man's boat?"

"No." Sejanus' eyes were furious.

"But the Emperor—"

"Later, Tiberius will think that the man was beaten with a crab. That is all that really matters. Shall I add insubordination to your other derelictions?"

"No, sir."

"Then do what you have been ordered."

Valerius nodded for the legionaries to seize the fisherman.

For a long time after the scream had plummeted to silence, the signifer stood at the balustrade, listening to the taunts of gulls. Then he shuffled toward the praetorium.

IV

CALEB hiked down the Jerusalem lane, which was more like a cascade of stone steps than a street. He averted the gaze of the centurion who was leading a Twelfth Legion patrol up the opposite way. Reminding himself that all Romans regarded young, strong-looking Jews with suspicion, Caleb did not bother to check over his shoulder as he strode across the square in front of the amphitheatre.

Then, out of the throng of passers-by and beggars, a white-headed man came puffing into view. "Uncle!" Caleb cried.

Matthias roused himself out of some musing. "Ah, Caleb—*shalom*."

"Where are you going?"

"The neighborhood of Mount Zion." Briefly, the old man hesitated before saying, "To see friends."

"The house of Caiaphas then?"

"No." Matthias' eyes dimmed. "I'm no longer welcome in that house." But then he shrugged off his sad expression. "And where are you bound, my nephew?"

"The Temple—for the school of *Rabban* Gamaliel."

"A just man, as becomes the grandson of the great teacher Hillel."

"Uncle," Caleb said slowly, "I've heard through a friend that you sold your house."

The old man smiled. "Yes."

"But *why?*"

"So I might buy this glorious feeling that I am embarking on a holiday—one without end." He laid his hands in blessing on Caleb's head and whispered "*Shalom*" before hurrying toward the upper city again.

Perplexed, Caleb took a few halting steps, then remembered the time. He ran toward the distant Temple, which loomed over the rooftops in the clear morning shine.

• • •

"You should've seen my wife's face—" Peter softly chuckled "when I told her I was leaving her, the children, the boats I'd hauled up on the beach—to go with our Lord. Later, I mentioned to Jesus that I wished he'd been beside me when I broke that news to the good woman."

"What did he say?" John asked.

"She too would be blessed—for her patience."

There was rapping at the door. Each of the eleven men in the chamber fell silent and looked to Peter. Quietly, he tread across the floor to the threshold. "Good," he sighed after peeking through a crack, "it's Joseph Barsabbas . . . and here comes Matthias as well."

"Peter . . . James," Barsabbas murmured, nodding at each face as he stepped inside.

Matthias then hurried through the doorway, his forehead pearled with sweat. "I'm sorry to be late. There were arrangements to be made before you might call me brother."

"And so—what of your worldly goods?" Peter asked.

"Given to the needy."

"Peter," James said, "they're both here. Let's get on with it."

"You grow no more patient with age." Peter clapped the man around the shoulders. "All right then, we won't put it off another moment." He was about to speak again when the cry of a rooster, far off, came to them over the street noises. He touched his side as if he had just experienced a sharp pain there. "When Jesus was with us he had many followers—but only twelve apostles. He chose that number because of the twelve tribes of Israel. Well, one of us died with our heart full of shame. And now there is the business of picking another." He smiled at the newcomers, who were seated side by side. They reminded him of elderly friends lingering in the Garden of Gethsemane on a warm afternoon. "Barsabbas and Matthias are good men—equally good, I'd say—"

"And they both were known to us during the ministry of our Lord."

"Right, Thomas." Peter looked slightly annoyed at having been interrupted. "We also think it important that this new apostle did witness our Lord's resurrection."

"Both Barsabbas and Matthias did indeed," James said.

Again, the rooster crowed. Wincing, Peter lowered his head.
"But only one can set right the number Jesus himself fixed for
us. Now, I must ask: Are we worthy to choose?" His face was
so full of self-deprecation that no one in the chamber answered.
"Chance, it is said, is the toy of God. I know toys are for
children. But didn't our Lord ask us to become like children?"
Peter opened his right fist, revealing three Roman dice. "These
were found under his cross. A guard tossed them to win his
robe, then forgot them." Seeing some doubtful expressions, he
quickly added, "The Essene wise men of Mesad Hasidim appeal
for guidance this way." He waited for any further objection,
but there was none. Striding to the table, he clenched the dice
and shut his eyes. "Lord, your gaze can pierce the hearts of
him. Show us which of these worthy two you have chosen."
Then Peter turned to Barsabbas. "Take them."

The ivory cubes clattered across the planks: The number
five was cast.

"And now Matthias—"

The old man received the dice with an air of humility, then
let them tumble without a moment's hesitation.

"Six," Thomas whispered.

Barsabbas was the first to embrace Matthias in congratu-
lation.

Peter took both of Matthias' hands in his. "You, whose
name means gift from God, listen to these hard words Jesus
shared with us: 'I have come to set a man against his father,
and a daughter against her mother—a man's worst enemies
might be in his own home! If you love your father and mother,
or your son or daughter, more than you love me, you are not
worthy of being mine...'"

The old man was peering over the crown of Peter's head at
the Temple of Herod. He was weeping without shame.

Caleb walked down between the twin rows of Corinthian
columns as quickly as he could without being admonished by
one of the Temple guards. He could see that *Rabban* Gamaliel
had already convened his school at the far end of Solomon's
Portico. A trumpet blared. Scowling, the youth glanced up at
the towers of the Fortress of Antonia, which abutted against
the outer wall of the shrine and gave the Roman sentries a clear
view of the courtyards. The guard was being changed on the
battlements. "One day..." he grumbled under his breath.

"Young Caleb," Gamaliel said with the brisk tone he used when displeased, "your fellow Zealot, Samuel here, and Seth—"

"A tedious Sadducee," Samuel half-whispered as Caleb sat beside him.

"—have been discussing the degree of compromise we, as a people living in a hostile world, should exercise. Not to adjudicate this issue before all the arguments are given, I will say only that I see a certain value in compromise—except in the case of tardiness."

"I beg forgiveness, *Rabban*."

Gamaliel lowered his eyes once, accepting the apology. "Now, my sons, throughout our history we have been challenged repeatedly to defend our inheritance—most conspicuously from foreign oppression, but also from our own emotional intensity and error." His gaze flickered down to his hands, then back up to his young audience. "As necessary as it was, our rejection of the claim made by Jesus of Nazareth once again revealed the bitterness of the conflicts among us." He pointed at the praetorians pacing back and forth across the parapets of the fortress. "And you may be certain that the Romans are also aware of these divisions."

One youth could hold his silence no longer. He waved for Gamaliel's attention. "May I speak, *Rabban*—please?"

"Who am I to stand in the way of such moral urgency? But I trust you will allow your mind to speak in concert with your heart, young..."

"Stephen."

"Oh, yes. Now I recall—our Alexandrian."

Samuel leaned into Caleb's ear but said so all could hear: "A nice fellow—but a Greek from a city built by Greeks."

"No, Samuel," Stephen said good-naturedly. "I am a Jew. And, like Saul here, the son of a Pharisee." He patted the shoulder of a student a few years older than the rest. This man had an expansive forehead—almost outsized—and a wan complexion. He peered back up at the Alexandrian with a stern glint to his eyes. "And I can understand," Stephen went on, "why Samuel resents that which is foreign—"

"What else deprives us of our freedom except that which is foreign?" Caleb asked.

Samuel gestured with a fist. "Caleb is right!"

"What else could your future brother-in-law be?" Laughter

followed Stephen's remark. "So, my brothers, do not blame me for the forces that scattered the tribes of Israel long ago. It is their fault I learned Greek."

"Tidily done," Gamaliel said with a soft chuckle.

Caleb grinned at Stephen. "It is also said you learned wrestling from one of their Olympic champions."

"He could teach you a thing or two, Caleb," a low voice said.

"Have him name the occasion. Then we'll see who's the tutor."

"Please, brothers, listen to me," Stephen said. "The Greek philosophers have glanced pieces off the truth. But they have yet to see the whole light. I abhor the idols they worship. Seeing their way of life has strengthened my beliefs—the wisdom we inherited as Jews."

"Indeed..." Saul stood. Modest in height and slightly stooped, he was imposing only because of his illuminative stare. "Our brother Caleb should be reminded that the Torah has already been revealed to the gentiles by our own scholars, who translated it into Greek. So it occurs to me that pagan culture can be made useful to our purposes..." He smiled with one corner of his mouth. "...although my own mastery of Greek is quite lame."

"Your point is well taken, Saul..." Seth paused meaningfully. "...or is it *Paul?* You also bear a Roman name and citizenship, I believe?"

"Like Stephen, I am a Jew first," Saul calmly explained. "My father lives in Tarsus of Cilicia. His father was a benefactor of that city. Rome bestowed on him its greatest honor—citizenship. You and I may think it more a blemish than an honor. But it was not I who acquired it. So spare me one more performance of this satire I have heard from you many times before, Seth."

"You misunderstand me, my friend. I'm no Zealot, like Caleb and Samuel here. Nor am I a Nazarene." Seth looked askance at Stephen. "Nor am I some Essene who turns his back on this corrupt world and retreats to Lake Asphaltites only to swat brine flies all day long. And I agree with you that there is value in knowing other places, other languages." Seth then angrily raised his voice: "But, in our appreciation of Greek philosophies and Roman roads, we must never lose sight of the fact that foreign customs can be infectious—"

Gamaliel had raised his hand. Seth quietly took his place beside Saul again.

"It would be dangerous enough if our divisions were doctrinal or political. But they go beyond that, don't they? There is uncertainty even among those of the same sect. And in this we forget, my sons, that we were called as a holy nation—*and that nation must be one!*" Once more, Gamaliel lifted his eyes to the Roman fortress. Then he asked Seth, "Do you understand, my young Sadducee?"

"Yes, *Rabban.*"

"And do you embrace my meaning with all your heart and mind?"

"Certainly. It is precisely what our high priest Caiaphas meant when he spoke of the menace posed by the false prophet from Nazareth: 'We must be ready for any sacrifice in order to prevent our nation from perishing!'"

"But *whose* sacrifice?" Stephen's face had grown flushed. "It was decided much too quickly by the priests and elders of the supreme Sanhedrin to hand the deliverer over to Pilate's butchers!"

"What deliverer?" Samuel asked contemptuously. "He came to Jerusalem like a conqueror, then preached submission and collaboration. I fault his execution only for this reason—we should give up no more Jews to Roman crucifixion."

"No, no." Saul shook his head. "You are missing the point entirely."

"Yes!" Stephen exhorted. "He died in our behalf!"

"*That* isn't what I meant either. The point is not that the Sanhedrin did or did not collaborate with the procurator to silence a rude carpenter from Galilee—"

"You sneer at his trade, Saul?" Stephen interrupted. "You yourself are a tentmaker."

"I stitch canvas because of our injunction to practice a skill. But I know other things—"

"It is enough to know love."

"Nor is the point whether or not this Jesus advocated either love or the sword as the solution to our political situation."

"Then what, Paul of Cilicia?" Caleb demanded.

"In a word—*blasphemy.*" Then Saul turned to Gamaliel. "Correct me if I am wrong, *Rabban.*" The young man reclined again. Unconsciously, he had done so in the Roman fashion: resting on his left elbow.

Gamaliel's face was pensive for a long moment. "We must admit that there was much in what Jesus said. Before we might improve our systems of rule, we must change ourselves . . . soul and body are inseparable—the body the temple of the soul which must be obedient to the Law of the Lord."

"A soul in chains." Caleb did not meet but could feel Gamaliel's stare.

"The chains can be laid to our numerous sins, interlocking in a length beyond our reckoning—even more so than to Tiberius' governors. And, my sons, do not disparage love. It may well be love that can save us. We Jews play into Roman hands by hating one another."

"So then, *Rabban*," Saul asked evenly, "are you becoming a Nazarene?"

"God forbid I should ever approve Jesus' desperate claim."

Saul smiled shrewdly. "Why, my teacher?"

The *Rabban* sighed. "As you have made clear—it is a question of blasphemy."

"Yes," Seth cried, "one so complicated it spans the generations of his family! It is even proposed that his mother—"

"Hold, Seth. Do not speak contemptuously of women." Then a spark visited Gamaliel's eye. "An emperor once said to a wise man: 'Thy God is a thief—to make woman he stole a rib from the sleeping Adam.' The wise man had no answer, but his daughter said, 'Let me see to this.' She went to the emperor and said, 'We call for justice.' The emperor demanded to know why. 'Thieves broke into our house in the night. They have taken a silver bowl and left a gold one in its place.' 'Ha!' cried the emperor, 'I wish I could have burglars like that every night!'" Gamaliel's face crinkled above his beard. "'Well,' said the girl, 'that is what our God did. He took a mere rib from Adam, but in exchange he gave him a wife!'"

The laughter of the young men reverberated down the length of the portico. Pilgrims, wrapped in their prayer shawls, glanced up to smile.

"Let us pray, my sons."

Following Gamaliel's example, his students came to their feet and turned toward the temple, then opened their palms to the sky.

"*Shemá Israel*. Hear O Israel. The Lord is our God, the Lord is one." Then, with a solemn gesture of his right hand, Gamaliel dismissed his school. "Go in peace."

Seth caught up with Saul in the blinding sunlight of the Temple courtyard. "Saul?"

The Cilician did not greet him in return.

"Saul, I learned one thing this morning. I think it is important we remain friends."

The man slowed his angry pace, then stopped altogether. He stubbed the ground with the toe of his sandal. "'A friend is more necessary than fire and water.'"

Seth's face brightened. *Ecclesiastes?*

"No, Cicero."

"A Roman?"

"Yes—a great one."

"A well-turned phrase, nevertheless."

"You see then, not everything that comes from Rome is evil."

"Agreed, my friend."

Saul cocked an eyebrow. "Don't give up so easily. How can we quarrel if you are so accommodating?"

Within a hundred paces, the young men were engaged in a barbless argument over whether or not all these present troubles might have been prevented had Jerusalem refused to submit peacefully to that first oppressor out of the west, Alexander of Macedon. And by the time they were traipsing past the hippodrome, they had moved on to a vigorous debate about the origins of the Jerusalem Sanhedrin, after which all Jewish councils were patterned. "But the elders themselves will admit that it can be traced back to the Greek *Gerousia.*"

"A Greek word does not always describe a Greek idea. What is more Jewish than a sanhedrin? God and politics in one body?"

"How temporally put! How Sadducee! How—!"

"A moment, Saul—look there." Seth pointed down a passageway at a small throng of youths raising dust in a sheep pen. "It's everyone from our school!"

They ran up the narrow corridor and vaulted over the low stone wall into the midst of their friends. Through a thicket of bare legs, Saul could see that Caleb had Stephen in his grasp and was straining to roll the Alexandrian over on his back. Saul tapped Samuel on the shoulder.

"Is this in anger?" Saul asked.

"No—in sport. Caleb is much stronger. But the Greek knows a trick or two."

"Who started it?"

"Both—by consent. They were smiling when they squared off."

Saul shrugged at Seth. "This is what comes of everyone being in such a tense humor."

All at once, Caleb was able to roll Stephen over and thrust the slighter man's shoulders into the thick dust.

"Twice!" Caleb cried, the sweat muddying his face.

The opponents threw themselves at each other again, and the thudding noise from the collision of their bodies made the spectators raise a hurrah that sounded over the rooftops. Caleb got a purchase on Stephen's arm and began wrenching it behind the youth's back. Stephen grimaced, squinted up into the sun, but did not cry out in pain. Finally he won back the use of this arm, but his quick fury of the first two bouts was now spent, and Caleb's knee was being pressed against his chest, forcing him slowly downward toward defeat.

Then Saul felt himself being hurled aside, and a voice said in Latin, "Clear the way!" The legionary's shadow fell across Caleb and Stephen. "Let him go!"

Caleb glanced up at the Roman, then returned his attention to pinning Stephen.

"Stop!" the Roman bellowed in Aramaic.

Then Samuel's voice rose above the others, sharp with fear. "Leave off, Caleb!"

Panting, Caleb grinned at Stephen. "A good contest." Then he spread his feet to rise, but had gotten no higher than a crouch when the legionary shoved him against the wall of the pen.

"Deaf as a milepost, are you?"

"Caleb—brother!" Samuel cried again, desperately.

But the youth had already leaped up and confronted the legionary, who pushed Caleb back with his left hand and moved to draw his sword with his right. Caleb caught the man's wrist in mid-flight, and the Roman's eyes widened in surprise at the strength of the youth's grip.

Caleb could see Samuel, his face agonized as he lurched against the many arms that were restraining him. "Brother?" he mouthed.

Then Caleb had a fleeting glimpse of cuirasses and helmets, crimson capes swirling in the air—before he felt the flats of Spanish short swords against his back. His breath was beaten out of him, and his vision bleared to the same shade of molten fire he had seen in the crucibles of Samuel's workshop. When he could suck in a little air again, he realized his hands were being bound behind him.

"March!" one of the legionaries cried in his ear.

Stephen, rubbing the dust out of his eyes, stumbled across the pen to Saul. "Stop this, please—use your influence, I beg you."

The Cilician stared at him briefly, then turned. "Corporal," he said with authority. "A word here."

"What now?"

"Forgive our friend—he's a bit overwrought. That's all. Surely an apology would be enough."

The legionary was still massaging his wrist from Caleb's fierce grip. "Who are you?"

"I'm a Roman citizen."

"A Jew."

"Yes," Saul admitted with the same confident tone. "But a citizen of Rome nevertheless. Paul, if you must know my name. It's duly enrolled—"

"Well, then it's a pity you weren't the one to attack."

"I don't understand."

"Why, you're a citizen, aren't you? That means we can't crucify you."

V

FOG pressed down on Capri, covered the island with cool, milky light and wafted gusts of mist down through the openings in the roof of the Villa Jovis. Two servants carried a brazier into Tiberius' study, and the Emperor gently laid his pet snake back down on the pillow beside him, cooing "My darling Columba" before warming his hands over the coals.

Sejanus, reclining on a couch across Tiberius, hid a frown behind his hand. "As I was saying, Caesar, there are those who are attempting to infiltrate your own family. The Lady Livilla— meaning no disrespect to her—is quite impressionable. She has lived a widow too long. If I may repeat—"

"No." Then, afraid he had been too curt with his praetorian prefect, Tiberius added more softly, "Her mother Antonia would never consent."

"What if she were to withdraw her objection?"

"She wants her daughter-in-law to keep faith with the memory of her husband . . . my poor Drusus . . ." Then, as if he could not yet believe it: *". . . dead!"* Tiberius picked up the snake again with his now chafed hands and kissed the creature on the back of its scaly head. "If you hope by marriage to become some kind of substitute son to me—"

"I would never dare to presume."

"And turn yourself into a candidate for the throne."

"Caesar, please!" Sejanus found himself looking past the serpent's flickering tongue in order to meet Tiberius' eyes. "That is the last thing I want."

"Good . . . keep your place. Keep your distance from all the insanity. You do your work well. Let things stay as they are."

Briefly, Sejanus' disappointed eyes were drawn to a painting across the chamber. It showed the Arcadian huntress, Atalanta, performing fellatio on Meleager. But then his attention returned to the matters at hand. "Caesar, I don't like to broach this particular—and distasteful—subject with you, but there remains the inquiry being made into the activities of Curtius Atticus and Cocceius Nerva. . . ."

"No, no, spare me that right now. They're my friends, even if they speak too bluntly from time to time." Tiberius took a noisy gulp of wine. "My astrologer says that soon the signs may turn favorable for me to visit Rome."

The prefect rose up off his couch rugs. "But I'm replacing these daydreaming legionaries with real guardsmen. You will be completely safe here."

"It has nothing to do with that. I should see Rome once again before I die. And perhaps Nerva is right when he talks of my duty to the Senate."

"But the dangers . . . the assassins . . . those who would have your throne . . ."

"Who?" Tiberius asked. "Gaius Caligula?"

"No, not really—but anyone can be tempted to commit treason. And I should tell you I'm keeping an eye on Herod Agrippa, a grandson of Great Herod. He dreams of ruling a free Judea one day."

"Speaking of—how are things there?"

"Certainly not quiet."

Tiberius blew a gust of air out of his cheeks, making the snake flinch. "Those raucous Jews. Is there no pleasing them?"

"But all is under control, Caesar."

"Except the Senate, my friend."

Sejanus stood up to go. "May I suggest that you address a letter to it? That will dispel any anxiety your enemies have aroused there."

"Hmmm . . ." But Tiberius did not answer. His eyes were frosty as his hand absently stroked the snake.

Quietly, the prefect slipped out of the chamber.

Valerius wiled away the hours playing dice with the praetorian charged with guarding him, a strapping Etrurian he had gradually befriended during his week of captivity. The back room of the praetorium had been lit only by one smoky lamp, but Pugnus—or "Fist," as he had been nicknamed—requisitioned another so they could accurately tally up the throws. As it became increasingly apparent that Valerius was doomed, Pugnus showed the rough kindness of a country boy: "Look here, friend, any business you need done in Rome, just let me know. My whole outfit rotates back to Rome in a week."

"Thank you. . . . I'll see what develops."

Pugnus nodded gamely. "Right. . . . You may see to it all yourself."

The door was thrown back against the inside wall, and Pugnus shot to his feet, dropping the dice to the floor and kicking them under the table. Then he saluted the praetorian prefect.

Sejanus ambled past the threshold. He appeared to be in a congenial mood and went so far as to give Valerius a thin smile. "Julius Valerius Licinius, standard-bearer of the Third Legion Augusta . . ."

"Sir." Valerius had also come to attention.

Sejanus waved for Pugnus to leave before he continued: "You served in Africa prior to transfer here with the Capri Cohort."

"I did."

Still smiling, Sejanus took one of the backless leather chairs. "You may be seated, Valerius."

He hesitated, hoping the pounding of his heart was not showing through his tunic.

"Go on, man, I mean it," Sejanus said with a friendly gruffness. "I think I have significant news for you."

Valerius resisted echoing the word *significant*.

"Your two men who failed to repel the intruder on Caesar's peace and security have been disciplined. Do you know the manner in which they were called to account?"

Valerius lowered his head once. Pugnus had told him. The two legionaries had been forced to run the *fustuarium,* two long files formed from the men of their own cohort, who lashed at them with cudgels while they dashed toward the impossibly distant end of this gauntlet. In his fitful sleep of the past week, Valerius had watched the pair stumble, fall, surge up again on the compulsion of their terror, ward off blows to their heads with crooked forearms—only to expose their backs and bellies—then, finally, see the futility in running. This was the worst part of these dreams: to hear the men petitioning comrades they had campaigned with, slept with, eaten with—prayed to the same gods with—"Mercy, Marcus . . . Servius . . . Quintus!" But no legionary feigned a blow. For, as Pugnus had reported, the entire cohort had been threatened with decimation. If there had been the slightest inkling that the condemned men had been coddled, all six centuries would have been disarmed while lots were cast selecting every tenth man, who would have been dragged out of the ranks by a praetorian as powerfully built as Pugnus — and beheaded.

Valerius wondered if he was losing his mind. In spite of this awful knowledge, he still wondered if he, of his volition, could have pitched that hapless fisherman over the cliff.

Sejanus had been carefully watching the young signifer during this silence. "They can be unsettling, these celebrations of discipline."

"And I have heard a rumor mine will be celebrated tomorrow." Valerius struggled to keep his voice level.

"No rumor, Valerius. Your colonel already holds the order."

"I see." Valerius sat straighter so the weight of his despair would not show in his broad shoulders. "I ask permission to write my father—to explain."

"He's with the Seventh Legion in Gaul, isn't he?"

"Yes, but how does the prefect know such a minor thing?"

Sejanus laughed gently and reached across the table to cuff him on the arm. Valerius felt such a surge of hope from this, he was instantly ashamed at how desperately he wanted to live. The feeling, he reminded himself in the midst of his misery, was un-Roman.

"Valerius, if I may speak to you as a friend, it was a foolish thing to frighten the Emperor in that way. That fish could have been a clever sheath for a dagger. But I've spoken to the Emperor in your behalf. It was a task, believe me, but I finally persuaded him to show mercy in your case."

Valerius became dizzy. He clutched the edges of the table with both hands. "I thank you for my father, a brave soldier who would have been dishonored. . . ."

"But *you* should be the one to thank me."

"You have my gratitude."

"Oh, I demand it, Valerius. From now on you're seconded to my service—at the Emperor's command, of course."

Valerius looked confused. "To the praetorian guard?"

"No, that might present administrative difficulties. You will perform a personal office for me." Then Sejanus leaned forward to confide: "Rome is in terrible danger. Even you must have noticed how very old our Emperor is. There are unanswered questions regarding the imperial succession. The young prince Gaius Caligula—you know of him?"

"Why, yes—a soldier. He visited our camp in—"

"Hardly a soldier," Sejanus chuckled. "Despite his boots. But the important thing is this: Caligula is a kinsman to the Emperor. He may one day be Caesar himself. And his noble grandmother, Antonia, is equally precious to me." All the humor drained out of the prefect's eyes. What remained there was cold, even vicious. "I must be assured that their lives are guarded—flawlessly." He continued to stare at Valerius.

"By me, sir?"

"By you. Watch them as if your life depended on it. Note all their comings and goings. Report to me regularly." Then Sejanus smiled again. "You must be eager to get off this rock."

"Prefect?"

"To see Rome again . . . your mother."

"Yes," Valerius answered—more fervently than he had intended.

VI

THE aging man sprawled on a couch that was still somewhat dusty from having been hauled out of storage. Impatiently, he popped dates into his large mouth and half listened to an adjutant who was lecturing him with the use of a vellum map of Judea.

"... So I believe we have found the fitting capstone to your tenure in Judea, Procurator—"

"Damn you, Calpurnius," he bawled, "you have already wasted more time than it took me to ride from Caesarea!"

"I meant only to suggest that Pontius Pilate's four years here have been so filled with achievement, it is difficult to arrive at—"

"*I* am Pontius Pilate!"

Calpurnius' grin was insipid. "I know that, sir."

"Then save these flourishes for the next fool Tiberius sends out here." Pilate pursed his lips and ejected a pit out onto the stone floor of the hall in the Fortress of Antonia. He squinted at the markings that indicated the mountainous regions of Samaria. His eyes seemed too small for his face, or perhaps it was their shrewdness that made them seem so—a narrowness of perception that shunned everything that was not practical or guaranteed to return some advantage to him. It was this same quality that, when displayed in its better light, made him seem fair-minded, or at least indifferent to popular hysterias. "Now, point out this redoubt of theirs."

"Right here, Procurator—Mount Gerizim."

"Run it past me again—the manifest of the treasure they supposedly hide there. But this time spare me the allusions to Virgil."

"Well, sir, there's gold and silver, Greek and Roman coinage and a veritable trove of gemstones—we believe."

In silence, Pilate ground the meat off another date with his

43

teeth. His gaze gravitated out the window of the tower and fell
upon the hammered gold and white marble of the Temple of
Herod. "How would they react to persuasion?"

"Meaning, sir?"

"I send an emissary . . . tell them to deliver up this hoard or
suffer our legions."

"I see. Not well: The Samaritans hold Gerizim to be holy.
In any event, they might appeal to the proconsul Vitellius in
Syria if such an attempt is made to extort their treasure—"

"Do not speak of extortion!" Pilate cried. "Or at least wait
until you are facing your own retirement!"

"Yes, Procurator," the man said meekly.

"We must simply wait for just cause, as we have in the
past."

"That's it. And then you are assured another commendation
from Lucius Aelius Sejanus—as you did for this messiah affair. . . ." Calpurnius' face became thoughtful for a moment.
"Is it entirely necessary that the cause originates in Samaria?"

"Speak plainly, man."

"Well, if we stir up the hotheads here in Jerusalem but then
strike at Gerizim, would Rome be any wiser?"

Pilate sucked on another date, then nodded. "No, this is all
seen as one hopeless Oriental mess. Do you have something
in mind—a plan?"

"Only today another Zealot fell into our hands. He attempted
to kill a legionary with his bare hands."

"Are you sure he's a Zealot?"

"Quite."

"Not a Samaritan, too, by chance?" Pilate asked.

"I'm afraid not. But our informers vouch for his loathing
of your government. If we set him free, there is little question
he will trouble us again."

Pilate swung his legs over the side of the couch and sat
there awhile, thinking. "During the past few days . . ." he started
to say, then frowned contemptuously at the officer who shared
his company. Strolling to the window, he peered down on the
courtyard of the Temple, ignoring the bearded faces that looked
back up at him. He had been about to confess that, recently,
he had begun to reproach himself for allowing the Zealot Ba-
rabbas to go unmolested. And although he put scant faith in
intuition, and tolerated soothsayers only for his wife's sake,
Pilate was yet haunted by the inkling that, of the two choices

that day in this very praetorium, the man called Jesus had posed a greater risk to the Empire. Pilate could not explain why—not even to himself. And this bothered him, had vexed his sleep of the past week. Yet, he had been relieved to the point of intoxication when his chief centurion had reported back to him that Jesus of Nazareth was undeniably dead, although the man had suffered the cross only six hours—a new record for Judean frailty.

"Very well," he declared at last. "Let's do it."

"As ordered, Procurator."

"Does this Zealot have a family?"

"His mother and two sisters."

"The girls—are they comely?" There was nothing lustful in Pilate's eyes.

"I am told they are young. Would the procurator care to see them for himself?"

"No. You check in my stead. If they are appealing, send them on to Caesarea and then Rome without delay. A bireme sails soon. My good friend Sejanus will appreciate the gift of young slaves." Then Pilate approached the map and stared longingly at the wedge-shaped mark that signified Mount Gerizim. "Also, put it out to the centurions to keep an eye open for Samaritan pilgrims here for . . . What's the name of that damned festival of theirs?"

"Shabuoth . . . the First Fruits of Spring."

"Yes, well, have them step on a few toes if they have to. I'd like a Samaritan or two marching behind our Zealot up Golgotha during . . ." He glanced to Calpurnius once again, his face full of irritation.

"*Shabuoth,* Procurator."

Samuel sprinted three paces behind Stephen, the bile rising in his throat, dodging pilgrims filtering back from the Temple through the darkened streets. He cursed himself for having waited on the steps of the Fortress of Antonia all afternoon with Saul, hoping to use the Cilician's Roman citizenship to gain an audience with Pilate, while his beloved Ruth . . . Samuel could not complete the thought without growing more sick at heart and falling even farther behind Stephen, who was still dust-covered from his wrestling match with Caleb.

"Wait!" Samuel halted at a covered passageway. "This way is faster!"

Stephen backtracked to him, his pulse quivering in his voice.
"I went to the house. To apologize . . . his mother."

"Did you see them taken away?"

"No . . . praetorians cordoned off the street."

"*Praetorians*—and not legionaries?"

"I'm positive."

Samuel nearly howled at this news: Invariably, the guard
did the procurator's dirtiest work. This added only one more
straw to his despair.

They turned the last corner and rushed up a steep lane, their
footfalls echoing off the stone faces of the house.

A sob flew out of Samuel's mouth when he saw that the
door was yawning inward and the rooms beyond were darkened.

"Ruth!" he shouted, tripping over a table in the blackness.
"Sarah . . . Leah!" But he knew no one remained within Caleb's
house.

"They've been taken," a neighbor said from the threshold.

Samuel dragged the old man back out into the lane where
he could see his face in torchlight. "What happened?"

"Easy, Samuel," Stephen said, "you'll choke him with his
own mantle."

The neighbor rubbed his throat before speaking. "The soldiers came at dusk. They made us all stay inside. But I could
hear Leah's Ruth screaming. . . ."

"Lord God," Stephen whispered.

"But Sarah argued. She said they had no right."

Samuel reared his head back and groaned. "But what happened to them, man? They were never delivered to Antonia;
we were there."

"No, my son," the old man said, snuffling now. "I overheard
one of the soldiers. Leah and her girls are being marched to
the coast. Directly to Caesarea. Heavy escort."

Samuel staggered over to the stoop, sank down with his
back rubbing the doorframe, then wept into his arms.

Stephen sat beside him. "The Lord will rescue us, Samuel.
He has come to our help in harder times."

"They will end up in Rome . . . in a slave market. My Ruth."
A breath seethed between his clenched teeth. "I tell you, Stephen of Alexandria, Pilate's body will feed the maggots for
this!"

"Samuel . . ."

"There are those in the city whose invitation I have declined before." He wiped his cheeks with his palms. "No more."

"You don't mean this. . . . The shock of—"

"I'd rather die than live with this shame any longer."

"You have no shame, Samuel. You have hurt no one."

He pulled back from Stephen's gentle face as if he suddenly found it repugnant. "Hurt no one *yet*. That will not be true before the Shabuoth is done."

"May he forgive you, for he hears you well. He has not forgotten us. But we spurn what he did for us when we kill."

Samuel rose. Delicately, he shut the door, as if recognizing that he would never again open it to see the smiling face of a girl. "Farewell, Greek." He then hurried down the lane toward the lower city and a house he knew where entry was restricted but to a special few: those who swore vengeance on Rome, even at the cost of their own lives.

"He hears you well!" Stephen's voice chased after him.

"I can now see their centurion," the youth whispered, his face stern with resolve. He lay back down behind the low parapet at the edge of the roof.

"Can you see Caleb?"

"No . . . the praetorians are just wheeling out of the square of Antonia." Then he added grimly: "But surely they haven't forgotten your friend on this day."

Samuel could now hear the drums of the Roman crucifixion detail. His heart was hammering, but he hoped that outwardly he appeared calm to the four other Zealots hiding prostrate on the roof. Insouciantly, he sniffed the palms of his hands: They reeked of the pitch and oil he and the others had kneaded into two long ropes. These they had then adorned with myrtle leaves and flowers so they resembled any of the other festoons hung along the streets for the festival—except that these two were far more volatile. One of the young men waited with a torch.

Voices welled up out of the lane below—Greek, Latin, Syriac, Aramaic and others Samuel did not recognize. He drew courage from the familiar Aramaic ones: The native Jerusalemites resented the sentence that would be carried out this morning on Golgotha, and the spirit of rebellion colored everything they said to one another.

The beating of the drums grew louder. Samuel could now feel the insistent tempo in his lungs.

"They approach!" the lookout cried in a hush.

Samuel crept forward to a rainspout, through which he could see the far end of the narrow street. Then he bit his lower lip to keep from crying out: He had stolen a glimpse of Caleb.

"Back from there!" the youth who was their leader said between his teeth.

Samuel crawled backward, too shocked to apologize for his infraction—the very thing he had been warned against during his thorough indoctrination.

But he had glimpsed Caleb plodding over the paving stones under the weight of a crossbeam. The stripes left by the scourge wound around his flanks from his back, which Samuel had no doubt was crisscrossed with welts. Yet, through his suffering, Caleb had remained defiant: His eyes were feverish with hatred, and unlike the four young men who trooped behind him, he appealed to no one for anything.

"You are not alone, my brother," he said under his breath, feeling the hilt of the knife he had concealed in his waistband.

Then, directly below, the tramping of Roman sandals brought all of Samuel's confused and hateful emotions into focus.

"Torch," the leader ordered.

The bearer leaned over the parapet and set fire to the two garlands. The flames shot along the graceful swoops.

Samuel rose to a crouch. In the breezeless morning, the smoke roiled not up but down in acrid billows that wafted across the ranks of the praetorians. The Romans began gagging and hacking for fresh air.

"Ready!" the Zealot who had lowered a rope over the side shouted to Samuel. "You will find Caleb straight away here!"

Samuel clambered down into the smoke. When it gusted clear for a moment, he saw Caleb standing free of the bewildered praetorians. His watery eyes widening when he saw Samuel racing toward him, he stopped choking long enough to swing his crossbeam around so Samuel could cut the hide thongs that bound his wrists to it.

Caleb heaved the timber into the thickest depths of the smoke, and a Roman cried out in pain.

Samuel seized Caleb by the scruff of the neck and guided him toward the rope. "Up—quickly!"

Swiftly, Caleb gained the top of the parapet, and anxious hands helped him over onto the roof. He spun around and stared back down, waiting for Samuel to come bursting out of the smoke. The rope hung limply; there was no tension in it. "Where . . . ?"

Then the smoldering mass began to wane, thinning enough for Caleb to be able to peer through it. Samuel was lying on the flagstones, his legs curled up under his chin. A praetorian was withdrawing his short sword from the youth's abdomen.

"Samuel!" Caleb screamed, preparing to drop to the lane again, when the leader of the Zealots sliced the rope. It fell away.

"Come," the hard-eyed young man insisted, "you must be out of Jerusalem. A friend of yours has made arrangements."

Pontius Pilate was on his feet at the window, overlooking the courtyard of the Temple, which had been turned golden by the late afternoon sun, when his adjutant Calpurnius led the praetorian centurion into the hall. The officer shook off a shudder as if he had found the sparsely furnished chamber chilly after the searing back lanes of Jerusalem.

Pilate tapped his lips with a finger thoughtfully. "Hail Tiberius," he said without emotion.

The centurion looked bemused. He had obviously expected a more strident reception. "Hail Tiberius!"

"Any luck?" the procurator asked in the same emotionless voice.

"I'm afraid not, sir. So far, at least. We've kicked in every door of the lower city."

"And the upper city?"

"Well, as you know, sir, the members of the Sanhedrin, all the substantial folk, live there. The going's a bit slower for us there—out of political considerations."

"Political considerations," Pilate repeated, but not sarcastically. He smiled at the officer, then crooked a forefinger. "Come here."

The centurion stepped lively. "Sir?"

Pilate gestured down at the masses of Jews praying on the colonnaded porticoes, queuing up to enter the Temple proper. "What would you say *they* are thinking about this morning's prank?"

"I'd . . . I'd imagine they're having a bit of a laugh at our expense, sir."

"A laugh at . . ." Finally, Pilate could feign coolness no longer. And perhaps before he himself realized what had hap-

pened, the procurator had struck the centurion across the face
with the back of his hand.

The officer glared back in amazement. A Roman could be
upbraided, scourged, even beheaded, but he was never slapped,
especially by another citizen. It could mean only one thing.

Briefly, Pilate's small eyes were remorseful, but then anger
seized them again. "I intend to write my good friend, Lucius
Aelius Sejanus, this evening. What shall I tell him of a centurion who misplaced a Judean agitator who was only two
hundred paces from crucifixion?"

The centurion's voice had been reduced to a croak. "Tell
him"—he struggled against the reflex to retch—"Sextius Cornelius has fallen on his sword . . . in the interests of his honor
. . . his children."

"It will be a pleasure. Dismissed."

The centurion stood gaping at the procurator for a moment,
then realized that nothing more would be said. He shuffled out
as if there were no sensation left in his legs.

As soon as the door boomed shut, Calpurnius scurried up
to Pilate. "You're not really going to write Sejanus *that*, are
you?"

"Of course not. That would amount to a confession of bun-
gling on our part." Pilate paused, his eyes hard on his adjutant's. "Are you?"

"Procurator?"

"Going to tell Sejanus what happened here?"

"No . . . please don't even think." Fright had made Calpurnius' voice shrill. "I would never—"

"Good, because if I fall, you fall with me."

"But how do we explain the centurion's death? He is a
praetorian, after all."

"Oh, I don't care. He was told he had a disease for which
there is no cure. I'll leave that to you." Pilate then spread his
hands on the window casement and leaned on them. "What
gives here?"

Below, a man in rough clothes had climbed up onto the
plinth of a column in the Court of Women and was exhorting
the pilgrims: "My Jewish brothers, men and women of Judea
and all that dwell in Jerusalem, give ear to my words. . . ."

Pilate watched with an amused smile as priests of the Temple
began infiltrating the crowd.

The speaker spun angrily on someone in the uneven ranks facing him. "I heard that! I'm not drunk. Neither are my friends, here. . . ."

Pilate chuckled. The man spoke such a lean and simple Aramaic, the procurator, for once, found himself understanding every word.

". . . No, this is no drunken talk. It is the giving forth of good news. Remember what was said by the prophet Joel: 'I will pour forth my spirit upon all flesh. And your sons and daughters shall prophesy. And your young men shall see visions . . . your old men shall dream dreams. And I will show wonders in the heavens above, signs on the earth below, blood and fire and vapor of smoke. The sun shall be turned into darkness, and the moon into blood when the day of the Lord comes, that great and notable day . . .'"

"Who is that fellow?" Pilate asked Calpurnius.

"I'm not sure. Do you want him apprehended when he leaves the Temple?"

"Mars, no. Let him stir the caldron. Never put your wedges on the shelf when you plan to split Jews."

". . . Yes, I say it again: The great and notable day is upon us. Jesus of Nazareth, a man approved of God by mighty works and wonders—"

"Ah," Pilate murmured, "here it is."

"—Jesus, crucified, slain by lawless men—"

Pilate frowned. "Now we begin to stretch out our arms for the cross."

"—God has raised him up. Of this, I, Simon Peter, among others, am a witness. . . ."

"Oh, yes," Calpurnius said, "chief adherent of the dead Jesus. A coward by avocation. He disappeared when things got perilous for his master."

". . . Therefore, he is exalted at the right hand of God. Let all the house of Israel know God has made him both Lord and Messiah—"

"Blasphemy!" a young man shouted from the center of the throng.

"Who is that little vial of vinegar?" Pilate asked Calpurnius.

"I spoke to him yesterday. He wanted to see you regarding the Zealot. His name is Paul, a Roman citizen from Cilicia."

"It is no blasphemy to fulfill the prophesies of old! Save

yourselves, men and women of Judea. The wonders and signs are upon you!"

"How?" a woman's voice sang out.

"Repent! Be baptized, each one of you, in the name of Jesus Christ. You shall receive the gift of the Holy Spirit. Save your souls." Then the speaker glared up at the Fortress of Antonia. "Save yourselves from this crooked generation!"

Pilate smiled, then stepped away from the window. "As predictable as the tides, these Jews."

VII

IN the weeks following his return from Capri, Sejanus spent more time at the Curia, where the Senate convened, than at the *castra praetoria,* the fortress he had convinced Tiberius to build for the guard. No matter how boring the proceedings, he steadfastly remained a study in attentiveness and resolution, leaning forward from his curule chair, handsome face propped on his fist. Never once did he show displeasure, even when Curtius Atticus muttered from the semicircle of benches across the marble floor, "Everyone of us is watched—in the baths, at the games, while we relax in our own gardens."

But, had the elderly senator looked closely, he would have glimpsed his own severed head spinning down through the frostiness of the praetorian prefect's stare.

From time to time, Sejanus peered up at the gilded image of Victory, wings flowing, offering a crown of laurel to the first taker. His lips parted on these occasions.

"And so," Cocceius Nerva, Atticus' ally and Tiberius' old friend, concluded a long oration, "it is therefore necessary that, without delay, this venerable Senate appoint a delegation, preferably of former consuls, to go to Capri and deliver unto Tiberius Caesar the appeal of his Rome, this orphaned city!"

There was an outburst of applause, which Sejanus politely joined. He did not add his voice to those he had instructed to mock old Nerva.

The *princeps senatus,* president of the Senate, stood on his low dais. Wincing, he shifted his weight on his gouty feet, then rearranged the gorgeously embroidered purple hem on his toga. "Conscript Fathers—"

"Speak louder," a freedman of his whispered from behind. It was this ex-slave's job to prompt the dotard during his orations.

53

"*Conscript Fathers,* you have heard the opinion of this noble man. One proposition is before you. Those who favor sending a delegation from this Senate to our Emperor, walk to the right. Those who so oppose, to the left."

Sejanus smiled gamely, although it soon became obvious after much shuffling of sandals and rustling of togas that Nerva's proposal had carried by a majority. Good-naturedly, the prefect shrugged at the men who had supported him in the debate. This also served as a signal to a praetorian centurion who had been waiting inconspicuously in the uppermost tier of the Curia and now stamped down to whisper in Sejanus' ear and hand him a sealed dispatch.

"Conscript Fathers!" The prefect boldly stepped out onto the floor, although he was not a member of the Senate. "I, too, have heard what the noble Cocceius Nerva has proposed. But it might run counter to the manifest wish of the divine Tiberius not to divert any of you from your duties in the city." Then his tone became threatening, although it was still wrapped in a veneer of respect: "He appreciates how you are totally absorbed in rendering loyal service to the Empire and its Emperor. However, I have just this minute received instructions from Tiberius that I am to convey to you his personal message. Consider my voice to be his." Then, so all could see, Sejanus broke the imperial seal. "'My lords, Senators of Rome. If I knew what to tell you, or how to tell it, or what to leave altogether untold for the present, may all the gods and goddesses in heaven bring me to an even worse damnation than I daily suffer.'"

Sejanus made broad business of searching for more—an explanation for this baffling document. He even went so far as to turn the scroll inside out. A smirk twitched at the corners of his mouth, but never emerged full-blown. Like the murmuring assembly before him, he displayed nothing but consternation.

Then, giving his strongest profile to the Senate, he strode out purposefully.

By evening of the same day, certain senators had invited the praetorian prefect to return to the Curia for an extraordinary meeting after the main body had adjourned. There, in the seats farthest from the doors, which were secured by praetorian officers, the patricians took an accounting of the royal family and found it bankrupt without Sejanus having to say a word:

"Who else, then? Julius and Drusus are exiled as the traitors they are. Gaius Caesar—"

"*Caligula?* Still a boy tramping around army camps in bootikins."

"That doesn't prevent some of our noble friends from licking those bootikins."

"Antonia's son . . . ?"

"Oh, yes, the limper, you mean."

"You're speaking of Claudius. A nitwit—not even to be considered."

"Hold now, Claudius is something of a historian. I read one of his books."

"What was the title?"

"Well . . . I forget for the moment."

"Enough said of Antonia's surviving son."

"So Rome must do without a head . . . unless—"

"We choose leadership, courage and express acquaintance with imperial power . . . over a tradition that now fails us."

All eyes gravitated toward Sejanus, whose brow became furrowed. "You all honor me, but I have never sought this."

"We know, Sejanus. But will you consider it?"

He hesitated as long as he dared without appearing to be balky. Then Sejanus nodded yes.

Yet, before leaving the Curia, he asked the senators to divulge none of this discussion, lest Tiberius hear of it. Sejanus made this request in a civil voice, although his eyes shone with violence for any man who might double-cross him.

Within the week, the prefect was glad he had taken this precaution, for it suddenly seemed that he might be able to achieve his aims without the help of the Senate.

This windfall, which had come from Tiberius himself, first came to Sejanus' attention while he was visiting Lady Antonia's house, plausibly to check on the matron's satisfaction with her new bodyguard, Valerius, but secretly to steal a few minutes alone with her daughter, Livilla, who had also arrived to visit. Antonia said she was pleased with Valerius, whom she described as a sensitive young man, but throughout her chat with the prefect she seemed agitated and distracted. At last, Sejanus was able to fulfill his carefully arranged tryst with Livilla in the *peristylium,* Antonia's shaded courtyard.

"You, woman, are as ripe as summer," he whispered, pressing her against his cuirass.

"Where have you been?" her breath roared in his ear.

"Being cautious . . . we must—"

"I love you."

"I—"

Footfalls, approaching at a run, made them step away from each other. A praetorian came sprinting around the fountain.

"Damn," Sejanus fumed.

"Pardon, Prefect. I've run all the way from the Curia."

The frown vanished. "What news from the Senate?"

"Good news, noble Marinus says. But you must come immediately to the Curia to learn what."

"Lucius Marinus has come to Rome from Capri?"

"Yes, sir."

Sejanus dismissed the man, then grinned at Livilla. "Then it's as good as if it's from Tiberius himself."

"What—?"

"I will know shortly."

"Will you send a guardsman to let me know?"

"Yes, yes, of course." He had taken a half dozen strides toward the atrium, when he remembered himself and hurried back to kiss her. "It is hard to believe what they say. . . ."

"What do they say?"

"That you were a plain child."

"I was, Lucius Aelius."

"Blasphemy!" Then he dashed for his appointment with the Senate.

Tiberius' whoremaster, Marinus, had divested himself of his vivid gowns and now wore a sedate toga with a thin strip of purple, which declared him to be a patrician. With Sejanus standing beside him on the floor of the Curia, he said in his silky voice, "Lords of the Senate, I bear to you news from Capri. A message from Tiberius Caesar." There was no sound in the hall but the rattling of parchment. "'In recognition of his many merits, of his faithful and loyal services to Rome and myself, its Emperor, I have decreed that our prefect of the Praetorian Guard, the noble Lucius Aelius Sejanus, the partner of my labors in ruling, be associated to me in the Consulship for this new year. I salute Sejanus, Consul of Rome, and exhort you, Lords of the Senate, to acclaim with me his virtues and valor. Hail and be well!'"

Sejanus' partisans unleashed a joyous cry, but the majority

of their fellow senators began applauding only when the hundred-strong praetorians ringing the back tier of the chamber raised a din by beating their shields with their swords.

The prefect smiled modestly all around him.

The office meant little of itself. Unlike in the days of the Republic, the two consuls wielded scant power, and then only at the discretion of the Emperor, who more often than not reserved one of the posts for himself. But this was a long-awaited omen for Sejanus: Tiberius, finally, was preparing the way for the prefect to be his successor. It almost seemed too good to be true.

Curtius Atticus, who had stubbornly refused to applaud the news, abandoned his seat and pushed his way past the praetorians at the doors. Sejanus made a mental note of this, but did not drop his smile for an instant. His keen eye also roved for Cocceius Nerva, who—probably having heard of the appointment beforehand from Tiberius himself—was not present.

But these were passing clouds on the brightest day of Sejanus' life.

And even before the applause had waned, he was thinking of a way to get secret word to Livilla. He ached to tell her she would soon be Empress of Rome.

VIII

CALEB refused to rest until certain he had left at least twenty Roman miles behind him. Only then, atop a ridge whose slopes glowed barren, cadaver-gray in the star shine, did he sit on his heels and recount all he and his family had suffered in the past three days—how swift this devastation to his world! Some images were too much for him to bear, and a soft gasp escaped him. Through weary eyes, he watched the dawn ignite the vapors rising off the mountains of ancient Moab.

After clambering over the rooftops of Jerusalem and racing pell-mell down its crowded lanes, the band of Zealots had arrived at a house in the lower city Caleb had heretofore known only by reputation. Reportedly, it was the secret headquarters to a handful of firebrands Caleb might have joined, except that he had believed it safer for his family if he waged a single-handed war against the Romans.

Caleb was flabbergasted to find Stephen from *Rabban* Gamaliel's school inside this nest of Zealots. "Don't tell me you are one of this—"

"No, no." The young man counted all the faces around him. "Where is Samuel?" And when the downcast eyes answered this for him, Stephen whispered, "I feared violence."

"He died bravely," the leader of the Zealots said, closing the matter. "Now we must prepare to slip Caleb out of the city at nightfall."

"And my family," Caleb added. "They must be put out of Pilate's reach. . . ." Immediately, from the discomfort of everyone in the room, he sensed that something was wrong. "What is it?"

Only Stephen would answer. "We are too late for that, my friend. They've been taken to the port of Caesarea. From there, it is said, they will go to Rome . . . as slaves."

"No! Why weren't they rescued, as I was?"

"It was not possible," the leader said simply. "They were guarded by both cavalry and infantry. Besides, you are more clearly a symbol of our struggle."

Caleb batted a pitcher off the table. It shattered against the wall. No one said a word to him, and he withdrew to a corner, where he stood alone, trembling with rage and hurt until Stephen finally crept up to him. "God will not abandon them."

"Where was he when they were taken?" Caleb's eyes were glistening.

"At their side . . . as he now is with us."

"I will take the road to Caesarea and find them."

"You will not," the leader said, anger in his voice for the first time. "Your comrade died in your behalf. You will not throw away his sacrifice by stumbling into a Roman trap. Your family is beyond hope: Accept it like a man, a Jew." He heaved a bundled robe at Caleb. "Put this on and eat something. As soon as that is done, we must move you out of this quarter and closer to the wall."

"Where will I go then?" Caleb asked quietly.

"Your friend will tell you."

"Mesad Hasidim," Stephen said, "on the northwest shore of Lake Asphaltites. Do you know of it?"

"I know of such a place, but it is on the Sea of Salt. Asphaltites is a Roman name."

"The same village." Stephen ignored the insinuation that he was, once again, the foreigner. "I have a friend there. He is called Ananias. He'll take care of you."

"Is he a patriot, like us?"

"No, he's an Essene, but you can rely on his people to protect you from the Romans. They are a pious lot, although I believe the answer lies in another way."

"Yes," Caleb hissed, flinching from the welts on his back as he donned the hooded robe, "the way of the sling, the sword, the spear."

"I was not thinking of arms, Caleb. The man from Nazareth—"

"Spare me," Caleb snapped. Then, a moment later, when he saw that his cross words had stung the young man who had put himself in jeopardy to help him, Caleb rested his hand on

Stephen's shoulder. "I thank you for what you have done."

"And Saul has been a friend to you as well."

"Saul?" Caleb cocked an eyebrow.

"He went with me to your uncle Matthias. We urged him to buy your freedom . . . that of your mother and sisters. . . ." Stephen did not go on.

"Well, what did he say?"

"He's joined the Nazarenes—and given all he owned to the poor."

"So that's why he sold his house." Caleb shook his head. "And his wealth could've saved us."

"No," Stephen said gently, "you will be saved by the mercy and love of the Lord."

And now, squatting on a rocky spine of the Judean hills, Caleb repeated bitterly, "Mercy and love. . . ." Below him, across a broken landscape quilted by the first rays of the sun to clear the mountains of old Moab, a huge, limpid lake had materialized out of the shadows. Its azure color was so like the blue of the sky, he could almost believe he was peering through a hole in the world—the void left by his family.

Caleb descended from these heights into a dry watercourse so steep in places he had to inch his way down crevices, with nothing underfoot but the morning breeze to catch him if he fell. At last, he reached a plateau perched above the briny waters of the lake and plodded across this sun-scorched terrace to a village. No one moved along the dusty footpaths, and the smoke of only one cooking fire—for a score of hovels tucked into stone crannies — trickled up into the sky.

Caleb hesitated on the outskirts, then concealed himself until he could be sure Roman legionaries had not beaten him to Mesad Hasidim.

After a while, a woman emerged from the largest structure, which was no grander than a laborer's dwelling in Jerusalem, and strolled to one of the outdoor ovens. Her motions as she removed loaves of bread were so placid and serene, Caleb knew that no Romans were waiting to seize him in this village.

He approached her through an orchard of gnarled and stunted fruit trees, clearing his throat and scuffling his sandals so as not to startle her. *"Shalom,"* he said when she finally glanced up.

She smiled but did not answer.

"I seek a man called Ananias. A friend of his sends me."

Pressing her finger to her lips, she motioned with her free

hand for Caleb to follow her. He trailed behind this lean figure in white linen, wondering if she might be a mute. It also bemused him that there were no shops to be seen among the houses.

She urged him up stone steps into the large building that proved to be a dining hall in which sat the entire population of Mesad Hasidim, silent except for the clicking of jaws and teeth.

"Shalom...."

Again, no one spoke, although all eyes in the long room were intent on his.

"I come looking for a man named Ananias. Do you—"

A man in middle age, garbed in the white linen that was apparently the uniform of the community, stood at his place along the table and, rather severely, shushed Caleb with the same gesture the woman had used on him. Then he waved for Caleb to sit down. A girl began serving the young man.

Caleb stared down at the fare: unleavened bread, although Passover had been over for weeks; roasted locusts; and water. He tried to nod appreciatively.

The meal was concluded with a Hebrew hymn. Then the same solemn man signaled for Caleb to accompany him outside, where he handed the youth a short-handled hoe. Caleb could not have looked more baffled had the man given him the fasces of Rome to bear.

"I am Ananias. Come."

He led Caleb out into the hardscrabble fields of the community, where spikes of barley and half-withered curls of lentil braved the sun and hot wind. It was only mid-morning, and already Caleb's robe was heavy with his perspiration.

"I am Caleb of Jerusalem. Stephen of Alexandria recommends me to you. I have had some trouble with the Roman governor." His voice came close to breaking. "They have taken my widowed mother, my sisters, as slaves."

"God protect them."

"I am in need of refuge for a short while. Then I will be gone."

Ananias bent over and began chopping up the salty-looking crust that had formed atop the field. "You are welcome. Now, stop tapping that hoe against your leg and help me." He gave Caleb a brief smile. "We live the very essence of our Jewish faith here. Ceaselessly, we strive for purity. We practice abstinence *and* continence."

Caleb began working faster. Obviously, the man had caught him eyeing the girl who had served him. "But these men—do they ever lie with their wives?"

"Most of us are not married. Those who are receive our encouragement not to breed."

"Why not?"

Ananias frowned as if he could not believe such ignorance. "The end of the world is upon us, young man. What do the priests at the Temple teach these days?"

"That we are on the verge of a new world: the building of a free Jewish nation."

"There is no time for such foolishness. Be careful, there: You are cutting off sprouts with the weeds."

"I have heard of your sect—"

"Sect, he says," Ananias grumbled, "as if we pray to Baal."

"—but I did not realize how removed you are from us."

"'Removed'? Have you heard of John the Baptist?"

"Of course I have."

Ananias shielded his eyes with his left hand and pointed with his hoe at a small stone hut at the base of a cliff. "See that house there? The one with the fig tree? Well, he lived there among us. Do you know any of the followers of Jesus of Nazareth?"

"Yes . . . my Uncle Matthias has just become one, I hear."

"Ah, then he must be the *one*." The man's eyes widened with interest. Then he shrugged and leaned over again.

"The one what?"

"A Matthias of Jerusalem has just been named the twelfth apostle of this Jesus—to replace the one who betrayed him."

"I did not know that."

Ananias smirked. "And we here are removed."

Caleb smiled back at him.

They labored until evening. Despite his weariness from having walked all night, Caleb found comfort in the mindless abandon that came from endlessly flinging his hoe, watching his own beads of sweat sparkle down and pelt the earth.

His features abstracted, Ananias was lost in his own meditations. Once, however, he suddenly dropped his hoe, hurried over to Caleb, and, with no explanation, seized the youth by the wrist and studied his palm. Unaccustomed to hard labor, it had erupted into several blisters. Ananias let go of Caleb's hand. He appeared to be confused. "You are no fisherman."

"No—nor did I say I was."

"Peculiar, then." Ananias went back to work.

Caleb had heard rumors that some Essene wise men could foretell the future. As the minutes passed, silent but for the sound of the iron blades striking the ground, his curiosity became intolerable: "*What* is peculiar, Ananias?"

"Well, I had a small vision in the midst of my contemplation: you defending yourself against violence with a net. But it makes no sense to me. Unless you were a fisherman and might one day have to defend your boat or something."

"I will defend myself, but with no fishing net."

"What are your plans, then, young Caleb?"

Instinctively, Caleb looked over his shoulder before speaking. "I was imprisoned in the Fortress of Antonia with some Samaritans. Revolt is brewing there, they told me. It's almost as if the Romans are forcing them into it."

"And you will join them in this bloodletting?"

"Gladly."

Ananias scowled and buried his hoe in a furrow. He held Caleb's eyes. "If you absolutely must sin, the least you can do is not go at it *gladly*." He then checked the position of the setting sun. "Be certain to evacuate your bowels before sundown."

"Why?"

"We approach the Sabbath. It would be sacrilege to do so before tomorrow evening."

"You joke." Caleb was grinning.

Ananias stared at the young man until his expression sobered.

He remained with the Essenes less than a week, for within those two Sabbaths another visitor arrived in Mesad Hasidim from Jerusalem. He claimed to be a Jewish pilgrim from Armenia returning to the kingdom after praying in the Temple, although his Aramaic was as accentless as Caleb's.

The pilgrim made no mention of the young Zealot's escape from crucifixion. If he could be believed, all the excitement in the city revolved around the small band of Nazarenes. "I saw this myself," the man said excitedly, "the fellow they call Peter. . . . He cured a cripple at the Beautiful Door of the Temple. The cripple actually danced! And then a strange flame appeared to these disciples—"

"A fire?" Ananias looked intently on the man. "Are you sure?"

"Well, I only heard this from others. But tongues of flame

rested upon his followers, enabling them to speak all the languages of the world."

"That makes no sense," Ananias muttered. "If this is to be believed, why, it means all men may partake of salvation." He shook off the thought as if it were ridiculous. "Only the sons of light will prevail and be saved." He then asked the pilgrim: "What do my old friends, the priests, say of all this?"

"They are concerned," the man said, his eyes guarded. "A young man of otherwise good reputation has been baptized by Peter in the Kidron." His eyes darted to Caleb's face. "Perhaps one of you know him. He is called Stephen."

"What does that matter to us? Stephen is a Greek name," Caleb said.

"Yes—Azariah, was it? Not a bold Jewish name like yours, but he is a Jew nonetheless."

"He means nothing to me." Yawning, Caleb took his leave of Ananias and the pilgrim as if he intended to go back out into the fields. Then he filled two water skins at the well and strode out of Mesad Hasidim—not on the road that coursed up the Jordan Valley, but into the Judean hills again, following the dry ravines, climbing over bluffs that were pocked with small caves. By the time he reached the crest, the last rays of the sun were shooting flat across the wilderness, and even the shadows cast by pebbles were as long as a man.

Without warning or apparent reason, Caleb was overcome by a feeling of sorrow he could not outdistance no matter how swiftly he hiked. The wind rose against him. Finally, he crouched in the lee of a great rock and wept out this bitterness before continuing north toward Samaria.

Sarah no longer gazed at the coast over the gunwale of the Roman bireme. The shoreline was always within sight, as even a sturdy naval ship such as this dared not venture too far out to sea for fear of becoming lost; but it had finally occurred to her that she and her sister, Ruth, would never see their homeland again. Bittersweet glimpses—like this morning's of snow-topped Mount Hermon, which she had once seen from afar as a child—only prolonged any agony she would have to put aside if she intended to survive.

And Sarah intended to survive. "Eat," she told her sister.

Ruth was curled up against a hawser, her face chafed red by wind and sun. They had been forced to live in the exposed deck, as the two levels below were reserved for the slaves who rowed the vessel. The girls had been permitted to follow the shade of the single sail, but even so, their pale skins had been brutalized wherever it was not protected by their coarse tunics or their metal slave collars, which had been riveted around their necks at Caesarea.

In one sense, the collars had been a blessing. They had saved the girls from being violated by the Roman marines who guarded them, for each had stamped upon it:

> I have run away. Catch me. If you take me back
> to my master, Lucius Aelius Sejanus, you will be
> rewarded.

One look at this, and the guards went elsewhere among the Rome-bound slaves to satisfy their urges.

"You must eat," Sarah again coaxed her sister, holding up the bowl that contained a little salt fish in vinegar. "You have not eaten since Caesarea. I do not want you to die."

"I began to die when mother died," Ruth said ominously.

Sarah closed her eyes. She was within a breath of cursing her sister. Now, when she needed to be fortifying herself against the coming night—when the ship would ride at anchor in Sidon harbor, silent but for the moaning of its timbers—she was being compelled to live that morning in Caesarea once more. . . .

. . . Again, the guard's hobnailed sandals clinked down the stone passageway. The door to the praetorium cell yawned open. Blinded by the sunlight, Sarah reached for Ruth's hand. She knew before the guard spoke. She had known the evening before, when her mother had been isolated in another cell. No one appreciated the gift of a female slave past her prime. "The old woman went during the watch before mine," the praetorian mumbled. "Follow. You two will board now."

Sarah thrust the bowl toward Ruth again. "Please . . . eat."

A marine cleared the way for two sailors who had been charged with securing a line. "Move to the other side," he ordered the young women.

Sarah padded first across the deck. Ruth shuffled along a moment later, brushing against the marine as she went. "Do you remember the story Uncle Matthias used to tell us?" she said to Sarah as soon as she had sat down again. There was a strange levity to her sister's voice that made Sarah look at her carefully.

"What story, my Ruth?"

"Of the king of old Israel who had come to hate life."

"No, I—"

"He said that the day of death is better than the day of birth."

"Do you believe that is so?"

Ruth said nothing, although her eyes were shining.

Then Sarah noticed the marine, who was craning his neck back to watch the work of the sailors, reach down out of habit to rest his hand on the hilt of his dagger. The sheath on his hip was empty, and he spun around in alarm, his eyes fixing on Ruth.

It was only then that Sarah saw the blade her sister was holding against her own breast, preparing to plunge it in.

"Hold, there!" the marine cried.

And when he took a step toward her, Ruth turned the point toward him. He skipped back a pace, holding up his forearms as if he meant her no further harm, and as soon as she lowered her grip a few inches he advanced again.

"Ruth!" Sarah screamed.

She swung the dagger in a clumsy arc at him. He easily nabbed her by the wrist, although the gleaming tip was stayed an uncomfortable distance from his throat. Baring his teeth, he wrenched her hand, twisting the blade back in toward her. "Lads!" he called to the sailors. "A hand here . . . so this one's not spoiled!" Then he cooed to her, "Drop it, now." Perhaps he expected her to do just that as he applied more and more pressure to her small hand, but suddenly the dagger slipped into her tunic, and her face began trembling in a ghastly way.

"Oh, damn the demons!" the marine wailed, holding her up by the elbows for a few seconds.

She shuddered, then went limp in his arms. "Damn the bloody demons!" He let her tumble to the deck. Hesitating briefly, he finally retrieved his dagger from her ribs. "Watch the others!" he barked at the sailors as he took off at a run. "There's rebellion in the air. We'll chain down the lot of them after this."

The sailors stood silent for a moment. Then one of them asked gently, his eyes moist with remorse, "Do you wish us to take her . . . ?"

IX

NOISELESSLY, Valerius stepped behind one of the columns in Lady Antonia's garden courtyard. He paused to listen. Over the splashing sounds of the fountain, the matron's voice wafted to him: ". . . an unexpected pleasure, Cocceius Nerva, my dearest friend. I have been anxious to see you."

"It is not easy to leave Capri. Tiberius clings to me . . . and then resents everything I share with him."

His face full of self-loathing, Valerius nevertheless sifted down another two pillars so he might better hear what was being said between the senator and the woman.

"How is the Emperor?"

"Trapped, my lady, in his own fears. There are times I think I can reach him, make him understand the situation as it genuinely exists. But then he quickly withdraws into his obsessions again."

"How does he look?"

"Oh, fit enough. But his eyes betray his confusion."

Valerius eased around the column so he could peer at the marble bench on which the elderly pair sat. They were still clutching hands long after their first meeting. Antonia, whose handsome features had been ennobled by her advanced years, wore a stately *stola*, the feminine version of the toga. Its draping folds were clasped together by buckles of silver inlaid with small gemstones; none was ostentatious. Over the ringed tiers of her white hair she had wrapped a shawl which trailed down over her left shoulder and nearly brushed the ground as she sat beside Nerva.

"So there is no hope he will return to Rome," she said with a sigh.

"Not as long as his fears are kindled by—"

"Sejanus." Her strong voice was contemptuous. "I couldn't

believe it when Tiberius appointed him to the second consulship."

"Neither could the Senate . . . well, most of it. But it's done. We have an emperor in self-imposed exile, and one in the making. Sejanus keeps weaving his plots."

Antonia chuckled as if reminded of something. "In his last letter to me, Curtius Atticus referred to our praetorian prefect as 'the spider.'"

"Curtius should be more careful. Sejanus doesn't forgive."

"Praise to the gods we still have a few brave men among us."

"Fewer each day, I fear."

"Then what can be done? How can Tiberius be persuaded to *listen*?"

"The Senate voted to send a delegation to him," Nerva said. "Then Sejanus cowed its members into postponing the crossing to Capri—indefinitely."

There was a moment of silence. Valerius peeked out again to see Nerva's kindly eyes fixed on Antonia.

"My dear lady, you may be our last hope."

"Me?"

"He respects you . . . loves you. He told me himself he's grateful to you for having loved his dead son as your own. And privately, at least, he blesses you for your steadfast refusal to allow your daughter, his beloved Drusus' widow, to marry Seja—"

When Nerva did not speak for several seconds, Valerius stole another look around the column. Two slave girls were approaching, bearing cups and a glass decanter of red wine. Antonia curtly dismissed the slaves as soon as she and Nerva had been served. "My father gave me an amphora of this wine when Livilla was born." She took a sip. "I wish my daughter had aged as nicely."

"But still you love her," the old man said gently.

"Yes, I do. Yet, I cannot forgive her." Antonia's face was downcast for a moment. "Well, Cocceius, let us toast to my Livilla. Long may she remain my daughter—but the day she weds Sejanus, she will no longer be."

Nerva raised his cup. "To valorous women . . . to my Turia!"

Antonia could have been expected to look gratified at this high compliment. Turia had been a famous matron who had saved her husband's life at peril to her own during the civil wars; she was remembered as the epitome of Roman womanhood. But, instead of wearing a dignified smile, Antonia seemed perplexed and anxious, as if Nerva's words had somehow slighted her.

Out of this distraction, she called for one of the slave girls: "Prisca!" And when the girl promptly appeared: "Ask Pallas to come to me at once. Have him bring his writing tablets." She turned back to Nerva. "I will dictate a letter to Tiberius—one I should have sent before this time. Pallas will take it to him in Capri."

"We must be careful. They may suspect Pallas, prevent him from approaching the Emperor. There must be someone who—"

Antonia's Greek secretary hurried out into the courtyard, carrying a strap from which dangled a satchel containing his wax tablets and stylus. "At your service, noble Antonia." He was polite and reserved in manner, although his obsequiousness revealed an underlying ambition unusual in a slave. He bowed to the senator. "And to see you in this house again, Cocceius Nerva, is a joy."

Nerva answered with a warm smile.

Antonia motioned for Pallas to sit on the bench across the slate walkway.

"Whenever the lady is ready," he said, opening his satchel.

Antonia took a deep breath. "Beloved Tiberius, my Emperor and friend: It is with a heart heavy with pain but filled with my concern for you that I beg you to heed what I am about to disclose to you. Read this as the truth, for love can only generate truth. And I love you dearly, as I love your son Drusus...."

Valerius squeezed his eyes shut and leaned the back of his head against the cold marble of the column. As he listened in horror he suddenly wanted to race out of the house, across the first bridge that spanned the Tiber and vanish forever into the snowy wilderness of the Alps. But—to his own discredit, he felt—Valerius did not. He remained. He memorized each word.

Tenderly, the old slave woman combed the small girl's hair. She appeared to delight in the feel of the silky locks between her fingers. "There now, Blandina, show your mother, here."

Momentarily, the child's smile softened her mother's aggrieved expression. But then the woman's features, once beautiful, solidified into their unhappy mask again. "Procula," she said to the elderly slave, "I do not like this gown. Call for another."

"Yes, Lady Apicata." She scurried to the door of the child's bedchamber, muttering to herself. "What is her name? Ah . . . Sirica. Sirica!" Then she turned back into the room, comb in hand.

"Sirica is in the kitchen." Another young woman stood in the doorway. She was striking-looking in an Oriental way that intrigued the slave and her mistress.

"And you are . . . ?" Procula asked.

"Sarah," Blandina answered her. "She played with me yesterday. She's from Jeru—?"

"Jerusalem." Sarah's dark eyes had brief glints for the little girl.

"Ah, yes, the new slave Pontius Pilate sent to master Sejanus," Procula explained to Apicata as if Sarah were not present. "There was a sister. But she did not survive."

"What do you wish?" Sarah asked the old woman.

"Blandina's saffron *tunica*. You were to clean it. Bring it here."

Sarah nodded and withdrew. Apicata stared after her. "I hardly noticed when Sejanus first brought her to me how beautiful she is. And genteel, too, as if well educated."

"Jewish girls learn to read and write when very young. It's a wonder, too, what with not having the good goddess Fabulina to help them learn the language." Carrying a washbasin toward the door, the old woman tripped on a few tiles that had worked loose of their grout on the mosaicked floor.

Blandina laughed shrilly. "You need the goddess Abeona to teach you to walk, Procula!"

The slave wrinkled her nose at her before leaving.

Sarah whisked back into the chamber with Blandina's *tunica* neatly folded over her arm. She fitted it down over the girl's head, then smoothed the folds. Apicata could not help but smile when she saw how lovingly the young slave admired her daughter.

"How old are you, Sarah?"

"Eighteen, Lady Apicata."

"What happened to your sister?"

Sarah's face remained emotionless. "She was killed on the ship that brought us here . . . stabbed by a marine."

"Your mother and father—are they still in your country?"

"I lost my father when I was very young. My mother died in the praetorium at Caesarea."

Apicata's eyes glistened, perhaps against her wishes. "It is difficult to be alone. To have no one with whom one might share . . ." She stopped, then self-consciously began primping over Blandina. "You have no one else left in your family?"

"A brother." Sarah was on the verge of saying Caleb's name, when she checked the impulse.

"Did you leave a love behind?"

"No. My sister, Ruth, was betrothed. But I had no time for love."

"Oh, you will, you will," Procula said, coming back in with Blandina's slippers, which were embellished with pearls. "Wait till you meet some handsome Roman lad with just enough touch of the purple to make him interesting. Then you'll find the time." The old woman giggled lewdly. "Juno knows, I did in my day."

"Procula!" Apicata said sternly, inclining her head toward Blandina.

"Oh, forgive me, lady."

Apicata glanced at the water clock: The liquid had dribbled down to the last mark on the glass. "Blandina, hurry, you'll be late for your lessons. And Euganor will be cross with me."

"Sometimes that Greek forgets he's a slave," Procula muttered.

Blandina took Sarah's hand. "Come with me. I must go and greet my father."

The girl led Sarah down a corridor that emptied out onto the atrium, the heart of the mansion, which was adorned with statues of their master, each amplifying his male beauty in a pose different from the others. A dozen slaves were scouring the floor with camel's-hair brushes, their strokes listless and often punctuated by long spates of gossiping.

Blandina checked behind the drawn curtains of the *tablinum*, the large alcove off the atrium where her father received his many clients. But only Sejanus' secretary and a praetorian colonel were within, counting coin before depositing it in the strongbox. "There's my lady," the colonel merrily cried out. "To what do I owe this honor?"

"Have you seen my father, Marcus?"

"Why, yes, I have. He's in the baths."

"Thank you." Then, after she had almost forgotten: "Hail Tiberius!"

"Quite," the praetorian chuckled.

Sejanus had finished his steam bath and a quick soak in the cold pool. A male slave was now giving him a massage, and he was groaning pleasurably as Blandina approached him, tugging at Sarah's hand for her to follow. The prefect opened an eye and grinned. "Tunic," he snapped at the slave, then covered himself and sat up on the table. "My lovely Blandina . . . ready for school?" He kissed her forehead twice. "Good Euganor must already be waiting on you."

Blandina looked down at her slippers. "Why do I have to learn Greek?"

Sejanus meant only to glance at Sarah, but wound up scrutinizing her. He finally smiled. "Well, you will one day be a great noble lady, and all the noble ladies must know Greek. Besides, you are part of an empire. And what is an empire if not a quiver of different languages?"

"I don't like Greek."

"But you must know it, my darling," Sejanus said, his gaze still intent on Sarah.

"But all the Greeks in our house speak as we do—except when they think we're not listening."

"No arguments now, lady." He turned to the slave who had been massaging him. "See to it she arrives in Euganor's care."

"Yes, Consul." The slave escorted a pouting Blandina toward the garden.

"Stay," Sejanus then commanded Sarah. "I am told Jewish girls know how to massage."

"That is not true," she said quietly.

"No? Well, you look intelligent. I'm sure you can learn."

Sarah hesitated, then began to slip toward the door.

"Come here!" He lay down. "Closer . . . closer."

Timidly, she approached the table, twisting the fingers of one hand in the palm of the other. She glared downward. He had shed the tunic once more.

"There's a pitcher of oil on the side table. Pour some on the sponge. There you go. Now squeeze that on my back and rub it in."

"With the sponge?"

"No, no—with your hands. I want to feel your hands on

me." His eyes languidly closed. "My gift from Pontius Pilate. Good man, princely gift . . . no, divine gift. I believe I could be induced to worship you. And I think I'll make my first offering—"

She had lifted her hands off his back and taken a step away from the table.

"Or I could shatter you as if you were made of clay. You are my gift." His long arm swung out and caught her around the waist.

Sarah broke free of him and dashed for the passageway, spilling over the table that held the containers of unguents and oils.

"You halt!" he cried, fumbling into his tunic.

She made it as far as the garden before she was stopped unexpectedly, pitched flat against the moist earth, the heels of her hands leaving twin gouges in a bed of moss. Rolling over onto her back, she saw that her foot had caught a rope.

"Now look what you've done!" an exasperated voice said. The tentmaker directed her attention to an awning he had been stretching between two stanchions; the canvas now hung limply on the ground.

Blaming her desperation, Sarah imagined the man to be of her own race. Then his eyes enlarged, and she was certain he asked in a Hebrew of some strange inflection, "Daughter, are you—?"

But at that instant Sejanus' voice boomed over the garden, "Go that way, Marcus—all the way to the orchard."

She scrambled to her feet again and dashed past the edge of the garden and onto a path that wound, sun-dappled, through the pine woods enclosing the estate. She was glancing over her shoulder for Sejanus' pursuit when she ran headlong into the arms of a legionary.

"No!" she cried, dazed, forming fists to pummel him when she realized he was as startled as she.

"What is it? Who are you running from?" The young signifer appeared to be willing to draw his short sword in her behalf. He glared back down the path.

And then, between the thickly-set trunks of the umbrella pines, the praetorian prefect could be seen, advancing at a run, his jaw in an angry set. "Ah! Here she is!" He ignored the signifer for the moment and glowered at his slave. "You," he growled, "report to Procula—at once!"

Sarah looked to the signifer, a plea in her eyes. But then, with the slightest of shrugs, he let her know there was nothing he could do. He, too, was in servitude. Sarah drifted back down the path toward the mansion, her arms dead at her sides.

"She broke half the vases in the house," Sejanus said affably, having recovered himself. "Still, I should thank her. She made me run like Apollo chasing Daphne. A soldier should exercise each morning, right?" He frowned: The signifer was still staring at the retreating figure of the slave. "Do you have a report for me, Valerius Licinius?"

Valerius came to attention. Then he recalled what news he carried, and his expression became sober, even troubled. He suddenly found it difficult to speak.

"Come, now," Sejanus murmured, leading the young man back to the garden. "You look positively sick. It can't be that bad."

"Cocceius Nerva came to visit the Lady Antonia. . . ."

"Yes?" Sejanus said with the same vague smile.

"They accuse you of treason. A messenger will leave for Capri with a letter from Antonia to Tiberius. He will have instructions to deliver it into the hands of Curtius Atticus."

Sejanus exhaled, then laughed softly. "Your loyalty and alertness will be duly rewarded, Valerius. I will—"

Apicata swept up to him in the midst of the roses. "Sejanus, I'm having difficulty with—"

"Later, Apicata." He brushed her aside.

Valerius avoided looking at her face, which he felt certain was still smarting long after the men had entered the house.

"I will have some token of appreciation for you tomorrow. Meanwhile, take a respite from your duties this evening."

"Thank you, sir."

"But resume your post at first light, when the good lady Antonia rises. Hail and be well."

Valerius was slowed by the push and crush of foot traffic as he inched along the narrow street. He fumed to himself that each of Rome's one million citizens had poured out onto the paving stones to impede his progress. And as if this were not frustration enough, the late afternoon hour had arrived in which carts were again permitted to creak up and down the congested avenues.

Just when he felt the last of his patience was expended,

Valerius found himself peering up at the Julia Victoria, the five-story *insula* in which his mother—and father, when on leave—lived. Having grown accustomed to the finest homes in the city, not to mention Tiberius' grandiose Villa Jovis on Capri, the signifer was momentarily taken aback by the sorry condition of the tenement. It sagged so heavily against the neighboring Augusta Victoria, timbers had been wedged in the diminishing space to keep the buildings separated. And there were cracks in the upper stories that Valerius did not remember seeing as a boy.

Reflectively, feeling haunted by the past, he passed through the main portal under the jaundiced gaze of the porter who had squatted there in his gloomy niche since Rome had been a Republic. Children were shouting for his attention in the courtyard, but first—out of distant habit—he leaned back his head and looked straight up. This was the same too: the square of evening sky rinsed of its deep blue by smoke.

A dirty-faced boy of nine or ten, half naked, boldly approached Valerius and translated the various uniform insignia to his friends: "Standard-bearer . . . Third Augusta. I could tell you more, but I'd have to see the streamers on his javelin." Then, with more heartfelt sincerity than he had seen in any praetorian, the boys formed a rank and cried in the echoing space, "Hail Tiberius!"

Valerius tried to return the exhortation. But when he did, all he could see before him was a naked old man leering goatishly at tiny gods and goddesses. So instead, Valerius said to the young legionaries, "Caesar requires volunteers for a foraging expedition. . . ." He had to enforce a stern look on himself; there was no lack of volunteers. "Does One-Eyed Caius still sell walnuts?"

"Yes!"

Valerius broke out a few *sesterces* and entrusted them to the apparent leader. "Centurion, go to it. The cohort is relying on you."

The children streamed out of the court through the portal, their shouts drawing a complaint from the porter.

Valerius continued on his way up the dingy stairs, each level crowded with more cubicles than the one below it, until he was standing before an open door on the fourth floor.

Within, roils of smoke were bumping against the ceiling, and he could hear his mother coughing. Quietly stepping inside, he watched as she tended the smoldering coals and vainly tried to fan the smoke out the door with a rag. He smiled and shook his head: The living quarters had no chimney above the charcoal stove, no openings facing the street; and this invariably happened on windless evenings.

Glimpsing him out of the corner of her eye, she gasped, her hands flying to her mouth. "I thought you were your father!" She rushed to embrace him.

"I take that as a compliment, Mother. He is the best man I know." Valerius unhitched his cape and hung it on a hook. "How is he?"

"Fine—due home from Gaul soon." She clenched her fists with delight. "I just knew you'd be here tonight. I made spelt soup—your favorite. The Penates whispered for me to do this." These were the spirits who guarded the household larder. "And they whispered something else...." Her eyes became mischievous.

"What now?"

"That soon I will be making a spelt cake . . . for your wedding."

Valerius said nothing. But he was smiling through a blush.

"Ah!" she cried. "There *is* someone, then!"

Valerius chuckled helplessly. "Well, perhaps. I saw her for the first time this morning."

"Just today?" She cut short a displeased look with a shrug. "So it was when I saw your father. If you love her, she has my blessing. This hearth is too quiet when your father is away—"

"Wait, Mother. I don't even know her name and you have her moving in with you." His eyes flickered downward. "There is something else: I believe her to be a slave."

Disappointment crumpled her face. "Oh. . . . I had thought . . . well, that perhaps one of the noble ladies in the house of Antonia or the prefect Sejanus had taken notice of my handsome—"

"This is all spoken too soon. I have no idea what this woman thinks of me."

Then his mother cupped his head in her hands and spoke rapidly as if afraid he might interrupt. "I am sure this girl is quite nice, to stir your feelings as she has. But a slave would be a bad awakening to your father. He wrote to me; his only comfort in the cold nights of Gaul is to dream of you marching ahead of him in the uniform of a colonel. We thought you were on your way . . ." Her voice trailed off.

"To what, Mother."

"Well, to win the favor of such a great man as Lucius Aelius Sejanus is such a good omen you will one day be a great man yourself. You are doing important work, and now to tie yourself to a slave . . ."

"Do you wish to hear about my work?"

She brightened. "Of course."

"I hide behind marble columns, or Lares' shrines, or in the folds of musty curtains, and listen to what people say."

"I do not understand."

"I'm a spy, Mother," he said, wiping his lips with the back of his hand as if erasing something foul there. "I steal secrets from people who trust me, then carry them under my cloak to Sejanus' house."

"Certainly there must be reasons. Sejanus is our prefect, our consul—the first man after Caesar himself."

"I trusted him, Mother, believe me. I even admired him, loved him as his men do. But only this morning I saw him as he truly is. He was running along a path in the woods. His face was that of a wolf."

She shuffled back to her stove, crouching below the thickest level of the smoke. Listlessly, she waved her rag in the air. "You must not leave without tasting some of your soup," she said, almost in a whisper.

X

─────────────

THE lightning flashed in through the window, over their bodies. In that instant, everything was revealed: their nudity, the damask quilt kicked down to the foot of the sandalwood bed, and—across the luxurious chamber—the pale stone Venus blessing them with her smile. By the time the accompanying thunder rumbled over Rome, all was in darkness around the entwined couple again.

"Oh, tell me, please," Livilla said, "all these hindrances will soon be behind us . . . and we will be as one."

Sejanus was silent for a moment. "But I am still married to another."

"It is no fault of mine. I would do anything"—the lightning found them once more; she flinched—"I have done everything, to become your wife."

"I've never doubted that."

"Then what can we do?" Her voice had become a girlish whine.

"Ask your mother again. Compel her to consent."

"I have tried."

"You must try again." He kissed her eyes, then the tip of her nose. "Learn from me: I have never been satisfied with no as an answer."

"But that makes for such an ugly quarrel. And I always lose my temper at the old woman. Perhaps I could ask Gaius to—"

"No," Sejanus said adamantly. "Do not involve Gaius Caligula in this. His eighteen years' posturing as a soldier are about to draw to a sudden close. Then Tiberius will see that only one choice remains for his successor."

"The choice that should have been obvious in the first place." She rested her face against his chest. "I am so tired of this waiting, I could scream."

"Then speak to Antonia."

When she began to protest, Sejanus covered her mouth with his, lightning glancing between their faces. *"Tomorrow,"* he sighed.

"My mother should be proud I have tamed the man who has mastered Rome."

"Tomorrow," he insisted.

"All right," she said at last, the night thundering down on them again. Livilla clutched his hand tightly.

Antonia stood from the bench and gathered her gown in her whitened knuckles. "No! You are wasting your time, Livilla. You were once married to one of Rome's finest sons. This should be honor enough for a lifetime. I did not bring you into this world to see your rank, your beauty, lowered into the grasp of a criminal . . . an enemy to Rome."

The strain of keeping a civil tone twisted Livilla's full mouth. "Sejanus' only crime is to work ceaselessly for a return to glory, to . . ." Her fingertips darted to her forehead as she grimaced. "Oh, damn, the glory of the Empire does not matter."

"What does, then?" Antonia asked coldly.

"I love the man—more than I ever loved Drusus."

"Don't you dare!"

And finally Livilla was shouting, careless of anyone who might be listening, such as Valerius. "I did not chose Drusus. I was handed over to him as if I were a slave. You must have enjoyed Tiberius' bed enough to want to sacrifice me on the bed of his son!"

Antonia began swaying on her feet. Her hand groped behind her for the bench, and she unsteadily lowered herself onto the marble top. "You . . ." She fought for her breath. ". . . you will never bring shame on your mother. Nor on the memory of your father, the only man in my life. You will not say one more word."

Valerius peered out from behind his usual pillar as Livilla angrily threw herself down at her mother's knees.

"I regret not having spoken so plainly before. . . ."

"Go, go. . . ."

"The truth frightens you, Mother. Well, here it is—the whole of it for you to relish. I despised Drusus—his soft skin, the brevity he called lovemaking. I hated him to the point I did not hesitate to hold the hand of Sejanus when he gave him the poison." Livilla held up her hands, fingers spread. "These helped murder Drusus!"

Valerius could not bear to look at Antonia's face as she rasped, "I know far more than you suspect. But to hear this from the lips I kissed so often . . ."

"How do you know?"

"You poor woman. Do you think any of us in this city can hang on to something as precious as a secret?" Then Antonia said with the calmness of extraordinary weariness, "You will leave this house at once. You will never return. You will forget that I was once your mother."

All at once, there was fear in Livilla's voice. "You're not going to repeat any of—?"

"Pallas!" Antonia called out.

Valerius realized that the secretary might approach by way of the portico on which the signifer hid. It took him only an instant to decide to quick-march out into the middle of the courtyard. "Noble Antonia, may I be of assistance?"

"Yes. See this woman to the portal. Once out, she is never to enter through it again."

"Mother!"

Valerius firmly took hold of Livilla's arm, earning a glare from her. But she went without further protest.

When he returned from the street, Antonia was slumping on the bench. She was not weeping or wringing her hands; instead, her anguish revealed itself in a fathomless stare. But her eyes had become quite hard by the time they drifted up to glare at Valerius. "What?"

"Forgive me, noble Antonia." While passing through the atrium, under the heroic gaze of Marc Antony, Valerius had come to a decision he realized might prove perilous. He would cringe behind no more columns for Sejanus. "You should know I overheard. . . ."

Her eyes narrowed. "Everything?"

Valerius nodded, shamefaced. "And not only today. I was posted here by Sejanus to spy on you and report to him."

Antonia studied the young man for a long moment. "What has made you change your mind?"

"The look on my mother's face when I told her of my duties here. And what I have seen with my own eyes."

"The very bottom of the pit, I'm sure. You are fortunate, young Valerius. You can climb out of it and be gone."

"No, my honor is at stake too." He lowered his voice. "I will escort Pallas with your letter to Capri. Sejanus will try to kill him, and others as well."

"Yes, Nerva must be warned. And brave Curtius Atticus. I will send a messenger at once." Antonia then patted the bench for Valerius to sit beside her. Although she spoke in a sad drone, her mind rose above the fresh grief of having expelled her daughter, and the old woman keenly examined the situation. She understood her grandson's importance in the coming struggle and, calling for her secretary Pallas, wrote to Gaius Caligula, urging him to return to Rome and the sanctuary of her house in all haste. "Sejanus would not dare assail my walls," she declared, overriding Valerius' doubtful expression. "And, Pallas, mention to Caligula that we must curry favor among some of Sejanus' subordinates in the praetorian guard. I rely on him to speak discreetly to Sutorius Macro."

"Caligula knows Sejanus' second in command?" Valerius asked, abashed.

"They are best friends." Antonia lightly touched Valerius' arm. "Ah, before I forget, my son Claudius must be alerted. Sejanus may disregard his infirmities and simply see Claudius as another possible heir to his uncle Tiberius. Go to him."

Valerius hesitated. Another mission to warn someone had been on his mind since he had come to his decision in Antonia's atrium. He wanted to speak to Sejanus' slave girl before the coming bloodbath, in which servants might well be executed along with their master. "Yes, but there is a person I must see before—"

"I beg you, young Valerius. His life is at stake."

He nodded. "Very well. Where will I find your Claudius?"

"Wherever there are books. First try Pollio's library on the Aventine Hill. If he's not there, look among the bookstalls behind the Temple of Janus."

"I go now."

But as Valerius began to rise, Antonia's frail touch stayed him a moment. She pushed a smile through the weight of her emotions. "You have a natural nobility that puts ours to shame."

A search of Pollio's library proved fruitless, so Valerius backtracked from the Aventine through the livestock market, where the flies besieged him in buzzing droves, and finally reached the fringes of the forum. He raced down a shaded lane and came upon the first of the bookstalls. These had attracted more than customers: Writers read from their latest works, apparently unconcerned if anyone listened; idlers or philosophers, depending on the liberality of one's view, argued in

small groups that would suddenly fulminate apart and reform
as parts of other groups along the lane. Valerius tapped a
bookseller on the shoulder. "I seek Tiberius Claudius."

"He was here a minute ago, drooling on my best scrolls.
Try the next stall."

But then, without asking again—from every description he
had ever heard whispered of the man—Valerius knew he had
located Antonia's son.

Claudius was not completely unattractive. His features were
pleasing, and his head of fine, white hair lent him dignity. But
he limped forward on spindly legs to accept a scroll from a
seller, and as he read with the aid of a magnifying crystal his
smile was punctuated by one of his famous facial spasms.

Valerius sidled up to him and said under his breath, "Noble
Claudius, the Lady Antonia told me to give you a message."

Claudius stepped back from him, startled. "You have a b-
book to sell?"

"No. You are in great danger. Return to her house at once.
Now I must go: I can't be seen with you."

Hurriedly, Valerius walked away, checking over his shoulder only once. Claudius was staring after him, still simpering.
Valerius was not sure the man had genuinely understood or
was just pretending in order to be polite. But, especially after
Livilla's costly fit of temper, Sejanus would have his informers
watching for any irregularities in Antonia's household, and a
signifer bearing messages like a lowly slave might warrant the
prefect's further attention. And now, to make sure that no
suspicion arose regarding his loyalty to Sejanus, Valerius would
rush to the prefect and report what Sejanus had probably already
heard from Livilla's lips. Yet, this was the lesser reason for
his sprint toward that mansion.

Sarah refused the first vendor's offer to sniff the herbs he
had crushed between his palms. But what the man at the next
stall held out was too tempting for her to stroll past: a spoonful
of honey. She sampled it, closing her eyes against a view of
the Temples of Saturn and Concordia.

"Good, eh?" He then gave some to each of the two slave
girls accompanying Sarah. "I will give your master an excellent
price if he buys in bulk."

Sarah shook her head no. Her companions suddenly giggled,
which confused her until she glanced over the marketplace

crowd and saw the signifer standing as straight as a javelin, gaping at her. His face flashed crimson upon being discovered, but then he took off his embarrassment and strode up to Sarah. "Do you recall me?"

"Yes," she said quietly, ignoring the pomegranates some merchant was trying to thrust upon her.

"Leave us," Valerius barked at the man. Then he shrugged at Sarah. "Procula told me I could find you here."

She began walking. He fell in step with her.

"And Procula also gave me some idea of the difficulty in which you find yourself."

"I am a slave. I must learn to accept this—in my heart."

"You must never accept it," he said fervently.

She studied his face, bemused.

"Procula promised me she'd watch over you. And Apicata, his wife, knows what happened. You'll be safe, at least until . . ." Valerius did not finish.

"Until what?"

"I cannot say right now . . . Sarah." He smiled. "What does it mean?"

"*Princess*. How little of one's destiny is in a name." But then she could not resist asking, "How are you called?"

"Valerius. It has to do with wishing others well. *Vale*—be well."

"Rome has not wished my family well. It has slain my mother, my sister."

"I am not Rome, Sarah."

"Your wear its uniform."

"Yes. . . ." Valerius did not know what to say for a moment. "I . . . I've been unable to put you out of my mind."

Sarah frowned. "They took the collar off to make me more attractive. But I remain a slave. I belong to another man." She was surprised to see how pained he looked after she said this. "I must return now."

"May I walk you there?"

"Yes, noble Valerius."

He smiled again, and she joined him.

XI

THE lantern on the imperial quay at Capri twinkled amber across the sea. Then, as the slaves rowed ever closer to the island, the light became steadfast and laid out a golden lane across the waters for the small boat to follow. Valerius was staring intently aft into the wake, as if the luminescence there held the answer to every fear he had felt since leaving Lady Antonia's house in Rome.

The wooden prow bumped against the stones of the quay.

Valerius stepped over the thwarts and was first to disembark. "Valerius Licinius, under the command of noble Sejanus," he said as insouciantly as he could to the praetorian who stood between the shore and him. "To see the emperor Tiberius—immediately."

The guard's pupils shone metallically in the glow of the lantern. He did not break off his glare for what seemed half the night. "Any swell on the mainland side?" he finally asked.

"None. Sea's like glass." Then Valerius glanced over his shoulder to make certain Antonia's secretary, Pallas, was following. However, the two men were only halfway up the trail that wound back and forth across the steep face of the cliff when a praetorian centurion, preceded by three of his guards, bearing smoky torches, hurried down from the Villa Jovis to intercept them.

Valerius was forced to explain himself all over again.

"Then give me the message," the officer demanded. "You and your slave..." The man's wary eyes alighted on Pallas' face once more.

"The name is Cratippus, noble Centurion," Pallas said with his convincingly servile grin.

"Cratippus...can stroll over to the praetorium and have yourselves a drop of mulled wine."

"I'm sure our prefect trusts you with this message. But my

84

orders were to deliver it personally." Valerius smiled. "And I have no wish to disobey Sejanus, even in the slightest."

The centurion considered this in silence, then said brusquely, "Come with me."

"And can you tell me," Valerius asked, "is Curtius Atticus on the island tonight?"

"Well, yes and no." The centurion was joined by his men in a grim chuckle. "Let's just say, part of him remains. But the more cranky portion must be across the Styx by now."

Reflexively, Valerius' hand felt for the hilt of his short sword. "What happened?"

"Why do you ask, Signifer?"

"Noble Sejanus had a message for him as well," he quickly lied.

"Ah . . . bandits got him, we believe. The lads are out now beating the thickets for them. But, as you well know, the brambles are dense, trackless, on this damned rock."

Tiberius dismissed the praetorian centurion and then scrutinized Valerius and Pallas for a moment before saying crossly, "You've insisted on an audience with me, young man, but now you will make it brief. This is a terrible night. . . ." He checked a sob before it could escape his lips. "My poor Curtius Atticus . . . bandits . . . my *own* island." His hand trembling, he took a quaff of wine. The skin of his face appeared to be afflicted with some rash Valerius had never noticed before. "Well, come on," Tiberius said impatiently, "what does Sejanus have to say?"

"We do not bear news from that traitor, Caesar."

Tiberius' eyes became panicky, as if he feared assassins. Before the old man could scream for his guards, Valerius swiftly added, "I bring a letter from Lady Antonia, who loves you dearly."

The Emperor's blemished face relaxed. "Antonia? Give it to me."

As he read his eyes grew moist, then glistened angrily and finally became tremulous with tears. He laid aside the letter and appeared to shrink into his couch rugs. "But for that noble woman, I am alone . . . so alone." Then, without the gradual incubation of rage Valerius might have expected, Tiberius exploded, "Sejanus will be seized—killed! He and his family. And Livilla—yes, the law demands! And . . . and . . ." He sputtered in search of another name big enough to fill his wrath. ". . . and anyone of whom we have the slightest suspicion!" He gasped on a sudden thought. "If Livilla could do *that* to my beloved Drusus, what of Antonia's grandson, Gaius? What is he capable of?"

"She has no reason to question his loyalty to you, Caesar," Valerius said. "In fact, she has written Caligula to return to Rome to help with your defense."

"Then that is enough for me."

"She has asked Caligula to explain matters to Sutorius Macro, his friend and your second in command of the praetorian guard."

"Gaius Caligula must come here to Capri at once. Macro will assume command of the guard." Tiberius covered his face with his hands and groaned. "And where in all this is my dear, sweet-tempered Nerva? Not gone like Atticus, I pray."

"No, Caesar," Pallas said, not flustered in the least to be speaking to the Emperor. In fact, he appeared to relish the opportunity. "Cocceius Nerva is safe with my mistress, Lady Antonia."

"Thank the gods."

Valerius quietly said, "If only we could have reached the quay in time to save noble Atticus."

"Yes, oh, yes," Tiberius moaned. Then he reached out and patted Valerius' arm with the warmth of a grandfather. "But I thank you for your courage and loyalty, young . . . ?"

"Julius Valerius Licinius, Caesar. And this is Pallas."

"I will remember you both." Tiberius then wrapped himself in his arms. "Now, make certain Caligula arrives here safely. And Nerva too. I so desperately need his friendship in this hour. These bloody convulsions—they just keep recurring, don't they? And when they have ebbed, I am more alone . . . always more alone."

Livilla was borne through the heart of the forum on her *lectica*. The purple curtains of the litter were not closed, as some ladies preferred in order to insulate themselves from the noisy throng and protect their alabaster skins from the sun. But Sejanus' mistress invited attention with a proud smile. Her retinue was enormous: Twenty slaves cleared the way, shouting passersby out of her path, even rudely jostling other servants aside; six strapping Cappadocian men, as carefully matched in height and build as trace horses, hefted the poles on their shoulders, accepting the shocks and jolts of the pavement in their legs so that nothing but the sensation of a smooth glide was conveyed to Livilla.

An elderly man with an insignificant pinch of purple running down the front of his toga hobbled alongside the litter, his legs netted by varicosity. "Be well, Lady Livilla!"

"Thank you, dear . . ." She leaned back slightly so her nomenclator could whisper a prompting in her bejeweled ear. ". . . Quintus Papinius. You served with my grandfather, no?"

"The greatest honor of my life!" The old man burst into tears. "The last of the Romans, Marc Antony was!" Then, his face blanching, he hastily added, "Until noble Sejanus, of course!"

"Yes . . . well said." Livilla then closed the interview with a wave of her ostrich fan.

Within a few paces, she was greeted with a burst of applause from a group of idlers waiting outside the Curia. Yet, above the praises for Sejanus and her, a strident male voice rang out, "Remember Drusus!"

Livilla started as if she had been pricked by one of her many brooch pins, but refused to dignify the moment by scanning the crowd for her taunter. Still, she appeared to have been shaken by the catcall, and only the sounds of marching troops stamping out of the Senate house relieved her of an anxious moment. She smiled as she glimpsed Sejanus' handsome head, unencumbered by a helmet, at the center of his praetorians. "Sejanus!"

When the formation reached her litter, she expected the guards to halt, step aside and give Sejanus space to approach her. They kept on moving.

"Sejanus!" she cried more urgently.

He glanced up from a deep distraction. When he finally smiled, there was nothing triumphant about it. It was sad, loving—and thoroughly terrifying to Livilla.

"Wait . . . please, if you will," Sejanus said to the praetorian *optio*, his respectful tones not even spent on a full centurion.

"All right . . . only a moment."

"Sejanus?" she asked, dazed. "What of Tiberius' letter? I had heard . . . What of the Protectorship? I'd thought it would be another honor . . . another stepping-stone."

Sejanus jerked his head toward a tumultuous argument within

the Curia. "My former allies thought so, too—before they slipped out the back. No, this letter was only a stepping-stone to the Stairs of Mourning." He spoke of the landing on the Tiber down which the bodies of traitors were dragged by hooks. "He betrayed his promise and accused me of treason. Macro is now praetorian prefect." He attempted to smile again for her, but it manifested itself as a grimace. "I am dead, Livilla. Save yourself."

"We move on now," the subcenturion barked.

Sejanus glared forward and straightened his shoulders. At last, after a dark moment in which his eyes moistened, he achieved the dauntless smile he had tried to give Livilla. "Remember this when you speak of me," he said from the corner of his mouth, not daring to turn and view her once again.

"Do we kill the slaves, then, sir?" the praetorian asked the *optio* who had just arrived at Sejanus' house with a squad of twenty, each man equipped with his shield and javelin.

"No, no, these are the choicest slaves in the city. They're to be transferred to the Emperor's household here in Rome by order of the prefect Macro." The officer had ventured into the atrium, when he halted on an afterthought. "Pass the word: Take care that a Jewess named Sarah isn't harmed. Don't ask why: Word slid down the standard from the Eagle himself, I hear."

"Caesar?" the guard asked, abashed.

"No—Macro, you fool. It's his talons you've got to fear from now on." The subcenturion then urged his praetorians to hasten as they fanned out into the chambers of the mansion. "Let's get this done and be back to the *castra praetoria*."

"A bit of gold dropping our way?" The guard grinned.

"Not as doltish as you look, are you, there, young . . . ?" The officer fell silent.

Before him stood Apicata, not a fold of her gown carelessly draped. She greeted the praetorians dry-eyed, although the old slave woman at her side was weeping uncontrollably. "Here, my Procula. . . ." Apicata slipped a gold bracelet off her wrist and thrust it upon the slave, whose despair was only deepened by the gift. "Keep this in memory of me."

Then Sejanus' wife went rigid: Blandina's cries were reverberating down the passageway. "You may tell the Emperor this from a dying mother: 'Tiberius, you are no better than the

murderer you send to the Tiber. Both of you have the blood
of innocents on your hands. Sejanus has Drusus'—'" Apicata
stopped short, her eyes flickering hysterically for the first time.
"Oh, my stupid, stupid anger, that I ever whispered to Antonia!" Then she composed herself again. "—and, Tiberius,
you have mine, that of . . . ?" Tears followed another distant
cry from Blandina.

Sighing and tipping back his helmet, the subcenturion pushed
past Apicata and stamped down the corridor toward the screaming. He burst into the bedchamber. "Look here, Pugnus," he
said heatedly to the guard within. "It's postponement that makes
one of these details so"—his eyes darted to the small girl—
"ugly." He stooped, his fist already around the hilt of his short
sword, and forced a smile. "Walk this way now, little lady,
will you?"

"What have I done? Please, if I've been bad . . ."

"That's it, love—this way."

". . . I promise I won't do it again." Blandina squared her
hand over her heart. "Jupiter, Venus, gods of my father—all
of you, help me to be good. Help me to be true. . . ."

The pallor of the youth's face became even more pronounced
when he peered up into the light of the full moon. His lips
were inebriated by a smile as he watched clouds scud in var-
iegated swatches past the glow. "Oh, each gown you don is
more beautiful than the last!" he exalted. "My Diana, let me
hunt you down!" He had the long, almost scrawny neck of a
fledgling, and—although scarcely out of adolescence—the hair
atop his head had thinned to a fine down. Despite his tallness,
his formidable brow, the young man still exuded all the spon-
taneity of a child. His skinny hands reached up to fondle the
moon. "Come down *tonight* so that I might make love to you!"

His head snapped to the side. Grinning moistly, he listened
to the bark of commands as the guard was changed around the
Villa Jovis. This suggested a new game to him, and he began
marching around Tiberius' swimming pool, his crisp, martial
movements wobbling on the black surface of the water. The
hobnails of his *caligae* clicked over the marble paving. He
laughed as if this sound suggested something significant to him,
his laughter carrying him down a colonnaded portico until he
was suddenly standing in the moon shadow of a bronze statue.

"Why, Uncle Tiberius—*father*. Pardon me while I help

myself..." Nimbly, he climbed up, making use of irreverent footholds, and snatched the gold crown of laurel from the Emperor's head. Then he slid to the ground. "... but I have an engagement with a goddess. And her standards are rather severe: She will only lie with another god ... or the *emperor* Gaius Caligula." He raised the crown as high as his arms would reach, then lowered it. It fell all the way past his face to his shoulders, but he did not appear to notice. "There," he whispered. "Now, where is she?"

Book Two

"THE TIDE"

I

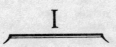

In the back room of a wine shop, the young men huddled around the Zealot from Jerusalem, waiting for him to speak again. His hair was shorn almost to the scalp, and he did not deign to shoo the flies that buzzed in through the window and lighted on his face. It was as if long ago he had given up any idea of personal comfort in his quest for revenge against the Romans. Now, making the Samaritans anticipate his next words, he stared out upon the summer-browned hills and absently took a sip of water. Finally he glanced back to the faces surrounding him. "You must understand their army from top to bottom. Tell me"—he pointed to a youth of perhaps sixteen years— "how many cohorts in a regular legion? I'm not speaking of those worthless Syrian auxiliaries."

"Ten."

"And how many legionaries in a cohort?"

"Supposedly six hundred, but most often about..." The boy faltered.

The Zealot snapped, "Quickly, someone else."

"Most often four hundred and eighty legionaries. And then there are six centuries in a cohort, each commanded by a centurion."

"Good. I want you to have no doubts that the Roman soldier is a capable fighting man." He glared down any objections. "The legionary drills with his shield and Spanish short sword until he drops. How many of you do that each day?"

After an uncomfortable silence, a Samaritan who had only a light haze of a beard asked, "But if Tiberius' troops are so fierce, how are we to defeat them?"

For the first time, the Zealot smiled. He brought a cloth bundle out from under the table and untied the leather straps, then unfurled a garment he revealed to be a *paenula*, the hooded cloak worn by Roman travelers. "I will show you how to humble a legionary. We meet again after sundown."

"But it is the Sabbath," one of the Samaritans protested.

The Zealot glowered at him so intently, the boy nearly slid off the bench onto the floor. "Then all the more reason for the God of Israel to favor us with victory. Go now: Ready your slings and sharpen your daggers."

And three hours later, when darkness washed over Samaria in waves of blue and purple, the group assembled again in a ravine that split the hills behind the city. Looking severe, the Zealot strode up and down the single rank in his *paenula,* sizing up each volunteer. He sent one boy home for being too young. "Follow me," he said at last. "And do it quietly."

They stole down the defile to a bluff that overlooked a small stream. Spanning the waters, which shone like quicksilver in the moonlight, was a Roman bridge, and across it paced two legionaries, dragging their sandals with boredom and weariness. Silently, the Zealot showed each of the Samaritans how and where to conceal themselves, then slipped away, leaving them to gawk this way and that in search of him, perhaps wondering if the stranger had only been a phantasm.

But after several minutes his hooded figure could be seen again. He was sauntering down the road toward the bridge, walking not as a Jew did but arrogantly, in the manner of a Roman. "Hail and be well!" he called out to the legionaries. His Latin was as clear and accentless as Caesar's.

"Friend," one of the soldiers said, sounding exasperated, "what are you doing alone out here?" The figure strode into their midst. "The Zealots like nothing better than—"

A dagger flashed in the moonshine, and the legionaries plummeted to their knees, clutching their throats with their hands before flopping completely prostrate.

The Zealot's solemn voice drifted up the slope to the Samaritans. "That was for my mother . . ." he said, ". . . for Ruth . . . for my Sarah."

Smiling vaguely to himself, Saul spread the three hinged tablets across his knees. On the inside of each citrus-wood panel was a thin coating of wax. These and the silver stylus had been purchased for him by his father in Rome years before. His eyes drifted to the notes he had scratched out earlier in the day: "Seven appointed to appease Hellenist followers. Will disburse poor fund of Nazarenes." Then he listed the names supplied to him by his informant, the landlord of a house in the Mount Zion quarter of the city: "Philip . . . Prochorus . . . Nicanor . . . Timon . . . Parmenas . . . Nicolaus . . . *Stephen*." He had underlined the last name.

Then Saul set aside his writing things and stood as the priests and elders of the Sanhedrin filed into the chamber. As soon as they were seated, the captain of the Temple guard led in the accused twelve, who, surprisingly, appeared to be more exalted than worried. Caiaphas duly noted that this was the second arrest of the followers of Jesus, that their numbers had been warned on the first occasion to stop specified practices. Now all were liable to the punishment of "forty lashes less one" for offenses against Jewish law. Then the high priest turned toward the side of the hall occupied by the Pharisees, in which Saul sat, and motioned for Gamaliel to speak.

"With your permission, Caiaphas . . ." The teacher positioned himself so that he was equidistant from both Sadducees and Pharisees. "I believe it is important to state that the aims of the Zealots and the Nazarenes are utterly opposed. The Zealots mean to inflame the hearts of the people with insurrection. The Nazarenes seek charity for all—even the Romans, if I understand their doctrines. Admittedly a dream—"

"The Zealots are still within our law, *Rabban* Gamaliel," Caiaphas interrupted. "When the followers of Jesus speak heresy and practice blasphemy, they are outside it."

"The *practice* of blasphemy," Gamaliel mused out loud. "Then it falls upon us to decide if healing the sick is a blasphemous act or simply a good dead."

"Or the cultivation of superstition." The high priest frowned at Peter. "There are those who believe their ailments will be cured if only they grovel in your shadow, Simon Peter. What do you say of that?"

"This, Caiaphas: We must obey God rather than men. The God of our fathers raised up Jesus, who died on the cross. After three days, he was resurrected from death—"

"Blasphemy!" a Sadducee cried. "There is no such thing!"

Gamaliel begged for silence by raising his hand. "Then are we to deny the words of Isaiah, who said, 'Fresh life they shall have, Lord, that are thine in death. Lost to us they shall live again. Awake and utter your praise, you that dwell in dust.'"

"God exalted Jesus at his right hand. This was to give repentance—as a savior—to Israel. It was for the remission of our sins, you see. And we are the witness of these things. So it is the Holy Spirit who has enlightened us." Peter smiled as if amazed by his own confidence in speaking these words. His pleasure was not cut short even when Caiaphas said with a scowl:

"You put yourself in peril of death with such blasphemy!"

"The peril of death is given over to the Romans. Are you ready to deliver us to them?"

"And now you challenge the authority of the Sanhedrin."

"Which is answerable to the occupying power," Gamaliel said simply, then slowly shook his head. "Men of Israel, we must take heed and do nothing we will regret. I say this: Leave them alone. . . ." He paused, his eyes darting to Saul's face, which shone angrily back at him. "If what they do is of men, it will collapse. But if it is of God, you won't be able to overthrow them. And you might find yourselves at odds with God." The *Rabban*'s eyes glimmered—almost mischievously, as if he sensed how appealing his logic might prove to the Sanhedrin.

Saul rose in the quiet that followed. He held up a trembling hand to gain the high priest's attention, but Caiaphas ignored him and said hurriedly to the twelve men before him, "You are charged to speak no more in the name of the man Jesus." Then he ordered the captain of the Temple guard, "Warn them by the tongue of the whip and let them go."

Clenching his tablets under his arm, Saul rushed through the departing Pharisees to Gamaliel, who regarded him benignly. "My son—"

"This . . . this leniency only encourages more blasphemy!" he blurted so loudly, even Caiaphas looked askance at him.

"Please," Gamaliel whispered, "if you have learned nothing else from my school, be moderate in your speech."

"*Rabban*, you are not aware of the intrigues being perpetrated by this cabal. Here, let me show you. . . ." Saul's excited hands tore open the tablets and held up that morning's notations for Gamaliel to examine.

"I see names but do not understand."

"No, no, down lower . . . right there."

"'I shall obey God rather than you'—Socrates," Gamaliel read. "A wise saying, but your point escapes me, Saul."

"This was said by the Alexandrian *Stephen*. And aren't these

words suspiciously like those spoken now by the Nazarene Peter
. . . here?"

Gamaliel studied Saul's face for a moment before looking
to the tablet again. "'. . . We must obey God rather than men.'"

Smirking, Saul waited for Gamaliel's reply.

The teacher sighed wearily. "Look to the causes of this zeal,
my son—for your own sake."

His eyes watering, Saul snapped shut his wax tablets and
rushed from the chamber.

II

"NOBLE Gaius Caligula!" a voice hailed him.

Halfway down one of the porticoes of the Villa Jovis, he slowly turned, a playful smile on his mouth. From his right hand dangled a leather ball on a short tether, which he snapped in the air as he watched the young signifer jog toward him from the direction of the praetorium. Then he let the toy hang limp as he leered at the legionary's body, locked at attention before him. "Ah . . . handsome standard-bearer of the Capri Cohort, Third Legion Augusta—and friend to the Emperor. Am I not correct?"

"Yes, noble Caligula—in all regards, I hope." Valerius hesitated briefly, feeling uncomfortable under the man's prying gaze. "Forgive me—"

"Already?" Caligula chortled.

"I dare ask you for a special favor."

"Dare, then."

"I am told you inherited all that belonged to the traitor Sejanus."

Again, the same giddy chortle. "Everything but his wife, daughter and *shame;* those went down the Stairs of Mourning into the Tiber."

Valerius struggled to show no revulsion. "There is a slave among the many who are now your property."

"Slaves?" Caligula asked with a yawn. "Oh, I gave those to my darling sister." He beamed as yet another voice called out his name.

"Yes . . . coming!" Caligula shouted back, then to Valerius: "Herod Agrippa waits on me. We must use the light while we still have some."

"Again, forgive me, but this particular slave—"

"We should discuss this at another time, my signifer. At length, I promise. Perhaps when we're both back in Rome"—

he hoisted his eyebrows over a broad simper—"and away from Uncle."

"If only noble Gaius might—"

"Really." Caligula sounded irked for the first time. After glaring at Valerius, he began running toward the garden, whirling the ball at arm's length and saying over his shoulder, "I cannot be rude to a barbarian who gives such marvelous dinner parties."

As the ball arced down through the dusk, its strap snaking behind it, Caligula suddenly uttered a sharp cry and began hopping on one foot, cradling the other in his hands.

"What is it?" the olive-skinned young man asked, genuinely alarmed.

"Wasp!" Caligula watched miserably as the ball thudded against the ground near him. "And you win!"

"No . . . I forfeited before it hit the earth, my friend."

"How good of you." Caligula limped over to a bench, his bottom lip quivering. Tears threatened his eyes. "You are much too generous."

"Let me tend to this wound."

Caligula watched morbidly as the Judean prince took hold of his pale foot and began squinting in search of a swelling. His dark eyes dolorous and sympathetic, he kept up the hunt long after the Roman's mind had drifted to other things. "Tell me, Herod, how did you think Tiberius looked this afternoon?"

"Hmmm."

"Please, we can speak frankly to each other. Aren't we closer than brothers?"

"Of course." Herod lowered his resonant voice to a whisper, but only after checking the approaches to the garden. "Tiberius looks *old*."

Caligula giggled. "It's his heart . . . brittle—ready to crack. You Jews and your revolts are doing it to him. Now there's trouble in Samaria, wherever that is."

"The country north of Judea."

"Wherever *that* is." Caligula cut short his laugh when Herod did not join him. "Oh, why the long face?"

"I hope Judea will fare better under your rule than it has under Tiberius."

"It will, it will."

"No, I am serious, Gaius Caligula." Then Herod attempted

to soften his words with a sad smile. "I have spent most of my days in Rome, so I know how things go with emperors. Your mistake is this: You do not know the Jews—"

"But you yourself are Idumean," Caligula interrupted. "Placed in power over Jews with the help of Roman arms."

"That was long ago. My family is thoroughly Jewish now. It is our faith that makes us so. The point is this, my friend: Rome attempts to govern Judea through procurators who can scarcely utter a syllable of Aramaic. What is needed is a—"

"Jewish monarch who is more than a mere tetrarch in the service of a divine Roman emperor."

Herod fell silent, his eyes hopeful.

Caligula winked shrewdly. "So you are opposed to the idea of a divine emperor, then?"

"In all cases but yours."

"Does that still mean you would believe in but one god?"

Herod chuckled uneasily. He finally set down Caligula's foot. "Meaning . . . ?"

"Meaning we shall play some marvelous games with each other when I'm installed in Rome and you're in your palace in Jerusalem. But I shall have to win always," Caligula added wistfully. "That is because I will be the Emperor and you will only be a king. But being a king is a step up from being a prince, yes? I hope you'll be grateful to me, Your Prospective Jewish Majesty."

"Lord of the Universe, I bow before you."

Caligula began massaging his heel—not the one Herod had been nursing. "You once told me there's a secret word in Hebrew for that—Lord of the Universe. What is it? Please tell me."

"I can't."

"Oh, tell me. What harm—"

"I can't, my friend. Only the priests know that name."

Caligula smiled engagingly, then sniffed some scent he had dabbed on his wrist. "You must beat the priests until they tell you."

"And if that does not work?"

"Line them all up. Behead the first one, and if the next does not reveal it, work your way to the very end. But, if I know men, you'll have that name in no time." Caligula sighed and leaned back on the bench, folding his knee under his chin. "Yet, what a disappointment it would be for you, Herod."

"For what reason?"

"You already know *my* name."

The young prince laughed uproariously, and Caligula shot him a look of consternation that made Herod hesitate, unsure if it was mocking or not. Then, when he had achieved the effect of sobering his friend, Caligula leaped on the prince and began gently pummeling him with his fists. Herod returned the feints with even less force. The two youths had seized each other's hands and were grappling for dominance when the tattletale clinking of military sandals approached over the paving stones of the path. Caligula gave the praetorians a fierce glare and appeared shocked when it did not deter their advance. "What is this? How dare you?"

One of the guardsmen stepped forward and saluted. "We have been ordered by Tiberius Caesar to escort Herod Agrippa—"

"*His Royal Highness Prince* Herod," Caligula said. "Where is he supposed to go?"

"Rome . . . to the Mamertine Prison."

Herod looked to Caligula disbelievingly. "You must not allow this!"

Caligula's eyes flared from their deep hollows. "I will go to the old buzzard himself! He will have some explaining to do!"

"Hold your tongue, Gaius Caligula. There are more cells in the Mamertine than there are princes in this Empire." The stout praetorian prefect came resolutely down the walkway, his hand positioned on the hilt of his sword. His hurried motion gave the impression that he had been detained by affairs more important than this, although he had been waiting from the edge of the garden, watching what would happen when the two young men were confronted by his guardsmen. The man seldom excruciated over his decisions, but he also appreciated how a Roman's career could pivot on his absence as much as his commanding presence. It now appeared that Herod would go along without resisting.

"Where have you been?" Caligula demanded.

"With the Emperor . . . trying to appease him."

"*Appease?*" Caligula sputtered. "Let him taste—"

"Hold. . . ." Macro planted his hand on the young man's thin shoulder and kept it there until he felt sure Caligula was in control of himself. Only then did he order his men: "Take

His Majesty away, and treat him with the respect he deserves."

"Aye, prefect. Hail Tiberius!"

"Hail. . . ." Macro had kept possession of Caligula's eyes if only to prevent them from fixing on Herod's face, which was confused and angry. When the prince had been led away, the prefect said quietly to Caligula, "Restrain yourself. Tiberius has had enough of Jews for one lifetime. And your friend has a big mouth in regard to Judean independence." He hoisted a forefinger as if he were reproving a child. "Caesar has many, many ears that listen for him."

"Including yours, my old comrade?"

"On occasion, yes. Now, it would be wise for you to be silent on this matter. Always yield to power when it might be costly to do otherwise. And then always exercise power once it even *appears* to be yours. Soon you can free your friend . . . if you will want to." Macro smiled to signal the end of the chastisement. "A little bird has told me something interesting."

"What?" Caligula asked, sulking.

"Cocceius Nerva has not been his usual buoyant self . . . and he has written a new will."

"So?"

"Tiberius' confidant senses he's not long for this corrupt world."

"Neither is Tiberius."

Macro seized him roughly again, his voice thoroughly exasperated. "Think that—revel in the thought—but never say it aloud. Do you hear me? Do you hear the friend who, more than anyone, has your best interests at heart?"

Caligula grinned defiantly as he stared past Macro's stern face. "Here's the old buzzard now, molting and covered with scabs."

Macro glanced behind him: Tiberius was strolling down the portico, conferring with his astrologer and physician, halting every few steps to gape around in bemusement.

"The least I can do," Caligula hissed, "is share my thoughts with my adoptive father." He broke free of the prefect and dashed toward Tiberius. Yet, still some distance from the Emperor, who was too engrossed to notice, Caligula shuffled to a halt, studied the old man, then somersaulted several times across an artificial meadow and disappeared into the woods, his laughter resounding through the pines.

• • •

Tiberius began to pick at one of the rashes on his face. But then, realizing he was in the presence of his physician, he resisted the urge and instead turned to Thrasyllus, asking a question he had put to the Greek twice before in the past few minutes: "Then you are quite sure?"

"Yes: Not only my reading of the stars, but the entrails of the peacock—"

"Right, right," Tiberius said crossly, suddenly recalling.

"The omens will never be better, Caesar."

"How many times, Thrasyllus, must you tell me that?"

"Forgive me, Caesar . . . I grow . . . senile."

"You do indeed, and I weary of it." Then Tiberius grew quiet. "Where is my Nerva?"

"He complains of melancholy, Caesar," Apemantus, the imperial physician, said. "I recommended bed rest . . . a tea from belladonna and woodruff."

Abruptly, Tiberius spun back toward Thrasyllus. "How are the winds?"

"Ah, winds are set fair."

Tiberius paused at a balustrade overlooking the sea. The waters had been chided into whitecaps by the evening breeze, and the haze of that morning had been swept away, revealing the Italian coast in sharp relief. The distant headlands were an inviting shade of green. Suddenly, the old man unclenched his jaws and declared, "I'll do it."

"Caesar?" Thrasyllus asked.

"I will go to Rome."

Apemantus looked shocked. "But why, after all this time?"

"Because I'm going to die soon." With that, Tiberius began ambling back toward the Villa Jovis, the wind lifting his white hair in fine tufts. "Now I want my supper: some nice fresh fruit. But no asparagus."

"But Caesar," Apemantus protested, "you complain of difficulty in urinating. I can think of no better—"

"I *said* no asparagus."

III

SAUL guided Caiaphas deeper into the crowd that had gathered in the inner courtyard of the Temple. Only when positive that the elderly high priest could hear every word that was being spoken did he gently draw Caiaphas to a halt.

"... Our fathers carried the sacred Ark in the wilderness, the testimony of their covenant with the Lord," Stephen cried, helpless not to grin now and again, his expression gradually exuberating the throng. "They carried it wherever they went, following the Lord's command. And the Lord rejoiced as his ark traveled with his people!"

"Now it comes," Saul whispered.

Caiaphas cupped a hand behind his ear. The twelve gemstones on his gold breastplate, each symbolizing a tribe of Israel, alternately glistened as his sunken chest crested and ebbed, then became still as he glowered at the young orator.

"I speak only according to the Scriptures. . . ."

"That remains to be heard," the high priest muttered.

"... The people of God are not in one place; neither is the home of their worship. The Lord revealed himself to Abraham long before he came to this holy land. And God gave his law to Moses when the children of Israel were yet wanderers in the desert. Was not the Ark of the Covenant carried for forty years through the wilderness? And was not a tent made of skins as pleasing to God as the temple of gold and stone that Solomon raised up? Ours is the faith of a pilgrim people. The earth is the Lord's and the Lord's people are of the earth. They are pleasing to Him *everywhere* they worship, not just when at one monument in a quarrelsome city. Did not the Lord say: 'Heaven is my throne, the earth my footstool'? When the Lord has already made His own temple with His own hands, what right have men to mock Him by saying *this*"—Stephen gestured at the towering edifice—"which arrogance has raised, is the Lord's place?"

"The Lord help him," Caiaphas sighed to Saul. "He blasphemes against the Temple." The high priest caught the eye of the captain of the Temple guard standing nearby, a squad of his men arrayed behind him.

"That is enough, Stephen of Alexandria!" the captain shouted. "Stop speaking and surrender yourself!"

Briefly, the young man was disquieted as the guards closed a ring around him. But when hands were laid on him, he smiled and said with a careless shrug, "This had to happen."

The crowd began to cry out in resentment. A hot wind blew across them, dithering the tassels of their prayer shawls. "Let him speak!" an angry voice boomed above the others.

The captain fixed his eye on the shouter, and the man said no more. The praetorians atop the Fortress of Antonia had rushed out to the crenellations to overlook the growing tumult. A trumpet bawled for the parapets to be reinforced.

Trying not to show his pleasure, Saul forced a frown on his lips and led Caiaphas toward the Temple.

"None too soon," the old man kept repeating. Then he looked at Saul as if with fresh eyes. "And no longer will I question your diligence, my son. You have saved us; I'm sure of it. Now, to convene the Sanhedrin..."

Within the hour, Saul was sitting again in the echoing chamber, wax tablets before him, listening to Stephen complete a long and elaborate defense. Ordinarily, the Cilician would have relished dissecting the scriptural arguments, then gloating aloud over their weaknesses. But Saul found himself absorbed by Stephen's face: it was lathered by sweat, split by an impudent grin—and utterly gratified. It was evident to everyone present that the Alexandrian knew his death was imminent and would do nothing to forestall it. *Rabban* Gamaliel had covered his eyes with his prayer shawl; even Caiaphas slumped under the intolerable weight Stephen's speech was heaping upon him:

"... You obstinate people! You always resist the Holy Spirit! Can you name a single prophet who our fathers did not persecute? You are the men who received the Law of the Lord by the hands of angels. And you are the men who have failed to keep it."

"Stephen... my boy," Gamaliel gasped.

Caiaphas had come to his feet and smoothed his *ephod,* the golden apron he wore, which, in the darkened chamber, was as dull as bronze. "No more—you are forbidden to speak any further."

But Stephen's gaze had vaulted out the single window, a round opening that gave him a glimpse of a thunderhead that had built up during the torrid afternoon over the Judean hills. Then his astonished eyes flew back from some frothy canyon to the priests and elders of the Sanhedrin, to the grieving Gamaliel and finally to Saul, who later believed what Stephen cried next was said directly to him: "Look! The heavens are opened and I can see the Son of Man standing at God's right hand!"

Saul resisted the temptation to look out that ocular window.

Caiaphas' voice crept out of the stunned silence: "You have wounded our hearts, Stephen. Only the Lord may forgive you. Your blasphemies have put clemency out of our humble reach."

The moist clouds were too distant to give relief to the sun-baked lanes of Jerusalem. His face reddened by the heat of the late afternoon and his own anger, Saul raced from synagogue to synagogue, starting with the one frequented by Cilicians, and repeated what Stephen had said before the Sanhedrin. Some pious men, desiring to hear no more, stuffed their ears with their fingertips. His fury acted upon him like an opiate. He ingested it with gluttonous haste; otherwise, the pangs of uncertainty, which he had so keenly felt in Stephen's presence, threatened to overwhelm him.

It was a Zealot who suggested stoning. "He shouldn't be handed over to the Romans, no matter how serious his offense. If he has broken our laws, he must suffer death in our way."

Saul seized upon the idea as if it had been his own. He sprinted back to the Cilician synagogue, his skin now dry and pale, to muster allies for this purpose. He had no sooner won the support of a half dozen young men than he experienced that first inkling of rigidity in his muscles, and he collapsed before the altar, racked by convulsions.

When he awoke after a few minutes, faces, twisted by revulsion, were staring down at him. "I'm sorry," he croaked, so ashamed he wanted only to bolt from the city. "The excitement . . . This has not happened in a long while. . . . I have avoided—"

"It is no matter, Saul," one man said quietly. "There is still something for you to do. If this is to be done properly, we should observe all the formalities."

"Agreed," Saul said, attempting to recover his dignity as he was helped to his feet.

"A witness to the blasphemy must be present."

"I heard everything."

"And traditionally, the witness cares for our garments while we perform the stoning."

"I will do this—gladly." Saul took a sip of water from a cup that was offered to him.

"Now," another volunteer said, "there remains the matter of the Temple guards who hold the blasphemer."

"I have already spoken to the captain." Saul rubbed the cool water over his clammy face. "I have been assured he and his men will look the other way."

"Then what is stopping us?"

"Nothing." Saul drew vigor from a new reason for hating Stephen and the Nazarenes: Their activities, and the agitation that accompanied them, had resulted in the disclosure of the very thing he had prayed would remain hidden from the eyes of his peers. In that moment, as he led the group of young Pharisees toward the Temple of Herod, he vowed incessant vengeance: pursuit of the followers of Jesus through all time. "Nothing is stopping us now," he repeated to himself.

If Stephen betrayed any apprehension at all, it was in his silence. Hands bound behind him, he was pushed and prodded in the hope he might say something argumentative; but he endured the taunts with a surprised expression, as if he could not quite believe the brutality of these men he had known for years, vaguely hoping it was a game they would soon put aside. The exalted mood he had savored while denouncing the San-hedrin had evaporated, and when he surveyed the mountainous thunderheads that ringed Jerusalem, graying the evening light, it was with dim eyes. He started whenever someone shouted in his ear. But he did not question the authority by which he was being dragged outside the city walls.

He smiled only once, but it was to no man. Directly ahead of him, lightning splintered down through a dark cloud. Stephen's lips crooked for an instant.

He spoke three phrases between his removal from the Temple and the rocky place of his death. The first was when he realized that he was being herded down the lane on which his mother lived. "Please," he asked the last man to have shoved him, "another way—for an old woman's sake." The request was denied, and she stood in her doorway, pleading for mercy, until Stephen was no longer in her sight.

Saul said to him, "See what sorrow you have brought on those who love you?"

Stephen did not answer. He did not speak again until they were through the gate and his tormentors were choosing a place with an adequate supply of stones. Then he raised his tethered wrists, indicating to Saul that he wished to be free so that he might pray.

Saul untied him, saying, "There's nothing personal in this, Stephen. I rather liked you," he said hollowly, then with more conviction: "But there can be nothing above the law of Moses if we are to remain the same people."

Stephen nodded that he understood. His gaze glistened in objection, but the young men were already bending over and picking up stones, having finished a prayer of their own. "God bless you," he said simply.

A raindrop glanced off Saul's cheek. He flinched as if it were molten lead. "I will ask them to be swift."

Stephen's mind was elsewhere. Then he sighed heavily and lowered himself onto his knees. "Lord Jesus, receive my spirit. Forgive them this sin," he said in a firm voice so all could hear.

Saul returned to the pile of cast-off cloaks he had abandoned to unbind Stephen. "Begin."

IV

TIBERIUS reclined on the couch in his *carruca*, his face growing more anxious as the luxurious traveling van rocked and clattered ever closer to Rome. The urine smell of the Spanish horses, the swaying and hard lurching of the carriage, the dormice stuffed with indigestible nuts he had sampled in the town of Tres Tabernae—all these now conspired to make him nauseous, and the only comfort he could find was in stroking Columba's head.

There was the crash of broken crockery, and he parted the curtains to peer back at his train of slaves. One of them had dropped a wooden box of dishes. Astride a handsome gelding, Gaius Caligula galloped up on the terrified bearer and commenced to whip him senseless, smiling all the while. Tiberius dropped the flap and cooed to the snake, "I'm nursing a viper for the Roman people." He chuckled phlegmatically. "Now, who said that, my Columba?"

The Emperor kept looking over the ears of the trace horses for a glimpse of Rome, although he knew well there was no vantage to the city this far south. But he continued to search, perhaps hoping there would be nothing flanking the Tiber but oaks and—where the Campus Martius might have been—a grassy plain. Suddenly, he was fighting heart palpitations in addition to his queasiness. There was no end to the ailments that city could inflict on him. He pined for the seclusion of Capri and blamed Thrasyllus for inventing auspicious omens for this ill-fated return to the Palatine.

Macro sidled his mount up to the van. He had difficulty managing his horse, and his frown accused the serpent coiled around Tiberius' forearm. The stocky man gave a cursory salute. "This, Caesar, is the seventh milestone from Rome. If you please, we can make entry before nightfall."

Tiberius considered this for a moment, then swung his ulcerated legs over the side of the couch. His eyes were flickering wildly. "I do not want to go on. Take me back!"

"*Back?* Where, Caesar?"

"To Puteoli."

"We're talking about more than one hundred miles." The prefect struggled not to sound too incredulous.

"Are we? Oh, yes. I see." Tiberius sucked on his bottom lip. "Well, find a place for me to rest. I'm exhausted and half sick."

"We could stop at the villa of Cortesius Naso."

Tiberius brightened. "Is Cortesius in residence?"

"Cortesius was executed five years ago . . . on your orders."

The Emperor slumped back on his cushions. "Damn . . . he would be such fine company tonight. Well, is there some other place?"

"A mile back—the villa of Dionysius."

Then the recollection darkened his features: He had ordered Dionysius' death even more recently than Naso's. "Cortesius' house will do." As soon as Macro had ridden away, Tiberius murmured, "I am so alone." Then Caligula appeared at his side, leering through the part in the curtains. "But not alone enough. What do you want?"

Caligula pouted. "Only your affection, Uncle."

"You will have everything else, but that I keep for those like Cocceius Nerva, whom I—" Tiberius blinked into Caligula's face, then asked timidly, "We . . . we did not kill *him*, did we?"

"No, Uncle."

"Thank the gods."

"He took his own life—don't you recall?"

"But why?" Tears filled Tiberius' eyes. "He knew how much I needed him. How could he?"

"He despaired."

"Of what?"

"You, Uncle: In the end, you disgusted him." Caligula shrugged as if to say he found it all baffling as well. Then, his lips quivering to erupt into a smile, he urged his horse forward.

Tiberius wrapped himself in his arms as the imperial procession passed down a length of the *Via Appia* that was canopied by lofty pines. When his carriage was pulled into sunlight again, he was still shivering, tugging at his couch rugs to cover himself with the hand not holding Columba. "Nerva had no right," he whined.

After a nap so brief the sun seemed no lower to him, Tiberius watched as his advance century of praetorians wound down a curved lane into the estate of Cortesius Naso. He was appalled at the condition of the mansion and its gardens until, once again, he remembered. Quickly, he sought distraction in the dream he had just had, a few fleeting seconds spent once again in the company of a Cocceius Nerva, rosy-faced and plump with youth. "Beware, Tiberius," Nerva had confided, "or the rabble will feast on your former power." Suddenly, in the same moment as his household servants swarmed past his halted carriage in their white tunics toward the villa, Tiberius wondered if the dream might have been a very grave omen. He had no sooner put this out of his mind than Macro dashed up and dismounted.

"What is it?" Tiberius' heart was thundering.

"A messenger intercepted me on the road, Caesar...."

"Yes, yes, what?"

The prefect's eyes were dark with foreboding. "Your lighthouse on Capri ... it has been destroyed by an earthquake."

Tiberius gasped. "I felt it last night in the Forum Appii; you told me it was nothing."

"I'm sorry, Caesar.... We all felt it but didn't want to alarm you."

Tiberius slowly smiled despite his anxiety. "You love me a great deal, don't you?"

"Ah, it goes without saying, Caesar...."

The Emperor moaned as the sea roared in his ears. Its surface was crazed by some monstrous agitation, and the waves ceased marching toward Capri's shore. They began breaking pell-mell against each other. Then the lighthouse, perched on its rocky headland, shook out its own lanterns and toppled over....

Tiberius bolted upright in the bed—that of a man he had had murdered, he realized. A fever racked him with chills. He looked to the window: First light revealed the rangy, overgrown orchards of the estate. "Apemantus!" he called for his physician.

Lifting the covers, he began searching for Columba, who ordinarily at this hour of the morning would be coiled up at the foot of the bed. The snake was not there. Tiberius touched his feet to the cold marble floor. His eyes darted around the chamber, then locked on a sight that made the old man press his knuckles against his teeth.

"Apemantus!" he shrieked.

The Greek physician burst through the door, his face still swollen with sleep. "Caesar, what—"

"There!"

The snake was dead on the floor. Legions of large black ants were feeding on it.

Macro and Caligula then hurried in and stood behind Apemantus, who finally approached Tiberius and gently forced him to lie down again. "Unfortunate, Tiberius, but it means nothing. All things must die."

"It means everything!" he moaned.

"Poor Caesar," Caligula whispered.

Macro shook his head. "I knew this trip would prove too much for him."

"I want to go home . . . to Capri."

"And so you shall, Caesar," Apemantus comforted him and, when the old man had closed his eyes, crept across the chamber to the door.

"How long?" Macro asked, hushed.

"A week."

"Should he be moved back to Capri?"

"It does not matter either way."

"Poor Caesar." Caligula clucked his tongue, his eyes downcast.

They visited him throughout the eternal day, drifted toward his bed out of a teary haze, each bearing the weapon of his or her choice. Mallonia, who had stabbed herself after a compulsory night with "that filthy-mouthed, hairy, stinking old man," lunged at him with a dagger, but dissolved into a wan glow before her blade touched his naked chest. The Parthian king, Vonones, whom Tiberius had eliminated for the treasure the monarch had taken into exile with him, traipsed around the bed, holding a garrote, waiting for Tiberius to fall asleep. Ever vigilant, Tiberius gave him no opportunity, and the king eventually melted into a wall mosaic of an Asian royal court. And as the light waned, Gaius Caligula appeared with a pillow in his hands.

Tiberius squinted up from his covers, trying to decide whether or not the figure was real or not. "But what have I ever done to you?"

"Nothing, Uncle."

Then the pillow fell over his face, blackly.

V

SAUL suspected that the Sanhedrin had not been frank with him about its true reason for sending him to Damascus. This made him sullen company for Seth on the first leg of their one-hundred-and-fifty-mile trip north, and he nearly growled the orders he gave to the escort of Temple guards that Caiaphas had provided him.

He ruminated constantly, scarcely aware of the stretches of desert between the small villages. "Tell me, now," he once said abruptly to Seth over the clatter of their horses' hooves, "is it not a measure of my effectiveness in Jerusalem that the Nazarenes have scattered to Syria and Asia Minor?"

"Certainly, my friend. Why are you so troubled about this?"

But Saul did not answer. He had hunkered down into his thoughts again, reliving events that helped justify his sense of betrayal. In his mind's eye, he was crouching outside that house in the lower city, a file of guards behind him. He listened to the voices within: They spoke Aramaic with a strong Greek accent, or entirely in Greek. . . .

"We thank you, Lord our Father, for the holy vine of David, which you have revealed through Jesus, your servant. Glory be to you. We thank you for the bread we break . . ."

Saul motioned for the guards to start moving toward the portal.

". . . for life and knowledge. As this bread was wheat scattered over the fields and then brought together and made into one, so may your church be brought together from the ends of the earth. Yours is the glory and—"

The foremost guard caved in the door with his shoulder, and the others surged in behind him. Saul held up his hands to stop the women from screaming. "All is well . . . all is well!"

He then smiled at the timorous faces surrounding him. "I apologize for disturbing your ceremony. On behalf of the holy council of the priesthood and the guarders of the Temple, I must make certain inquiries of you. Who will speak for you?"

"I will," a man said softly. "My name is Nicanor."

"Ah, one of the Table of Seven."

"*Six,*" Nicanor corrected Saul, referring to Stephen's death. "And we need no introduction to you: Saul of Tarsus is well known among us."

"Good—then you have some idea of the issues that concern me. Would you say that it is idle and idolatrous to worship in a temple made by human hands?"

"There is no harm in such worship."

"But no good, then?"

The man exhaled, exasperated. "If you expect me to contradict the words of our brother Stephen..."

"I expect nothing more or less than what lies in your hearts."

Nicanor stood straighter. "Do you wish to arraign us—as you arraigned him?"

Another of their number spoke up: "Yes, are we to be taken before the Sanhedrin simply for swearing to the truth?"

"The council will sanction what I already know, Timon." Saul smirked when he saw the man lose his color at being identified. "You have all condemned yourselves out of your own mouths. Captain, arrest this entire assembly."

A child began wailing, and Nicanor asked, "Our children— how can they be anything but innocent?"

"You are responsible for their sins." Saul paused, wavering, then turned to the guards. "Take only the men."

While Saul's retinue was occupied in separating the women and children from the prisoners, a male Nazarene elbowed his way past two guards and ran headlong into the night. He was out of sight in the instant it took Saul to reach the threshold. Saul decided not to give chase. "Well, he won't get far." He said to the women, "You may tell...Philip—isn't it?—that this might be overlooked if he promptly surrenders himself to the authority of the Sanhedrin."

"Is this not more so the authority of Saul?" Nicanor demanded as he was jostled outside. A moment later, he could be heard from down the lane: "Do not shove! I am a good Jew who has simply found the Messiah!"

• • •

Now, watching the shadow of his horse glide over the pebbly road to Damascus, Saul reminded himself what a harvest of blasphemers he had cut and stacked for the sake of his faith, only to be politely rebuffed in the guise of this warrant "to seek out transgressors in our ethnarchy of Damascus and to deliver them to our justice." But whose justice? It was questionable whether Caiaphas, as high priest in Jerusalem, had the right to meddle in the affairs of Damascus' Jewish community. As to Roman law, Damascus lay within the jurisdiction of Syria, of which Judea was only an annex supervised by a procurator. This administrator was subordinate to the proconsul in Antioch, so Paul could not rely on the support of the Roman authorities as he had in Jerusalem.

Yet, Saul had an inkling that this assignment had more to do with Roman politics than Jewish.

Pontius Pilate was finally receiving what he had long deserved for his treachery and greed. The Samaritans, outraged by his massacre of innocent religious celebrants, had appealed to the Syrian proconsul Vitellius. At the same time, Jerusalem was on the brink of revolt because Pilate had permitted imperial standards to be brandished through the streets to the Fortress of Antonia. Vitellius saw to it that Pilate was recalled to Rome. The former procurator was now awaiting trial by the new Emperor, Gaius Caligula.

But Pilate's replacement, Marcellus, might have been the cause of Saul's sudden journey to Damascus. Saul had heard through his sources that the new governor considered the young Pharisee and his squad of Temple guards to be as much, if not more, a menace to the peace than the Nazarenes. "Typically, this is the blind eye Rome casts on our affairs," Saul muttered.

"Quite," Seth agreed drowsily from the saddle.

So, the Sanhedrin, which certainly approved of Saul's prosecution of Nazarene terror, suddenly found it more expedient for him to carry on *someplace else*.

The second day on the road found Saul in a deep depression. He could not believe that his diligence had been so rudely spurned. Refusing Seth's repeated offer of food, he rode onward in silence, head bowed to the sun. His expansive brow was burned red, but he seemed too far along in his dejection to be bothered by discomforts of the body. When the party encamped at dusk, he plodded across a dry riverbed and up onto a bluff. There, he prayed alone half the night.

Dawn saw him in better spirits. "I have been childish," he told Seth. "No more will I quibble with the opportunities God lays before me."

"That's the spirit, my friend."

"It's on to Damascus, where I'll carry out my duties as always."

Seth was looking over his shoulder. The Temple guards had fallen behind; two of their mounts were lame. "I'm afraid your pace of the past month has exhausted them."

Saul and Seth wheeled their horses and cantered back to their escort. "Your hearts don't seem to be in this mission," Saul said.

"Nothing to do with heart," the senior guard answered, although his eyes said otherwise. "It's more a matter of horse-flesh."

Saul turned to Seth. "We're still nearer to Jerusalem than to Damascus, aren't we?"

"By my reckoning."

"Very well. You men may go back to the Temple. Take your time. Be kind to your horses." Saul smiled. "And tell Caiaphas that, in due time, I shall be marching to Jerusalem at the head of a legion of Nazarenes."

"Good luck to you, sirs." Without another moment's delay, they turned and started south.

"Why are you so eager to be rid of our only arms?" Seth asked, looking after the retreating guards.

"I don't know what secret instructions Caiaphas has given them. Besides, their presence may be resented in Damascus." Then Saul led Seth up the road again at a lively pace. The late morning had grown humid, and the hills on both sides of them were banked with cumuli, burgeoning whitely from within. An errant cloud drifted out of this mass, sheeting rain across its own shadow.

"It's pleasant to see you in such a good humor," Seth remarked.

"I'm impatient to get there, my friend." Suddenly, Saul clapped his hand to his nape. "This is peculiar. . . ."

"What's that?"

"The hair on my neck is standing."

• • •

"He's a bit too ardent for my taste," the senior guard said, checking over his shoulder to make sure Saul and Seth were out of earshot. "And it's a good thing he let us be on our way home."

"Why, Ehud? Do you take issue with his methods?"

"I will say just this: In time, this Saul will bring trouble on *our* heads."

"How is that possible?"

"Mark my words: Somehow, no matter that we are praised today, we will be blamed for the things he is doing."

"Are we far enough yet?"

The senior guard chuckled slyly. "No, wait a few more minutes. These stallions can take another mile or two with those coins wedged in their soles."

"Ehud, look at this!" one of the men cried, peering backward from his saddle.

In the distance, Saul and Seth were riding through an island of shadow. Above them, from the gray underside of a cloud, globes of white fire were slowly descending toward the ground. Before they lighted upon the small figures of the riders, who appeared to be unaware of their approach, these dollops of intense light exploded into a festoon that seemed to scorch the desert for minutes. Then the conflagration faded, leaving all as it had been before—except for the two men who had been northbound on the road. Seth was desperately clutching the harness of both terrified horses to keep them from rearing. Saul was prostrate on the shingle of the knoll they had been trotting across when the passing cloud had caught up with them.

One of the guards finally opened his mouth. "Should we—?"

"No!" their senior cried. "It was a sign! To Jerusalem!" And he bullied his lame horse into a gallop. "Do not look back!"

Saul could feel Seth's gasping breath on his face. "Seth . . . is that you?"

"Yes, of course—can't you see?"

Saul groaned pathetically. He was resisting tears. "Then the night is not on you as well?"

"No—noon blazes."

"Did you hear?"

"Yes . . . awful noises. My ears are still ringing."

"No, I mean . . ." Saul fell silent. "You must lead me."

"Yes—back to Jerusalem."

"No . . . to Damascus." Through his back, Saul could perceive the skittish first movements of the horses. Then their hooves thudded the ground and receded until the vibrations became imperceptible. "Gone?"

"Gone," Seth repeated desolately.

"No matter; I must get to Damascus without fail."

"*Why?*"

"You honestly did not hear?"

"I think not, Saul."

"Help me rise."

Seth could be heard removing his cloth girdle. He tied one end of it to Saul's own waistband. "I will pull you in this way, if you think you can travel."

"Yes—quickly." And Saul said no more until the sounds of a city rose around him and he shed the pensive expression he had worn continuously across the wastelands. "Describe this street to me."

"It is quite wide and as long as I can see."

"Is it straight?"

"Perfectly."

"Then ask for the house of Judas from Jerusalem. He will have lodgings for us."

Seth stirred first in the sparse chamber. He glanced over at Saul, who was still sleeping on his pallet, a moistened rag laid across his eyes. The man had thrashed from side to side all night in the throes of some bedevilment. And whenever his breathing had finally grown deep and regular, it was soon interrupted by a soft whimpering, during which Saul shielded his face with his forearms, buffeted by invisible missiles.

Now, he threw off the cloth and blinked directly at Seth, seeing nothing. The startled expression slowly wore off his features as he recalled. He sighed.

Gently, Seth pushed him back down against the pallet, then dipped the rag in a bowl of cool water and reapplied it to Saul's eyes. "Can you tell me anything yet?"

"Are you sure you did not hear the voice?"

"I heard *something* . . . our horses . . . thunder, perhaps."

"No, no, it was definitely . . ." Then he dropped his angry

tone. "Forgive me; I took no refreshment from this night. Such sad . . . persuasive dreams."

"What did you hear on the road, Saul? I will understand."

"It was the Lord's voice."

Seth raised an eyebrow. "What did he say?"

"'Saul . . . Saul, why do you persecute me?'"

"But in what way have you offended God?"

"No . . . it was the Lord Jesus."

Seth stared at his friend, disbelieving. "What are you saying?"

"I will no longer persecute his followers."

Seth was silent.

"You may go back to Jerusalem," Saul said.

"You mean our work is over?"

"My work. You are your own man."

"I will stay with you."

"Seth—I am to become one of them."

His hair still wet, Saul sat across the table from the old man who had just baptized him in the water trough of the stable. Their embarrassment at being in each other's unexpected company made them stiff-backed, and between long silences they fired staccato questions at each other. Both men strained not to make these inquiries sound like accusations.

"You are not the Ananias of renown from lake Asphaltites?" Saul asked, munching down the last of his bread.

"No, I am not."

"Of course, I am familiar with the priest Ananias of the Temple."

"Yes . . . I am sure."

"It is a common enough name among our people."

"It is."

Saul shooed away a chicken that had perched on his bench to peck at his fallen crumbs. "Will you repeat for me what you said as you . . . ?"

"I just said it is."

Saul laughed self-consciously. "No, I meant as you baptized me."

"Oh." Ananias nodded gravely. "'I baptize you, Saul, in the name of Jesus, to the remission of your sins and in the fullness of the grace of Most High.'"

"Yes...." Saul smiled back at him placidly, scrutinizing every aspect of his frail person: the man's wizened face, his hawkish nose and, most intently of all, his liver-spotted hands, which had caused the blindness to fall from Saul's eyes only this morning. It did not seem possible that those fingers, now busily shredding a chunk of bread into pieces the man's few teeth could handle, had brought light back into Saul's head. Nor did any of the astonishment that had quavered in Ananias' voice remain in it when he presented himself at Judas' portal, explaining in confused snatches of words that God had commanded him to seek along the street called Straight a man of Tarsus named Saul.

Already, it seemed to Saul that the reality of these moments had faded. They had become memories of dreams.

"Do you think it would be fitting," Saul asked, "if I took a new name with me into this new life?"

"It might." Ananias nibbled, pensively. "What do you have in mind?"

"Paul.... From now on, I would like to be called that."

"Very well. I shall introduce you this evening as Paul. But they will still remember who you were."

"So will I, Ananias, and for this I will work doubly hard in our Lord's behalf."

VI

SARAH hesitated beneath the awning, unsure whether or not to chance the uncertain sky once again. She and her two fellow slaves had just dashed across the forum through a hard rain that had splattered as high as their knees. Each of the young women was now drenched. Shivering, they peered out from under the canvas. Sarah, especially, regarded the squall-washed air with suspicion: There were other heavy clouds billowing over the roofs of the temples toward them. Then lightning forked down behind the Capitoline Hill, and Sarah was startled by the rumble of thunder, when a voice said behind her: "I'm sorry. . . . Did my approach frighten you?"

"No, I—" It was the signifer, Valerius, whom she had last seen here in the forum months before. "Ah, it is you . . . Sejanus' man."

Valerius frowned. "I hope I was never really his man. But that is all past now. Are you cold?"

"Always . . . Rome is cold." She began trying to rub the gooseflesh off the backs of her arms.

"And you're wet." He began to unhitch his military cloak.

"No!" She said this so sharply she felt the need an instant later to smile in apology. "Thank you, but I'm fine, Julius Valerius Licinius." Then she quickly turned away to hide her blush from him.

"I'm happy to be with you again, Sarah."

"Why?"

The frankness of her tone made his expression thoughtful. "Well, have you forgotten what I said?"

"To forget, one must first remember. I do not wish to remember anything." She feigned rapt interest in the passing of an ornate litter bearing a vestal virgin.

"You never thought of me?"

"No . . . I have tried to keep you out of my thoughts."

"Tried?" A smile tugged at his lips. "I attempted the same, yet I did not succeed."

Her eyes became tender but no less troubled. "I am sorry, noble Valerius. I will confess I have been reminded of you often. But this is not meant to be. There are too many things in the way of our . . . our friendship." She took a step forward, but he gently clasped her arm.

"Things will change, I promise." He was on the verge of saying that he enjoyed ready access to the most powerful men in the Empire, but then realized that, while true, it still rang too much like a boast. And he was trying to pick his words as carefully as he would gemstones. "You will be able to leave your service."

"To go and serve another master?" She slipped free of his grasp.

Valerius half trotted to catch up with her. "Please . . . give me time."

"I can't give you what is not mine to give. And I beg you, as the good man I think you to be: Do not see me again."

Valerius halted, his face smarting. Then he compressed his lips and surged between Sarah and one of her friends, who had stepped in to protectively flank her. "Why?" he demanded. "Because I am a Roman and not a Jew?"

She refused to answer.

"Well, the gods gave me no choice in the matter."

"Did your gods choose for you to become a soldier as well?"

Valerius' eyes darted back and forth in search of an answer. His sigh told her he had settled on the truth. "No," he said quietly, "I decided to follow my father. A family tradition. But I could have said no . . . I think."

"So you carry a sword. You believe in its power. My brother did too. He was fighting you Romans. We were punished in his stead."

"I have never raised my sword against a Judean."

"But one day you could be called upon to, Valerius. What would you do then?"

He hunched his shoulders under his cloak. "I don't know, Sarah. I would have to decide at the time. All I know is that I could never hurt you."

The rain began pelting them again. They seemed unaware of it, although Sarah's friends had hurried under the cover of another awning. Sarah considered something, then shook her head, firmly. "It would never do—an officer . . . a slave."

"Perhaps. But an officer and a freedwoman is another matter."

"Then we are back to a Roman and a Jewess, Valerius. Don't you see the hopelessness of this?"

Their progress across the rain-slick forum was checked by a cohort of praetorian guards returning to the *castra praetoria* after a tour of duty at the imperial household on the Palatine Hill. They were resplendent as they tramped past in their polished cuirasses and red capes, but Valerius was disconcerted by the spectacle and kept glancing at Sarah out of the corner of his eye until the last silver helmet was past. Only then did he say, "Would it be so hopeless if I loved you . . . and you came to love me?" When she did not reply for a moment, he quickly added, "My freedom would be yours. I only ask that you do not forget what I am saying, Sarah. These differences you—"

She had rushed ahead. His heart sank. But then she spun around as she continued on her way and gave him a radiant smile he had not seen before. "I will not forget, Valerius Licinius."

Caleb leaped off the prow onto a stone quay in the Roman harbor of Puteoli even before the small boat had landed. He did not turn to give the merchant ship that had brought him from Caesarea one more glimpse; he had wearied of it during the past two months. The Romans lining the harbor paid him no attention: They were watching the departure of a quinquereme, an enormous warship with five banks of oars, that was bound for Illyricum to subdue pirates.

The first man he asked directed him toward the road north to Rome.

It was only through happenstance that he had learned of his mother's death. A Zealot from Caesarea, wanted in that city by the Roman authorities for indiscretions of his own, had joined Caleb's group in the Samaritan hills. Learning where the new man came from, Caleb pressed him for any word he might have had about the fate of his family. "Friend," the Caesarean said, his eyes growing sad, "if I am truly giving you news about the same people from Jerusalem, I bring you sorrow as well as another sword. The old woman died her first night in the Roman prison. The girls were put aboard a ship the next morning."

In that moment, Caleb vowed to go to Rome.

"But what will you do?" a comrade asked. "Jump off the boat and immediately start cutting throats?"

"No . . . but I will have my revenge—after I find my sisters."

"There are men of considerable fighting skill in Italy," another young man said. His parents had once been slaves in Rome.

"Then I will learn those skills."

"How?"

Caleb felt their eyes pressing on him—these youths whom he felt he had weaned of their mothers. "I will go to one of their schools."

"You mean become a gladiator?"

"If need be."

"Caleb, please, you are the best fighter in Samaria. We need you here."

"I will become the best in the world."

"Then what will you do?"

"Strike at the heart of their Empire: Rome."

As a foreigner, he had expected to be challenged by Roman soldiers at every town along the straight and level road that shot across the verdant countryside. But, encountering so many non-Romans—Armenians, Cretans, Egyptians and a dozen other peoples that he did not recognize—Caleb began to wonder if the Italians were the minority in their own country.

Yet, it was not long before he strode into a handsome town populated by sturdy-looking people who had gathered in the small forum. Caleb quickly surmised that a trial was being conducted, and one slightly bored elderly man in a toga was doing the work of the entire Sanhedrin. Caleb was finally in the presence of the natives, and he eagerly observed their rituals.

"Who is accused of what?" he asked an old woman, who did not blink an eye at being addressed by a Jew in a worn and soiled mantle.

"Furius Cresinus yonder." She pointed to a weather-bronzed man in early middle age, obviously a farmer. "And this prosecutor is from Rome—a regular Cicero, we hear."

"But what has he done that—"

She shushed him with a good-natured tap on the arm.

The noted counselor from the capital took the rostrum, a slab of marble that afforded him some elevation over the heads of the throng. "Furius Cresinus, as I have just heard," the man said with the officious tone of a *rabban,* "rejects all these accusations. But allow me the privilege of summing up the facts we all know. Furius was freed from slavery six years ago. After his manumission, he went to work in a small factory and ingratiated himself with the owner, also a freedman. When this man died, Furius inherited the factory. In the subsequent two years—a period, I might add, in which Fortuna failed to shine her face on the rest of this region—he made a fortune and retired to the life of a country gentleman on a farm formerly owned by a knight famous to you good people. . . ."

"Still," Caleb whispered to the old woman, "I see no offense in any of this."

"Shhh . . ."

". . . Drought came and diluvial rains after it. The harvests of his neighbors were claimed by these calamities. But his fields, his trees, bore all their fruits as if armored against misfortune. How, then, can this be explained except by the command of sorcery, of which Furius Cresinus is reputed to be an expert by the most reliable personages in all of Volsci? This enabled him to attract the ripeness to his harvests and shunt onto others the violence of nature so he could grow ever richer while his neighbors became as poor as slaves. He performed sorceries on his field, secret incantations known only to associates of demons, who, long ago, perused the now irrevocably lost six books of the Sibyls. All these I have mentioned are crimes punishable in accordance with our ancient law of the Twelve Tables. Noble Magistrate—" he turned to the elderly man, who was losing the battle on his curule chair against a spate of drowsiness, but propped open one eyelid—"I appeal to you to fulfill the law."

When the old woman joined in the polite applause, Caleb asked her, "Then you agree that the accused has used witchcraft?"

"Not at all. It's just that the prosecutor is so well spoken. We seldom see such talent here."

Then Furius Cresinus bound up onto the rostrum. He stood there not speaking, smiling, until the crowd grew restive. "Say something in your defense," the magistrate scolded him over the rattle of an approaching ox cart.

"I am." Furius then gestured toward the wooden cart, which was drawn by two snow-white, meticulously groomed oxen. Within it were seven boys, as deeply burnished by the sun as their father, and a woman of proud carriage with hair light red like kernels of spelt wheat. Each had come to Furius' defense armed with a farm implement. Yet, they raised their ploughs, scythes and sifters not in mutiny but simply to show the crowd how their success had been won. "My family, my working tools, my good animals—these and only these are my witchcraft. I regret I can't bring as my witnesses the sleepless vigils, the toil and the sweat. But these saved my harvests. These made me prosper."

The people around Caleb burst into applause, crying for dismissal. The magistrate granted them their wish and motioned for the grinning farmer to go home.

The old woman cackled in Caleb's ear, "See? Roman justice lives yet!"

"Perhaps here." Then he continued north on the road, somewhat unsettled by the thought that these Romans were not vastly different from the people of Judea or Samaria; he had assumed that all of Caesar's countless minions were either legionaries or corrupt officials.

As he neared the imperial city Caleb was seized by the fear that he was too late, although he could not decide for what, as Ruth and Sarah—for all he knew—had been Roman slaves for years now. But, in the throes of this anxious feeling, he could no longer justify his failure to come here immediately to find them and steal them back to freedom, if need be.

At last, he was standing in the forum before the Golden Milestone, a pillar jacketed with a gleaming bronze from which all roads in the Empire issued. He tried not to be overly impressed by the forest of columns, the gilt statuary and soaring temples that surrounded him; his weariness helped him in this effort. But it also occurred to him that he had eaten nothing since some berries he had foraged alongside the *Via Appia*. And he had no money. Nor did he know the whereabouts of his sisters.

Caleb confronted a man with no purple stripe on his toga. "I am a Jew."

"My felicitations."

"I mean, where might I find my people?"

"Judea, I believe."

Caleb struggled to hold his temper. "In this city."

"Ah, *now* we make ourselves clear. I once commissioned a tentmaker called Aquila. Go around that building there—the Basilica Aemilia—and follow the lane to where it ends. That will be the Street of the Ten Shops. Ask for Aquila."

"Shalom," Caleb muttered.

"What's that?"

"Peace be with you."

"Ah . . . peace, yes."

Caleb was mildly surprised that the awning outside the tentmaker's shop was the most faded he had yet seen in the city. But this was quickly forgotten in the pleasure of speaking to someone of his own race, even if it was in Hebrew and not his more familiar Aramaic. Aquila, a man of almost exquisite gentleness, had been born to Jewish parents in the kingdom of Pontus in Asia Minor. Having never traveled to Jerusalem, he asked Caleb question after question about the holy city, but especially about the death of Jesus, which Caleb had witnessed.

"Then it is not a large hill? That was my impression—a commanding mount outside Jerusalem."

"Oh, no, Aquila, Golgotha is more a heap than a mount. It's all of fifteen feet high." It did not take Caleb long to surmise that the man and his kindly wife, Priscilla, were Nazarenes. If only in gratitude for their hospitality, he did not confront them with his suspicions. Nazarenes were like Zealots in that they were cautious in a fresh acquaintanceship until sure the other party could be trusted.

"And now, over dinner," Aquila said, leading Caleb back past stacked bolts of canvas and an expansive cutting table to his living quarters, "you must tell us why you have come to Rome."

And after three cups of red wine Caleb told them about his family's misfortune—but did not mention how he had offended the Romans in Jerusalem. He was also silent about his rebellious activities in Samaria. ". . . So I don't know where to start looking in Rome. But I'm grateful to you both."

Priscilla's eyes had filled with tears.

"The Lord wants us to help one another." Aquila looked to his wife as if for approval. Furtively, she gave him a slight nod, and he then said to Caleb, "I always need another pair of hands in my line of work. Why don't you stay with us?"

Priscilla smiled. "Making tents, awnings—it's not as difficult as most think. You will learn quickly."

"I thank you, but I must keep faith with my own trade."

Aquila nodded respectfully. "Of course. I understand completely. And what is your trade, young Caleb?"

"I am a swordsman." He finished the last of his wine. "I want to join a gladiator's school."

In silence, Aquila and Priscilla glanced at each other.

"You would have to sacrifice to their gods," Aquila said.

Caleb laughed carelessly. "I've learned how to pretend. That's how I survived in Judea."

"My friend, if you think you can use your sword to free your sisters, you are wrong. A gladiator is no more than a slave. Few live long enough to enjoy their successes. Roman people are addicted to the excitement of the games. The more victories you collect, the more they will want to see you fight. And always against stronger opponents."

"I am not afraid."

Priscilla touched his arm. Like Aquilas', her hands had been toughened by canvas. "God will be help enough for you to find your sisters—believe me."

"Do you have any idea where they were bound in the city?"

"Only rumors, Aquila, from travelers I met through the years."

"What was said?"

"My sisters were a gift from Pontius Pilate to a man called Sejanus. But then I heard that Sejanus had been executed as a traitor."

"Yes, that is true." Aquila's eyes dimmed briefly as he appeared to recall something, then lost it. "But this may be a beginning. We can inquire into what happened to Sejanus' property." Suddenly, the man realized what he had said. "Forgive me. . . . This is what comes of association with Romans. I did not mean—"

"They *are* property—until I can free them. Where can I find Sejanus' family? They would know."

Priscilla's eyes flickered downward. "They were murdered and thrown into the Tiber."

Caleb could not speak for a moment. "Is it possible . . . Were his slaves . . . ?"

"We do not know, Caleb, so let us trust in the Lord's mercy." Aquila swiftly changed the subject. "Tell us, please, during your years in Jerusalem, did you ever meet a man called Stephen? He would have been a Hellenist."

"Certainly." Caleb brightened as the exuberant face came to mind. "We were in *Rabban* Gamaliel's school together. A good wrestler—in the Greek style." Then Caleb's expression sobered. "When I was in Samaria, visiting friends, I heard how he had been condemned by the Sanhedrin and stoned to death. Saul's doing, it was said."

"Would that be Saul the Cilician?" Priscilla asked.

"That's right . . . a Roman citizen from Tarsus."

The man and his wife once again shared glances. "Caleb, a Greek brother stayed with us recently. He had just come from Syria. He told us this same Cilician now calls himself Paul and has preached for the Nazarene in the synagogue at Damascus."

Caleb smirked. "No . . . your Hellenist friend has the wrong Paul. The man I knew was a Pharisee. He despised the Nazarenes."

"And you?" Aquila had begun tracing his forefinger around the outline of a fish that had been carved into the table.

"What about the followers of Jesus? I have no quarrel with them. But you'd never find me on my knees, praying, while the stones were flying. I'd have a good short sword in my fist." Caleb lifted his chin at the etching. "What's that?"

"A fish," Aquila said noncommittally.

Priscilla frowned. "Tell him, husband, he has a good heart. I know it."

Aquila simpered. "All right. This is the work of our Hellenist brother."

"What is that word inside the fish?"

"*Ixthus*—it is Greek for fish. But each letter is the initial of another word: *Iesus Xristos Theou Uios Soter*—Jesus Christ Son of God the Savior."

"I still do not understand," Caleb said.

"Well, Jesus asked his first followers to be fishers of men," Priscilla explained.

Caleb shrugged. "This all means nothing to me, but I do not mind that you are Nazarenes."

"No . . ." Suddenly, Aquila threw up his hands, grinning sheepishly. "Yes, no—what am I to say? There is so much we need to understand first. But our hearts are willing, and, before God, that is the truth." His eyes darted to his small water clock. "And now I must reopen the shop. The Romans

have finished their afternoon rest. They will want to do a little
business before the revels of the night. Caleb, it would delight
me to share more of your company while I work."

"Thank you, Aquila, Priscilla, but your meal has refreshed
me, and I am eager to start searching."

"Ah, of course. May the Lord direct you."

Thunderclouds were rolling across the sky as Caleb marched
down the Street of the Ten Shops, squinting against a gust of
wind that promised rain any moment. Hurrying toward the
forum again, he scrutinized each female face that glided past
in the opposite direction. Some smiled at him invitingly, which
he found shameless. Judean women shyly averted their eyes
from a strange man's gaze.

Gnashing his teeth at the thought, he wondered if the humiliation of slavery had changed Sarah and Ruth, blighted their
youth beyond recognition.

A figure fell into step with Caleb, who instinctively feigned
indifference when he glimpsed the military cloak. He yawned,
then slowed his pace and pretended to take great interest in a
fruit stall. The signifer continued on his way, grim-faced, apparently too deep in his own concerns to take notice of the
Judean.

Caleb smiled to himself: Rome was less dangerous for a
Zealot than Jerusalem.

VII

AFTER three nights of sleepless fretting, Valerius finally decided when and where to approach the Emperor. He would steal a few brief words with Gaius Caligula in the vestibule of the dining chamber at the imperial palace. Caligula would be in a festive mood and, eager to traipse into his cavernous banquet hall, might generously approve any request made to him.

But, as he took up his post in that passageway, flanked by statues of the gods Mercury and Mars, a flushed Valerius suddenly realized how risky his plan was.

The first months of Caligula's reign had seemed an answer to the prayers of Rome, especially after the benighted last years of Tiberius' rule. Young Caesar was pious, sober and respectful of the least freedman in his Empire. He abolished unfair taxes, restored wronged kings to their thrones and recalled all exiles to enjoy their former lives. But then this wave of light crested and began waning, leaving dark whispers behind it. Caligula had been observed having a one-sided argument with the marble Capitoline Jupiter, which had ended with the Emperor screaming: "If you do not raise me up to heaven, I will cast you down to hell!"

Yet, Valerius steeled himself to speak to the Emperor, reminding himself that Gaius Caligula was no more than a man.

Some cloying scent floated down around Valerius. He peeked inside the hall: From the uppermost balconies, slaves were spraying unguents on the guests.

Then he heard a cadence of heavy footfalls, and a dozen German praetorians escorted the Emperor down a corridor and into the vestibule. Caligula's eyes were vapid and red-rimmed. He staggered slightly as he moved at the center of his guard. Valerius knew at a glance that the man was inebriated, but he braced himself and saluted before saying in a firm voice, "Bear patience with me, Caesar. May I remind you of your promise?"

Caligula waved a limp hand for his procession to halt. He studied Valerius for a long moment, then smiled, lightly clenching the tip of his tongue between his teeth. "Which promise?" Unexpectedly, his eyes appeared to focus. "Oh . . . my handsome signifer . . . Tiberius' Horatio, who single-handedly fended off Aelius Sejanus."

"Caesar, this is about a slave. . . . Do you recall?"

"Of course, I do. . . ." He weaved through his Germans and hung his hairy arm around Valerius' neck. "The fellow belongs to my beloved, beloved sister, yes?"

"No, Caesar, I am speaking of a girl. And she has now come to this household with your noble sister."

"She's beautiful, I suppose?"

Valerius hesitated, briefly. "I believe so."

"Oh, that's not good enough. Now I will have to take a look for myself." Caligula turned to his centurion. "I want this—" He stopped. The statues of the gods lining the corridor had caught his fancy. Conspiratorially, he whispered in Valerius' ear, "Do you know what the Jews believe?"

Panic brought the taste of bile into his mouth. In the confusion of the moment, he imagined that Caligula was teasing him, having already taken Sarah to his bed. "No, Caesar, I do not."

"They believe there is only one god. Clever people, the Jews. And I intend to get on their good side. That's why I sent that oaf Pontius Pilate into exile." Caligula flagged his hand irritably in front of his own face. "But that's beside the point. . . ." He lifted his eyes to Mars' stone countenance. "Let me confide in you, my lovely signifer, what I plan to do."

Valerius nodded, his mouth too dry to form words.

"I'm going to cut off the heads of these lesser gods . . . and put mine there."

Behind Caligula's back, the Germans were grinning broadly as if thinking: *Finally, here's an Emperor with a little dash.* Caligula slowly turned toward them, but the praetorians did not stop beaming. Then, astonishingly, they all chuckled together.

Valerius felt heady from the exposure to such dazzling madness. "Caesar," he finally croaked, "if you might just—"

"Yes, I might just," Caligula answered playfully. "I want

the entire Empire to sit up and take notice, because I might just." Then he whisked into the hall, giggling at the hysterical ovation that greeted him.

Valerius leaned back against Mars' pedestal.

The Emperor plopped down beside Herod Agrippa on a wide couch built for three diners. Herod's dusky eyes frowned at Caligula over the lip of a wine cup.

The Emperor's gaiety dissipated, and he sneered back at the man. "Never satisfied, are you?"

"My dear Caesar?" Herod's voice was level.

"Not gratified, even after I set you free."

"An Emperor should keep *all* his promises."

"Don't you tell this Emperor what he should and shouldn't do. The whole point of being an Emperor is the total freedom it confers on one. *Total*. And that includes the freedom to break promises. Be satisfied with what you have, Prince Herod the Little."

"My throne should be in Jerusalem, not in your court."

"Fill your mouth with food."

"Caesar?"

"Do as I command!"

In smarting silence, Herod stripped a piece of flesh off a roasted pheasant and tasted the meat as if it were offal.

Caligula was smirking again. "Swallow...."

Herod did so.

"Imagine how delicious that would have tasted to my Aunt Livilla, who my grandmother, the noble Antonia, locked in her room and starved to death." Affably, Caligula patted the prince on the back. "You are fortunate to have survived those terrible days, my friend. Let that be enough for now. Judea remains under Roman rule. The Senate so decrees, and I have made it a point to listen to the Senate. Haven't I, Uncle Claudius?"

The white-maned man wiped away a pearl of drool that had formed at the corner of his mouth and nodded. "S-sometimes, Caesar."

Caligula laughed as if this were hysterically funny. "Entertain us with a little eloquence, Uncle Claudius, if you'd be so kind."

Without a moment's hesitation, Claudius rose up off his

couch and limped to the center of the hall, where—without changing his languid expression—he launched into a recitation:

> "Right on the threshold, in the jaws
> Of Orcus,
> Pain and the vengeful Cares have
> Their dwelling. . . ."

His eyes darted askance at Caligula as he overheard the Emperor delivering the lines along with him:

> "And sallow Sickness and Senility,
> And Fright and Craving that lead men
> to kill—"

"No, no, no," Caligula interrupted Claudius and himself. "Virgil can be too morbid for a dinner party. I want something a little less hackneyed, but a bit more uplifting—in the moral sense."

When Claudius spoke again, it was after a brief interlude in which his eyes had become plaintive. "He who is all-powerful is free to perform both good and evil acts. And because g-good is harder to accomplish than evil, he will best show his power in the enactment of good. He who performs nothing but evil is enslaved to evil and has forfeited his power of choice. The evil ruler is no ruler at all." He then appeared to be unmoved by the ghastly silence he had created in the hall. Smiling inanely, he hobbled back to his couch.

Caligula shook his head and chuckled. "And which one of your constipated stoics wrote that, Uncle?"

"An unknown philosopher of b-both good and bad family."

"Wealthy?" the Emperor asked.

"Only in books."

"Damn . . . I would have seized his estate for writing such seditious rubbish. But if he has no property, why bother?"

"Yes, Caesar, w-why bother?" Claudius began swallowing more easily.

"Now," Caligula announced, "my friend Prince Herod Agrippa the Little will oblige us with some Hebrew poetry."

"All our Hebrew poetry is sacred, Caesar."

"Well, so am I. Oh"—Caligula made a soft gasping noise—"how thoughtless of me, Herod." He then snarled at his guests:

"Each of you, plug your ears with your fingers!"

"I mean," Herod continued, "The Psalms of David are not a garnish for lobster and suckling pig."

"Why is everyone so tiresome tonight?" the Emperor whined, beating his forehead against his couch rugs. *"Why does everyone insist on being such a spoilsport?"* He scanned the other couches again, this time glaring at the expressionless faces. "Very well. If you will not entertain your Emperor, your Emperor must entertain you. My whip, please."

A slave ran it out to him. Caligula gave the black leather hilt a caress, then sprang out into the arena formed by the circle of couches. Wavering slightly as he stood on his tiptoes, he ran his leer past senators, knights, magistrates and their matrons, in search of some mischief outrageous enough to suit his mood. A female slave, unaware of him, darted among the guests, dispensing cream from a pitcher.

Caligula let the whip fly, and she looked up, startled, as the vessel exploded in her grasp. A flurry of cream splattered an ex-consul and his wife.

The other guests began laughing hesitantly.

But Caligula's attention had been captivated by the slave. "Where are you from, my dear?"

Sarah let the shards of the pitcher remaining in her hands clatter to the floor. "Judea."

"Judea!" Caligula said brightly, turning to Herod Agrippa. "She's one of yours. Tell me, Your Majesty, what was the name of your grandmother again?"

"Salome, Caesar."

"Salome the dancing girl? I loved that tale."

"No, that was another Salome, a stepdaughter of my uncle."

Caligula tittered as if in parody of the modesty he had recently shown. "She danced naked, did she not?"

"In a manner of speaking, yes."

"And she was given a prize for dancing so exquisitely, was she not?"

"The head of—"

"Oh, don't bore me with Jewish history. Somebody's head—that's all that really matters." Caligula cracked the whip over Herod's head. Resolutely, the king did not flinch. "Well, Your Majesty, you have to admit, *that* was imperial entertainment." Then he rested his chin on his shoulder and smiled at Sarah. "Whose head do you want, my dear?"

She did not know what to say. The hem of her tunic was betraying her trembling.

"Well, we can decide after your dance. Music! Ready? Dance!"

Sarah stood dumbfounded, unable to budge. Her arms hung at her sides.

But then movement drew her eyes to the vestibule. There, Valerius, his face pale, devastated, appeared to be on the verge of rushing into the hall and confronting the Emperor. She began to dance, clumsily at first, as if trying to recall the steps that had been effortless in happier times. Gradually, her body became less rigid, and she was enticed to sway her hips by the trilling of the flutes. This only served to make Caligula more impatient.

"Something faster . . . faster!" he screamed at the musicians.

She could still see Valerius agonizing in the vestibule, but kept him there with a flash of her eyes.

Caligula shook his head with disgust. "Oh, no, that's no way to dance, Salome. Like this! Music!" He lowered himself onto his knees, drawing her down until she was nearly atop him. Below the waist, he began undulating, bumping his pelvis against her until she matched his motion. Caligula grinned in an arc of flashing teeth. "Applause . . . applause!"

There was short-lived clapping, then the guests lapsed back into their petrification, each terrified to so much as scratch his nose for fear of attracting the Emperor's gaze.

"Please," Sarah said to him, "no more."

"You will dance," Caligula whispered ominously, wrapping the whip around her neck. "I have my guests to think of."

"I beg you—"

Caligula gave a vicious tug on the whip, and her head snapped back. Sarah collapsed to the floor and lay still.

"Applause!" Caligula cried.

Everyone obeyed wretchedly.

Valerius' eyes bulged; he was so horrified that he could not move.

"Now, dear Salome, you shall have a severed head as a reward for dancing so well. Whose shall it be?" Caligula ignored her lifeless form and began taking stock, one by one, of all the faces in the hall, cackling at each fresh manifestation of panic. He leaned over and picked up Sarah's hand. He let go, and it flopped to the floor. "Oh, damn," he said remorselessly, "she broke ... and I'm so bored again."

Valerius had quietly assumed the stance he adopted whenever awaiting a military inspection. His expression was composed, and while his anxiety had not completely let go of him,
it was now more like a keen alertness. Only moments before,
he had been prepared to draw his short sword, fight past the
ring of German praetorians inside the hall and hurl himself on
the person of the Emperor, whom he would hack to death.

But Sarah had stayed this assassination with her little finger.

Valerius' hand had been on his sword hilt and his eyes on
her corpse when, suddenly, he spotted something that made
him gasp. Her ashen cheek was lying across her left hand,
which was hidden from Caligula's view by the fall of her hair.
All at once, she lifted a finger. She did this again a moment
later, so Valerius would be sure to notice.

Caligula was now occupied with the young patrician woman
who had defied him with her bold stare. "You—," he declared
as if he were bestowing a great honor, "—will share the imperial bed for a celestial union."

"Most divine Caligula," the elderly man beside her said,
punctuating his words with a meaningless chuckle, "my daughter, Corinna, she is ... she is so young, a virgin."

Caligula raised his voice so everyone could hear him. "I
can think of no condition that is more satisfying to remedy."

His remark was greeted with chortling and applause, which
appeared to give him immense delight. But the young woman
named Corinna, although extraordinarily pretty, seemed to please
him less than she had in his first sight. "You ..." he said
contemptuously, "... must rid yourself of that audacious glare
if you ever hope to win a man."

"I will see to it," her father prattled when she refused to
speak.

In the meantime Caligula had noticed that a fold of a woman's gown had slipped from one of its clasps, revealing a glint
of ivory-white flesh. The woman's husband slid his arm around
her waist as the Emperor trod toward them, lurching now as
he came, forgetting the martial primness he had just been exhorting. "You," he barked at the man, "take your hands off
my wife!"

"With respect, Caesar, my wife." The man simpered, waiting for the Emperor to declare it all a joke with a boisterous
laugh.

But Caligula became no less insistent. "I find her worthier for my embrace than that one"—he jerked his thumb toward Corinna—"and you mortals must learn to live with the whims of gods."

"Caesar, she *is* my wife."

"She will be yours again tomorrow." Caligula took her by the hand and led her back to his couch. He was about to plant a voluptuous kiss on her throat when something made him glance back down at the vacant floor. "What has happened to my dear Salome?"

"One of your guards removed her body, Caesar," Herod said morosely. "She was . . . broken."

"Well, we still have need of a head. I promised these people a head." Caligula leveled his gaze at the glum husband across the hall. "*Yours* will do."

Valerius would not put her down until he was outside the imperial palace, awash in the clean air of the night. "We are alone," he said at last, his voice breaking.

She opened her eyes as her feet touched the street, and then clung to him, shuddering.

"I despise it all . . . but especially my part in it."

"Please keep me warm," she whispered.

He enveloped her in his cloak. "As of now I am a Roman no more."

"You will always be a Roman, Valerius: That cannot be changed."

"The bastard! The monster!" he seethed. "What it must have been like to lie there all that time!"

"I was not frightened for myself."

"Then you are much braver than I, Sarah."

"I was terrified *you* might do something rash. I opened my eyes a little . . . and could see the look on your face."

He smiled up at the faint stars. "Then it is not so hopeless for you and me?"

"Look at me, Valerius Licinius . . . so I may tell you I love you."

Yet, in that moment, Valerius could not meet her eyes.

A figure had strolled out of the shadows. When Valerius' hand darted for the hilt of his sword, the man said, "Don't be such a fool, Signifer." He approached the couple, his own blade drawn and held ready against the side of his leg. "She could be crucified and you beheaded for this little trick."

It had not occurred to Valerius that Sutorius Macro, the praetorian prefect, might be skulking somewhere on the fringes of Caligula's lunacy. In this way the man could keep track of happenings with less risk that the Emperor, in one of his rash fits, might demand his head.

"What does the noble prefect intend to do?" Valerius asked, torn between running with Sarah into the night and striking Macro down on the spot.

"I have to take her back."

"No . . . she's not being returned to Caligula . . . or his sister, who actually owns Sarah."

Macro's jaw muscles were rippling under his heavy jowls. Then he chuckled dryly. "Very well, Signifer, this sounds like a matter of the heart."

"It is."

"If the good *lady* will pardon us, a word alone with you . . . Valerius, isn't it?"

His hand still on his sword, Valerius walked with Macro to a circle of torchlight across the street. "Whatever you wish to say, she is not going back to the palace."

"Hold your bloody temper; perhaps we can work something out." Macro sighed wearily. "The truth is, I'm not in such good graces with Caligula myself. I could use another pair of ears next to the Emperor. A few minutes' warning, could save my life . . . my family's."

"What can you do for me?" Valerius asked impatiently.

"Caligula's desperate for money to finance an invasion of Britannia."

"What does that have to do with—"

"It could get you your lady."

"I already have her."

"No you don't," Macro said. "This is theft from the Emperor. Do you really think it won't be found out?"

Valerius did not answer.

"Now, in the next few weeks, that maniac is going to seize all property that rightfully belongs to his sisters; the whole lot's going on the auction block. Your woman could be among those other items." Slowly, so Valerius would not misunderstand the movement of his hand, Macro reached inside his waistbelt and produced a leather purse. "Here's enough so no one can outbid you—or, better yet, your agent."

"What happens to Sarah in the meantime?" Valerius asked quietly.

"I'll take her forthwith to one of his sister's lesser households—one Caligula is not likely to visit before he departs for Britannia."

Valerius stared at Sarah, waiting alone, her hands clasped together. "Give me a moment to explain to her."

"But only a moment, Signifer. Just as I was watching you, there is someone watching me."

VIII

PAUL kept vigil in the marketplace that was wedged between the Hasmonean Palace and the western wall of the Temple of Herod. He scrutinized each man who hurried past. But he held his cloak across his own face as protection against the billowing dust and recognition by the Temple guards, who knew Saul of Tarsus on sight better than anyone else in Jerusalem.

At long last, an elderly man stepped up to a fruit stall and dropped his shawl from his nose and mouth as he squeezed the pomelos to feel how juicy they were.

Hesitantly, Paul approached him from behind. "Joseph Barsabbas?"

"Yes, what——?" Barsabbas' eyes hardened when he recognized the intruder. "I must go."

Paul caught him by the arm. "Please, has no news arrived here from Damascus?"

"Yes, Saul. But it is not easy to believe what we have heard."

"You *must*! Even my name is changed——believe it!"

"We know you are now called Paul. But that proves nothing."

"Please, Barsabbas"——Paul tried to swallow the desperation that kept rising in his voice——"I'm unarmed, alone. . . . Already I have paid dearly for my faith. When I spoke before the synagogue——"

"I'm sure you found many supporters," Barsabbas said bitterly.

"They reviled me. Seth, my companion, was slain by those who came at us with daggers in the night. There was only one way for me to leave Damascus: over the wall in a basket." Paul held up his hands as if he did not know what more to say.

Barsabbas blinked against an onslaught of dust. "Saul, we have heard from a dozen pilgrims every detail of your conversion. But it's too sudden for us to accept. A man doesn't change that quickly."

141

"Unless the Lord wills it."

Barsabbas pondered this for a moment, then sighed through the lamb's wool of his shawl. "What do you want, then?"

"Will you take me to the brethren?"

"And next thing they're brought up before the Sanhedrin. One traitor was enough."

"I beg you." Then, swiftly, Paul covered the lower half of his face with his cloak. His eyes were frantic.

Barsabbas glanced back to see a troop of Temple guards fighting against the gritty wind to return to their garrison. The old man smiled at Paul's discomfort. "All right, I will take a chance . . . and pray I am not wrong."

Peter stared intently into Paul's eyes. "What I don't understand is this: If you were so afraid of the priests taking vengeance on you, why'd you come back here to Jerusalem? Why'd you put yourself within their reach again?"

"I needed instructions. I was cut off from knowledge in Damascus."

"This is all too neat for me to accept it." Thomas, who had been pacing the floor ever since Barsabbas had returned with Paul in tow, now drew back a corner of the linen blind to check the lane below for the third time. A blast of dust made him recoil. "There is no doubt in my mind that Caiaphas is privy to all of this. I suggest that, one, Saul be shown the door immediately; and two, we find some other room in the city, now that the Sanhedrin is familiar with this house."

Paul lowered his face into his hands. "I did not come to drive you deeper into hiding."

Thomas stood over him. "Well, that is precisely—"

"Hold, hold, please," Peter said wearily. "We have been made suspicious because things happen too fast lately, yes? And there are those who have converted for the wrong reasons"—he smirked as he crossed his thick forearms over his chest—"like Simon Magnus, who wanted to buy the secret to our 'magic.'"

"Or that Ethiopian whom Philip converted with absolutely no authorization," Thomas said incredulously. "A *gentile,* yet."

"So," Peter continued, "let's go at this with a bit of patience until we understand what the Lord has intended for Sau . . . Paul, here."

"What do you want me to do?" Paul asked quietly.

"First, eat and sleep. I was a fisherman: I know exhaustion when I see it." Peter smiled to soften his next words. "Then leave Jerusalem."

Saul looked crestfallen. *"Why?"*

"Well, to think things over."

"There is nothing to think over, as you say." Tears welled in Paul's eyes, and he was clasping his hands together to keep them from balling into fists. "There is no need when one is struck blind by the Lord Jesus on the road to . . ." He could not continue without risking the escape of a sob.

A man left the corner of the room where he had been sitting quietly and crouched before Paul. "He lives within you, doesn't he?"

Paul nodded fiercely. "You are . . . ?"

"James."

"His brother?"

"Yes."

Paul studied the gentle face as if to glean something he realized could never be retrieved.

"Peter is right," James said. "You must go. And it is not that we wish to be rid of you. The priests would deal more ruthlessly with you than any one of us, for they once trusted and respected you. Go, Paul."

"Where?"

"Home," Peter said. "Return to Tarsus. Meditate. Prepare your heart for what is to come."

"Don't any of you realize? I am ignorant of his teachings."

"Barnabas and Thomas will go as far as Caesarea with you. They will tell you as much as we know."

"Not I." Thomas returned to the window.

"Then, James, will you?" Peter asked.

"Gladly."

Decimus Marcellus, the newly appointed procurator of Judea, strolled atop the semicircular seawall with Cornelius, his chief centurion. The officer had just acquainted the governor with the aqueduct system that brought water to Caesarea from springs on Mount Carmel, thirteen miles distant, and now the two men had come down to the harbor to scan the horizon. They were expecting a ship from Rome. In its hold, they knew from land-borne dispatches, was a gilded hunk of marble that might well plunge the region into revolt.

Marcellus had immediately liked and trusted the centurion. Privately, he did not believe himself capable of managing a hotbed of strife like Judea, and so he thanked the gods that he had been given a competent, forthright adjutant in the person of Cornelius. Marcellus was not exactly sure how he had received the imperial appointment, except that he was a distant cousin of the Syrian proconsul Vitellius, who had undone Pontius Pilate. The disgraced procurator, at last report, had been banished to Rhaetia, a wasteland of snow and ice.

Marcellus had been afraid to mention to the emperor Caligula that he scarcely knew his cousin. The only things he could recall of Vitellius were that the man was a glutton and he belched loudly whenever he felt the urge, regardless of the company he shared. Other than that, Marcellus knew little about the proconsul.

Now, perhaps because of some mistaken notion that he and Vitellius were the closest of kin, Marcellus found himself the governor of Judea. He did not know Aramaic. Nor was he proficient in Greek. And he thought Jews had an unpleasant odor.

"Ah, here she comes, Procurator." Cornelius pointed to a sail skirting the coast to the north.

"What am I to do?"

The centurion frowned. "I don't know—temporize... delay... hope that Rome will reverse the decision."

"Do you think it will?" Marcellus asked hopefully.

Cornelius' face grew sad. "No."

"Then what will happen?"

"There will be a bloody, foolish massacre. As much as I pray to God, that is truly what I think will come."

Marcellus looked askance at the centurion, then smiled. "My friend, did you just say *God* or *gods*?"

Cornelius chuckled. "It's possible I've been out here too long, eh? Sixteen years this coming Saturnalia."

"Simply explain this to me: If they believe in but one god, what's wrong with pretending this image of Gaius Caligula is that god? I mean, what's the real harm in putting the statue in their temple? They can ignore it if they want... let it gather cobwebs, for all we care."

"That, Procurator, would still be a blasphemy to them. They maintain that their god has no image."

"Ah, now hold there, dear Cornelius," Marcellus said authoritatively for the first time. "I understand that, according to a new Jewish sect, God transformed Himself into a man. A slave called Chrestus. Am I not correct?"

"A slight confusion there, sir. Chrestus is, I grant, a common enough name for a slave."

"Yes, what else to call one but *cheerful, helpful, useful.*"

"But the name you mean is Christus," Cornelius went on. "This man was not a slave but a son of the royal house of David. He was Joshua to his kin. But we heard of him as Jesus of Nazareth. And his followers are called Nazarenes. Christus means 'anointed with sacred oil' . . . like a king. They called him the king of the Jews, the Messiah."

Marcellus threw up his hands. "Enough of this, Cornelius. I would like a repast and a bath. Then I suppose I must come back here and supervise the unloading of the deified Caligula."

"They're really not so difficult to understand—these Jews, I mean. Just make a bit of an effort to speak to them, sir."

A few minutes later, as they were ambling along the busy quay, Marcellus took the centurion's advice and nodded in greeting to a man in travel-worn clothes who was waiting to board a ship. "Where are you bound?" he asked congenially.

The Jew seemed so terrified, he could scarcely speak, although when he finally did his Latin was more than adequate. "Tarsus . . . my home."

"Been to Jerusalem, then?"

"No. I mean to say yes . . . briefly."

"Well," Marcellus said, walking on, "safe voyage to you." *"Shalom."*

Then the procurator muttered to his centurion. "Funny people . . . I'll never get used to them."

"Nor they to us, sir."

IX

"IT isn't often we have a free man enroll in our little school,"
Serpenius, the *lanista*, or keeper and chief trainer, then smiled
to let it be known that no wool was being pulled over his eyes.
"*Metellus*, is it?"

"Yes," Caleb said.

The Numidian black ran his fingers through his salt-and-
pepper hair. "Why'd you think of us and not one of the imperial
schools?"

"They are not as good as this one." Caleb did not mention
his real reason: The public institutions were under the control
of the Emperor, and he did not want to serve that butcher in
the slightest. But he had spoken the truth about this private
school, which was owned by a unnamed group of speculators,
in that it was known for producing the best fighters in Rome.

"There's a reason free men don't join us," Serpenius went
on, "although we've had more unusual recruits than you, believe me. To the criminal, this place is a blissful alternative to
the cross or the ax. To the slave—well, he's got no choice.
But a free man—"

"I am used to discipline," Caleb said with a vague smile.

"Are you, now?" Serpenius crooked a finger that had been
hacked off at the first joint. "Then follow me, young Metellus.
I want you to see something before you finally decide."

Caleb put his tunic back on; he had removed it to show the
lanista his musculature, and Serpenius led him at a stroll out
into a sandy courtyard that was closed off by colonnaded porticoes on all four sides. There was not a hint of breeze in this
enclosure; yet, the nearly naked men there were training at a
furious tempo, unmindful of the heat.

"This is where you start . . . if you still want to." Serpenius
gestured at a pair of youths in loincloths who were swinging
wooden swords at each other under the watchful eye of an
obvious veteran of the ring.

"Why wood?" Caleb asked.

Serpenius barked with laughter. "Oh, you will be great fun, I'm sure." He then invited Caleb to step inside a darkened chamber along the cloister.

Caleb waited for his eyes to adjust to the shadows.

"Welcome to the guardroom, Metellus," Serpenius said.

Slowly, Caleb could make out the silhouette of a man slumping in a sitting position, his wrists and ankles rubbed raw by the stocks that held them. His face came into focus: It was hollow-eyed and gray in color.

"Why are you here?" Serpenius demanded of him.

His voice was a croak. "I did not . . . show initiative."

"Will you in the future?"

"Yes . . . please . . ."

"Well, another week—then I may believe you." Serpenius jerked his head for Caleb to step out into the sunlight. "Now, young Metellus, do you still want to join our school?"

"Today—if I can."

Serpenius let loose with his canine laugh again. "Good, I like that."

Within a few days, Caleb had shown enough promise to his boxing and fencing masters that Serpenius himself was sent for. The *lanista* came promenading out into the courtyard as if reliving the afternoon on which Tiberius Caesar had bestowed upon him his wooden sword, signifying that the gladiator had to risk his life no more.

"Well, Metellus, it's time you learn what this is all really about." Serpenius waved for Caleb to join him in the shade of the portico, where they sat together on the same granite step. "The games are really only one thing. They are *not* lions or panthers prancing about the arena with arms and legs sticking out of their jaws. Nor are they a flooded pit and a mock sea battle. Frills for the mob—and never forget it." His eyes locked on to Caleb's. "You've got what it takes to be a first-rate gladiator, so listen closely now: The games are a balanced match between two completely different manners of fighting men—"

"Retiarii and Thracians," Caleb said quietly.

"There you have it." As if by magic, Serpenius produced a pomegranate from somewhere within his tunic and bit open the tough outer layer of skin, the red juice dribbling down his chin. "The retiarius—may the gods bless his pitiless heart—

strides out into the arena armed only with a net and a trident. If he gets cornered, it's all over for him. So he can never back off a pace, never lose the initiative. Why? Look at what he faces: a man suited in armor from helmet to the greaves on his shins, who bears a round shield and sword—or sickle, if he prefers." Serpenius grinned, his teeth stained crimson by the fruit. "*This* is what should truly interest the crowd—advantage and disadvantage perfectly offset by disadvantage and advantage. Lightness versus heaviness. Poise against power." Then he said without a moment's pause, "You're a Jew, aren't you?"

Caleb hesitated, then shrugged. "What does it matter?"

"Not in the least. I'm a bit of an outlander myself." Serpenius spat out some pulp. He studied Caleb's face. "I'm going to groom you to be a retiarius. Shed that helmet and breastplate." Then, without apparent cause, the Numidian chortled to himself. "One week from today, I will test you. Now go—there is much to learn."

As soon as Caleb was handed his first net and felt the almost sticky meshing entangle itself around his forearms, he smiled, recalling the vision the Essene holy man, Ananias, had had about Caleb defending himself with such a thing. The thought amused rather than disconcerted him. Then a veteran Thracian combatant cried, "Are you ready, brother?"

The entire *familia*, as Caleb had learned to call his fifty-odd fellow fighters at the school, was lined along the porticoes, awaiting the arrival of the Thracian who would face Caleb's net and trident. The sound of horse hooves on the street outside made the men fall silent, and a moment later, when the fighter strode out onto the sands, the *familia* burst into cheers of approval.

Caleb could not understand their enthusiasm. The hinged halves of the Thracian's visor were closed over his features, but he appeared to be lithe and of moderate height. Caleb had expected a more massively built opponent.

Serpenius strode between them. "Now, this is just an exhibition for the entertainment of our family." He could scarcely keep from chuckling. "So it's no steel today and no mending tomorrow. Right?"

"Aye," Caleb grunted.

The helmet across from him dipped once.

"Go to it."

Caleb immediately snapped his net out toward the Thracian, who—although forced to jump backward—advanced again with birch short sword whooshing through the air. This time, Caleb only feinted a cast of the net, but the Thracian correctly guessed it to be a ruse and drove for Caleb's abdomen. Inches from what in the arena would have resulted in his disembowelment, Caleb shunted the blow with the handle of his trident.

His next cast nelted him the Thracian's round shield, which he yanked out of his opponent's grasp, then kicked aside. Behind him, Caleb could hear the *familia* making wagers, updating the odds after each exchange of thrusts or parries.

The Thracian eluded two rapid swirls of the net, but a third wrapped around the fighter's upper body. Caleb pressed his blunt-tipped trident against the exposed throat.

"Finished!" Serpenius shouted.

Accepting the cheers in his behalf with a grin, Caleb lowered his trident and gave a pull on his net, which brought the Thracian's helmet along with it.

Caleb gaped at the young woman, who freed herself from the last strands of the net, then swept her long hair back from her face and down over her shoulders.

"You are quite good," she said matter-of-factly.

Caleb could think of nothing in reply. Slowly, he became aware that the men on the porticoes were doubled with laughter. The corner of his mouth twitched. He broke off his stare and marched straight for the armory, where he broke the trident over his knee, then sank onto a bench.

Serpenius appeared at the portal after a few minutes, each hand filled with a cup of wine. "Let's drink to your victory." There was no derision in his voice.

"*What* victory?"

"Don't tell yourself otherwise: She's good . . . quite good."

Caleb finally accepted his cup, then drained it in two gulps. "What kind of oddity is she?"

"They come along every few years—patrician women who plead with me to teach them our skills. Old Augustus would never've stood for it. But Tiberius hid on Capri, and Caligula probably thinks it's good fun."

"Does she actually fight in the arena?"

"Of course—that's the only reason we take somebody on. This school turns out gladiators, not rich athletes."

"But she's a *woman*."

"A *Roman* woman, lad," Serpenius said. "I don't know how things are in Judea, but these here are the most independent women in the world—I'm sure of it." He squinted at Caleb. "Now tell me, in your country can a matron go off on a holiday—if you catch my drift—by herself, without telling her husband?"

"Certainly not."

"Can she sue or be sued in the courts without his knowledge?"

"Never."

"Can she carry on a little romance behind his back, as long as it's kept discreet?"

Caleb laughed at the absurdity of the notion. "Only at the risk of being stoned to death."

"Are you jesting about that?" Serpenius asked with raised eyebrows.

"No. What would happen here if an adulteress were—"

"Found straddling? Why, she'd probably tell her poor cuckold, 'Take away your property!'"

"Then he'd divorce her?"

"What do you mean, lad? With those few words, she would be divorcing him."

Caleb sighed and began stripping off his sweaty tunic. "And how long has this one been disgracing her husband?"

"Who, Corinna? She's not married, Metellus."

"Caleb," he said as if cross with himself for lying in the first place. "My name is Caleb."

"I thought it'd be something more like that." Serpenius came to his feet. "But, after your victories, there'll be plenty of noble wives asking for you, I can see that already. Just use your head. Don't do what I almost did. . . ." He shook his head as he recollected.

"What was that?"

"Nearly eloped with one of them. I still shudder when I remember, considering what her husband is today."

"Tell me."

"No, that's my secret. You'll have enough of your own in due time." Serpenius paused at the threshold. "The Lady Corinna wants a word with you. She's waiting in the passageway to the street." Then the former gladiator allowed himself a boisterous laugh.

• • •

Caleb strode up to her, his jaw thrust out and his eyes hostile. "You wished a word with me?"

"Yes, Metellus, I—"

"You may begin by calling me Caleb. That is my name." No longer distracted by embarrassment, he confirmed what he had suspected during those confused moments in which he had pulled the helmet off her head: She was lovely. She now wore a transparent veil over her flaxen hair, and her gaze was so lucid, he felt silly when he murmured, "You are Corinna."

"Yes. . . . I was afraid that my presence shamed you before the *familia*. I fought believing they had told you about me."

"And spoil their own joke?"

"I am sorry, Caleb. It was not my doing."

He accepted her apology with a nod—despite himself. "You have no one to fight for you?"

She held up her head. "There is no one brave enough—not in Rome, at least."

"I'm glad to hear that."

She smiled. "You are?"

"Yes, where I come from there are too many brave Romans."

She tried to hide her disappointment. "Where is that?"

"Judea." He fought the temptation to stare at her. When he realized it was too strong for him, he turned to go. "Well, we must fight again sometime."

"Wait."

Slowly, he spun to face her. "What?"

"Next week . . . this same day . . . will you train with me? I still have difficulty with a really accomplished retiarius. I would be grateful."

Caleb began sauntering back toward the courtyard. "All right," he said over his shoulder, seemingly as an afterthought.

They rested on the stone bench that circumvallated the fountain in a niche off the exercise yard. Caleb lay on his back, peering up into a hazy morning sky, although peripherally he could see Corinna washing the sand off her legs. "Are your parents still living?" he asked.

"My father."

He could tell by her tone that they had recently quarreled.

Smirking to himself, he pressed on. "What does he think of your . . . sport?"

"It does not matter what he thinks."

"I simply asked, Corinna."

She exhaled, exasperated. "There is a poem circulating. Another senator slipped my father a copy. He was beside himself with anger."

"How does it go?"

She planted her hands atop a knee. "'Hear the gladiatress grunt as she slashes and batters . . . see her face in rose as she plunges to kill.'" Then her features became so grimly pained, he expected to see tears, but none came. He sat up, and she held his eyes. "All the shame should be his alone, Caleb. He could have said no when Tiberius had me dressed as Venus when I was yet a child. My father could have found his courage when Caligula ordered me to his bed."

Caleb could not help but to ask, "Did he . . . ?"

"No. But only his fickleness spared me."

"Well," Caleb said philosophically, "such a thing can be endured, even forgotten in time."

"You don't understand. I would have killed myself. You don't know what Rome has become. At an imperial banquet, I saw the Emperor break a girl's neck: He murdered her. Then he ordered a man beheaded who'd offended Caesar by not gladly handing over his wife. There isn't a patrician who isn't living from day to day"—her eyes shone with pride—"but only I have chosen to do it with dignity."

"On the contrary, Corinna, I know your Empire all too well. You Romans killed my mother. And somewhere within this filthy city my sisters are slaves."

"Which household?"

"I'm still searching. . . . Friends are helping me. It has not been as simple as I thought. They might even be at someone's villa in the countryside."

Lightly, she touched his hand. "I did not take part in your mother's death, and I detest those who did."

Caleb nodded, withdrawing his hand. "Serpenius tells me I will fight for the first time by the end of the week."

"Good news. Here in the arena?"

"No, Pompeii. Games are being staged to celebrate Caligula's expected victory in Britannia."

Her pretty mouth formed a scowl. "A triumph even before he marches. We've become buffoons as well as cowards. There is a rumor the Emperor is poisoning senators and knights for their estates, all to finance this expedition. And no one says a word." She glanced at Caleb again, her expression softening. "In Pompeii . . . don't get hurt."

"I will ask you not to speak this way. One day we may face each other in the arena, and this kind of talk . . . it might only confuse us."

Her lips became thin. "That day is in the future. We must not be so foolish as to live it now. I would like to say more, Caleb—"

"Back to work!" Serpenius bawled from the center of the courtyard.

The gladiators, who had been sprawled out across the shaded porticoes, shook off their drowsiness and reached for their weapons again. A few of them had formed a file and were trooping over the sands with mock solemnity. "*Hail* Serpenius! Those who are about to die salute you!"

"Get on with it, now," Serpenius said, biting into a ripe plum.

Caleb trotted out into a clear space among the other fighters and began tapping the butt of his trident on the ground, waiting for Corinna to don her breastplate and helmet, then join him. The sun broke through the overcast, and he squinted up at it, his face hard, resentful.

"Ready," she said curtly.

His net made a soughing noise through the air—and missed her. With surprising agility, she closed on him and, after a brief sequence of fencing moves, exposed him to a thrust that—had she carried through with it—would have finished him then and there.

Caleb glowered at the glints of her eyes that shone through the visor. Abandoning any pretense of fighting with finesse, he dropped his net to the sand and charged toward her, brandishing his trident as if he were swinging a staff in a Jerusalem street brawl. Knocks resounded in the courtyard as her wooden sword caught and repelled his blows. She performed this so deftly, his attack became doubly vicious, and he sought to overcome her solely through superior strength.

Then his most forcible strike yet snapped off her dented

blade at its hilt. He was unable to control the swing: His trident clouted her leg below the knee, and Caleb stepped back, appalled by what he had done.

Corinna dropped to the ground, moaning. The handle of his weapon had opened her skin, and she dabbed at a smear of blood with her fingertips.

Serpenius jostled his way through the gladiators, who had suddenly closed ranks around Corinna and Caleb. "What gives here?" he demanded.

"He threw away his net," one fighter explained of Caleb, "and went at her like a demon."

"Is that so?" Serpenius asked Caleb, who shrugged, his face full of shame. "Well, there'll be no more of this. I'd cool you off in the stocks for a week, but all of Pompeii is counting on seeing some splendid new retiarius. You..." Serpenius said sternly, "...you will fight only as you were taught here."

"Yes. I apologize to the *familia*"—Caleb helped her to her feet—"and to Lady Corinna."

"All right, then," Serpenius said, "I want to see some sweat."

Corinna took a step, winced, then continued on toward the street, expressionless.

Caleb caught up with her. "I have an anger."

"Yes, you certainly do."

He looked at her intently, but no more words came out of his mouth.

A slave was lounging in her chariot, which was not greatly different from the racing type Caleb had seen raising dust in the Circus Maximus. Corinna seized the traces from the man's grasp and was preparing to go when Caleb leaped up beside her. He hesitated, bewildered with himself, then kissed her, his arms inching up from his sides and entwining around her back.

Book Three

"THE WIND"

I

SEASHELLS crunched under the sandals of the two legionaries.

Valerius only half listened to the young military tribune he had befriended on the march through Gaul. The signifer's thoughts were back in Rome all the while Manius was prattling about invading the country whose chalky cliffs were shining across the waters of the channel.

"Britannia . . . Britannia. But what do the natives call it?"

"I understand there's no one name, Manius. Each barbarian tribe has its own little region and fancies theirs to be the only realm of any importance in the world."

"And now the mightiest realm of all rushes in. Think of it—from their point of view. Soon they will know law and roads and clean drinking water. Say, do you really think some of them paint their naked bodies blue?" Manius waited for an answer. "Valerius?"

He glanced up, "Forgive me, friend, my mind wanders so easily."

"Still thinking of that mysterious woman?"

Valerius nodded.

"Come on, you scoundrel, tell me her name. I can be trusted with a secret."

Valerius pretended to be offended. "A lady's honor is at stake."

"Ah!" Manius cried with glee. "A noblewoman, then."

Valerius peered across the mud flats at hundreds of small open boats that had been hauled up onto the beach. These were the invasion craft, and their crews were loading the last provisions aboard them.

"No, Manius," he sighed at last, "she is not a noblewoman."

"A dancer?"

Valerius shook his head no.

Macro's prediction had been correct.

In the past month, Caligula had appropriated all the property that rightfully belonged to his sisters. These holdings included hundreds of household slaves. None had gone to auction by the time Valerius had been ordered to join the Emperor's campaign against Britannia, but the young signifer had begged a family friend to loiter around the slave market and buy Sarah in the event she went on the block before he could return.

And then, as if intentionally to add to Valerius' anxiety, Caligula had stripped Macro of his office as praetorian prefect in the hours before the Italian-garrisoned legions marched for Gaul. Valerius had caught up with the former prefect as he was slowly ambling away from the palace.

"Sutorius Macro, I assure you I heard nothing about this."

"Nor I. Well, it isn't the ax yet. I'm dispatched to Egypt as an envoy."

"Then I wish you luck there."

"And I you. We could've been useful to each other, Valerius Licinius."

Valerius had then rushed to the mansion that had just been sold out from under Drusilla, Caligula's sister. The new owner had allowed her slaves to remain as long as it took them to empty the chambers of her possessions, which were also slated for sale.

In the garden courtyard, he found Sarah kneeling at the small shrine, which surprised him until he saw that she was packing away the Lares, exquisitely carved deities of both sexes that she handled with obvious distaste. She turned at the approach of his footfalls, and he realized how frantic she was by how she flew to his arms. "Where have you been? I have been mad with worry."

"There's madness outside these walls as well. Tomorrow, I leave for Gaul . . . and then Britannia."

She was incredulous. "The slaves—all of us—are to be sold!"

"I haven't forgotten that. . . ." Then he told her about the arrangements he had made with Gracchus, the family friend. "I honestly believe I'll be there to do the bidding myself. Word has it that Caligula will show his face in Britannia for a day or two, then scurry back to Rome. I will be returning with him and the rest of the imperial staff."

Tears came to her eyes. "But why are you taking part in this conquest?"

Valerius did not give her an answer. Instead, smiling, he pressed her body against his and whispered, "I love you. I'll be back before you know. But, if for any reason I'm delayed, send word to Gracchus. Now, once again, where can he be found?"

Listlessly, she repeated the name of the lane on the Esquiline Hill, then said in a thin voice that still cut him weeks later, "But why are you cooperating with them?" At that moment, a canvas worker had shuffled out into the courtyard. Clutching an awning under his arm, he started to ask where he might find the new master of the house, when he took notice of Sarah. Valerius guessed that the tentmaker was also a Jew. Giving Sarah a farewell peck on the cheek, the signifer took advantage of the interruption and slipped away. To his back, he heard the Jew politely asking for her name.

Now, scuffling through seashells on the coast of Gaul, Valerius finally gave Sarah the reason why he had chosen to "cooperate" with Caligula's invasion: It was for Marcus Licinius, his centurion father. Valerius' desertion would have broken the man's heart. "You don't understand," he muttered. "My family—yours, soon—has honorably served Rome since the days of the Early Republic." Sarah's face was vivid in his imagination. "My great-grandfather was with Gaius Julius Caesar at the battle of Pharsalus."

"Indeed." Manius was grinning. "*My* family soon? I knew you were fond of me, dear Valerius, but I had no idea you intended to adopt me."

Valerius' face reddened. "Be patient with me, friend. I'm beside myself."

"I hadn't noticed."

"Get me back to Rome and I'll be excellent company."

"Are you sure you don't want to unburden yourself?"

"Yes," Valerius said too sharply, then smiled and clasped the man's shoulder. "Perhaps later."

Manius exhaled. "Well, I suppose I must continue to endure a fellow who mumbles in his sleep—and now in his waking hours as well."

A trumpet blasted shrilly over the *castrum* of tents on the bluff above the shore. It was joined by another, and then several

more, until every quarter of the vast encampment was being
stirred to assembly.

"Do you think . . . ?" Manius did not finish. His eyes were
very wide.

"I have a strong inkling."

They started running. Manius' voice was quavering as his
eyes swept the coastline opposing them. "You were in Africa,
no?"

"Nine months."

"How . . . how many battles?"

"Half of one. It was against a small band of rebels. We
rushed forward behind our cavalry. I snatched the standard
from my *aquilifer*, that's supposed to be good form for a signifer to do that—passion of the fight and all. Then I tripped
over a dead rebel, they later told me, and struck myself on the
skull with the standard." Valerius smirked. "Half a battle."

Manius gave the story a heartier laugh than it deserved,
Valerius thought to himself—especially for a fabrication that
had been invented on the spot to make his friend feel better
about facing the wild men of Britannia today.

Within ten minutes, over nine thousand legionaries had
formed ranks on the broad beach. Following what seemed to
Valerius to be an eternal flourish of trumpets, the divine emperor Caligula came galloping down from his imperial tent on
a splendid white gelding. Caesar was flanked by a colonel of
the praetorian guard named Cassius Chaerea, a man Valerius
knew to be sober, although slightly effeminate, but an exem-
plary officer by all accounts. Habitually, Cassius wore a disgusted expression whenever in Caligula's presence, and it was
a wonder to Valerius that the Emperor had not had the colonel
beheaded, simply for the offense of having a vinegar face. Yet,
as Manius had pointed out, Cassius' almost matronly dourness
gave Caligula comedic opportunities he would otherwise lack:
The Emperor's latest delight, when requested by Cassius to
give the watchword for the night, was to utter some profane
word, then giggle as the colonel's face turned to stone.

Caligula gave his own staff a cold stare, then rode out into
the cohorts and began inspecting them. He did this for three
hours, oblivious to the fact that he had ordered the legionaries
to present themselves in full panoply—nearly a hundred pounds
of weapons and gear. Even veterans, who had learned long

ago not to lock their knees when at attention and thereby impede
the flow of blood to the brain, were beginning to waver in the
hot morning sun. Here and there, men pitched facefirst into
the muddy sands.

But Caligula continued up and down the ranks, a vague
smile on his lips.

It gradually occurred to Valerius that the Emperor was less
interested in the readiness of his forces than showing off his
skill at maneuvering his horse by almost imperceptible movements of his hands and feet. Then someone else caught on.
From the first cohort, a voice Valerius recognized as belonging
to the *primipilus,* the head of this legion's corps of centurions,
cried out, "Caesar, if I might be so bold as to speak..."

"Speak!"

"Your genius over horseflesh is more than human."

There was silence. Valerius dared not look aside to catch
Caligula's expression.

Then the Emperor said, exasperated, "Nine thousand and
only one has any idea." He sighed heavily. "As a god, I can
speak any language, human or animal. I can put thoughts in
your heads as easily as I do this miserable horse. Right this
moment, if it were my will, I could make you all draw your
short swords and slit your own throats!" He lowered his voice
to a whine. "But that would be doing you too much of a favor.
Noble *primipilus,* have these ignoramuses stand at ease."

The centurion gave the order. There was a clinking of armor
as the legionaries tried to budge their deadened limbs into more
relaxed postures. Valerius' feet felt as if ants were swarming
over them, and Manius' skin looked clammy.

Caligula was smirking down at them from his saddle. "Soldiers of the Empire," he cried, beginning what was obviously
a rehearsed oration. "Your brave hearts and fine bodies have
gathered here on the shores of Gaul, tremulous for the..."

Staring up at that arrogant, pallid face, Valerius realized
what a captive Caligula had made of Rome. No one in the
ranks sniggered, as might be expected in the midst of such an
overblown speech. No one dared even cough. The legionaries
listened raptly, as if to a god—and perhaps Roman cowardice
had truly made Gaius Caligula an equal to Jupiter.

"...and from here you shall embark for the wilderness we
call Britannia. Together, we shall trample its savages underfoot. The riches of Britannia shall..."

Valerius and the men around him started as a half dozen large tents on the bluff were swiftly collapsed by slaves, revealing ballistae and arrow machines—both among the deadliest devices in the Roman arsenal—that appeared to be aimed at the cohorts.

"Good Mars," Manius whispered, "he's going to slaughter us, isn't he?"

"Quiet!" Valerius hissed, although he was thinking the same thing. Sarah had been right: He shouldn't have come. There was no way in which to honorably serve a demented emperor. She had known this. Now, he would die ridiculously. And worse than that, he would never see her again.

"This is a solemn occasion. Soon, we shall wrest a new imperial province out of darkness. But first, there is another battle to be waged. . . ."

Caligula slid his sword out of its scabbard and raised it over his head. Valerius looked away, up into the azure sky: He did not want that jaded countenance to be his last sight. Manius flinched, and by this Valerius knew that the Emperor had dropped his short sword. Swarms of arrows whistled through the air, and—a heartbeat later—the heavier missiles of the ballistae could be heard humming wickedly in flight.

"Juno protect us," Manius said, dazed. "They're all going into the sea!"

Valerius spun around and watched as the next salvo splashed into the waters beyond the surf.

"Halt!" Caligula cried, chortling now. No one joined him, for no legionary understood the Emperor's reason for joy. "I thank you all for this great victory."

Only Cassius Chaerea had the courage to ask, "Over *whom*, Caesar?"

"Why, Neptune, of course."

Then, even the praetorian colonel became speechless.

"These shells spread along the shore here," Caligula shouted, "they are the spoils of my campaign against the god Neptune." Then he repeated contemptuously, "*Neptune*, who taunts me day and night! Well, we've thrashed him properly, so start gathering my booty, dammit! We will have to prove to Rome that we have conquered the ocean!"

No man moved. The *primipilus* looked to Cassius, who cleared his throat and asked Caligula, "How many will Caesar require . . . to establish our claim that we have vanquished Neptune?"

"All of them, of course!"

Cassius took a breath to calm himself, then passed the order along to the centurions. In seconds, the flawless ranks were reduced to eddies of stooped legionaries, duckwalking across the beach, filling their helmets and tunic-laps with shells.

In the course of his own hunt for Neptune's treasure, Valerius meandered back and forth until he was collecting shells only a few yards from Caligula and his most elite retinue.

Cassius was asking, "But Caesar, the hour is already past noon. The boats are ready. When do we embark?"

Caligula spread his fingers across his cuirass. "Embark?"

"For Britannia."

"You!" Caligula bellowed.

Valerius realized with a sinking heart that Caligula meant him. "Hail Caesar!"

"Yes, yes—come here before . . ." Caligula paused. "Ah, once again we steal a moment in each other's company."

Valerius' face was searing under the accusatory glares of the general officers.

"Give me your helmet, Signifer." Caligula accepted it with a smile, then ran his fingers through the sandy shells as if they were gold coins. "One conquest at a time, Cassius. Today, I have seized Neptune's trove; another day, Britannia's. Let our ships sail."

"But *where*, Caesar?"

"Back to Rome, you idiot! You, as usual, did nothing while I humbled Neptune, making it safe for our ships to voyage home."

"Then I take it Caesar will also return by ship."

Caligula's eyes shone with terror. "No! Are you out of your mind? Neptune would shipwreck me before I could clear Lugdunensis!" He giggled away his tension as he handed Valerius back his helmet. "Here, my handsome Signifer. Go happy, go rich!"

Valerius pretended not to notice Cassius' furious stare, which tracked the Emperor as he urged his horse back up the slope and into the camp. Then the colonel turned toward the clicking sounds that came from shells being pitched into thousands of helmets. He watched in silence, his eyes moist with rage.

II

PETER and Thomas plodded up the steps one at a time. A few minutes before, they might have bolted deeper into Joppa along the twilit lanes, had not a dozen residents of the coastal town pled with them to mount the stone stairs and at least make the attempt. They had heard that Peter had healed a man in neighboring Lydda who had long suffered from paralysis, and these people of Joppa had faith in what the Nazarenes might do.

They argued with tears in their eyes that the woman "waiting" in the upper-story room had justified her days with charitable works, and the memory of those works now made those days seem too brief. But, in the end, it was her name that apparently swayed Peter. "Tabitha," he repeated, "a lovely name ... *gazelle*." Then he motioned for Thomas to follow.

They hesitated at the door. "I'm not certain we should have consented to this," Thomas whispered.

"Please, help me. Long ago, in Galilee ..."

"Not so long ago, Peter."

"... the child—"

"Oh, yes," Thomas said solemnly, his eyes recalling.

"What did he say? The *words*, Thomas."

"Only you, James and John went inside the house with him."

"I know, but you remember *everything*."

Thomas smiled. "*'Talitha cumi'* is what he said, according to James, at least. 'Rise up, little girl.'"

"*'Talitha cumi'* ... Tabitha *cumi*." Peter smiled at the coincidence of the rhyme, then eased open the door.

Using the dim light from a high window, they crept across the floor to the bed. "Do you smell anything?" Peter asked, hushed.

"No."

"Don't you see? They washed her, but didn't anoint her."

"One would think—" Then Thomas saw Peter's point. "This frugality means they believe, doesn't it? They're not about to waste expensive oils and spices on someone who will rise."

"Yes." Peter studied the dead woman's face. It seemed irrevocably still; yet, an instant later, he was left wondering if her right eyelid had twitched minutely. Taking a dove feather out of his waistband, he held the downy base of it under her nose. The fluff did not stir.

Thomas looked at him quizzically.

"That is what *I* had to believe: She is among the dead." Peter lowered himself to his knees. "Whatever happens from this moment on, it will not be of our doing." Then he addressed the corpse: "Tabitha *cumi* . . . rise up in the name of the Lord." Peter held his breath until his ears began ringing. Then he shut his eyes, his lips busy with prayer for several moments. "Tabitha *cumi*," he said with pleading in his voice.

Thomas touched his arm. "Nothing."

Peter slowly came to his feet. "Well, it wasn't for us to do."

"I thought so."

Peter turned toward the window and listened to the nearby surf. It soughed rhythmically.

"Peter?" Thomas moaned.

Only then did Peter realize that the sound he had taken for the sea was issuing from Tabitha's mouth. Her eyes were on his. She extended her hand, and Thomas, overcoming his terror, helped her rise to sit.

"Quickly," Peter snapped, "we must go."

"Yes . . . at once. They'll descend on us—"

"In the hundreds."

"Hundreds, nothing, Peter—the thousands." Thomas gave the blinking, astonished woman an expression that was more a wince than a smile. He let her hand drop to the covers and followed Peter through the door. They came down the stairs abreast and, ignoring the throng of expectant mourners, burst out onto the lane, where unintentionally they parted company until Peter shouted, "Thomas, this way!"

"Are you certain?"

"Yes—we can use our noses. This Simon is a tanner."

"Then his place is unclean."

"Do you prefer to sleep in the street?"

Then, an exultant cry from Tabitha's house convinced Thomas to fall in behind Peter, who was already huffing down a passageway toward the harbor. The sea was laid out before them like hammered copper, and half the sun had already been eclipsed by the horizon.

"I'm getting too old for this," Thomas panted.

"There can be no other life for us. And we should be thankful." Then Peter hunched over and wept in fear and awe—and from the bone-weariness that followed years of privation.

Voices echoed down the lanes, calling to them: "Peter! Peter, the Nazarene!" And it was delirious hope in those voices that made Thomas shunt his sobbing friend down an even narrower corridor, where they hid until all was quiet in Joppa again.

The tanner had cluttered his small courtyard with wooden tubs and stretching frames. So he had then converted the flat roof of his house into a place for rest, rigging an awning on four ropes to block out the harshest sunlight.

This piece of canvas flapped overhead in the onshore breeze. If Peter closed his eyes, he could easily imagine that it was the sail of his boat in Galilee. And this filled him with homesickness.

But noon was the hour for prayer, not wistful daydreams, and Peter tried to rub the heaviness out of his eyelids.

More passersby, obscured from his view by the parapet of the roof, called for him to show himself—to cure them of boils, of piles, of ringworm, of mange . . .

"Are you still hungry, Peter?" Thomas peered over the lip of the crawl-space on the roof.

"Yes, thank you, but I'll wait until my prayers are finished."

"Call and I'll bring a bowl up to you." Thomas then lowered his voice: "There's still a line of people below, waiting to be healed. Each one of them expects a miracle."

"Tell them it's blasphemy. Tell them to pray." Peter eased back down onto the pallet and rolled his face away from the sunlight that was creeping around the edge of the awning. "I am nothing. They could heal themselves if only they had the faith to. . . ." He began to breathe deeply through parted lips.

Thomas crept down the wooden rungs of the ladder without letting them groan.

The sun inched up Peter's throat, over his beard, until his

eyelids were twitching from the glare. He tried to use his forearm as a shade. But there seemed to be no way to block out this persistent shimmering; it shone through his arm as if the flesh had turned to papyrus. Grunting, Peter sat up—and looked in astonishment as four linen furls lowered out of the sky.

Thomas set aside the bowl he had carried to the roof. One glimpse told him that Peter had seen something marvelous. "Did you see *him*?"

"No . . . a vision . . . a voice."

"Are you certain it was not a dream? You were sleeping soundly when I left you."

"I only shut my eyes for an instant and then"—Peter indicated the salt marshes at the sea's edge—"a great white cloth was let down by its four corners *there*. . . ."

Thomas glanced overhead at the awning. When the breeze was not buffeting it, the canvas lay slack on its four ropes.

". . . And on it were the animals we're forbidden to eat— swine, salamanders, deer. A voice said, 'Rise, Peter. Kill and eat.' But I answered, 'No, Lord—'"

"Are you sure it was—?"

"'—why should I eat something that's common or unclean?' But he said, 'What God has cleansed, you must not call common.'"

"A bad dream, Peter, brought on by an empty belly." Thomas reached for the bowl again.

"No, I believe it means we mustn't be afraid of breaking bread with the gentiles. We have to go into their homes, eat their food, if we want to bring them our news."

"Get yourself properly awake before you speak."

"Remember that time Jesus argued with the scribes about what we should or shouldn't eat according to the ancient laws? He said it's not what goes into our mouths that defiles us, but what comes out." Peter slowly turned toward the salt marsh again. "Now I understand."

The centurion Cornelius had not expected the arrival of an envoy from the new governor of Syria. But he tried to make Publius Petronius' tribune comfortable in the courtyard of his house: "Please help yourself to whatever you desire. Here is fruit, wine. And excuse me while I try to gather my aides."

"Of course—and I thank you. The hospitality of the Italian Cohort is famous."

Once he had padded into the privacy of his atrium, Cornelius let the polite smile slip from his face. In truth, he had never felt more agitated in his life. It was worse than the sleepless night before a battle.

That afternoon, he had been at prayer in this very chamber, peering up through the opening in the ceiling, when a platinous light had flowed down through the aperture and suffused his body like chafed honey. Immediately, it had come into his head that he was to send to Joppa for a man called Simon Peter.

Even now, as he tried to think of a way to deal with Publius' representative, Cornelius was pestered by a mental voice that kept crying, "To Joppa! Simon Peter!"

It was the same inner beckoning that had made him a secretive man, which he was not by nature.

His superior, the procurator Marcellus, had been recalled to Rome after only a few months in Caesarea. Cornelius blamed himself for the man's downfall, for he had persuaded Marcellus to delay installing the statue of the divine emperor Caligula in Jersusalem's Temple. He had done this in the hope that something or someone would convince Caesar of the folly of this blasphemous act, and in fact a deputation of Jewish leaders from all over the Empire had sailed to Rome to plead with the Emperor. Caligula had offered them a new tetrarch, Herod Agrippa, but had refused to back down on the issue of his image being mounted on a pedestal before the Altar of Burnt Offering. When the Jews continued to protest, Caligula called for a whip and proceeded to chase them off the Palatine Hill, thwacking them bloody with great delight.

After this, there was no doubt in Cornelius' mind that the Zealots and other hotheads would eventually win the sympathies of the Judeans. There would follow a Jewish revolt—a ruthless one in which no quarter would be offered by either side. Yet, Cornelius knew that there was nothing he could do about that which God had ordained. It was now time for him to lay down these burdens of a world he had privately renounced and save himself, his family and those in his household who believed as he did.

Cornelius did not feel remorse because he had manipulated Marcellus as he had. The procurator had served the interests of God, even if the Roman had not realized it. But the centurion felt less than honest because he had never confessed to Marcellus that his respect for local religious customs went far beyond his giving alms to the destitute and praying three times a day. Years before, Cornelius had become what the Jews called a "God-fearer"—still a pagan in their reckoning, but far more respectable than an idolater.

Cornelius roused himself out of these recollections. An hour before, he had sent for his orderly, Kaeso. The young legionary had since failed to report, and Cornelius now fretted that he had departed for Lydda on his own volition to investigate reports of a healing performed by the Nazarenes there. Kaeso, like the centurion he served, had a fascination for any information about the new sect, and had mentioned last night his intention to visit Lydda in the next few days.

Cornelius was on the verge of detailing more soldiers to find the orderly when the man himself came bounding through the portal, his cloak more brown than red from the road dust.

"I apologize, Cornelius. I was on my way to Lydda when your messenger overtook me."

"I thought so. Please, man, let me know when you come and go; things are heating up—quickly too."

"What is the situation?"

"There is a tribune in my courtyard at this moment. He comes from Publius Petronius."

"The new Syrian governor?" Kaeso suddenly lowered his voice.

"None other. It appears that Marcellus will not be replaced in the immediate future."

"So who are we responsible to?"

"You are responsible to me. And I will answer directly to Publius in Antioch." Cornelius' eyes became downcast. "It is already suggested that we move to Jerusalem to assure Gaius Caligula that there are no hitches with the placement of his idol in the Temple." The centurion then smiled, seemingly without good reason.

"Terrible news: There will be bloodshed. Why—?"

"Why am I so relieved? Because I intend to resign from this insanity." Cornelius emptied his lungs of all their air. His eyes became glassy, but his smile remained, more ardent than ever. "There, I finally said it. You cannot imagine what this feels like, dear Kaeso."

The orderly scrutinized his officer's eyes for several seconds. "Something has happened," he whispered. "Something marvelous, yes?"

Cornelius nodded. "The Lord spoke to me. I now have instructions."

Kaeso could barely suppress his excitement. "No—now *we* have instructions."

The tanner answered the loud knocks on his door. His face hardened when he saw the legionary confronting him. "I seek a man called Simon."

"I am Simon."

Kaeso grimaced as some sharp odor drifted out of the house and assaulted his nostrils. "The man I want is a follower of Jesus . . . a Nazarene."

Simon the tanner lowered his head. Then, after a brief quibbling within himself, he gazed directly into the eyes of the young legionary. "I am a disciple of our Lord." The old man steeled himself for the worst.

"So am I, friend, or at least hope to be." Kaeso slowly scratched his chin. "Then *you* are Simon, also known by the Greek name Peter?"

"Oh, no . . ." But Simon fell silent. He no longer knew what to say without betraying the presence of his guest.

A voice from the rooftop spared him further agony. "I am Simon Peter, the apostle of our Lord." Gravely, Peter looked down over the parapet at the legionary and the two servants who had accompanied him. "And in the moments before you pounded on this door, I had a vision: I saw myself on the back of a horse. This is something I have never done in my life."

"Yes," Kaeso said, his mouth agape. "I have brought a horse for you, and one more for a brother."

"Surely, this all means I must risk a new thing. Please, Simon," Peter said to the tanner, "offer them your hospitality for the night. In the morning, I leave for . . . ?"

"Caesarea," Kaeso answered him.

"Right," Peter said, sounding a little awed despite his willingness to go, "Caesarea."

"Ask them to slow down!" Thomas hissed across the space between the two galloping horses.

Peter shrugged with one hand that, finished with the gesture, darted down again to clutch the mane of the dappled mare. "I can't . . . not again . . . not without them thinking we're cowards."

"Who cares what they think? They're uncircumcised."

"Thomas—"

"And I do not care for the idea of entering the house of this centurion. We would be stepping into a dwelling of the uncircumcised. Our Lord never did that. It's against the law."

"Which law? The one that's been persecuting us?"

Thomas gritted his teeth following a jolt that had nearly sent him to the ground. "We are Jews. The followers of Jesus are still Jews. We keep the law."

"There is the matter of my vision."

"Your *dream*. Tell me, Peter, would you really place pig flesh on your tongue? Lobsters?"

"I know what the vision meant. We are now speaking of a new law. Perhaps it began when Philip baptized the Ethiopian—"

"Have you changed your mind once again? I thought we agreed Philip had no right."

"What is your objection to this poor Ethiopian?"

"He is uncircumcised."

"*He is a eunuch! What more can you ask?*"

They ignored each other until the party halted in Caesarea before Cornelius' house, which—with its colonnaded front and red roof tiles—was decidedly Roman. Two stalwart legionaries of the infamous Italian cohort were posted at the door. Thomas whispered to Peter, "We will end this day in a praetorium cell, believe me."

Peter prayed briefly before stepping through the portal on Kaeso's heels. It was cool and seemed dark in the atrium after the glare on the broad streets of the city. Gradually, Peter's eyes adjusted to the shadowy light—and nearly gasped at what he saw: the centurion on his knees in reverent welcome.

"Up," Peter said. "I am a man like yourself. *Shalom*. I offer you peace, according to God's commandments."

Still, Cornelius did not rise. "I know the commandment of your leaders, master—"

"Not *master*, please—I beg you."

"—that it is unlawful for you to mix with Romans—that you may offer hospitality to us but not receive it. There are those who might suggest you have defiled yourself by entering my house. . . ."

Peter looked askance at Thomas, giving him a slight frown.

"... And for me, my friends, you have defied these ordinances. I thank you, Simon Peter," Cornelius finished.

"It is clear God is no respecter of persons. Every nation that fears him and does right seems to be acceptable to him." Peter found himself smiling at the Roman's earnest, almost pained expression. His next words came effortlessly: "Do you seek baptism in the name of the Lord Jesus Christ?"

At last, Cornelius stood. "Yes."

"Do you know of some place nearby?"

Cornelius led Peter and Thomas past a century of legionaries, who earned a tongue-lashing from their *optio* for gawking at their highest-ranking officer in the company of two scruffy Judeans.

Then, the subcenturion's own jaw went slack as he watched his superior of sixteen years follow the Jews into the brackish waters of the pond that had formed behind a buttress of the seawall. Dazed, the *optio* shuffled down to the reed-choked shore. He frowned a moment later when he realized that the eighty soldiers under his control had broken ranks on no one's authority but their own and joined him. But he didn't bark at them. The men at the rear of the crush began hopping on their toes to get a better look.

When the larger Jew took hold of Cornelius *in his hands*, the legionaries began clamoring for an explanation.

"Quiet there!" the *optio* whispered. "How in the name of Mars am I supposed to know?"

"Receive this cleansing water," the Jew said. "I baptize you in the name of the Lord and of the Son and of the Holy Spirit." Then he lowered Cornelius beneath the surface of the waters.

"That bloody does it!" The *optio* undid his helmet and let it clatter to the ground. "I'm getting out of here on the next bireme. I've got one year more than what I need for an *honesta missio*. So I'm taking my honorable discharge and my three thousand sesterces before—" He turned in the midst of his hasty retreat toward the praetorium and jerked his thumb toward the pond. "—before I invite some barbarian to drown me!"

III

VALERIUS' night-long watch at the imperial palace had been uneventful. The Emperor had retired shortly after dinner to his most private chambers, complaining of a "murderous" headache.

The signifer now trooped wearily through the rose-lit streets of Rome, which seemed inviting for their calm. He was heading up the lane that would deliver him to his garrison when sandals slapped the pavement behind him. Grasping the hilt of his sword, Valerius wheeled around—and faced Gracchus.

The old man recoiled and cringed for his life. "No—please!"

Valerius held up his right hand to show he had not drawn. "I'm sorry, Gracchus, but never greet me like that again."

"What makes you so suspicious?"

"The palace," Valerius said. "Everyone who lives or labors there has been poisoned by suspicion." He sensed bad news in the way the old man fidgeted with the hem of his frayed tunic. "What is it? Does she go on the block today?"

"Yes. . . ."

"Have you lost the coin I gave you?"

"No, no"—he patted a bulge in his waist belt—"it's all here, but it may not prove to be enough."

"Why not?"

"Well, hanging around the slave market as you asked, I picked up a rumor—"

"What kind of a rumor?" Valerius' eyes were frantic.

"Another bidder has surfaced . . . a serious bidder." Gracchus tapped his lip with a forefinger as if searching for the most delicate phrase possible. "An ex-consul who has an appetite . . ." He scolded himself with a shake of the head. ". . . no, I mean a preference, for Levantine and Jewish women. He was borne on his litter to Drusilla's former house, and there examined—no, I mean glimpsed—your Sarah from afar. My source says the noble ex-consul is *intrigued*." Finally, the old man appeared satisfied with his choice of words. "He might well open bidding at the full amount you have entrusted to me, young Valerius."

He covered his face with his palms for a brief moment, then seized the old man by the shoulders. "Go back to the slave market. I will be there myself shortly. If she is first on the block, pay whatever you must: I will find the gold and silver."

"Dear Valerius, they accept no promissory notes."

"Then I'll have to hurry, won't I?"

"Quite right, my boy."

Valerius raced through the now awakening streets, beleaguered by a city of early risers who had meandered out onto the sidewalks to yawn and scratch—directly in his path. "Out of the way!" he shouted. "Clear the way!"

"Filthy army," an old plebeian woman muttered to his back.

At last, his lungs burning, he reached the dilapidated hulk of the Julia Victoria and spent his remaining strength pounding up the four flights of stairs.

His parents, like most of Rome, had already risen, but his father was still in loincloth. The scars Valerius had traced so often with boyish fingers were visible—the one put in his father's back by the javelin of a mutinous auxiliary, and the shoulder cut from a German broadsword that had retained its lividity through the years. The man stared at his son while munching on a piece of bread garnished with olives and dipped in red wine. "Do I know you?" he asked gruffly. "Or do you bring word from Caesar that I must open a vein?"

"Father," Valerius gasped, "I need money."

Marcus Licinius stared across the table at his wife. "Three years I don't see him, and what are the first words out of his mouth?" He glanced his remaining scrap of bread off the wall into the coals of the stove. "But I should count myself fortunate. Why, if not for greed, my son would have no reason to come calling at all."

"Father, I've just finished my watch. I had planned to catch a few hours' sleep, then hurry here. At the palace last night, I learned your cohort had arrived back in the city."

"Come here, you lying blackguard."

And when Valerius approached, his father wrestled him into a fierce, loving hug that misted the eyes of both men. But Marcus must have felt the tautness in his son's body. He pushed

Valerius back slightly so he could see his son's expression. "Aye, there's trouble coming. Out with it now."

"I have no time—"

"Naturally."

"The world is changing—"

"Here we go now, Mother." Marcus winked knowingly.

"Has it changed so much that you must marry a Jewish slave?" she asked, her voice sharp.

Valerius frowned at her. "I wanted to explain myself."

She waved toward Marcus. "Explain, then."

Valerius tried to ignore the fact that his father was listening to him as if hearing out a prisoner of war. "Slavery is not a sign of low birth or lack of good qualities. Sarah is of good family—"

"Royalty, then?" his father asked.

"Well, no, but neither am I."

"But *you* are a Roman." Marcus smiled triumphantly.

Valerius fell silent for a few seconds. Then his nostrils flared and he began gesticulating with an axlike hand. "Rome is not what it was. The only refuse in this city used to float down the *cloaca maxima* into the Tiber. Now, it sloshes from chamber to chamber in the imperial palace. I know. I have to endure its stench ten hours each day. So you must pardon me if I have a rather low regard for Rome and a high one for a well-born Jewish woman who goes on the auction block any minute!"

Valerius expected his father to strike him. His wanton rage even welcomed the blow. But the man only pursed his lips and vented a low whistle. His eyes flickered sorrowfully at his wife's. He sat down. "The first dawn of my honorable retirement. I must've spent a thousand hours dreaming about this morning. At different times, of course—on marches, digging breastworks, trying to nurse a flame out of wet firewood. And now"—he held up his hands to take in the smoky room—"here it is."

"I am sorry, Father. I love her. . . ." Valerius' voice threatened to break. "And I am frightened for her this morning."

"What was wrong with Helvidius Cimber's daughter?"

"Nothing. I did not love her."

"Oh." Shrugging, Marcus turned to his wife. "He did not love her." Then, unexpectedly, the man leaped to his feet and for the first time growled in terrible anger: "I understand love, for I have known it. But I will never understand treason. I gave you breath; I will take it away if ever I hear such talk against Rome again!" Still glaring at his son, he backed off and then scraped loose one of the stones forming the charcoal stove. He brought out a leather purse and blew the grout dust off it. "Four thousand sesterces—all we've got, your mother and me. Yours, if you swear on your grandfather's ashes never to dishonor or strip off that uniform."

Valerius squeezed shut his eyes. "I swear."

The heavy purse thumped against his chest, and he stooped to recover it from the floor. "I will spend the rest of my life thinking of ways to repay you, Father."

"Don't bother," he spat. But then, against his most wrathful intentions, a small chuckle escaped Marcus Licinius. "My grandson will avenge me . . . probably on a morning just like this."

"Is that the final bid on this girl from Jerusalem, golden city of Judea?" the auctioneer asked. "She speaks Latin, dances, sings. Broken in, if you gentlemen know what I mean. Is all this to be had for a measly five thousand *sesterces?*"

His lips trembling with indecision, Gracchus began to raise his hand but then thought better of it.

The darting eyes of the auctioneer noted the old man's failure to top the last bid, and they glided across the crowd to the lean and gray ex-consul, who flashed a small smile of satisfaction. The auctioneer shrugged. "Then five thousand—"

"Hold, please!" Gracchus cried. A boy had raced up to him and thrust a purse in his hand, whispering that it held another four thousand. "Six . . . I will go six."

"Six thousand sounds more like it." The auctioneer lifted his chin at the ex-consul, waiting.

"Six and five hundred!" a Greek slave announced for him.

"Seven!" Gracchus tried to mask the desperation in his voice, knowing it would only encourage the patrician.

The auctioneer slid his hand down the smooth skin of Sarah's arm and hoisted his thick eyebrows at the ex-consul. Gracchus could not bear to glimpse her expression.

"Eight and five!" the Greek sang out.

Gracchus clutched the purse as if it were a talisman and muttered a prayer to Mercury, the god of trade. "Nine . . . nine."

"*Nine* and five," the slave answered for his master—without a moment's hesitation.

Gracchus could feel Sarah's gaze on him. His mouth was open, but no sound escaped. Then, lightly, a hand touched his shoulder. Behind him stood an easterner—a Jew, perhaps—who whispered, "Freedom is not cheap in Rome: Go as high as you must." When Gracchus hesitated, the stranger opened his fist, revealing a handful of gold coins.

"Ten!"

"Why, you old lecher," someone said from the throng. "No wonder you must dress in rags."

No one laughed harder than the ex-consul, who then bid with his own voice, "Eleven . . . whatever."

"Thirteen," the stranger chuckled to Gracchus, "and watch his *whatever* vanish like the smoke it is."

"Thirteen," Gracchus declared.

The ex-consul wrapped his left hand in the folds of his toga. As if on some furtive cue, his Greek murmured something in his ear. The patrician's expression became outraged. *"Why was I not told this?"* he fumed, and the slave lowered his face obsequiously. "No—absolutely—I will not take on another headstrong one." With that, the former consul of Rome tramped back to his litter and was carried away.

The stranger handed his coins over to a bewildered Gracchus, who rushed forward and paid the auctioneer's own slave, a sneering Parthian who counted each piece as if it were destined for his own coffer and not the Emperor's. Sarah was herded down off the block and instructed to stand beside her new master. Outwardly composed, she was nevertheless pale, and her dark eyes were glassy with humiliation.

Gracchus glanced back toward the crowd to wave his thanks to the easterner, but the man was nowhere to be seen.

Several minutes later, after the old man had delivered her to a secluded courtyard two streets distant from the slave market, Sarah was still impassive. The only change was in her eyes: They now had cold, stellar glints to them. She did not share in Valerius' delirious relief and accepted his embrace in silence.

"I thank your god we had enough money!" Valerius cried.

"But we didn't," Gracchus admitted.

"What?"

"A stranger gave me the four thousand we were short, my boy. And then he departed before I could thank him."

"I know him," Sarah said quietly. "I will thank him."

Soberly, Valerius looked at her. "Who is this . . . benefactor?"

"A Jew. A friend to my family."

Valerius smiled again. "Well, I will want to show my gratitude. Who is the fellow?"

"I have told you—a Jew." Then, her hand flew to her mouth, and she wept with more bitterness than Valerius had imagined possible.

Mercifully, the ceremony of manumission was brief. Sarah stood before a corpulent praetor, whose lictor scurried forward at his command and gave her a light tap on the head with a rod, crying, "I declare this woman is free!" Gently, Valerius took hold of her shoulders and turned her around so she faced him. "And I desire that this woman should be free," he said, giving her the weak, ritualistic slap on the cheek. The magistrate perused Sarah's bill of sale one last time, then declared, "And I adjudge that this woman is free." He patted her face with his plump fingers. "Go, *libertina*, and prosper."

Sarah did not return his smile.

Outside the basilica, Valerius halted her, his expression as grave as hers for the first time. "I know none of this has been pleasant for you, Sarah. But it has been more than a few Roman formalities. You see, at this moment you are genuinely free. You are owned by no man. You may go as you please—and I will not stop you."

After a long pause that hardened his face, she asked, "Where in Rome does a *libertina* live?"

"What do you mean?"

"A slave lives with her master. Where can a freedwoman go?"

"With her husband—if she chooses."

"Her new master, then."

"No," he said tersely. "Her husband. The choice is hers."

"You have never asked me to be your wife."

Valerius stared off, calming himself with a few deep breaths. "I wanted to wait until now—the moment in which you are free."

"I am free, then. Your praetor said so." She ventured a thin smile.

"Will you be my wife?"

Silence.

"Sarah?"

"Yes, Valerius?"

"Did you hear me?"

"Of course, I did."

He was aghast. "What are you doing?"

"I am savoring my liberty before surrendering it—gladly, with all my heart." She flowed into his waiting arms and snuggled the crown of her head beneath his chin. "It is terrible to be a slave, and then frightening suddenly not to be one; these feelings are not waved away by your lictor's staff."

"I will be patient."

"For that I love you." She sighed, then smiled more happily. "I would like to find a place to live—a *home*, Valerius."

The week she was a *sponsa,* or bride-elect, Sarah stayed with Aquila and Priscilla. Valerius made the acquaintance of the Jewish couple on the day he came to present Sarah with her betrothal gifts. Placing a ring on the third finger of her left hand, he explained to all with a shy grin, "A nerve runs from this finger directly to the heart." Then he thanked Aquila for his generosity in helping secure Sarah's freedom.

The tentmaker answered curiously: "I did it for the sake of a fish."

Valerius appeared to take it as some Judean folk saying and excused himself without further delay, as was proper during this week.

"He respects you, Sarah," Aquila said, watching Valerius march down the street, square-shouldered in the Roman manner.

"A considerate man." Priscilla gave her a hug.

Sarah nodded absently, twisting the ring around her finger. "Yes, and for those reasons I should tell him."

"There is plenty of time for that," Priscilla said. "Do not complicate this happy time for yourself, child."

Aquila picked up his shears and began cutting canvas along a faint chalk line. "And as for Caleb, he has another month of games in Pompeii. He will find it easier to accept that which God has already blessed."

"Yes," Sarah whispered. "I hope so."

The rooms they rented were so small and cluttered, the wife of Marcus Licinius had wheedled him into descending the stairs of the Julia Victoria in only his mufti tunic and knocking on the enviable ground-level door of his first cousin. The man, whom Marcus had always treated with disdain for never having served the Empire as a soldier, had acquired a modest fortune by speculating in squalid lodgings for sailors in the port city of Ostia. Therefore, his residence—by the standards of the Julia Victoria—was spacious and well-appointed. There was a mock atrium in that the roof of the main chamber had been recessed and the "opening" painted a sky blue. The Corinthian columns had only been brushed on the walls, but after a cup or two they resembled pink marble. And it took several cups of *calda*, a hot spiced wine, for Marcus' cousin to consent to open his abode to the wedding party. Laughing heartily as he said his farewells and staggered back up the stairs of the tenement, Marcus secretly vowed that someday he would reek vengeance on his cousin for all the begging and toadying he had been forced to do in Valerius' behalf. But the important thing, as his wife remarked, was that their son had a more dignified place in which to say his vows.

It was into this artist's copy of an atrium that Sarah stepped on the afternoon of her wedding. Valerius' mother had fretted over her since dawn, making certain that the young Jewess at least looked like a proper Roman bride. Her hair, which had been parted with the tip of a javelin, was a likeness of the style worn by vestal virgins during their period of service. The significance of the saffron cloak, silver collar, vivid orange veil and wreath of myrtle leaves and citrus blossoms, she had forgotten by the time she had descended the stairs. But she steadfastly recalled the ancient formula by which she would agree to become Valerius' wife.

Glimpsing Aquila and Priscilla, she smiled, reassured, and this in turn brought warmth to Valerius' face.

She had been forewarned by Valerius, but still Sarah found it difficult to hide her revulsion as an old *auspex*, the neighborhood diviner his family had used on all its notable occasions, inspected the steaming entrails of a lamb. Earlier, while patiently suffering the primping of Valerius' mother, she had heard the victim bleating miserably in the courtyard below.

"I have examined the entrails of the sheep you have sacrificed. It is indeed just and propitious to tie this marriage bond."

Sarah had not expected Valerius to wear his signifer's uniform, but he now stood forth in full regalia, his brass and silver gleaming. "Father, Mother, my friends—I call on you to be my witnesses. I ask this woman, Sarah, to become my wife."

His mother then handed her a spindle and a distaff. "These are the symbols of the virtues you will exercise in governing your home."

Sarah was relieved of these objects by her bridesmaids, Valerius' cousins, the oldest of whom served as the *pronuba*— patroness of this marriage. The plain-looking woman officiously rested Valerius' right hand atop Sarah's.

This, Sarah realized with an imperceptible start, was her signal to speak. But then she erased her nervousness with a deep breath and met Valerius' eyes. She took unexpected pleasure in the words "Where you are, Gaius, I, Gaia, will be." All at once, she found herself wishing there were more she could declare to him. There had been brief moments of doubt in the past months, but now there was none: she loved this gentle Roman.

Valerius was grinning boyishly, and his uniform vanished in the brightness of it. "Where you are, Sarah, I, Valerius, will be."

They embraced.

IV

PETER massaged his eyes with his fingertips. Briefly, he had imagined the faces confronting him to be those of the Sanhedrin, hands cupped behind ears to catch the faintest whisper of blasphemy. But these men were his brothers, he again reminded himself. "I've told you everything in order. What more can I explain?"

"We don't need a new explanation, Peter," James said, his voice quiet, reasonable-sounding. "Everything is laid down in the Scriptures. The law of Moses is not changed by your new law."

"Do you mean I must turn a Roman centurion into a Jew—circumcise him—before I can invite him to join us?"

"You can't turn a man into a Jew. One must be born a Jew. Then he can become one of our number. It's really as simple as that."

"And so we ignore the gentiles, James?" Peter flashed his smile around the room, hoping to disarm a few tempers before saying what he did next: "I baptize a few Romans who believe as we do, and I'm in the wrong? Is that how it is? If a man eats a piece of beef and washes it down with a cup of goat's milk, is he then unworthy to hear our Lord's word?"

"Please!" Thomas gagged. "We have just supped!"

"Then you would turn away the world for the sake of your supper?" Peter chuckled. He was the only one to do so.

At that moment, there was a sequence of raps on the door. It was obviously a code, and Peter—who had been traveling on the plain of Sharon for the past months—smirked at the intricacy by which John gained entry into the room. "If it becomes any harder to enter the church of Jerusalem, even I will find myself locked outside."

John's face and hands had been chafed by the cold. "The problem is not over the church of Jerusalem, Peter, but its Temple."

"Has the statue arrived?" James asked.

"They hauled the idolatrous thing through the streets a few minutes after nightfall."

Matthias carried a basin of water to the threshold and began to wash John's dusty feet. "Is it in the Temple now?"

"No, but close by, in the square of the Antonia."

"So Publius stalls once again . . . hoping," James mused out loud.

"Aren't we doing the same?" John asked, patting Matthias' shoulder in thanks. "Shouldn't we join the others—the Pharisees, Sadducees, Zealots, even some Essenes, I'm told—who will die for the Temple if it is violated?"

Peter shook his head in disgust, then tapped his fingers over his heart. "Here is the Lord's temple."

John leveled his gaze at him. "We're still Jews, Peter."

"That is in question tonight," Thomas said.

"It shouldn't be. Not tonight, when all Jews are uniting as brothers. That's a miracle in itself." John received a bowl of mushy lentils and ate thoughtfully for a moment. "I think we should fight."

"Over a statue?"

John gestured with his wooden spoon. "Do this for me, Peter. Go to the square. Look at that thing—at all the Roman and Syrian soldiers who must stand in a ring to keep the righteous anger of the people from destroying it. *Then* come back here . . . tell me what you truly feel."

Peter answered the man's fervor with an amused smile. "Very well, I can use the walk. . . ."

The night was mist-shrouded and—although there had been a drought in Judea for several months—the gusts of breeze were rain-scented. So Peter was not caught unaware when big drops began striking the paving stones around him; he kept to the passageways that were arcaded. By the time he reached the square, a downpour was making the Roman torches gutter in the darkness. The statue of the divine emperor Caligula was no more than an oversize silhouette, lording the night over an army of dwarves bristling with spears.

"I feel nothing," Peter said, sounding relieved.

He glared up at the lamp glow from the windows of the Fortress of Antonia.

"I truly feel nothing."

• • •

"I know everything before you say it, Caiaphas—" Publius Petronius cut short his weary rasp of an argument and glanced toward the window. "By the goodness of the gods, is that rain I hear?"

"After ten months . . . yes." The high priest had hurried to the opening after the first swirl of mist had drifted inside the fortress hall. "But it comes down in torrents, Proconsul."

The Syrian governor joined the priest, and together, in silence, they overlooked the darkened grounds of the Temple. Wherever torches dimpled the blackness, water could be seen pooling. The surfaces of these tiny ponds were being agitated by a harder and harder fall.

"Perhaps this will cool a few tempers," Publius said, wistfully.

"You know otherwise."

"Yes, I do." Wiping the tiny drops off his face, Publius returned to his couch and slumped across its rugs and pillows with a soft groan. "I have known since I left the coast with the thing and thousands came out, lined the fields, begging me to go no farther with it. These were not the fanatics we both decry every chance we get. No, these were the very people I have considered the friends of my government."

"Indeed, you and the good man you succeeded—Vitellius—are known by all responsible Jews to have been our friends. So why—?"

"Caiaphas, Caiaphas . . ." Publius took a long draught of wine. "If I were Emperor, I'd be free to follow my own inclinations in this matter. Then everything you have said and are about to say this evening would be aptly spoken."

"Our anger is justified."

"Agreed. But I am not Caesar. He has dispatched his orders to me, and I must execute them."

"Orders you know to be murderous to the peace in Judea."

Publius glared at the priest. "Don't threaten me. Not only is disobedience useless, it will prove fatal to all Jewry. I *shall* carry out Caesar's decree, come what may. Otherwise, I am destroyed. You cannot save me; therefore you cannot convince me."

Caiaphas stiffened his back. "Tomorrow, then?"

"Damn!" the governor exploded without warning. "What is

wrong with installing the bloody thing in one of your lesser courtyards?" Then, seeing the high priest's implacable expression, Publius smiled sadly and sat back again. They had picked over this barren field a thousand times before. "I am sorry. I am exhausted. I wish to retire for the night."

"Tomorrow, then, Proconsul?" Caiaphas persisted.

"No, I don't think so."

"May I ask your plans?"

"Yes, certainly. We require logs—straight and round ones—to roll the divine Caligula across the temple floor without marring its polished stone. Your Jerusalem pine is too gnarled for the purpose, your oaks too stunted. I must send men north to Mount Hermon for lumber that is up to the task. And now I learn there is a shortage of axes and saws in Judea. . . ."

"I thank you for another day of life, Proconsul. But you cannot tarry forever."

"What else can I do?" Publius asked.

Caiaphas' eyes glimmered with the answer.

"Well, whatever we Romans do"—Publius gave the high priest his back as a sign that the interview was concluded—"we seem to bring more Jews together. But make no mistake, Caiaphas: Whatever you do to oppose us, it will not work."

Aquila greeted Sarah at the door of his shop and pressed both of her hands in his. His voice was hushed, and it gave her the eerie feeling that someone who had lain dead within this house had just arisen and asked for her. "Praised be the Lord, who reunites what was divided."

"Where is he, Aquila?"

"In the back."

As she followed her friend down the aisle between the bolts of canvas toward the lamplit chamber, she was suddenly tempted to halt, wheel around and rush back out into the darkened streets of Rome. She was dressed in a modest *stola*, and although its clasps and pins were simple bronze rather than gold or silver, Sarah realized that she was the very image of Roman wifehood. Pulling her shawllike *palla* down off her head and around the ornamentation, she hesitated in the shadows and let Aquila go on before her. What she had done to make herself less conspicuous in the Claudia Victoria, the tenement in which Valerius and she had made their first home, now smacked of treason to her Jewishness. The man waiting for her in the next chamber would see this in an instant and break her heart with his stare.

Nor could she decide what to say to him in these first brittle moments.

"Sarah?" Priscilla coaxed from beyond the waiting threshold.

She crept inside. A solitary oil lamp had never seemed brighter. Then she was astonished to see that the young man wore his dark brown hair in the Roman style. His tunic was no different from the one Valerius donned when he took off his signifer's uniform. But most amazing of all to her was his face: Less the deep olive color imparted by the sun and its somewhat suspicious eyes, it was her father's. *"Shalom,"* she said and stumbled into Caleb's embrace with a faint sob.

He held her fiercely, and she could feel the gasps of his breath striking her neck. His body was shaking as it denied itself release, and from this Sarah knew that he had learned of Ruth's death. She glanced at Aquila, who looked miserable.

"I am sorry," his voice croaked. "He had such hopes, and I thought it wrong to falsely deny what God has willed."

"No," Sarah wept, "you were right to do so . . . and I was wrong to ask you to wait." She grasped her brother's face. "And there is Mother—"

"I learned that when I was in Samaria." Caleb sat against the bench and gently drew her down beside him. He wiped his eyes with the back of his hand. "And they paid dearly for it."

"They?"

"Romans, Sarah, and their Syrian auxiliaries. I was nearly crucified as a Zealot, so I became one after brave Samuel rescued me."

Already, she felt Valerius' presence between Caleb and herself. She did not want to broach the subject, but a check of Aquila's expression told her that he had remained silent about her Roman husband. "How is Samuel?"

Caleb did not know what to say for a moment. "He died saving me."

Sarah closed her eyes. After a moment, she said, "I must tell you something. You will not find this pleasant—"

"His name is Julius Valerius Licinius." Caleb looked stern. "He is a signifer of the Third Legion Augusta attached to the palace guard."

Her gaze accused Aquila and Priscilla.

"They did not tell me—intentionally, at least. I asked where you lived, and they told me the block. I went there this afternoon, asked a few questions. I saw him as he departed." Caleb turned her chin toward him. *"Why?"*

"He rescued me . . . tried to protect me from the very beginning. You do not *know* . . ." She sighed as Caleb's angry face dissolved into a watery blur. "I had no hope you were alive."

All at once, Caleb sounded more cheerful. "I see. . . . Then it was necessary to . . . to befriend him in order to save yourself. And now that I am here—"

"No," she said quietly. "At first, I myself wondered if that was the reason for my affection. So I denied what I felt in my heart."

Caleb shook his head. "A little time in *my* protection, Sister, and you will understand this infatuation for what it is: an act of desperation."

"I love Valerius. I will always love him."

"Truly," Priscilla said, "he is a kindly man, and he treats your sister with great respect."

"Also," Aquila simpered, "not to betray a confidence—for all of Rome is talking about the lady Corinna and her fellow gladiator, Metellus—but haven't you yourself been less than a Zealot toward the Romans in their capital?"

Caleb blushed. "That is different. She came to me. And she has all but renounced being a Roman."

Laughing softly in relief, Sarah touched her brother's forearm. "Nothing is different: Valerius' first loyalty is to me. It has been that way from the beginning."

"We shall see, my Sister."

V

VALERIUS could not shake off his strong sense of foreboding. And every happenstance served to feed it, make him doubly anxious—such as when he left the Claudia Victoria for the palace. A young man—a Levantine slave, perhaps—had been loitering in the wide portal to the tavern across from the tenement, sipping his hot wine and failing in his attempt to appear inconspicuous. Valerius had little doubt the Levantine was or had been a gladiator. No ordinary household slave had a chest and arms like that, and farm slaves were overworked to a stringy leanness, their shoulders slightly stooped by their labors. Valerius also knew that the emperor Caligula had further outraged his own praetorian guard by insisting that gladiators of all races be admitted to the elite force. It had been enough of an insult to the all-Latin officer corps for Caesar to demand that his innermost ring of protection be composed of half-civilized Germans, who—used to their own mad chieftains—saw nothing improper or unusual about Caligula's eccentricities.

Marching toward the Palatine Hill as if to his own execution, Valerius was thankful Sarah would be away from the Claudia Victoria tonight. She had mentioned something about visiting Aquila and Priscilla, and he now reminded himself to let Manius know of her whereabouts. Valerius had made a secret pact with the tribune he had befriended during Caesar's triumphant campaign against Neptune: Should either of them be summarily arrested or cut down on the spot, the other would sprint to warn the man's family. Life in Caligula's retinue had become that precarious, and no one honestly expected to be alive at the next Saturnalia.

Now, passing through the vaulting atrium of the palace, surrounded by dozens of statues—their original heads decapitated and replaced with Caligula's—Valerius caught up with the tribune.

"Well," Manius said in a tone of mock levity that everyone around Caesar now used, "we've had a pretty good watch, all in all." He paused, waiting until a brace of Germans had glowered past on their way toward the imperial apartments. "Yes ... and may you both choke on your mustaches. But"—he turned back toward Valerius—"Caesar developed another of his headaches after breakfast. He kept calling for Drusilla, and all of us ran about the house, shouting ourselves hoarse for the poor dead woman."

"Did anyone remind him ... ?"

Manius raised his eyebrows. "That he had killed her with his own hairy little hands? Come, now, my friend, I expect to die, but would prefer it not to be immediate."

"That's how he controls us all. We keep stalling, hoping against hope."

"Whatever, Valerius. But to continue—after supervising the garroting of the dozen slaves who had prepared 'too heavy a breakfast' for him, Caesar retired to his bed. He hopes to be refreshed by the time his games begin tomorrow."

Valerius tried not to sound as terrified as he felt. "I am being watched."

Manius blanched. "Who?" he whispered. "Here at the palace?"

"No, outside my *insula* ... a gladiator guardsman, I'm positive."

Manius nodded. He tried to smile reassuringly but failed. "Where's your wife? Not still at home, I trust."

"No ... within the hour she'll be calling on friends. Aquila, a tentmaker, and his wife—they have an establishment on the Street of the Ten Shops. Get her out of Rome if—"

"Don't worry. I doubt it'll get to that, really."

"Just get her out of the city," Valerius repeated hoarsely. "I beg you."

Manius clapped his friend on the shoulder. "Relax ... these are the sweetest days of your marriage."

"A bachelor tells me about marriage?"

"Who more fully understands the subject? That's why I'm yet a bachelor." Manius cuffed him again; the blow was harder, less jocular, and burst forth from his own panic, which had been tightly wrapped in the meaningless grin. "This sort of needless fretting is bound to affect your performance."

"She must be so confused," Valerius said under his breath.

"I make love so desperately, each time as if the last time."

Manius was silent, his eyes downcast. "I have no wife. Just two aged parents, whom I love and honor more——"

"Valerius Licinius?!"

He stared up into the pockmarked face of a praetorian centurion. "Hail Caesar!"

"Hail Caligula! Follow me."

Manius gave Valerius' arm a painful squeeze; then the signifer fell in behind the centurion, who quickly led him down an endless corridor to the chambers that housed the officers of the cohort in residence at the palace for that month. Valerius did not attempt to chat with the man. No one risked idle talk anymore; one thoughtless word and a soldier could forfeit his life.

I do not regret what I have done, he told himself, a bold resolve taking hold of him, dispelling his fear. It was over—— the endless worry, the sleepless nights. Valerius was glad for it, and from this sprang a fresh courage: He would die like a Roman. He would not grovel or beg. With an amused smile that surely would be reported to his bereaved father and mother, Valerius would open a vein or, nobler yet, fall on his sword as Brutus, the last true Roman, had done. In these moments, his and the centurion's footfalls resounding down the passageway, he could not force himself to think of Sarah; that was the one loss that was too agonizing to dwell on.

His unfamiliarity with this officer suggested one thing to Valerius: The Colonel Cassius was already dead. Caligula's spies had discovered everything.

Still, god of all men, I do not apologize for my part in this, Valerius mused, his smile becoming more ardent with each step. The instant he had promised his father that he would remain in service to Rome, Valerius had known that he would have to help overthrow the deranged Emperor. Otherwise, he could never live with his Jewish wife in good conscience.

At first, he had expected only to join what other Romans would start. He had been sure some cabal of nervy officers would strike down the Imperial Beast. Valerius then planned to ratify their mutiny with his own sword. But it soon became clear that no one wanted to be the first to draw his *gladius*. It was a matter of trust: No officer dared reveal his intention for fear his comrade would quick-march off to the Emperor to collect a handsome reward.

And Caligula continued to thin their ranks with ever mounting cruelty.

Yet, it was Valerius who had been first to break this spell the Viper had cast on his victims. He had caught Cassius Chaerea alone in a rare moment in which the colonel was exhausted, despairing aloud: "Rape, mutilation, confiscation of property," he said from his couch, kneading his brow with his fingers. "And I am no better . . . you, young Signifer, are no better."

Valerius had clasped his hands behind him and glared at Cassius. "What is the colonel suggesting?"

The man suddenly remembered himself. "Nothing."

"Certainly it is something, sir."

Temper showed in the officer's face. "*Nothing*, Signifer."

"If noble Cassius Chaerea is suggesting that we hold ourselves up to the world as something better, I am for it."

The colonel said nothing for a long moment. Then he smiled from the depths of his weariness and disgust. "There's a reason they chose you as standard-bearer, isn't there?"

Valerius had released a sigh louder than he had expected. "Yes, sir, my centurion said it: I tend to become impulsive under great pressure."

But now, trailing the stern-faced centurion into the headquarters of the palace cohort, Valerius was stunned to see Cassius Chaerea in the flesh, not a scratch on him, looking disgruntled as always. The sight did not assuage Valerius' misgivings: It compounded them. His heart was racing. The old suspicions reared their Gorgon heads. He believed for an instant that Cassius had betrayed him. He wanted to plunge his sword into the man.

The colonel brusquely dismissed the centurion, then strolled around the chamber to make certain no one was lurking in the alcoves before he whispered, "Tomorrow."

With that word, Valerius trusted him again. "If I may ask, why then?"

"Why not?"

Valerius considered the dangers for a moment, then realized that no day would ever seem auspicious for such a task. He nodded. "I am ready."

"Good. I was counting on that reply."

"Where, sir?"

"Certainly not inside the palace—too many bloody Germans. We were thinking of the games. As always before Caesar ventures to his amphitheatre, I will require someone trustworthy to inspect the locality where our divine Emperor will *alight* to dispense the favor of his presence."

"Understood. May I take the tribune Manius with me?"

"Can he be relied upon?"

"I believe so." Valerius then gave the colonel a long stare. "But we really won't know about any of us until tomorrow evening—will we, sir?"

Cassius took a thoughtful sip of wine. "Go to the Palatine Games, Signifer. Bring me back a plan—one that will work."

Due to his night-long watch at the palace, Valerius had no sleep. So, he moved through the events of the next morning as if in a dream. At dawn, while bracing himself with a second cup of hot wine, he learned from Manius why Cassius had not delayed: "A soothsayer has warned Caligula, 'Beware of Cassius.'"

Valerius paled. "Do you think he has gotten word of our plan?"

"Who knows? Too late now."

"Cassius is a dead man any second."

"Not quite, my friend." Manius chuckled feebly over the lip of his cup. "You see, the augur didn't come up with a surname for this Cassius. So the Emperor sent word for Cassius *Longinus,* the proconsul of the province of Asia, to be executed. But it won't take him long to get around to every other Cassius he knows."

"Just when I think no other madness is possible—"

"Madness is inexhaustible, Valerius. It's reason that has always been in short supply around this palace."

"Good luck, Manius."

"What else?" the tribune asked with a smile. "And if not, it's a noble way to die."

Two hours later, Valerius was waiting in a tunnel of the amphitheatre. A roar went up from the direction of the arena. He stared down the length of the *vomitorium,* the bosses of the mortared stones reflecting the light at the mouth of the passageway. At this moment perhaps, directly above that portal in the imperial gallery, Cassius was saying the words to the Emperor that would set everything into motion: "Caesar, I have a message from the Oracle of Fortune at Antium. He has ridden all night to arrive and begs an urgent word. . . ."

Valerius could imagine Caligula's deep-set eyes bulging at this news: too coincidental to be ignored even for a moment! "Where is he?" Caligula would ask, feigning complete indifference.

"We delayed him in the *vomitorium,* Caesar. He is such a famous soothsayer, I was afraid his appearance at your side might alarm the crowd."

Simpering with his liver-colored lips, Caligula would then pat Cassius' hand and murmur something like: "Excellent thinking, as always. Lead the way."

Cassius had suggested the ploy—not Valerius, although the signifer had understood at once why the colonel had done this. By all but confessing to the Emperor that he was the Cassius to be feared, the man was in the same bold stroke reminding his fellow conspirators that this was their only chance. Death for all would follow failure; no one could expect mercy. By implicating himself, Cassius was also exhorting his comrades to use every last vestige of their courage.

Curiously, Valerius did not experience the sickening tension he had anticipated. He even laughed under his breath from time to time. He had thought these moments of waiting would be much worse.

And then, as if he had dreamed it all before, Valerius watched the distant figure of his friend, Manius, step into the portal, stretch and dab a wide yawn with his fingers.

Valerius relayed the signal by scraping his sword twice in his scabbard. A score of praetorians, mostly officers but a few guardsmen who had sworn vengeance on the Emperor, trooped out of an alcove in the passageway and lined both walls.

Caligula burst into the *vomitorium,* jabbering something to Cassius, who was directly behind the Emperor. To their rear was a contingent of Germans, only a half dozen strong, due to the limited space on the imperial gallery, marching somewhat discontentedly after being forced to leave off enjoying the games.

"Hail Caesar!" Cassius' praetorians cried.

Valerius vowed to himself that those would *not* be the last words the Beast would ever hear. And then it came back to him. As they had his first time in battle, his knees felt tremulous, and he had to stiffen them against betraying any unmanly motion. His hand longed to grasp the hilt of his sword—prematurely. In the blinking of an eye, his heroic calm had vanished, and once again he was simply a man preparing to do something extraordinarily terrible—and necessary, he reminded himself in the same moment that Gaius Caligula began to sniff the peril awaiting him in the passageway. His buoyant stride weakened to a shuffle, and he leered aside at Cassius. "Just where *is* the Oracle, Colonel?" his voice echoed.

"Don't you see him, Caesar? Past your guards there. He's dressed as Charon."

"Charon?" Caligula's voice was on the verge of quavering. There was a pathetic, almost childish quality to it that made Valerius' stomach lurch. "Am I . . . dead, then?"

"So be it!" Cassius screamed, the outrage of years exploding out of him. His first strike caught the Emperor along the lower jaw, and he collapsed, squirming to the stones.

As planned, the two files of praetorians did not finish off Caligula but instead charged past the prostrate figure to engage the Germans, who bellowed in angry surprise, "Kaiser! Kaiser!"

Next, it was the moment for Valerius to do his part. He prayed for the dream state to sweep over him again to blunt the revulsion he so keenly felt. It did not, and Caligula lay at his feet, gurgling, "I am still alive . . . alive!"

Cassius barked at Valerius, and the shout went through him like a blow: "Strike again!"

Caligula's glassy eyes shone upward, pleading.

"For Rome . . . and for Judea!" Valerius hissed.

In the instant before the blade was buried into the side of his throat, Caligula looked bewildered, and he whispered, "Ju . . . is this because . . . the statue?"

Valerius was staring downward, transfixed, vaguely aware of the clash and scrape of swords, when Cassius roughly seized him and cried, "Go to the palace! Complete the plan!"

"Manius . . . the tribune Manius . . . is he ready to go—?"

"Dead—the Germans got him. Go!"

Valerius did not rush directly up the Palatine from the games. Somehow, too addled by sleeplessness and the events of the last hour to understand how, he made his way to the Tiber and became too sickened to go on. Between bouts of nausea, he would murmur, "How little satisfaction . . . how little."

A *vigil,* one of the city's combination firemen-watchmen, ambled up and asked if all was well. Obviously, the man was not yet aware of the tumult in the nearby amphitheatre.

"Yes . . . fine," Valerius said, not wishing to draw attention to himself. "I've just had a bit much to drink. . . ." But after the watchman had moved along, the signifer said, "And I'm not used to the taste of blood."

He stared down into the gray waters of the river until he imagined a corpse bobbing past. Then, spinning on his heels he continued toward the palace, his face ashen. He met no one's eye along the crowded street.

Cassius had tasked him with mollifying the palace garrison and, if necessary, subduing any forces that might persist in their loyalty to the dead Emperor. At the previous night's conference, the colonel had believed that, rather than avenge a Caesar of no further use of them, most of the guardsmen would be interested in finding a new one. It was a question of their jobs: no Emperor, no guard. While not a praetorian himself, Valerius was nevertheless respected for his loyalty to the imperial family: His part in assisting Lady Antonia with the downfall of Sejanus and Livilla was now common knowledge in the halls of the *castra praetoria*.

But the young signifer no longer had the heart to carry through with this mutiny. He thought himself craven, a worthless example to his future children, but he could not compel his feet to move fast toward the palace now looming in his sight. He prayed that everything—especially the executions of Caligula's immediate family—was concluded.

Two evenings before, while Sarah and he had lain in their bed at the Claudia Victoria, trying to ignore the sounds of quarrels and revels that welled up through the central courtyard, their conversation of whispers had meandered to the subject of the *Christiani*, whom Sarah had called the Nazarenes. Valerius confided in her that the praetorian guard was gathering information on their members in Rome, believing them to be a threat to the person of the Emperor.

She was silent for a moment. "Then you *know*?"

"About Aquila and Priscilla? Yes, I realized a few days after the auction, when he told me he helped us for the sake of a fish. A centurion at the palace explained that the *Christiani* use the symbol of the fish as a kind of code."

"Did the centurion also know that Nazarenes hold all life to be sacred—even the monster Caligula's?"

Valerius was on the verge of sharing everything with her— his words with Cassius, the assassination that surely would

come, the dangerous weeks that would follow until a new
Emperor was installed on the Palatine by the guard and the
legions—but then he sighed instead and ran his fingertips down
across her darkened profile. "Are you sure—*even* Gaius Caligula?"

"Is that so hard to understand, my Husband'.

"Yes . . . impossible."

Now he understood—and was filled with shame. He had
expected to feel noble, a contemporary Marcus Junius Brutus,
driven to extremity only by *patria,* an intense love of country
and the tradition of Roman liberty. It was uncanny, stupefying:
He could no longer recall the reasons that had convinced him
to plant his sword in Caligula's neck.

Arriving at the palace, he turned away from the imperial
apartments, mortified to imagine he might discover Caligula's
widow, Caesonia, and her small daughter. He could not kill
them, as had been ordered by Cassius; but he was also hoping
that others, blessed with stronger stomachs, had already decided the matter.

The atrium was deserted, although its gleaming floor was
littered with chunks of white marble—the remnants of Caligula's statues. This, with no accompanying sense of relief,
indicated to Valerius that Cassius' people had already prevailed
here and had departed for the Curia. There, the praetorians
would humble the Senate and make sure none of its dotards
suggested the restoration of the Republic.

Every trapping of success was present—except joy.

Footfalls made Valerius halt and step behind a column.
Around its edge, he glimpsed three Germans stamping down
another corridor, their bearded faces full of loathing. Each of
them carried a gold chalice or some other valuable, but Valerius
had no doubt that, if confronted, their interests would change
from looting to murder. Picking up his sandals as he went, the
signifer darted noiselessly into the nearest chamber, one of
several libraries in the household, and waited just inside the
threshold, listening as the Germans marched out of earshot.

Before he even noticed a quiver of the purple curtains,
Valerius sensed that he was not alone in the chamber. He crept
along the tiers of pigeonholes that held the scrolls and drew
his sword, wincing at a tattletale clink of metal. This forced
him to remain stationary for a few minutes until he felt confident
that his progress toward the hiding person could not be heard.

He was reaching for the purple fabric when voices in the corridor made him freeze. A group of praetorians, both Germans and Latins, burst into the library, half drunk and laden with booty, which they let drop to the floor when they saw Valerius drawn, reaching for the curtain.

"What is it?" one of them asked.

Valerius shrugged, then seized the drape and yanked it aside.

The white-haired man was cringing, fending off the blow he expected any instant with a scroll.

"Why, it's Caligula's poor daft Uncle Claudius," the same praetorian chortled. "A scholar."

"Then let's give his head a rest . . . on the floor," another said.

"Oh, p-please! Not me!" Claudius begged.

The praetorians were closing on him when Valerius raised his short sword—not to attack the old man but to salute him. "Hail Caesar!" he cried suddenly.

Claudius blinked at him. A drop of saliva trickled down his chin.

The first reaction of the praetorians was to laugh, but then their mirth died away as they considered the possibility.

Afraid to hesitate for even a moment, Valerius pulled Claudius out of hiding by the hand. "What is Caesar's pleasure?"

"P-please don't kill me."

VI

THE light snow falling over Jerusalem was unusual enough to entice Publius Petronius and Caiaphas to the window overlooking the Temple. The courtyard grounds were smooth and unblemished, except where a guard had paraded across the stuff, leaving a trail of bluish pocks. Both men watched without speaking; they had exhausted words in their efforts to come to agreement.

Publius held two sealed dispatches under his right arm. In truth, he did not care to open them. These missives had arrived in Judea by different means, one by ship and the other by road across Asia Minor. Both had been delayed in Ptolemaïs when the roads south were ravaged by torrential rains.

They bore the imperial seal.

Publius savored the clean, snow-chilled air. "Really quite lovely, the city like this."

"Yes, I look forward to these gentle storms."

"Is there such a thing in this part of the world?" Then the proconsul of Syria strolled back into the hall and enjoyed a glass of good wine, tasting each sip with complete concentration. Finally, he opened the first dispatch and read, his lips mouthing some of the stronger words. Slowly looking up, he met Caiaphas' inquiring gaze with a wan smile. "Caligula has instructed me to take my own life. He will tolerate no further delay."

"I am sorry . . . Publius Petronius."

"I knew this was the peril from the beginning. So it is not unexpected." His face now colorless although his voice remained calm, he cracked the second seal with his thumb and gave a cursory glance at the epistle. His pupils stopped moving, then backtracked to a phrase he appeared to scan several times. Then he giggled—ineffably, weakly—and wheeled around before collapsing on his couch.

"What is it?" Caiaphas asked.

"Caligula is dead—murdered. The praetorian guard and the Senate have invested Claudius with the Throne of Augustus."

"Praised is the presence and appearance of God!"

"Well, whatever," Publius said matter-of-factly, his dignity restored. "Now we can get back to normal in this part of the world."

The slender young man glanced over his shoulder before venturing into the dimness of the Temple of Astarte. His left arm was hefting a wooden box, but with his right hand he picked self-consciously at the wrinkles in his chiton, a Greek-style mantle. The thick incense smoke appeared to strike him as being more reminiscent of ordure than perfume. His fingers were reaching up to pinch his nostrils shut when the priestess approached him, smiling in a way he found immodest.

"Choose your own servant of the goddess"—she gestured at three reclining women in cubicles formed by panels of sheer rose-colored curtains—"and make your offering."

"I am not a . . . *devotee*," he whispered.

"Then what are you?" She no longer sounded pleasant.

The young man seemed willing to give this question some serious thought, when he remembered where he was. "I am Luke, the physician you summoned for one of your . . . *attendants*."

"It is said that you are the most capable in Antioch. Is that true?"

"I know my trade," he said quietly.

"This way. . . ." The priestess led him down a row of transparent cubicles, and he averted his eyes from the scenes within them. "Are you a Hellenist Jew?" she asked.

"No, I am Greek-born, of this city. Why did you ask that?"

"You have the aspect of a Jew."

"I was not aware."

"This is the girl." The priestess then sauntered back to the temple entrance.

Luke crouched beside the young woman's bed. She was doubled with pain, her knees tucked up under her chin and pale buttocks facing him. "Where is your distress?" he asked.

She craned her neck to look. Her eyes were suspicious until she saw him open his box, revealing glass vials filled with colorful liquids and sprigs of herbs. "I ache all over." But she was clutching her abdomen.

Gently, he brushed her hands aside and began palpating her smooth belly. She flinched once and then again. He scrutinized her eyes and had her blow a breath in his face. Then he frowned. "You have an impurity. This is not a clean occupation." He reached down and selected two vials. "Take this draught. And apply this ointment to your person. Give up this trade."

Her brown eyes were large, doelike. "This is not a trade. I am consecrated to the goddess. I am placing my body in her service."

"You are putting your body in the service of lust, nothing more." He smiled to show that he meant her no offense. "Try to understand: Your body is like a precious vase. It holds your spirit, the gift you received from God. If you had a fine unguent from Capua, would you shatter the glass that holds it?"

"Of course not."

"So, by selling your body, you waste your spirit." Luke rose. "My medicines will relieve your pain. But your ailment stays as long as you remain here. Leave this place."

She did not reply, but he could feel her curious stare on him as he withdrew through the curtains.

Outside on the street again, almost feeling cleansed by the warm sunlight, Luke was strolling aimlessly, given over to quiet musings, when he espied an elderly man striding ahead of him through the throng. The young man rushed forward as fast as he could, but his haste was thwarted by the density of the crowd along the colonnaded thoroughfare, and the gray head disappeared into the synagogue before Luke could close the distance.

Shifting the heavy box to his other arm, Luke mounted the worn stone stairs but was halted by the overflow of *tallith*-clad men standing in the entryway. A snaggletoothed old Jew muttered, "When a reverent man cannot even get into his own place of worship because it is crammed with gentiles..."

"You," another said to Luke, "yes, you, the Greek—it is time to find another entertainment."

Luke chuckled affably. "I saw the one called Barnabas come this way. Is the Tarsus man also here?"

"Of course, preaching resurrection and curing the sick." The old Jew flashed his solitary tooth in a grin. "You'll be losing some patients."

This news made Luke even more impatient to get inside. Then he had an idea that turned his eyes mischievous. Nudging

his way up one more step, he said urgently, "Physician . . .
please stand aside . . . I am required within . . . please . . . physician."

Once inside the synagogue, he peered through the thicket
of shawl-covered heads at the speaker, whose prominent brow
had been weathered to the color of walnut shells. His style of
orating was enthusiastic but not florid, as was the eastern preference; Luke found it decidedly Roman.

"Some of you are Jews, some of you gentiles yet fearers of
God. Others of your number have worshiped stone idols. But
I bring the good news to all. The Son of God, who lived among
us as a carpenter in Nazareth, died for us. And, most won-
derfully, he has risen again from the dead. He left us a
word—"

"Only one, Saul?" a voice asked dryly.

"The name is now Paul," he said good-naturedly. "And yes,
one magnificent word: *love*. This is the simple truth of his
victory. He has conquered death with love, and we are invited
to become his partners in that conquest. Love denies death its
agony. Be baptized in the water of life!"

"As promised, we have heard you again, Paul," a venerable-
looking man said. "Now we wish to worship in our accustomed
way."

"Of course, *Rhabbi*, and I thank you and the men of Antioch
for the great courtesy you have given me." He included the
entire assembly in a gesture of blessing. *"Shalom."*

Paul was answered with silence.

Yet, when Barnabas and he took their leave, two gentiles
ran after them and begged to be baptized. Luke, who followed
at a distance, saw that this greatly cheered the two Nazarenes,
who led the Syrians down through the city to the Orontes River.
Hidden within a copse of poplars, Luke watched the proceedings with a faint smile, but he never revealed himself.

For the next three days, he trailed the pair of Nazarenes,
interrogating those who had come in contact with them, but
never confronting Paul and Barnabas directly. Carrying a satchel
of wax tablets, he took copious notes, converting them at night
onto papyrus. Vaguely, he had some kind of narrative in mind,
but it was also his nature to be methodical in his approach to
all his interests, which embraced verse and painting in addition
to medicine.

He had learned that, the year before, the disciple Barnabas

had been dispatched by the church of Jerusalem to help organize the growing following in Antioch. This Jew from Cyprus had, in turn, called upon Paul of Cilicia to help him. It was not clear if Paul had yet established a substantial church in his home of Tarsus, but he willingly journeyed to the Syrian provincial capital. With half a million people, it was the third largest city in the entire Empire.

Of course, Luke was mostly interested in these men because they had knowledge of Jesus of Nazareth. But there were peripheral questions that aroused his interest, such as the proper name of the new sect. Paul, Barnabas or other important followers referred to themselves as brothers, disciples or saints. Most Jews called them Nazarenes. Yet, a new term was being applied to them: *Christians.* No one seemed certain of the origin of the word, but Luke privately believed it was derived from the Latin *Christiani,* meaning the adherents to Christ. Paul, who was rumored to be a Roman citizen, would be able to clear this up, Luke felt, making another note to himself.

Then, on the third evening, as Luke loitered at the edge of their presence Paul and Barnabas broke off a hushed conversation. The Cilician strode directly toward the young physician, who feigned insouciance and leaned over the balustrade of the Orontes bridge. *"Shalom,"* Paul said, seeming no less imposing because he was smiling.

"Good evening ... oh yes, and may peace be with you."

"You are not a Jew?"

"No."

"Forgive me, but I have seen you in the synagogue before."

"Along with many other gentiles who come to listen to you," Luke pointed out.

"That is true. The Lord opens the way for Jews and gentiles alike." The Cilician offered his right hand in the Roman fashion. "I am Paul."

"I know. I am Luke."

"There are no calluses on your hand."

"I am a physician." Then, like many young men who must have their ideas heard, Luke blurted, "I approve of your philosophy of healing the sick. Most often, a cure is a matter of confidence, which you would probably call faith."

Paul smiled at the conviction with which the Greek spoke. "Are you finding faith?"

"I think so." Luke watched in thoughtful silence as the Orontes rippled past.

"I have also seen you spying on our baptisms twice now." Luke simpered, then confessed with a nod.

"Are you ready for the waters?" Paul asked.

"They are chilly this time of year."

"Your faith will not feel them."

Luke's eyes became moist as he grinned. "*This* is why I have not approached you, Paul of Tarsus."

"Because you knew I would say 'Be baptized, Luke,' and you would be baptized. Then I would say 'Follow, Luke,' and you would follow."

"Yes!" the young man cried, laughing. "Tomorrow—here— if you would be so kind."

"Tomorrow we will be on the road to Jerusalem. Come. . . ."

Obediently, Luke mimicked Paul's brisk stride down to the shore, kicked off his leather sandals and waded into the dark green waters.

Luke did not ask why they were walking to Jerusalem until Barnabas, Paul and he were several miles south of Antioch.

"A moment and I will tell you," Paul said. Then, groaning, he removed a heavy satchel that hung off his shoulder on a strap and handed it to Barnabas, who smiled and bore the burden for a while. "There. . . ." Paul rubbed feeling back into the deadened muscles. "We were pleased for more than one reason that the Lord sent you to us last evening."

"Yes," Barnabas said, "there is safety in numbers."

"Safety from whom?"

"Robbers, Luke." Paul patted the satchel now carried by Barnabas. Its contents clinked. "We bring coin for our brothers in Jerusalem. Judea has suffered three bad harvests in a row. Grain is available, but only at a dear price."

"It is all part of what Agabus has foretold," Barnabas said.

Agabus, Luke recalled, was famous for his forecasts, which would neatly fulfill the prophesies of the Scriptures, if only they might come true. "What does he think will happen?"

"A famine will strike the Empire," Barnabas continued. "And this will herald the last days of the world."

"Judea's plight might well be the beginning," Paul said, wiping his sweaty forehead on the shoulder of his tunic. "But whatever follows, our Lord charged us to feed the hungry."

"Why doesn't the emperor Claudius send relief to Judea?"

"To know the answer to that, you must understand Rome, my friend." Sudden life came to Paul's eyes: It was obvious he enjoyed discussing Roman affairs. "The people here in the eastern provinces tend to think of all Romans as being wealthy. That simply is not so. Many are sustained by free grain that is distributed by the Emperor's government. I am talking about one third of Rome's citizens. So Claudius must see that his own masses are fed first. Otherwise, he faces revolt, and that nearly happened, I hear. A mob caught up with his litter in the forum. The people pelted him with stale crusts of bread, and this was over just a temporary shortage of grain. Imagine what will happen if the drought continues in the African grainfields."

"Could Rome actually collapse?" Luke asked, relieving Barnabas of the satchel.

Paul chuckled sadly. "No, but Rome can be changed. I hope it never entirely collapses."

"Forgive me, but aren't those strange words for a Christian?"

"Not at all, Luke," Paul said. "The Empire, its roads and unity, will make it easier for us to spread the good news."

"Then you plan to go among the gentiles?"

Paul nodded at the young man. "Soon."

VII

VALERIUS had believed that Sarah, as wife to a Roman legionary, would not be affected by the imperial edict that expelled all Jews from the city of Rome. Then, unexpectedly, he was told otherwise. The praetorian centurion, who served as Valerius' superior in the absence of any Third Legion officers at the palace, confronted the signifer in the atrium. A blunt man from a farming family in Campania, he came right out with it: "You're married to a Jewess, aren't you?"

In the year since Caligula's assassination, Valerius had often wished that Cassius Chaerea were still alive. But Cassius and the other conspirators has been executed on the new Emperor's orders; all except Julius Valerius Licinius, who—in his desperation to save a harmless, fifty-year-old man's life—had inadvertently bestowed the Throne of Augustus on Lady Antonia's least-favored son. Valerius had never expected the guardsmen, who were in a seething and confused mood, to wholeheartedly support the notion of making Claudius Emperor. Next, Herod Agrippa, who saw advantages for himself and Judea in Claudius' rule, endorsed the project. Finally, the candidate himself rose to the occasion and—astonishing all of Rome with his eloquence and aplomb, which he had been masking for years in order to survive—persuaded the Senate not to restore the Republic immediately, which had been seriously considered. For launching all of this, Valerius had received a reward no grander than that given any other member of Caesar's guard: one hundred and fifty gold pieces. But there was one noteworthy bonus: He had been spared when others, whose swords had never drawn Caligula's blood, had been beheaded. And although no promises had been uttered, Valerius believed that he could call upon the Emperor for a favor if the need ever arose.

But now, as he glared at the praetorian centurion, he was

stunned by the possibility that his Sarah might be ordered out of the city. "You already know about my wife's race, sir. She is a freedwoman. I have the documents of manumission—"

"Hold, Signifer. Exceptions are being made."

"I should hope so."

"All you must do is establish—before witnesses—that she has renounced her superstitious beliefs."

"How is this done?"

"Oh, some kind of oath. Then she must sacrifice to the house of Jupiter. The law's quite lax in that regard; she may choose our gods to her own liking."

Valerius thought to remark that the centurion didn't know what he was asking of a Jewess, but held his tongue. "Very well, sir. I will see to it at once."

The officer winked at the signifer. "That's it, Valerius. You and your witnesses report to me when the business is concluded." Then the centurion strolled away, appearing satisfied that one more item could be scratched off the day's agenda.

But Valerius did not go straight home. He headed for the sumptuous chambers where he might find Pallas. The former slave was no longer a lowly secretary. After Lady Antonia's death, he had passed into Claudius' possession and, in a short time, had proved himself an invaluable adviser. The new Emperor had freed him and now relied on him as one of his foremost ministers.

As chance would have it, when Valerius burst in on him, Pallas was perusing one of the many applications for citizenship that Messalina, Caesar's wife, was offering to Jews at a staggering fee that was far beyond the means of a signifer. "Hail and be well, Valerius Licinius," the Greek said absently.

"I am not well."

"Oh?"

"My wife is to be included in this idiotic decree."

Pallas frowned. "Lower your voice and follow me."

They withdrew from the man's reception vestibule into a more comfortable chamber that was furnished with couches. A well-groomed slave poured them each a cup of wine. "Pallas," Valerius said angrily, "I will not permit this, and I expect Caesar to exempt her without delay."

"Had anyone but you just said that, Valerius," the Greek said smoothly, "I would report him to the guard for preaching mutiny. Do we understand each other?"

Valerius answered him with a glare.

"Now, so I can appreciate your situation, has the woman refused to renounce her former convictions?"

"I haven't asked her yet."

"Then, my dear Valerius, why all this fuss?"

"Because I will not have her suffer the indignity of a trial in her own home." Valerius set aside his cup without drinking. "Nor do I see good cause for the decree in the first place."

"Politics," Pallas said smugly.

"What does that mean?"

"Well, I'm willing to admit to a close friend like you, the Jews really haven't caused all that much trouble in Rome."

"Are you willing to argue that to Caesar?"

"Mars, no." Pallas chuckled behind a napkin, then dabbed the purple off the corners of his mouth. "And the disturbances have been limited to the vicinities of their temples—"

"Synagogues."

"Whatever. Nor do I care that this has all been instigated by the followers of this Chrestus."

"He is correctly called Christus."

"What an authority on things Jewish you have become. But I'm sure you've garnered all this under most pleasant circumstances." Then Pallas' expression sobered. "These fools have brought it on their own heads. They couldn't have chosen a worse time to draw attention to themselves. In case you're unaware of it, we're having considerable difficulty finding corn and wheat for this city. The harvests of Syria and Judea were first withered by drought and now are washed away by floods. The province of Africa has not seen rain in over a year now. Who is to blame?"

"No one."

"Ah, if only the riffraff in the streets could see the problem through your enlightened eyes. But they don't. When there is no one to blame, they heap their abuse on the Emperor. That's precisely what happened several months ago in the forum, and Claudius nearly lost his life."

Valerius stood. "Do you mean to tell me that this is being put on the Jews?"

"Oh, nothing as bald as that. It's merely been suggested that the political strife in Judea has contributed to the problem."

"That is a travesty."

"No, my friend, it's politics. Now, my advice to you is

what it would have been to the Jews in Rome: Don't call
attention to yourself. I am considering your best interests when
I say: Claudius should never learn that you have a Jewish wife.
Go gather your three witnesses and get it over with. It is always
preferable to be rewarded by Caesar than punished by him.
Look what his gift of one hundred and fifty *aureum* got you—
a nice little house on the Janiculum Hill."

It had also enabled Valerius to repay his parents, he recalled
sullenly to himself. "All right, Pallas, I'll speak to her," he
said at last.

"Here's the sensible man in you talking. I think you're
making too much of this. After all, she had a Roman wedding
ceremony, didn't she? How is this any different?"

When he had exhausted all other arguments, Valerius admitted to Sarah that he had lied: It was no safer for him in the
emperor Claudius' court than it had been in Caligula's. The
Palatine was aswarm with whispers of new plots; there was
even rumor of a conspiracy implicating Caesar's wife. So Sarah's refusal to renounce Judaism could leave him prey to one
faction or another.

She sat quietly on her couch in their small courtyard averting
his eyes while she considered her answer.

Valerius was left to wallow in his bog of deception. In truth,
he was less concerned for himself than for her. It was his
experience that one form of Roman persecution usually gave
rise to another, always sterner. But to say this to Sarah was to
ignite her fierce pride. She would only agree if she believed
that her husband would be put in jeopardy otherwise.

Listening to the cheerful liquid noises of the fountain, he
thought to himself: *I do not want to lose all this.* Pale blue
shadows were filling the courtyard as the sky dimmed with
evening, but these served to make Sarah's skin tones even more
soft, luminous. She caught his eyes. She dipped her head once,
almost imperceptibly.

But a few seconds later, as they entered their modest atrium
hand in hand, she halted and started to pull away from him.
"I cannot do it. I will never do it."

Immediately, Valerius glanced at the three witnesses. Gracchus and the two cronies he had found in a wineshop smiled
back at him with sympathy and mild embarrassment. Then they

resumed their solemn poses and wrapped their left hands in their togas, a patrician affectation.

Gently, Valerius took hold of Sarah's wrist to keep her from fleeing. He whispered, "You are not asked to believe—just prove your loyalty."

"I stand accused of practicing a foreign superstition. But then I am asked to fake acceptance of *your* superstition."

Valerius could hear the witnesses murmuring among themselves. *"Please,"* he begged her.

"We have heard your wife, Julius Valerius Licinius," Gracchus announced. "We are convinced that there is no treason in her heart or mind. And she is loyal to you, a soldier of Rome."

"We will report that you have judged your wife and found her worthy to stay at your side," one of Gracchus' comrades said.

"Thank you, my friends." Valerius was so relieved, he embraced each of the men.

Sarah quietly slipped out of the atrium.

The witnesses made the same declaration at the palace before the praetorian centurion and a magistrate who had been summoned from his house to officiate.

Sarah and he had made plans earlier in the afternoon to visit Aquila and Priscilla and offer what help they could to the Jewish couple. But when Valerius hurried back to the Janiculum from the palace, he found Sarah in their bedchamber, already retired for the night. He lit a lamp to rout the gloom that surrounded her. "Will you come with me to the Street of Ten Shops?" he asked.

"No." She had been crying.

"Your friends will be pleased to see you."

"I am ashamed."

"Why?" Valerius chuckled to show her how incredulous he was. "You renounced *nothing*!"

"It was reported that I did. Aquila, Priscilla, Caleb—they wouldn't have allowed even that."

Valerius sighed. "Then I will go. I will say you were feeling ill or something."

"Valerius?"

"What?"

"Thank you . . . for not demanding."

Crossing the Tiber in the darkness, the waters black, Val-

erius recalled his unease several months before when Sarah
had drawn him out to their courtyard with the sobering words
"There is something I should have told you long before this."
All kinds of ugly pictures were dancing through his head, most
of them involving Gaius Caligula, until her eyes moistened and
she blurted, "My brother is alive. He is in Rome." Then she
looked astonished as Valerius began to laugh.

He had not yet made the acquaintance of his brother-in-law.
Caleb, who he learned, was a gladiator fighting under a Roman
name. So far, all his contests had been in Pompeii, or so Sarah
said. Valerius discovered that a retiarius named Metellus had
fought several bouts in the city and belonged to the school of
a Romanized Numidian called Serpenius. But he did not blame
Sarah for withholding the entire truth: It was obvious that her
brother had no desire to meet his new Roman in-laws, and she
was only trying to spare Valerius' feelings. Regarding Caleb
himself, Valerius had no opinions, other than a mild curiosity
he suspected would never be satisfied. There would always be
some excuse for his not meeting the elusive Metellus.

So he was surprised when Priscilla answered his knocking
on the shop door and led him back to the living quarters, where
a young Jew sat beside a striking-looking patrician woman
Valerius had seen before at palace banquets. She smiled pleasantly at the intruder, but her companion resolutely ignored him
until Aquila said simply, "Caleb, your brother-in-law—Valerius Licinius."

"*Shalom aleichem.*" The Roman forced a grin.

"*Aleichem shalom,*" Caleb muttered, not lifting his eyes
and going directly on with his argument to Aquila. "Don't you
see the real purpose behind this? That whore these Romans
call their Empress is selling citizenship to rich Jews. She's
making a fortune. So where does that leave a gladiator with
no means?"

"You have the means through me, Caleb," the woman said,
smiling again at Valerius as if ashamed of the way her companion was snubbing him. "He is too proud to become a Roman
citizen."

"Valerius," Aquila interjected, "Lady Corinna."

"Just Corinna—please." She studied Valerius for a moment.
"I saw you do a remarkable thing some time ago. It was in the
palace during Caligula's reign."

"Remarkable?" Caleb asked, almost contemptuously.

"Yes, this man carried your sister away after Caligula and all the rest of us believed the Emperor had killed her. I have learned since that she was only feigning death. Did you know?"

"I did: She moved a finger to let me know."

"Tell me," Caleb said, meeting Valerius' gaze for the first time, "how has my sister dealt with this edict?"

"And where is she tonight?" Priscilla asked.

"Slightly ill—she sends her apologies." Valerius folded his hands atop the table. "Sarah has refused to renounce."

"Good," Caleb said, beaming.

"So we were quite fortunate that the witnesses lied in her behalf."

"As a loyal Roman, you allowed that?"

Valerius stared back at him. "My first loyalty is to the wife I love."

Swirling the remaining wine in his cup, Caleb said nothing.

"Which brings me to why I have come here. . . ." Valerius turned to Aquila and Priscilla. "What will *you* do now?"

Aquila patted Corinna's hand. "Corinna has offered to hide us on her country estate in Etruria. But we cannot accept."

"Besides," Priscilla said, "we want to go back to Corinth. It was our first home after we left our native Pontus."

"Men preaching the words of Jesus are traveling from city to city in the eastern provinces." Aquila's face brightened. "Great things are happening. The followers of Christ are becoming legion. It is a good time to lay aside your weapons, Caleb."

"It seems I have no choice—in the arena, at least."

"What may I tell Sarah of your plans?" Valerius asked.

"Corinna leaves for Etruria tomorrow. I will follow in a few days with supply carts."

"From retiarius to teamster; my brother-in-law is a man of many skills," Valerius said affably.

Caleb shrugged. "I probably could have stayed at the school. My *lanista*, Serpenius, would have protected me. But he is a good man. I want to bring him no trouble." He then lifted his chin defiantly. "And it is time I think about Judea again."

"What would you do there?" Priscilla asked.

For the first time since Valerius had appeared, Caleb smiled. "Now I must help Corinna farm her land in Etruria. But one day she will be working for me on mine."

Aquila poured more wine for all. "A good and peaceful occupation."

"Caleb, I would ask one favor before you leave."

The young man glared at Valerius. "Go on."

"Please come to the Janiculum and see your sister."

"I do not step inside Roman houses."

"It isn't a Roman house. It's where Sarah lives."

Caleb finally lowered his eyes. "Perhaps."

VIII

"Do you know who I am, Cleopas?"

The middle-aged man narrowed his eyes at the face that swirled in and out of focus. Once, in the midst of this effort, he let out with a gasp of joy. Glints of milky light were playing on the countenance that was only a few inches from his own, and Cleopas imagined that he was being confronted by someone he had seen long ago on the road to Emmaus. But then the face became a far different one.

"Do you know who I am?"

Cleopas nodded, drunk with the pleasure that overwhelmed his senses whenever the Temple guards stopped wrenching his arms out of their sockets.

"Say it," the resonant voice commanded.

"Herod . . . Agrippa."

"*King* Herod Agrippa."

"Yes," Cleopas rasped. "King." Tears filled his eyes: He felt great love for Agrippa, but was troubled to think that it was only the sudden absence of torment and not the Lord's injunction for his followers to love their enemies.

"Now, for the last time, where is the one called Simon Peter?"

"I do not know . . . *King*." Cleopas tried to stretch the syllables as far as he could, realizing what would follow these words. He screamed as the guards twisted his arms in a way they were never intended to be bent.

"Where is Paul . . . the man once known here in Jerusalem as Saul?"

"The Cilician?"

"Yes . . . that's the way, Cleopas. Where is he?"

"Gone."

"Gone where, my dear subject?"

"He came with money . . . to feed the starving. Then departed away."

"Where?"

"I do not—" Cleopas gnashed his teeth to keep from screaming again. He had not realized how thoroughly his own sounds could frighten him, weaken his courage.

"Oh, my brother Judean," Herod said quite warmly, "do you have any idea of the difficulties I face?"

"No, Your Majesty."

"I was installed here by the Roman Emperor to put our Judean household in order . . . to end all this religious bickering. How can I do these things without your help?"

Cleopas choked down his tears. "But I know nothing."

"And God save our country if I fail: Rome will take all authority out of Jewish hands and invest it once again in some procurator who knows nothing of our customs. Do you want to see that happen to our Judea?"

"I know nothing—"

"Oh, yes, I'm afraid you do. Yesterday, you were seen with one of them. Tell me his name . . . and there will be no pain."

After a silence of several seconds, during which his sweat pattered against the stone floor, Cleopas whispered, "James."

A new voice snapped at him. It was thin with advanced age. "Is this James the brother to John?"

Cleopas lifted his head and tried to fix on the figure across the darkened hall. But all he could glimpse through the eddies of blur was a gold breastplate, its inlays of jewels winking at him, and a brittle-looking fist, its veins and knuckles showing through the translucent skin. "Yes . . . that is . . . the James."

"Where might he be found, Cleopas?" Herod asked, his voice increasingly gentle.

"I don't—"

Herod Agrippa assisted the high priest up the steps to a sunlit rampart of the Jerusalem palace. Painstakingly, Caiaphas lowered himself onto one of the king's Roman-style couches. "You, young Herod, have rubbed elbows with the Caesars too long."

"I have never had a choice in the matter."

"Ah!" The high priest's laugh had been reduced to a cackle. "Precisely what your grandfather would've answered."

"It is possible for one to profit from his association with Romans. So far, Claudius has given me a free hand to do what I must."

"But how long will Claudius himself survive?"

"Not long, I fear." Then the king shrugged off a troubled silence. "But that fate hangs over all our heads. What is important is that I show Rome results in quieting Judea. With that will come more and more sovereignty for us, and perhaps eventual independence."

"I once thought that."

"No longer?"

"I have no more thoughts . . . just aches." The high priest smoothed his white beard with a palsied hand. "The man James, for whom you have sent—how has he greatly offended our law? Indeed, in what way have any of the Hebrew Christians transgressed? Speaking of late, I mean."

"It is Peter we want. The beheading of James will smoke him out of hiding."

"How?" Caiaphas' eyelids had grown heavy.

"There will always be those, like poor Cleopas, who will talk. We simply need to frighten them a bit."

"But many of them are now old men."

"And old men have no fears?"

Caiaphas smirked through his drowsiness. "They are afraid of everything . . . everyone. Having lived so long and so well makes them that way."

Perhaps because he had spent most of his days in the deep rift that held the Sea of Galilee, Peter had developed a certain sense. Deprived of expansive horizons, a Galilean had to rely on faint inklings, even a change in the very texture of the air, to warn him that a storm was about to swoop down off the western hills. This faculty, which now awakened in Peter as he hiked up a serpentine lane of the Mount Zion neighborhood, had both served him admirably and been the cause of his deepest shame. Yet, however he felt about it, this was as indelible a part of him as his reddish-brown skin. "Lord, how it buzzes in me," he muttered, forcing himself to continue onward and not flee blindly wherever his feet took him.

Numerous sandals scuffed the stones behind him. But he did not spin around. He kept striding, smiling to himself now.

"Simon Peter?" a voice demanded.

He halted. "Yes . . . ?"

The captain of the Temple guards marched around him and blocked his way. "You are to come with me."

"Will I be put with our brother James, whom you took a week ago?"

"Yes, in due time." The man smirked. "He was beheaded yesterday morning."

Peter doubled slightly from the waist as if he had been struck in the abdomen. He had difficulty breathing until he took several deep gulps of air through his mouth. Then he offered a tremulous smile to the captain, who had been sobered by the effect of his news on the hardy-looking man. "Well," Peter said, "he never promised our cause would triumph without imprisonment . . . without death."

"Then, follow, Simon Peter." The captain turned to his contingent of guards. "And don't mock him as we go. I respect a man who refuses to harbor false hope."

"*False* hope, yes," Peter whispered.

And the next morning he was still alive.

The captain then told him that no action would be taken in his case until the festivals of Passover were concluded, although King Herod Agrippa was already in the city. To discourage any thoughts of escape the prisoner might have in the meantime, sixteen guards were assigned to oversee Peter's captivity—not in rotating watches, as was the usual practice, but all at the same time. These men were posted within his cell and along the corridor that offered the only access to freedom. He found it impossible to engage them in conversation, and from this he realized how intent they were that he ultimately answer to Herod.

Their silence created an illusion of privacy, and so on the sixth night—once again, filled with the premonition that a storm was on the wind—Peter knelt in the narrow space left on his pallet by the two guards who slept beside him. They each opened an eye on him.

"Lord," he prayed, "that night long ago . . . you said, 'Not my will but your will be done.' Those are my words now. Yet, you called me the rock. You told me to feed your sheep. I have work to do, and I want to do it. But all is in your hands. Not my will . . . but yours. May my enemies be forgiven. May the faith live. May I see your heavenly kingdom. But not until I've finished your work. Amen."

Peter lay back down. He closed his eyes.

• • •

It was the most exhilarating dream he had ever experienced. The window was drawn on the floor in moonshine, and the air murmured like a honey tree. When Peter floated up to his feet, the guards on the pallet did not stir. Nor did the other pair of soldiers slumped against the wall.

He was sure he could flee and no one would be the wiser. Yet, as in any dream, there was the moment of hesitation, that last inner obstacle before abandonment to fancy. His resistance melted, and all things became possible. *You are asleep,* the overruled self whispered, then echoed to silence.

A torch throbbed in the corridor, flickered through the crack under the door. Then that iron barrier swung open, and a young man was revealed—luminous, drifting forward with the smooth cadences of the stars. He whispered—no, Peter later decided, the youth simply made it *plain* without the use of sounds or gestures—"Come . . . follow me . . . come. . . ."

And Peter took a few giddy steps toward the young man, but then halted. Fear had seized him once again.

The young man offered his hand. It was exquisitely warm, like that first feel of the hearth after a winter's afternoon on the sea. This heat undulated up Peter's arm and diffused throughout his entire body. He began traipsing over the prostrate forms of guards in the passageway outside the cell. His fear was gone. He felt safe, coddled . . . loved by immense forces.

"You are awake." Peter realized that the voice was his own.

The paving stones beneath his bare feet were hard, cold. A full moon flared over the tops of the houses at the end of the lane, but there was nothing mysterious about its light. The young man had vanished, although Peter could not recall him having taken his leave.

A dog yapped in the lower city.

"I am awake!" Peter cried under his breath, and with these words the fear came back to him. After one confused glance at the building that had served as his prison, he began running toward the first friendly house he could think of: that of Mary, mother of John Mark. They were relatives of Barnabas'.

He rapped softly on the door for several minutes before a groggy female voice asked, "Who is it?"

"A friend," Peter hissed. "Open—please, quickly."

The door yawned back no more than two inches. A moonlit

eye, glistening with suspicion, showed in the crack.

"Please, let me in. I am Peter."

There was a loud slam, and Peter saw that he had been shut out. From within the house came a hysterical scream that erupted his skin into gooseflesh and made him look up and down the lane for Temple guards. "Please . . . please don't," he begged.

"It's his ghost," the woman was wailing. "Peter's ghost is on the threshold!"

"What are you saying, Rhoda?" a man asked.

Peter recognized the voice as belonging to James the Elder, and thinking of what had befallen the man's namesake made him all the more desperate to get safely inside the house. "Let me in!" he whispered.

"Is that really you, Peter?" James the Elder asked from the other side.

"Of course . . . please."

"Are you corporeal?"

"Am I *what*?"

"Are you still in bodily form?" James demanded in all seriousness.

"Yes."

"How can we be sure?" Rhoda was blubbering.

"Because," Peter answered between clenched teeth, "if I were a ghost, I'd pass through this door and throttle every last one of you! Open up!"

"What of this Christian Zealot who eluded you in Jerusalem, Your Majesty?" the Roman envoy asked, not lifting his eyes from the gladiatorial combat taking place on the grounds of the Caesarea palace. "Have you recaptured him?"

"I am not familiar with this affair." Herod Agrippa chuckled pleasantly as he wondered how the Roman had already heard of Simon Peter's inexplicable escape. The negligent guards had been executed, and Caiaphas had instructed his priests to say nothing about the matter of Peter's arrest and imprisonment. "Like your own Emperor, I cannot be aware of each petty criminal case."

"On the contrary, Your Majesty, our Emperor follows these legal proceedings with great interest."

"Does he, now?" Again, the obsequious chuckle. "A man of inexhaustible attention to detail, I'm sure." Herod rested his right hand on the left shoulder of his glimmering silver tunic.

At this signal, the Jewish tetrarch of Galilee stood up from the midst of the reclining nobles on the tier below Herod's. "Your Majesty, if I might have a word?"

"Speak; these fighters are boring me."

"May you always be benevolent to us. Heretofore, we have respected you as a man, but from now on we are agreed that you are more than mortal to us."

There was a smattering of applause, although Herod noted that the priests had not joined in. "You are too generous in your praise to a mere servant of his people. Please, enjoy your leisure and rest assured that I will always remain propitious toward my Judea." Herod then looked askance to make certain his Greek scribe had gotten everything down on his wax tablet.

The Roman envoy was smiling. "It will please Caesar to hear how beloved his client is in this kingdom."

"Oh, it is not just me but my entire family." Herod gestured at a handsome young man on the lower gallery. "I share the affection of my people with my son—who, Caesar granting, will one day succeed me."

"Yes, I should like to meet Herod Agrippa the Younger."

"And so you shall this evening." Herod's jaw dangled as he stared upward. An owl was perched on an awning rope. "How unusual, to see one this early in the day."

Then the Roman noticed the bird. "An omen certainly."

Herod smiled uneasily. "Good or bad?"

"I'm no soothsayer, Your Majesty."

Herod turned back to the games, although his gaze kept darting up to the owl until it fanned its wings and flew over the top of the palace.

"Pardon me, Your Majesty," the Roman said delicately after a while.

"Yes, Consul?"

"You look feverish. Are you well?"

"Yes, of course . . . quite all right . . . except for an undecided stomach." There was sweat on Herod's upper lip as he curled it into a grin. "I cannot dine as exuberantly as I did in my younger days with your royal family." He started to clutch at his abdomen but then forced his hand to remain at his side.

"Herod Agrippa!" a shrill voice cried from the throng of commoners who sat under the hot sun.

Perplexed, the king glared down at an ancient man garbed

in unbleached lamb's wool. Then he waved for the captain of his guard to see that the proud figure was silenced.

"Herod! You may usurp tetrarchies as you please, but never the kingdom of God!"

The envoy looked for Herod's reaction, but the king had bent forward, his beard almost touching his knees and his hands kneading the soft tissues of his belly. A shudder rolled up his trunk, and he vomited before collapsing to the marble floor. Crying in alarm, his retinue encircled him so tightly, the royal physician had to thrash his way to the writhing Herod.

Aloof, expressionless, the Roman stood off some distance with his adjutant. "Have a message sent from the praetorium."

The aide came to attention. "Consisting of, sir?"

"Herod Agrippa is dying. We request instructions."

"Can we be certain, sir?"

"*Look* at the man, Tribune."

The adjutant marched for the headquarters without another word.

IX

CAUTIOUSLY, Valerius trod down the corridor, deeper into the mustiness of perfumes that had lost their freshness. He knew the reputation of this house: A legionary of his cohort had earned a dagger slash in the back and lost the three thousand *sesterces* of his discharge pay in one of these cubicles.

A woman's laughter sifted through a panel of curtains, then denigrated into moaning. Valerius, who had halted and reached for his sword, continued walking.

He might not have ventured into this place, except for the last words of the plebeian woman who had accosted him outside the palace: "To refuse, Signifer, could prove dangerous."

Now he regretted not having told a trusted friend his destination, for the same plebeian shrew stepped out of the last cubicle along the dusky passageway and glowered at him. "This one," she ordered.

Valerius ducked through the slit in the curtains, hand ready on the hilt of his short sword, and nodded gravely at the young woman sprawling half naked on the thin bed. She wore a wig of a thousand golden ringlets; banks of them reared up off the crown of her head. The only thing that made her distinct from other women of her occupation was a pure silk shawl, which she had snugged around her bare shoulders. It was worth more than what any common prostitute could afford.

"Come closer, Signifer." She patted the rumpled bedding she had nested beside her lap. "Please sit."

Valerius hesitated.

"You will sit," she said ominously.

"Who are you?" He lifted the oil lamp to see her better. "I know you . . . don't I?"

Coquettishly, she veiled the lower half of her face with silk. "So you think you know Licisca?"

"Perhaps not."

"But I remind you of someone?"

Valerius shifted the glow back and forth across her features.
"I thought for a moment—"

"Someone at the palace maybe?"

"Not . . . !" He couldn't finish—not aloud in this place.

She laughed at his indignant expression.

So the rumors were true. He set the lamp back on its tripod
table. Grimly silent, he watched his shadow pulsate on the
wall. He should never have come, but now it was too late. He
was compromised no matter what happened after this moment.
It might be difficult enough to save his life, let alone keep his
honor intact.

Valerius was neither appalled nor perversely delighted at
the prospect of making love to the Emperor's wife. He felt
only weary and trapped. Once again, it was made clear to him:
the impossibility of serving any of these recent Caesars without
being contaminated by the vileness of their private lives. Had
it always been so, and the truth glossed over by historians like
Livy? Was the glory of Rome a golden bedsheet thrown over
an endless orgy that had been inaugurated the day Gaius Julius
Caesar had crossed the Rubicon River, dooming a republic in
which men and women had valued one another for their fidelity
and restraint?

Valerius sighed. "What do you want of me?"

"Not what you think. I need your kindnesses."

"I am at the Emperor's service," he said listlessly.

"Oh, of that I'm sure, *Brutus* Valerius."

He winced at the nickname he had garnered after his involvement in Caligula's assassination. "It is *Julius* Valerius,
Lady."

"Don't be so sensitive; I know *everything* about you. I
admire you and have great plans for your career. You're a
brave soldier, the first to exalt Claudius after helping to murder
the last emperor."

"I killed a monster. He was no emperor."

"Well said. It is not easy to find a man who can strike down
a monster—not in today's Rome."

"Whatever the lady has to say to me, it is best said on the
Palatine." He turned to go.

"You will not go yet," Messalina said quietly but firmly.

And he halted, enraged, frightened. She was right.

"Does this house make *Brutus* Valerius uncomfortable?"

"I . . . I do not understand."

"Come, sit; I will explain."

Valerius lowered himself onto the foot of her bed. He was well aware of Claudius' debaucheries, which stopped at nothing but relations with men and boys. On several mornings over the past months, the signifer had suffered taunts as he escorted a veritable troop of courtesans from the palace and through the streets to their designated neighborhood on the west side of the Tiber. Yet, of Messalina's activities he had only heard stories, and these had seemed fanciful even by imperial standards. By no reckoning could he imagine that the apparent Empress of Rome was selling herself to the public, even after a praetorian of his acquaintance claimed he had coupled with her in one of the less expensive establishments across the river. Valerius had thought the guardsman mad for uttering such improbable slander. Now, it appeared he had been one among hundreds who had lain with her.

"Do the *others* here know who you are?" Valerius asked.

"Some. What does that matter?"

He did not know what to answer.

"This is my escape from boredom." Her grin was vaguely girlish—until she licked her teeth. "Oh, I tried spinning, but wool makes my skin itch. And an Egyptian taught me painting, but after the first lesson we never picked up a brush again. You have seen the Emperor. You have stood close enough to smell his old body. Surely, you realize . . ." Then Messalina proceeded to confess her innermost sorrows to Valerius. Although she clutched her breasts in a gesture of anguish, she spoke languidly, completely without emotion. Valerius grew more anxious as he began to realize his own plight: He was in the reckless sway of a ruthless and foolish woman, a bad actress only a dotard, who had blunted his otherwise keen intellect with gluttony and drunkenness, would fail to unmask as the Circe she was. And unless Valerius vanquished her first, she would transform him into another of her slavish animals. ". . . I was married to him when I was sixteen. I bore him two beautiful children, Octavia and Britannicus. And it is only for his son that he tolerates me."

"The Emperor loves you," Valerius said woodenly. "He often praises your beauty, your—"

"Then why does he fall asleep as soon as he lies down in our bed? Not that this is anything but a relief to me."

Gritting his teeth, he agonized that the afternoon might go on forever like this: locked away in the fetid cubicle with her, hearing state secrets tumble off her voluptuous lips as carelessly as drivel to a handmaiden. He resolved to draw the interview to a close. He was beginning to despise her. "Claudius is my Emperor. I'm bound to him by oath. You still haven't told me what you want."

Effortlessly, she manufactured tears and let them quiver for a moment on her lower eyelids. "I have no friends on the Palatine, Valerius—none I can truly trust. Claudius' ministers intend me nothing but harm. Narcissus would do anything to become the wealthiest man in the Empire. Pallas would like to see another woman take my place."

"Who?"

"Why, Agrippina, of course."

"But what worry do you have there? Such a union would be incestuous. She is Claudius' niece."

Giggling, Messalina touched a knuckle to her lips, then stroked the back of Valerius' hand. "You are so delightfully old-fashioned."

He withdrew his hand, quickly.

"My husband is weak, and Agrippina is seductive." Yawning, dry-eyed now, she reclined against her cushions. The long sweep of her leg showed through the transparent material of her *tunica*. "You will have to choose, my quaint friend."

"Between what?"

"Between *whom*—a waning Emperor or a waxing Messalina." She tilted her head to the side and smiled. "An admirer—a poet—wrote that for me."

Valerius rose. "This is treason. I've heard none of it."

"You are married."

He stopped short of the curtains. "Like many."

"But how many have a Jewess for a wife?"

He lowered his chin against the cold metal of his cuirass. "That bloody palace," he whispered.

"How fortunate she was not deported with the rest of her kind."

"It was all within the law. . . . Roman law saved her."

"As it will condemn you, Julius Valerius Licinius," she hissed, her cruelty no longer hidden but now triumphant, gloating on her face.

"On what grounds?" he demanded. Murder had just crossed his mind like a grass fire, and his eyes were still smoldering with the thought. "For what offense of the Twelve Tables?"

"Adultery with the Emperor's wife." With great pleasure, she watched his face turn ashen. "Please, please, Valerius, let's put aside these cross words and forget them."

Dazed, he tried to nod, but his head twisted to the side. His voice was a dry rasp: "What . . . are your requirements?"

"Your loyalty, which my friends and I will prize more than you can imagine."

"Friends?"

"You'll meet all of them in due time." She sprang up off her disheveled bed and excitedly seized his hands. "Oh, my new guardian, so boyish in appearance but so cunning of mind. You can't fool Messalina. Never once did you misstep while hundreds faltered and died. You predicted that Sejanus would fall when all of Rome was wagering otherwise. Then you cut down Caligula before he could do the same to you. And of a dozen conspirators only Valerius figured out how to save himself: He raised up Claudius." She pulled him closer to her. "I am surprised that *you* did not come to *me* . . . you who can so clearly sense a change in the wind."

"In those unfortunate events you have just described," he said very deliberately, "I was guided by the sense of honor my father instilled in me, not by hopes of gain."

"How cleverly put! Never lose this pretense of sincerity. It will serve you well in the years to come." Moistly, she kissed him on the mouth, then hurried to wash at a basin in the corner. "You have *gravitas,* as my father used to say. You know what I mean—seriousness . . . dignity."

Valerius knew only that he felt confused and ashamed. In the gloaming across the cubicle from her, he was struggling against feelings of arousal he had never expected to burgeon out of his contempt for her. The woman, he mused in an effort to reassure himself, was a witch, an enchantress.

"And let me tell you this much"—she tossed her wig on the floor and was lathering the pasty makeup off her features— "Lucius Geta, our noble praetorian prefect, is as feeble as the Emperor he serves. I have discussed the matter with my friends in the guard. They are agreed: You would make an acceptable prefect." Her face glistening, she looked over her white shoulder at him. "Well?"

Valerius swallowed hard, then tried to appear pleased. "But I'm not even a praetorian."

"The Empress can make a scullery slave the consul of Rome,

if that is what she desires. So, turning a respected legionary into an even more respected praetorian is no great feat." She let her *tunica* fall around her ankles, then stepped out of it before approaching him. "I've seen to it that you are assigned to me. You will look after me. You will come to care for me."

"I will never betray my wife."

She kissed him again, but less intently this time. "Of that I'm sure. You love your wife too much. I can read that in your eyes. I approve of such love, Valerius. It can give us rebirth when everything around us has grown stale." She half closed her eyes as if some delicious sensation was filling her. "And I thank the gods that *finally* it has come to be. And tomorrow, my Signifer... my Prefect, you shall escort me to the place of flowers and blue sky where I will be reborn."

Then the Emperor's wife donned her matronly *stola*, her eyes flashing at Valerius with elation all the while.

Valerius began to fight drowsiness in his brushy place of concealment outside the villa window. Within, the sounds of passion had crested an hour before and then ebbed to meaningless chatter between the lovers. Now, Valerius supposed, Messalina and Gaius Silius, the lean polished noble she had visited at three different country estates in the same number of days, were sleeping.

The late morning sun poured down on Valerius. Flies razzed the silence as they circled the rotten figs that littered the ground. Idly, the signifer broke off sprigs of rosemary, crushed them between his fingers and sniffed the scent to stay clearheaded.

Then Silius could be heard groaning pleasurably, obviously stretching as he awoke.

Messalina murmured something, but Valerius could not make it out.

Then the patrician said quite clearly, "We don't have to wait until the drooler dies of old age."

"But we ourselves must appear to have been innocent of his death, no matter how long it takes."

Silius chuckled. "We are not innocent, my love. Only the innocent can have long-term strategies. Our kind of guilt calls for audacity."

"You have such courage," she sighed. "Even more than I do. Perhaps that is why I find you irresistible." There was silence for a moment: A turtledove cooed from its depths. "What does my Gaius suggest?"

"End this absurd pretense. Bring it all out into the open. The bolder we are, the better."

"And how will Claudius respond?"

"I think you will be pleased by the panic in which he will find himself."

After a brief pause, Messalina laughed brassily. "Oh, let's do it. All of it—I mean, poison Agrippina and that affected son of hers, Nero. And announce what we have already done in secret. Tomorrow. What fun it can be." Then the hard edge came to her melodious voice: "But what of my Britannicus?"

"I have no children of my own; you know that. It would please me to adopt both your son and daughter."

"Oh, my husband, how deeply I love you."

Refreshed by their nap, the lovers began exciting each other again with murmurs and kisses. Valerius slowly rose so his knees would not crack and, picking the clear ground in the garden, crept back to the path. Marching briskly up to the squad of bored praetorians lounging around a portico, he accepted a cup of diluted wine from their subcenturion.

"Where've you been?" the *optio* demanded jocularly.

"Out in the hills, the woods . . . patrolling."

One of the guards shook his head. "Old Valerius—always doing more than he really has to. It's going to get him in trouble one of these days."

"Yes," the signifer said, his face grim, "it's inevitable."

An hour later, Messalina rushed alone from the villa and motioned impatiently for Valerius to join her in the *raeda* that had been brought out into the countryside from Rome. This carriage was far less ostentatious than her usual *carruca*, but even so, she insisted that he draw the linen curtains for her.

Then, in the yellowed light, which made her face appear jaundiced, Messalina glared at him.

Valerius pretended to be indifferent, although his pulse had quickened.

"What is *this*?"

"Lady?"

She leaned forward from her couch and plucked the dried fragment of a fig leaf off his cloak.

"Ah," he said, as if heedless of any danger, "I was scouring the woods for intruders."

"Did you see any?"

"No."

"How stupid of me."

"Lady?" His voice was reduced to a whisper.

"Your *gravitas* is genuine, isn't it?"

Valerius could not answer—not without condemning himself to death on the spot.

Yet, surprisingly, as the *raeda* was pulled up the Palatine through the imperial gardens, she brusquely told him, "I will no longer need your services, Signifer."

"Today, Lady?"

"I mean, you are to return to the Emperor's personal contingent."

"Have I displeased you in some way?"

"No." She feigned a warm smile. "On the contrary, you have revealed qualities I hope to emulate."

Valerius knew he was now talking to save his head. "Such as . . . ?"

"Why, your steadfastness . . . the honor your father gave you." When the carriage halted, she kissed him with tenderness. "Go home, Valerius . . . savor the company of your lovely wife."

"Thank you, Lady Messalina."

And from this he immediately knew that he had little time. As soon as he was out of sight of the palace, he raced toward the Janiculum Hill. His first urgency was to make sure Sarah was safe. Then he would gain the Emperor's ear through Pallas, who—according to Messalina—had hopes that Agrippina would be Claudius' next wife.

While crossing the Sublician bridge, he suspected that two men—Parthians, by the looks of them—were following him. Rather than lead them back to his home, he opted to decide the question then and there.

Valerius halted and pretended to be engrossed by the waters of the Tiber, which had been varnished rose and purple by the twilight. Stepping into a recess between the pedestals of two statues, he drew his *gladius* and concealed it under his cloak. The Parthians passed him by, gossiping in their language, seemingly unaware of the Roman legionary standing rigidly at the parapet.

Entering the atrium of his home, he heard Sarah and her brother chatting out in the courtyard. Valerius smiled at the levity in her voice. He had not heard her sound so cheerful in weeks, and he blamed himself for that.

"Well, I must be on my way," Caleb said. "Corinna will be worried."

"If by that you mean you've outstayed your welcome here—"

"No, no, but it is well past the hour carts can use the streets again. And to tell the truth, I am anxious to join her again." He laughed self-consciously.

"I am pleased you have found someone in Rome, Caleb."

"Yes, so am I. Their Empire is a sham, but the ordinary Romans are all right."

"I'm glad you recognize that, my brother-in-law," Valerius said, plodding out into the courtyard, his face drawn. "Still, Rome is foul with corruption. And unless we Romans rise to end it, we are no better than our masters. Caesar moves to conquer Britannia, adding yet another province, when it is too much for him even to govern his own household—" His voice broke.

Sarah flew up from her bench into his arms. "What has happened? God protect us, something is terribly wrong."

Desperately, he held her, his eyes tightly closed. Then he broke the embrace and approached Caleb. "Do you know where the Julia Victoria *insula* is?"

"Sarah has told me."

"Take her there, quickly. My parents will care for her until—"

"What?" Caleb asked gently.

Valerius smiled at her. "It is safe for a Roman to love a Jew in this city again."

She pressed against him once more. "I will not leave you."

"You must for a little while, so I am free to do what needs to be done." Valerius winked over her shoulder at Caleb, who nodded and pried her away from her husband.

"Be well." Then Caleb led Sarah out of the house. She turned back once, her eyes glistening.

Aimlessly, Valerius roved around the chambers, a cup of wine in hand. There was nothing he could do for a few hours yet: Claudius had gone to Ostia for a religious celebration and was not expected to return to Rome until late evening. Valerius did not want to be seen in Pallas' company until the Emperor was back in residence on the Palatine; otherwise Messalina would be forewarned and able to take action against them before Claudius knew what was happening.

He had just ambled out into the courtyard again and was staring vacantly at the small shrine there when one of the Lares

figurines caught his eye. She wore a lascivious smile not unlike
Messalina's. Lashing out with his forearm, he scattered the
tiny gods across the tufa paving stones, then slumped over the
monument. "My Lord, please, a way out of this. I can no
longer endure it. And my sadness grows. I would abandon
everything but Sarah to be at peace with myself...."

He could not shake the premonition: Somewhere along these
streets, dark except for a dim starshine and the spill of lamps
from rare first-story windows, he would be struck down and
left for dead.

Yet, he made it across the Tiber and halfway beyond to the
Palatine's slopes without incident.

He began to feel foolish. There was always the possibility
that Messalina herself was loyal—but for a few sexual esca-
pades—to the Emperor and had only been testing the signifer,
who, after all, had helped murder the previous Caesar. If that
was the case, Valerius had done well and would hear no more
of it.

Then, within sight of the Circus Maximus, three figures
darted out of a passageway and arrayed themselves in a line
across the street before him. They were already drawn.

Valerius knew he could kill two of them. But a third assailant
was beyond his capabilities.

"*Shalom*," a voice said from behind.

Valerius leaped aside two paces, expanding his fighting
front to include what he imagined to be a fourth attacker—
until he saw the young man hold the threesome at bay by
flashing his short sword in the face of their advance.

"My sister sent me," Caleb said from the corner of his
mouth. "You Romans walk too fast. I had a time trying to
catch you."

One of the assailants lunged forward, attempting to run
Valerius through. Swiftly, Caleb gave the man a shoulder cut,
and Valerius finished him with a thrust to the abdomen. Equally
matched now, the two pairs of swords rang out in the night.

"Who are you?" Valerius growled at his opponent, who
remained silent, his features lost in the shadows.

There was the decisive clatter of a *gladius* landing on the
stones, and Valerius looked askance, hoping it had not been
Caleb's. But his brother-in-law was looming over a collapsed
figure, wrenching his sword free from the rib cage of the body.

The third man saw no further purpose in remaining. He spun around to flee. But Valerius could not let him warn Messalina. The first blow hamstrung the man, sent him sprawling. It also cost Valerius his balance. So it was left to Caleb to deliver a merciful end, which he did with gladiatorial precision. The man's sword, which had been raised for one final strike, fell back against the street.

Caleb then helped Valerius to his feet, and together they dragged one of the assassins into a round of torchlight. Valerius scrutinized the face.

"Do you know him?" Caleb asked.

"No, but I'd swear he's a guardsman."

"Have you seen him at your palace?"

Valerius shrugged. "Perhaps—I don't recall: There are nine thousand of them in the city."

"They certainly fought like praetorians. I have always found you legionaries to be tougher."

"Why is that?"

"Well, you expect resistance. These poor fools think their reputation will do their work for them."

Valerius clasped Caleb's forearm. "Thank you."

"It was for my sister"—Caleb wiped his sword on the dead man's white tunic—"and you, I suppose. Just never stop loving her as you do now, Valerius Licinius."

"There is no danger of that."

"Then I must go. If it has not departed for Etruria without me, a train of carts is waiting along the *Via Flaminia*."

Pallas laid down his jeweled stylus. After listening to Valerius for only a few minutes, the Emperor's minister had become too excited to take notes. He intertwined his fingers to hide their agitation from the signifer. "And you're positive it was not a common robbery?"

"Pallas—"

"Patience, friend. I must be sure of everything you claim. It could mean her head—*finally*."

Valerius sat down in a curule chair to keep from pacing. "From what she said this afternoon, I knew she would try to silence me. Had my brother-in-law not been following me—"

"Yes, yes, brave fellow, I'm sure. Did anyone see you enter the palace now?"

"I don't think so."

Pallas came to his feet. "It's time that the Emperor hears this."

"Do you want me to go along?"

"Of course, it's absolutely necessary. He knows I abhor the harlot. Everything I say about her is suspect for that reason. But you—"

"Who am I to Caesar that he'd believe me?"

"Don't underestimate his regard for you. Shall we go? Or do you want to fish for more compliments?"

As Valerius strode beside the Greek down a main corridor lined at intervals with praetorians, he was only slightly less anxious, knowing that Messalina had departed from the Palatine at dusk. A legionary named Gavius, who had helped Valerius enter the palace unseen, had told him this, adding that she might have gone to a house she maintained in the city. There, over the past years, she had entertained her many paramours.

Even with Messalina away from the household, there remained praetorians who might be loyal to her. Valerius realized that any one of these expressionless guards might suddenly break his rigid stance and cut down the two men rushing toward the Emperor's study.

Pallas noticed that the signifer was ill at ease. "I have always made sure my access to Caesar is guarded by praetorians friendly to me," he whispered. "My worries begin when we are closeted with the Emperor."

"Why?"

"He may not believe us—or want to believe us. We are gambling that his mood is favorable to our cause. Sometimes, he is quite mawkish about the whore. Others, he appears to understand what she truly is. Let us pray to the gods that he is of the latter inclination this evening."

The guardsmen posted at the vestibule to Claudius' most private chambers failed to bat an eye as Pallas and Valerius whisked past them. The Greek took a few deep breaths, then smiled for luck as he rapped on Caesar's bronze door.

After a long moment, a muffled voice said, "Enter."

Claudius and his niece, Agrippina, stood ten feet apart, their faces flushed, although the chamber had not been overheated by its small brazier. The Emperor's tunic was a skein of wrinkles narrowing from his knees toward his midriff, and he grinned nervously.

"I beg the Emperor's pardon"—Pallas was careful to give Agrippina nothing more than a polite nod—"but something of urgency has arisen."

"Oh, yes." Claudius turned and beamed at the woman, who was well past her first youth. "Child, if you will excuse us."

"Of course, Uncle." She gave him a peck on the cheek and withdrew.

"I spoil her."

"I understand completely, Caesar," Pallas said. "After all, who was more dear to you than her father, the good Germanicus?"

Claudius' eyes misted. "Yes . . . you *do* understand." He appeared to take notice of Valerius for the first time. "Why, it's you," he said with mild surprise. "How have you been?"

"Troubled by things I have seen and heard, Caesar."

"Troubled, Signifer?" Claudius ran his fingers through his white mane as if he were already anguished.

"What Valerius Licinius is about to reveal to you," Pallas explained as if to a bright adolescent, "has been corroborated by other witnesses who have approached me."

Valerius tried not to frown at what he suspected was an outright lie.

"Well?" Claudius was staring at the signifer.

Valerius stood at attention. Almost paralyzed by the fear that, at any instant, the Emperor might interrupt and order him to his death, Valerius resorted to the terse military manner of reporting. Between phrases, he studied Claudius' eyes for some reaction. At first, they glistened, which was understandable, considering the heartbreaking news he was hearing about the mother of Britannicus and Octavia. But gradually, they lost their sheen and became indifferent, even slightly bored.

"Caesar," Pallas said emphatically, "this is the second report I have received confirming that Messalina has married Consul Silius! She will use bigamy to pry you from your throne!"

Claudius nodded absently. "The world is more evil than any man can know. Every day there is some new surprise, some new p-putrid revelation. This age should be washed, scoured, begun anew. But no one knows how." His wet lips curved into a self-effacing smile. "I thought I knew; what effrontery to the gods."

"Caesar, the criminal couple must be apprehended!"

"Yes, see to it, Narcissus."

Exhaling loudly, Pallas glanced at Valerius, then said slowly and deliberately to Claudius, "I am not your other minister—"

"See to it, see to it." The Emperor was now exasperated. He grimaced and vigorously rubbed his nose with his hand. "All the way back from Ostia you ranted about this illegal marriage, spoiling what had been a delightful day. Come here, you two...."

Pallas and Valerius followed the limping figure to a table cluttered with scrolls and charts. Claudius riffled among them until he found the one he wanted. "The auspices were taken for the completion of my harbor at Ostia. I wish you could have seen your way clear to attend, Pallas—" Then he froze, eyes filling with knowledge. He clutched Valerius' cloak to hold himself up. "Signifer, you will see me to the *castra praetoria*—immediately."

"Caesar?"

Claudius ignored him and turned to Pallas. "Find Narcissus . . . tell him I will grant him his request."

"Which was, if I might ask . . . ?"

"To be appointed my praetorian prefect."

"What?" Pallas asked, almost insolently.

"Just provisionally, until this wicked business is disposed of." Claudius began to weep, but then quickly controlled himself. The lucidity in his eyes, dimmed briefly by this surge of emotion, returned. Then, imperiously, he glowered at the two men. "I have spoken!"

Reflexively, Valerius saluted. "I will arrange for a litter for Caesar."

"I will summon Narcissus," Pallas said, walking backward toward the door. "We will join Caesar in the safety of the praetorian fortress."

Claudius slumped down onto the table. "Such a vile way to reward my passion for her," he moaned.

Half trotting down the passageway, Valerius asked Pallas, "*What* is going on?"

"We've won. The whore is dead, unless he changes his mind between here and the *castra praetoria*. But I don't think his cowardice will let him. Just keep nurturing this sudden fear he has of her; our lives may depend on it."

"Did Narcissus already tell him the same news I brought?"

"Obviously."

"And Caesar *forgot*?"

"In a manner of speaking, yes. And that is why we must hurry while he remains in a clear mind."

"But who runs this Empire, then?"

Pallas, Lady Antonia's former slave, smirked. "It would not be politic for me to answer that."

"God, what I'd give to get out of Rome."

Pallas crooked an eyebrow. "Are you serious?"

"Yes!"

"It can be arranged," the minister said simply. "And I owe you something for coming forward with this evidence against Messalina." He chewed on the inside of his cheek for a moment. "Claudius has been persuaded to give Herod Agrippa the Younger a few of his father's tetrarchies. Would you care to bear the imperial missive to Judea?"

"If it will spare me involvement in the coming bloodbath here in the city, please."

"That's where you and I are different, Valerius. I wouldn't miss witnessing this slaughter for half the Empire. The most exciting games have always been staged right here in the palace." Then the Greek chortled again and gave Valerius a comradely slap on the back. "Go ahead and make plans to embark for Caesarea. And may *god*, as you so amusingly put it, grant you fair winds." Then he halted on a sudden thought. "Oh, and would you care to have a centurion rank?"

"Of course—it has been one of my father's fondest dreams."

"Consider it done. I'll have Claudius sign it along with the order for Messalina's execution."

X

"STAND firm against trials!" There were so many cries in the synagogue against him, Paul had to repeat himself to be heard. Then he smiled, hoping that it might mollify the more angry Jews, who had begun to shake their fists at him. "Share with those who are in need, open your houses to them. Be happy with those who are happy, weep with those who weep. Remember that everyone who calls upon the name of the Lord—"

"Not *everyone*!" someone cried from the worshipers, his Hebrew heavily accented by the Greek of Achaia. "Do not dare to say everyone!"

"—will be saved. Everyone," Paul said placidly. "I realize I am reproached because I bring the good news to the gentiles. But listen to the words of the prophet Isaiah: 'I have been found by those who did not seek me and have revealed myself to those who did not ask for me.'"

"Agreed, Paul—we did not ask for you."

Once again, he attempted to conciliate them with his wan smile. "I am a Jew, descended from Abraham through the tribe of Benjamin. We are loved by God as the chosen people. God never revokes his choice. But just as our ancestors changed from being disobedient to God and were forgiven, so those of you who are now disobedient will find mercy in God. To him be the glory forever. Amen."

"Amen!" a middle-aged man cried in a loud voice, as if to shame those who had dogged Paul from the moment he had opened his mouth.

Outside the synagogue several minutes later, the same kindly-looking Jew sidled up to Paul. The man might only have been squinting against the flat rays of the afternoon sun; nevertheless, his eyes appeared to be laughing. "This is not the same Corinth I so fondly recalled," he said to the clearly exhausted Christian.

"You are newly arrived like me?" Paul asked hoarsely.

"A few months. My wife and I lived here many years ago, before we moved on to Rome."

"I see. You are victims of this new dispersion."

"We think ourselves fortunate; the emperor Claudius sent us to you, Paul, whether he knows it or not."

Paul stared off toward the waters of the gulf, which were limpid and golden. He crooked a finger and pressed it against his lips to keep them from trembling. "You must forgive me."

The man smiled consolingly, although he seemed bemused as to why the renowned teacher had been so moved by a simple declaration.

"Just when I begin to weary . . . to despair . . . I am reminded like this. . . ."

When Paul could not finish, the man said, "My name is Aquila."

"Latin for eagle. The Lord sends an eagle to soar above my self-pity." Paul dried his eyes with a corner of his *tallith*. "I would ask you to guide me to lodgings."

"Difficult to find at the moment, I'm afraid. Our quarter is filled with expelled Jews like Priscilla and me. Please, come home with me, meet her. Break bread with us."

"I praise the Lord for generous men."

Paul was led up a straight and wide street of the city that, in the last two hundred years, had been both destroyed and rebuilt by Romans. It lay on an isthmus that connected the mainland of Greece and the Peloponnesian peninsula, and a refreshing seabreeze now poured over this sinew of land. He enjoyed the evening coolness and said little. He was also feeling somewhat ashamed, for he had forgotten the admonition he had made to himself as he entered Corinth: *Do not be afraid.* Entry into a strange city had become no easier with experience, even though in the past years he had ventured through the gates of Lystra, Iconium, Pisidian, Antioch, Troas, Philippi, Thessalonica, Athens and now Corinth. It was always done with a dry mouth and the inkling that he might lose his life in this new place. Then, inevitably, there would be the hecklers and those who would trot off to the Roman authorities to report the stranger from Tarsus for this or that offense.

Aquila halted and waved for Paul to enter a courtyard. "Welcome to my home."

Seeing the wooden vats and dyed canvas hung in the breeze,

Paul cried, "You did not tell me you were a tentmaker!"

Aquila shrugged and held up his stained and calloused hands. "I thought you would notice these."

"In truth, I saw no farther than your heart."

A woman brought them a wine jug and two cups.

"My wife, Priscilla. This is Paul, who preaches the gospel, who saw our Lord."

She put Paul at ease with a warm smile.

"Here," Aquila offered, "you will drink some Greek wine, yes? I've cured its sourness with honey."

"Just a cup of water, if I may. I've had a thirst since coming into this city."

"You were teaching in the synagogue?" Priscilla asked.

"Yes," Aquila interjected, "when he was not being shouted at."

Paul rubbed his large forehead as if to erase the day's tumult from his mind. "I spoke . . . briefly. And before that I walked a great deal through the streets, looking for lodgings." He accepted his water and drank it down quickly. "I am surprised by the many people in Corinth."

"Oh, it's a popular town with visitors from all over Greece." Aquila's expression became sad. "Pleasure-seekers. But honest men come here too."

"But surely it is smaller than Athens."

"Oh, yes, Paul. Have you been there?" Priscilla asked as she poured him more water.

"Recently."

"Tell us if the Athenians accepted our Lord's word—please, if you are not too weary."

"Well, at first they thought of me as a babbler: The word comes from a little bird that flits around the gutters. . . ." Then Paul told Aquila and Priscilla how he had been taken to the Areopagus, a hill on which the judicial council convened. He was summoned not so much to answer charges but simply to explain the doctrines he was teaching in the streets. "The Athenians love anything new, and my message is the most novel in the world," Paul said, softly chuckling. Facing a crowd that was awash in the brassy sunlight, he had praised them for being extremely religious: So fearful were the Athenians of neglecting any deity they had built a roadside altar on the outskirts of the city and dedicated it "to an unknown god." Paul suggested to them that, in this way, they had already honored the Lord of heaven and earth. "Not all present appreciated my point."

"What was the outcome?" Aquila asked.

"I never know until some months, even years have passed." Paul listened to the canvas panels flapping in the wind. "You use more linen than we do in Tarsus. Most of our cloth is made from goat's hair; we call it *Cilicium*."

"And we do less leather-work on this side of the Aegean Sea. Romans commissioned us only to do awnings and bed-hangings. But the toil is much the same everywhere, even in my native Pontus. We were delighted to hear that you practice the same trade."

"And I will continue doing so, for it is improper for a *rabban* to ask a fee for his teachings."

"So you wouldn't object to making tents and awnings here?"

"Are you offering me something, Aquila?"

"There's work enough for two. And we have an unused room behind the shop. It's very little."

"I am grateful."

A centurion and two legionaries jostled him over the raised stepping-stones that served as islands on which to cross the flooded street. Paul had been lying on his pallet in his cramped room, listening to the cloudburst beat against the roof tiles, when the Romans entered the courtyard and awoke Aquila, who hemmed and hawed until he himself stood in peril of being arrested. At that moment, Paul had emerged to tell the officer that he was the "follower of Chrestus" the man sought.

Now he and his escort had to negotiate the runoff from the immense thunderhead that had passed eastward, leaving a clear night sky dazzled with stars. "Is it true what I heard?" the centurion asked over his shoulder.

"What is that?" Paul asked.

"Your god sent an earthquake to deliver you from imprisonment in Philippi. But you and your comrade did not flee."

"It is true that we did not run, although the wall had been breached by the shaking."

"Why not?"

"Our warder would have been executed. And besides, we trusted in the Lord that we would be set free by those who had accused us."

The centurion led the way through the foot-deep waters, not speaking for several minutes. Then he dropped back and fell in step with Paul to ask in a whisper, "What became of the warder?"

"Why, he is one of us now. The man and his family were baptized that very night." Paul could feel the Roman's stare on him, but he did not turn his face to confront it. Instead, he gently smiled.

"We must talk sometime."

"It would be a pleasure, Centurion."

The proconsul had an austere face despite his full lips and somewhat bovine eyes. "I am Gallio," he said from the far end of the hall, then pointed to a couch. "Recline or sit, whichever is your fashion."

"I am a Roman citizen. My name is enrolled at our basilica in Tarsus."

"I had heard that. . . . Interesting." Gallio approached him, holding two steaming cups of spiced wine. He gave one to Paul. "Well, I've been here in Achaia all of a few weeks. The only thing people seem to talk about is *you*, Paul." He motioned at the couch once again. "Please, be comfortable."

Paul lay down in the Roman fashion, resting his weight on his left elbow. "Peace be with you."

"It is to secure the peace that I am here." Gallio took a thoughtful sip. "You are accused of blasphemy by your Jewish peers. Personally, the issues in this squabble mean little to me. No matter which side prevails, both you and your detractors will always benefit from reason and restraint."

"Excuse me, noble Gallio, but you talk more like a philosopher than a governor."

The proconsul nodded pensively. "That may be true. I come from a family of thinkers and poets. My brother Seneca is well known, and my nephew Lucan is gaining recognition for his verses. But make no mistake, Paul: I am a proconsul first. I will not tolerate a fist raised against Rome."

"I understand the distinction you make between blasphemy and treason." Then Paul asked, "Are you son of the elder Seneca of Córdoba?"

"I am."

"Your father may have known mine."

"In Spain? What was a Jew doing there?"

"Trade. You are Spanish and Roman. We are Jewish and Roman. The wings of the eagle are wide. If you will satisfy my curiosity, Proconsul, what do you know of our Christian faith?"

"Some of it I liken to the philosophy of the stoic. Do right, even when the state counsels wrong. Be prepared to suffer for your convictions. Be proud in the certainty that right predominates."

"I do not counsel pride."

Gallio sat up as he began warming to the argument. "It is a proud man who dies for his faith—as your Jesus did."

"He went as a lamb to the slaughter. We are prepared to follow him. We Christians trust in God."

"But which? The one of your accusers?"

"There is only one God. Even our enemies can share in his love."

Gallio slowly got up off his couch and strolled to the pool at the center of the hall. Positioned under an opening in the ceiling, it had been flooded within an inch of its lip by the rainfall. The proconsul eased down onto the parapet and ran his fingers through the cloudy waters. Carp shimmered under a raft of water lilies. "Of course, Paul, there are those who say you are not a blasphemer . . . that you are merely insane . . . or a drunkard of such long duration, you can no longer reason clearly."

Paul chuckled. "What did the stoic Zeno say? 'No person who is drunk is entrusted with a secret. The good man is entrusted with a secret. Therefore, the good man will not get drunk.'" He then joined the proconsul beside the pool. "I have been entrusted with the greatest secret of all, Gallio. Now it is my duty to impart that truth to as many as who will listen. If, as it has been charged since the day I started preaching in Damascus, I am persuading men to serve God contrary to the law, I will remind the proconsul that it is not *Roman* law of which we speak."

Gallio scrutinized the man for a moment. Then he drew his hand out of the waters and wiped it on his tunic. "What is your attitude toward the Emperor's government?"

"Our Lord Himself preached that we should give Caesar what is his."

"Tullius!" Gallio abruptly shouted, then fell silent until an aide breathlessly appeared and saluted. "Inform the accusers of Paul that I decline to judge matters purely of Jewish interest." The proconsul turned to Paul. "You are free to go."

The youth half dozed over the scroll, his soft, almost pretty face cradled in his hands.

"Nero," a voice intruded on him.

His eyelids rolled open to reveal irises of pale blue.

"Nero," the voice persisted, "I asked you to name two things to avoid. The first you have given me: *Avoid that which is ratified by the mob.* And now, the second, please."

"I don't recall," Nero mumbled.

"Try."

"Enough philosophy. It's time for my music lesson." Nero obstinately closed his eyes again on the old man's square face, its querulous expression. "Avoid all that which does not impart pleasure."

"No, no, and if you must paraphrase Epicurus, do it within the context of his philosophy. When he spoke of pleasure, he did not mean the basest kind." The old man folded his arms across his toga. "I will persevere until I am properly answered."

The youth sighed in defeat. *"Avoid that which is a gift of chance."*

"Yes," Seneca said fervently. "Don't you understand the importance of these tenets, should you assume a position at the highest levels of state?"

With his fingers, Nero fluffed out the reddish fringe that wrapped around his jawline. "But I want to become a great actor, singer, dancer. I will be responsible to the arts, not the state."

"That would not be a moral responsibility."

"Oh, it's so stuffy in your chambers." Nero stood up from the curule chair and fanned himself with the sheer wings of his silk gown. "Deep down, you know that, somehow, my mother will find a way to marry my great-uncle Claudius. And you hope to gain from it."

Seneca frowned. "That would be impossible for Agrippina. Not even an emperor can wed his own brother's daughter. There is an ancient prohibition against incest that no power can reverse."

"I'll wager money on that. One hundred *sesterces?*"

"I don't have a hundred *sesterces*."

"So Seneca is unsure of himself?"

"I do not wager. Betting is frivolous."

"Immoral?"

"That depends on the sum bet. Your mother will not become Empress. On that I will wager you a tenth of a *sesterce*, to show you that I can unbend like anyone else. But I will not have to pay it."

"Oh, you'll pay, noble Seneca—mark my words." Then Nero began to sing a Greek song. His was a lithe tenor voice.

Book Four

"THE FIRE"

I

THE pack surrounded the old plebeian on a torchlit corner of the Vicus Tuscus. He stood tall in his shabby tunic and glared at the young men. It almost seemed for a moment that his bluff might prevent them from attacking him. But then, one of their number—his face feminine except for a thin russet-colored beard—strutted forward and slapped the old man across the jaw. This excited his comrades to hurl their own blows, and within seconds their victim lay across a stepping-stone, groaning.

The band of youths sallied forth again, celebrating their victory with laughter.

Down the street, a silhouette emerged from the shadows and began following the young men. He paused briefly to help the plebeian to his feet.

"Are you hurt badly?"

"No." The old man's mouth was bloodied. "But I'm off to see the *vigiles* about those ruffians."

"Don't," the man in the hooded cloak said. It was not so much a threat as a warning. "A few loose teeth are a small price to pay for an encounter with that crowd."

"Who are they?"

"You don't want to know."

The old man examined the stranger's earnest eyes for a moment, then shuffled away without another word.

The hooded figure hurried on toward the guffawing and caterwauling that marked the progress of the revelers. But his thoughts were in Etruria, where Caleb and Corinna had lived the two years since he had last seen them. Valerius was delighting in the notion of overtaking this patrician offal and beating them soundly with the flat of his sword. Then he would quickly gather up Sarah and their year-old daughter, Ruth, to flee through the brisk night toward Corinna's country estate, as they had been invited to do a dozen times.

But there was no escaping Rome. The Empire was as big as the world. Bigger.

Valerius had known at once from the praetorian prefect's expression that he was being assigned to another "extraordinary detail." By this, Burrus meant that the newly promoted centurion was to shadow the Emperor's adopted son, Nero, and make sure no harm befell the pustular youth while he bullied half of Rome. "I keep hoping he'll try to push around some retired legionary or drunken Goth, but no such luck," the prefect had muttered. "Just make sure he doesn't see you. Otherwise, he'll complain to his mother that I'm spying on him. Of course, it's my head if anyone cuts him in two at some wineshop."

And Valerius was wishing that precisely that would happen as Nero steered his fellows into a noisy all-night tavern.

The Inn of Horatio was of the lowest variety, and, slinking into the throng, Valerius recognized the clientele as consisting of thieves, runaway slaves and thick-chested bargemen. While Nero and his band became no less raucous, they were not so foolhardy as to molest any of the patrons. They reserved their viciousness for the helpless and infirm.

After several minutes of sharing undiluted wine from the same enormous goblet, the youths encouraged Nero to stand and sing. Primping his blond ringlets first, the young man did so, but the words of his ditty were lost in the cacophony of rough voices—although Valerius imagined that it, like most of Nero's songs performed outside the palace, described some debility of the emperor's. Whenever in Claudius' presence, he lovingly referred to Caesar as Father, using the endearment more often than did Britannicus, the Emperor's son by Messalina. But once off the Palatine, Nero's remarks bordered on treason.

Stung by the absence of applause, Nero sat down and sulked until it occurred to him that it would be fun to give one of his comrades a shower of *calda*. Giggling, he opened the spigot on the urn in which the wine was heated, while his friends kept the foppish patrician from wriggling free. The boy began to scream and the keeper shouted to break up the disturbance, but Nero silenced him with a large gold coin.

The Emperor's adopted son eventually tired of the game and turned off the flow. The crowd applauded his antics. Beaming, he bowed graciously, ignoring the whimpering of his scalded friend. Then he led his followers out into the street again.

Valerius trailed them across the Tiber and up to the threshold of the very house in which he had made the acquaintance of the late Messalina. While Nero pounded on the door and demanded entry, Valerius recalled the woman with disgust and sadness, plus vague stirrings that attested to the power she had been able to exert over men. In truth, she had not even been pretty.

Pallas, as good as his word, had made sure Valerius did not have to take part in the executions that swiftly followed the disclosure of her bigamous marriage. Messalina had died in the arms of her mother, an image that struck Valerius as being plaintive when held up to the depravity of her days. But on the night this occurred, the centurion had been at sea, several hours out of Puteoli and bound for Caesarea with a dispatch that would give Herod Agrippa the Younger a handful of minor tetrarchies. Pallas had insisted that the ship voyage at night, which the captain had not thought safe. But the minister had wanted Judea assured, as soon as possible, that Claudius was still firmly in control, as mutinies in Rome often incited revolts in the provinces. Watching an orange moon rise off the summit of Mount Vesuvius, listening to the banks of oars slap against the waves, Valerius had found only one cause for joy after the convulsions of those days: His Sarah was safe.

But returning to Rome two months later, the centurion found his situation at the palace no different. He was still caught in the midst of endless intrigues; only some of the royal faces had changed in his absence. Agrippina and her son, Nero, had come to the forefront; they were obviously vying against Britannicus for the Emperor's crown. Everyone realized this—everyone but Claudius, who had grown even more distracted since the death of Messalina.

Valerius realized with a start that, while he had been ruminating, Nero and his fellow carousers had entered the house. The portal was vacant, and Valerius knew he would not see them again until dawn, when they would be turned out to stagger back to the palace or the wealthiest mansions of Rome. He wrapped himself in his cloak and hunkered down onto the curb. He planned to fill the long hours by conjuring up visions of Etruria in spring—lush meadows ringed by oaks, apple blossoms, peerless skies. . . .

Two nights later, Nero had recuperated sufficiently to go out into the city again. But this time he was not accompanied

by any of his dandies. He slipped into the darkness with only
one of his mother's female slaves at his side. Favoring the
quieter streets, they went together as far as the forum but from
there the girl continued on alone. Nero stood idly by, apparently
awaiting her return. He sang in his cloying voice to the empty,
moonlit square.

Valerius decided to pursue the slave and nearly winded
himself trying to catch her. She wasted no time walking to a
substantial house within hailing distance of the forum and rapped
softly on the door. A woman answered, her features lost in
shadow. But her accent was not Roman. "Come in, child, and
my compliments to your mistress."

The door groaned shut. Valerius trusted that the house was
large enough to have an atrium. Hoisting himself up onto the
garden wall, he followed the narrow parapet to the edge of
the roof and, stepping gently across the brittle tiles, crept up
to the opening. The chamber below was dimly lighted, but he
could see the slave's back as she stood facing the older woman.
". . . That is what my mistress desires," the girl said, hushed.

"Sudden, she says . . . but not *too* sudden?"

"Yes . . . she wants it to seem natural."

"Ah, well, the subtle beauty of Sleep-Bringer lies in its
convincing imitation of nature. Does your mistress know how
to administer?"

"She knows, Locusta."

"Will one vial suffice?"

"Yes—only one."

"Give me a moment, child. Then you may be on your way."

Valerius scuttled backward off the roof and lowered himself
to the street. He did not return to the forum but instead ran
toward the palace. But then he slowed his pace and finally
halted: He did not know what to do once he arrived at the
Palatine. Who was the intended victim? He had assumed the
Emperor himself, but the praetorian prefect was also a logical
candidate. Agrippa and Nero despised him. And Nero could
not hope to become Emperor unless Britannicus was out of the
way.

The signifer slowly turned toward home. He had decided
to wait, having seen too many men forfeit their lives because
of one careless word. Suddenly, he hungered to see his baby
asleep on her *lectulus*, the tiny sleeping couch he wished she
might never outgrow.

• • •

Agrippina kissed him full on the mouth, passionately, her eyelids closed. "See what an obedient boy you can be if only you *try*."

Nero pressed the vial into his mother's palm. "Tomorrow then, will we relieve him of his misery?"

"No—tonight. It is best to conclude it quickly. You must learn to trust no one. At this very moment, the sorceress Locusta might be offering the same potion to Claudius' agents. How else did that witch get herself such a handsome house except by selling to both sides in every dispute?"

"But how will you get the stuff down him? He has already glutted his dinner like the flatulent pig he is."

"Claudius can always be talked into one more repast."

Nero accepted her caresses with a thin smile, but she was too engrossed with his throat and earlobes to notice that his eyes were glazed with indifference.

"I must go to him now," Agrippina said. "Announce to Britannicus and Octavia that he desires their company at a late supper. . . ."

She found Claudius moaning quietly on his couch, a moistened bandage laid across his forehead. "My dear husband!" she cried, rushing to him.

"Oh, it's n-nothing."

"Surely it is something terrible to make you suffer so."

"A pain . . . an ache of no one organ. An aging body reminding itself that it will never be young again."

"Such gloomy thoughts."

He covered his eyes with the cloth. "Sometimes I feel so culpable. . . ."

"But why?" Her lips twitched slightly before she forced herself to kiss his cheek.

"Oh, so many reasons—that you are both my niece *and* my wife . . ."

"Love is always stronger than convention."

". . . that I leave Rome no better than when I came to power . . ."

"Nonsense, your lovely new harbor at Ostia, the aqueduct, the—"

". . . and, finally, that I allowed myself to be the instrument by which you will make your son Emperor."

Agrippina said nothing, her eyes fixed on the dripping cloth.

"It is so unfair to Britannicus. He is a man of few vices."

"You disapprove of Nero, then?" she asked coldly.

"I approve or disapprove of nothing anymore, my dear wife. I merely feel culpable. I preferred it when I thought myself simply as a hapless victim."

"But you *are*, my beloved Claudius—believe me."

He chuckled, almost knowingly.

"Well," she sighed, "I have caught you in a black mood. Nothing I say will console you." She moved toward the door, then stopped. "Oh . . . I almost forgot why I disturbed you. The recent rains—"

"Dismal," he murmured.

"Yes, but they have brought one blessing: a fresh crop of wild mushrooms in the Etrurian woods."

Claudius threw off his compress. "Really?"

"Shall I order them prepared for tomorrow's dinner?"

"No, no." He sat up, forgetting his previous complaints. "They're like flowers. Always best savored when fresh. Give the word: I'm on my way to the dining hall. Have all our children join us."

"Nero as well?"

"Yes, I don't wish to be alone tonight. Nor do I want enmity under my own roof. A man's family should be a lasting comfort to him."

Pallas and the young man wound through the winter-brown gardens to a balustraded rampart that held back the sea. The waters were pestered by a gale out of the northwest and colored gray by a solid cloud cover. Both men had to clutch at their togas with both hands to keep them from unraveling, and finally sought refuge from the wind behind a funerary wall honey-combed with niches that harbored urns stacked upon urns. The young man regarded these arcades of the dead with grim eyes that were very much like Messalina's, Pallas decided.

"I will never understand," Britannicus said.

"What, my friend?"

"Why was Nero chosen over me?"

Pallas nodded gravely. "Perhaps your father was on the verge of explaining his reasons when he suffered his stroke."

"Perhaps." Britannicus lapsed into an unhappy silence.

"I don't think this serves any useful purpose—to keep coming out here to your father's old villa. You are cultivating, not mastering, your sorrow."

"I come to Ostia, Pallas, in search of an answer." The

youth's eyes were now glistening. "What did I do wrong? Is there some glaring weakness in my character I don't see myself?"

"Oh, no, I wouldn't take this as an occasion to doubt your own abilities."

"I would have made a splendid emperor," Britannicus said fiercely.

"No one believes otherwise. Most were as shocked as you when your father's wishes were made known—"

"Six days after his death."

"Well, yes," Pallas said evenly. Then, after a thoughtful pause: "Do you doubt the authenticity of the will?"

"Does it matter? Nero has already been confirmed as Emperor-designate by the praetorian guard. What chance have I now?"

"Realistically?" The Greek shrugged. "None . . . unless civil war is to your liking."

Frowning, Britannicus shook his head no. "I wish there were someplace I could go—and simply *be*."

"There is, my young friend. It is called the Palatine Hill."

The youth smirked but added nothing to Pallas' remark. "Is it true what they say about my uncle Germanicus?"

"Which legend of that great man do you wish for me to corroborate?"

"That after he was cremated, his heart was found intact among his bones and ashes?"

Pallas exhaled and did not take another breath for a few seconds. A raindrop pelted his bald spot, but he did not seem to feel it. "I have not heard that tale."

"Oh, it's no tale. I have it on good authority from several who were there at the time in Syria."

"Really?" the man said too quickly to sound nonchalant.

"Is a poisoned heart proof against flame?"

"There must be those who believe so."

"Did anyone examine the ashes of my father's pyre?"

For the first time, Pallas glanced up at the urns. "This place has turned your thoughts morbid. Forthwith, you should return to the bosom of your family. *There* you will find solace."

"Yes," Britannicus said with a raw grin, "in the arms of Nero, who is both my brother and brother-in-law. I should not feel sorry for myself. Octavia bears the worse fate: to be that preener's wife."

"Come now, your carriage waits." Pallas led Britannicus

by the arm. "We should dwell on our most joyous memories."
He clasped the young man around the shoulders. "Why, I recall
them as if they had been held this morning, those Palatine
Games. Your mother brought you to your father, who had just
been declared Emperor. The crowd began clamoring for a better
look at you, so Claudius held you out as far as his arms could
reach. He cried, 'Good luck to you, my boy!' and everyone,
patrician and plebeian alike—even a wounded gladiator—exhorted the same proud words."

Britannicus' eyes had filled with tears. "Were there ever
such times?"

"Many, my boy. That is what is forgotten about your great
family: It has known moments of happiness like any other."

Britannicus was pensive and bleary-eyed until Pallas and he
were ensconced in the *raeda*. He listened to the tapping of the
horses' hooves over the wet paving stones, then shook his head
before laughing sadly. "I envy you, Pallas."

"But why?"

"You have the marvelous ability to manifest your will."

"What in the name of Jupiter do you mean?" Pallas kept
his eyes on the Via Ostiensis.

"You make things happen the way you want them to. That's
a gift. You wanted your brother, Felix, to become procurator
of Judea, and so he became. You wanted Agrippina to become
Empress, and so she became." A final thought had formed in
his eyes, but Britannicus did not reveal it.

II

PAUL started as he felt a hand seize him by his scruff hair. He twisted free and was turning to glare at his assailant when a Jew in Mesopotamian dress clenched his forearms around Paul's throat and cried, "Men of Israel, this is the man—the one who has brought a gentile into the Temple!"

"It is the renegade Saul! He has defiled the Temple!"

More hands reached out to grasp him. "I have done no such thing!" Paul shouted, but his words were lost in the growing uproar. Then he was cuffed across the face, and when the buzzing shock had worn off, he realized that he was being jostled and prodded back out into the Court of the Gentiles.

In his confusion, he wondered if Luke had ignored the warning and slipped past the low wall of demarcation. Yet, Luke had read the Greek portion of the sign out loud:

> "Whoever is the follower of a foreign religion is
> forbidden to go any farther. Anyone who tres-
> passes beyond this gate will be killed. He alone
> will be answerable for his death."

And, seeing the young man's stung expression, Paul had further explained, "It's an old law, my friend. Not even the Romans can touch it. Indeed, a new quaestor—interested in the Temple treasury, no doubt—was stupid enough to disregard this notice. He was stoned to death on the orders of the priests. Not even the intervention of the procurator could save him. You go your way, Luke. I must perform the rite of purification."

The young physician had smiled, then ambled back toward the streets of the city, and Paul had continued alone into the heart of the Temple complex.

After his warm reception by James and the elders of the Jerusalem church, Paul had wanted to reassure these, the most

Judaic of Christians, that his years among the gentiles had not made him forget his upbringing. For more than a week he had been trying to find some graceful way to establish this. Finally, he lit upon the idea of purification of the Temple. And had gone there with no plan of preaching to the crowd of worshipers.

Paul took a hard blow to the small of his back, and his vision whitened as if it had begun to snow in the courtyard. When his sight was restored, he found himself trapped in a whorl of angry men. They were roaring at him, driving him toward the gate, but it also seemed likely to Paul that they might suddenly halt and beat him to death with their fists. He glanced up at the Fortress of Antonia: A trumpet was bawling for the legionaries to muster.

Momentarily, he imagined that he was back in Ephesus. The mob that had been incited to riot by Demetrius, the silversmith, had somehow finally caught up with him. Paul shouted, "I know you make your living by fashioning idols of the goddess Artemis! And I understand that my preaching in this city has lessened the demand for your work! But listen to the words of our Lord. . . ." Then Paul saw that he was in Jerusalem. Confounded by the Christian's words, one of the Asian Jews holding him wrenched his arm all the harder.

So much had happened in the years since that day on the road to Damascus—the countless tribulations and hairbreadth escapes. Perhaps he had come too close to death too often, for now it seemed as if past and present had been breached, and one blended into the other without distinction.

"The priests! Someone should go for the priests!"

"Indeed," Paul murmured, his terror now revealing itself as a slight giddiness. Shoved forward, he flickered through light and shadow along one of the porticoes. A grimace had taken hold of his face and made the cheek muscle pulse every few seconds. He tried to raise his hand to rub the spasm away, but his captors grappled it down again.

They burst into sunlight. Paul could see nothing. Repeatedly he licked his lips. He knew that, for the first time in years, he was close to that awful humiliation. Hundreds, even thousands, would witness it now, and believe that the man from Tarsus was possessed by devils, that his teachings were only some demonic babble. "O Lord," he prayed, "please deliver me from this—"

"Hold!" a voice cried in Greek.

Paul could hear hobnailed sandals scraping down over stone steps. He opened his eyes on the two flights of stairs that connected the Court of the Gentiles to the Fortress of Antonia: Dozens of legionaries were rushing down them and fanning out to encircle the unruly throng. Their tribune shouted at the men who were holding Paul: "What gives here?" Again, Greek rather than Latin.

There was such a confusion of explanations, the tribune raised his sword for silence. "It's the facts of this affair I want, not your foul wind. Centurion, take possession of the prisoner. . . ."

As Paul was quick-marched up the stairs, he touched his fingers to his brow, thinking the moisture there was sweat. It was blood.

The tribune had been frowning at him. "That's right. See what a quarrelsome nature earns a man?"

Minutes later, in the cool interior of the limestone fortress, the officer apparently assumed that Paul only spoke Aramaic, for he said to his centurion, "These fools always pick the perfect time to stir up trouble—Passover, as if there aren't enough problems as is." He glared at the battered man. "Wait, could this be the Egyptian who mounted the revolt against us three years ago?"

"I am not an Egyptian," Paul announced.

The tribune swallowed his surprise. "Then what are you?"

"A Jew, born in Tarsus."

"Well, my Cilician, you've created quite a row with your cousins here in Jerusalem."

"If you want the crowd quieted, let me speak to them."

"That's right, and urge them to attack the Antonia. No, thank you." He turned to the centurion. "Take him away."

"Aye, Tribune Lysias."

"Did it appear to you," Paul asked, "that I was in any position to lead a mob? It was my blood they wanted, not yours."

Lysias smirked. "That's true enough."

"Let me say just a few words to them, and the interests of the peace will be served."

The tribune motioned for his subordinate to wait. "All right. But if he preaches revolt in the slightest degree, Centurion, strike his head from his shoulders. Just make sure the rabble doesn't see."

The breeze soughing through the coarse wool of his tunic,

Paul stood in a crenel of the uppermost battlements until the crowd in the Temple grounds below recognized the figure perched in a notch of the Roman tower. Quickly, voices were raised against him, and Paul sighed deeply before crying down, "Fathers and brethren—"

"Blasphemer! Leap to a righteous death!"

"Listen to me!" he begged. After a moment, perhaps only because their curiosity was as keen as their hatred, the men of the gathering quieted themselves. "I am a Jew. I was born in Cilicia, but my real life began here in Jerusalem at that very spot"—he pointed to Solomon's Portico—"where I sat at the feet of Gamaliel and learned to be zealous for our God and the law. I am a Jew who persecuted his own brothers—sometimes even to their deaths. But then, one day, I heard the voice of our Lord telling me to stop my persecution, to follow him— the true Messiah!" He paused and glanced down and then skyward, as if realizing, for the first time, that he was speaking from a great height. He smiled. "It was said to me: 'The God of our fathers has appointed you to know his will, and to hear him speak. Arise, and therefore be baptized, and wash away your sins, calling on his name.' I have obeyed the voice of the Lord of our fathers. How can I have angered you when I have not offended God? For again it was said to me: 'Depart and bring the word to the gentiles—'"

A sound—a shrill blend of shouts and screams and moans— flew up as if Paul had just tossed a torch onto the roof of the Temple. "Please, listen—"

But from that moment Paul's words were drowned out, and pebbles began clicking against the walls of the fortress.

The centurion yanked Paul back down behind the battlements. "I care less who's right or wrong. It's your motive that intrigues me. Why are you stirring them up? Follow—I intend to find out."

In the dusty yard of the fortress, Paul was bound to the whipping post. At the direction of the tribune Lysias, the Syrian auxiliary who would administer the "examination" approached the prisoner and showed him the *flagellum*. This was seemingly done as a courtesy, as if the questions about to be put to him would be more understandable if only Paul might inspect the instrument of his torture. Three leather thongs sprouted from the end of a wooden rod; attached to these short whips were pieces of bone that looked sharp enough to tear flesh.

Paul craned his head back and caught Lysias' eye. "May I speak?"

"After the first blow. Then you may chatter all you want." The tribune chuckled to the centurion, "That's the only way to get at the truth of this business. I agree with you: There's more to this than some religious bickering."

Then Paul cried in a loud voice, "It is unlawful for you to flog a man who, firstly, has been condemned of no crime and, secondly, is a Roman!"

"*You*, a citizen?"

"Yes . . . it can be readily proven. If you flog me, I promise it *shall* be proven to the satisfaction of the procurator Felix in Caesarea."

Paul could hear the soldiers murmuring; then footfalls crunched over the yard toward him. It was Lysias. "That's a dangerous thing to claim," he whispered confidentially. "It costs a heavy purse to buy citizenship—at least it did for me. Frankly, my friend, you don't look rich enough."

"I was *born* Roman."

The tribune breathed noisily through his nostrils for several seconds, then strode back to the centurion. Again, utterances whisked back and forth between the Romans. The Syrian, out of boredom or the mounting suspicion that he was about to be denied his favorite amusement, snapped the *flagellum* at Paul's naked back, missing him by inches.

Finally, Lysias said, "Untie him. Lock him up for the night. We'll see what the Sanhedrin has to say about all this in the morning."

Upon being trooped into the presence of the council under a heavy Roman escort, Paul was heartened to see that Caiaphas was no longer the high priest. Yet, one glimpse told him that the latest man to wear the splendorous breastplate was no less severe than his predecessor. Paul had known Ananias all too well from his own days in the service of the Temple. The new high priest was notorious for his quick temper, and the insolent tone of his introductory remarks made it difficult for Paul to sound respectful when it came time for him to speak.

"Brethren"—Paul shook his head with exasperation—"I see the men who make up this assembly. I see the Sadducees. I see the Pharisees. Now, what do the Sadducees believe? That there is no resurrection: Death ends our earthly torments. But the Pharisees, who are even more rigorous toward the law than their Sadducee brothers, accept resurrection. Today, I am being questioned because I proclaim the resurrection of the dead. And what is my answer? I am a Pharisee and the son of a Pharisee!"

"That," Ananias cried shrilly, "is *not* why you are accused!"

A Pharisee tapped the butt of his staff on the floor. "Then is he condemned simply because he is one of our sect?"

His face clouded with anger. "I will not have the issues clouded by divisions we have lived with for years!"

An Asian Jew shook his fist at Paul. "He defiled the Temple!"

"My Greek friend went no farther than the Court of the Gentiles," Paul said, "which any pagan can enter with no fear for his life. I went yesterday to the Temple for the holy purposes of purification!"

"Cuff him!" Ananias ordered the captain of the guard. "Cuff the profaner soundly across the face!"

Paul was grinning in astonishment. "I cannot believe that the high priest of the supreme Sanhedrin has commanded such a thing!"

"Stone him! Stone him!" the Asian contingent began chanting.

Then, through the mounting din, came a sound that compelled the assembly to immediate silence: The Roman legionaries, at the signal of their tribune, had struck their shields with their swords. Lysias then strolled down the aisle dividing the sects and took hold of Paul by the wrist. "Come—before someone foolishly decides to do you violence." The officer then smirked at Ananias. "You have no idea how much you have just improved my estimation of the Roman Senate."

Paul tried to keep a deferential expression on his face despite what he knew of the Roman governor. Greek-born, Felix had secured the Judean post through the offices of his brother, Pallas, the late emperor Claudius' minister. Like many ex-slaves who had risen to power, he wielded his authority with cruelty and severity. He had, in the two years of his rule, solicited more bribes that Pontius Pilate would have ever dreamed possible. His countenance was bloated and smug, his eyes soulless. Yet, it was within his power to send Paul back to Jerusalem—and that meant death.

In the weeks since Paul had been dispatched by the tribune Lysias to Caesarea, the Nazarene's enemies had won out in the Sanhedrin. And, not trusting a Judean to impress upon the imperial governor the gravity of Paul's offenses, the high priest had hired a professional orator of Roman blood to plead the council's case.

This man, Tertullus, was now concluding an epic compliment to the virtues of the governor. Paul was thankful for a cooling breeze that blew inside the praetorium from the nearby sea.

". . . and so, illustrious Antonius Felix, under your governance we enjoy much peace, and by your providence many evils have been corrected in this territory . . ."

Felix was supporting his cheek on his fist, which had stretched one side of his mouth into a sneer.

". . . and we accept the judgment you shall be pleased to make. I will be brief and put off all tediousness and say merely that we have here a most pestilent fellow, an insurrectionist who spreads his fire among all the Jews throughout the Empire, and a ringleader of the Nazarene conspiracy. Another matter: He plotted to desecrate the very symbol of Jewish piety, the Temple, hoping that in the disorder that would surely follow such an outrage, his sect might reap gains at the expense of imperial order—"

"Please," Felix interrupted, "your oratory is like spelt cake: One piece is enough. Let the accused speak."

"I know, Procurator, you have been a judge of this nation for many years. Therefore, I make my statement to you cheerfully and with confidence. . . ."

Felix looked no less suspicious than when he had been listening to Tertullus.

". . . I spent no more than twelve days in Jerusalem," Paul continued. "I stirred up no crowds. I never profaned the Temple. The Jews of Asia who started this accusation against me are not here this morning. If there were any truth to their claim, they would be in this chamber. And those of Jerusalem who abet that false accusation can really only find me guilty of one thing—something that is already accepted by the Pharisaic sect, whose members are admitted to the holiest councils of Israel."

"What thing?" Felix asked impatiently. Then, momentarily,

he was distracted by the entrance of a handsome Judean woman into the hall. Flashing a toothy grin, he waved for her to join him on his couch.

Paul waited until the woman had reclined, then said as if solely to her: "That after death there is resurrection. Believing this, I do not offend the ancient convictions of our people."

She stared back at him, her head held high.

Felix leaned over and whispered in her ear. She did not respond, other than to look troubled.

Paul smiled at them. "Justifiably, the procurator wonders if there is more to this than a minor disturbance at the Temple. It concerns him that I might prove a greater threat to the Roman peace than these trifles would indicate."

Felix laughed alone—loudly. "You are more Pharisee than Nazarene, Citizen Paul." Then his eyes became small and shrewd as he addressed the high priest and Tertullus. "This is no simple matter, as the accused himself has said in so many words. I will hold him until I receive the answers I need. Centurion, clear the hall—except for the prisoner."

Felix then gestured for his servant to pour Paul some wine and offer him some small quince cakes. "Well," the governor said in a more relaxed tone of voice, "you are indeed a Roman. I received confirmation from Tarsus. If you could afford citizenship, that surely means you have money."

"I have no money," Paul said, eating hungrily after a recent diet of salt fish.

"Come on, Paul, you can speak frankly: You're among friends."

"I was born a Roman. The honor was bestowed on my father for services rendered to the Empire."

Felix's smile faded. "A pity. Money always triumphs where justice fails. Now, we are guaranteed entanglements, delays. If only you had friends who might..." Purposely, Paul felt, the governor let his voice trail off. Then Felix sighed and said, "May I present my wife, the lady Drusilla?"

"I am honored. If I might be so bold, are you not the youngest daughter of the late king Herod Agrippa?"

"Yes," Felix answered for her, "she was, but now she prefers to be known as the consort of a Roman procurator."

"I see."

Felix rose. "She has questions for you about the man Jesus."

"Ah," Paul said, "it would delight me... although when

one speaks of our Lord, it naturally follows that justice, self-restraint and the coming judgment must be discussed." He leveled his eyes on the couple.

"I will excuse myself," Felix muttered. "These are Jewish affairs, I'm sure."

III

CALEB inched out of Corinna's arms so as not to awaken her. He padded in his bare feet across the wooden floor to the only window in the mill. Ordinarily, the thick, bubbly glass annoyed him for the way in which it distorted the view of the fields and woods beyond. But on this dawn he took pleasure in the rose tint it gave to the snow that had fallen during the night. The stuff was already melting and dripping off the roof, pattering in a muddy line alongside the outer wall. This would not last— the haunting light, their life here in Etruria . . . everything.

"What is my husband thinking?" she asked from their bed, stretching.

He smiled. Denied permission to marry by her father, they had exchanged vows to each other alone under these dusty beams. *Where you are, Gaius, I, Gaia, will be. . . . Behold: You are consecrated unto me, according to the Law of Moses and Israel.*

"I'm thinking how glad I am the noble senator never let us live in his villa across the stubble there. It's the only thing here that is too Roman."

"It is still rightfully mine."

"When he dies. But who cares? We'll be in Judea by then." Her expression became sad. "It never ebbs, does it?"

"What, Corinna?"

"The dream of revenge. Sometimes while you sleep, I see it come upon your face like a fever."

"You would understand . . . if you shared my nightmares." Then he returned to the bed and her embrace. "This begins to sound like a quarrel."

"Is it?" she asked quietly.

"No." Tenderly, he kissed her. "I'm not so foolish as to fight a Thracian who knows my every secret. I was fortunate enough to catch you once in my net."

For a long time—until the cold-looking sun had risen higher than the hills and its light was glittering on the fields—they held each other, silent, listening to the liquid noises of the snow melt off the eaves.

"What do you want to do?" she finally asked in a whisper.

"Each day I feel more restless."

"I know." She took his hand in both of hers and pensively began caressing it. "Do you want to go to Judea?"

"That isn't possible—not right away. I have given this much thought lately. We have no money. And your father will lend you none as long as you are with me. Now that the emperor Claudius is dead, Jews have begun to trickle back into Rome."

"And you think we should join them?"

He smiled at her use of *we.* "Perhaps. I could go back to Serpenius' school . . . fight in the arena again. I could earn enough for our passage on a ship—well, a bit more than that. I don't want to arrive in my country a pauper."

"I have friends who might loan us enough—"

"No," Caleb said adamantly, "I will not be indebted to Roman nobles."

"But we could then leave—"

"Quiet." He had turned his face toward the window. Faintly, someone could be heard sloshing across the wet snow toward the mill. Caleb sprang up and stepped behind a *catillus,* one of the large grist devices. Donning a woolen robe, Corinna hurried to the oversize door and, before peering through a crack in the weathered boards, reassured herself that her short sword was still propped upright in the corner.

"How many of them?" Caleb hissed.

"Be still." She moved back and forth, trying to expand her view. "One . . . and he's unarmed, it appears. Wait—it's Linus."

Caleb walked out of hiding. "He's harmless enough."

"Please!" she whispered. "Get back there. I've known him all my life, and I tell you he's been acting suspiciously these past weeks."

Caleb sighed and ducked behind the *catillus* again, although he saw no reason for it. The young patrician, whose Etrurian estate bordered that of Corinna's family, was like a conquering Roman only in the way a kitten is reminiscent of a lion. He now came through the door, shivering, his cloak thoroughly soaked.

"Forgive the intrusion, Corinna."

"Linus, how can one get so drenched in less than one mile? And the sky is clear this morning. Does the roof leak in your father's villa?"

"I have no idea, Corinna. I have not lived there in months," he said soberly.

"I don't understand."

"Well, it would require a great deal of explaining to make you understand."

"Then explain."

"Is it enough to say that you are not the only one to displease your father?"

"No, it is not," Corinna said cautiously.

"May I shed my wet things—within decency, of course?"

"Surely . . . and I will get you a blanket."

Caleb tried to draw her attention without making a sound. He was debating whether or not to slip outdoors with his trident: Across the field in the leafless oaks, a wisp of smoke was rising into the still air. Linus had not come alone.

But Corinna had retired with the young man to the far side of the mill, where she fired the hearth and urged him to hug the flames. "Now, why did you spend the night in the woods, Linus?"

"I *live* in the woods . . . or with friends in Rome."

"Ah, like the Rufini with whom your family has always been great friends."

"No." Linus chuckled unhappily. "The Rufini pretend I have died; so do all the others now. And the truth is, I have been reborn." He paused. "I see I am confusing you."

"Somewhat."

"When my father sent me to Athens, I learned far more than Aristotle, dear Corinna. It was there that I heard a follower of Jesus speak. From Athens, my father had intended that I go on to Alexandria to study at the library. But I missed the ship to Egypt—intentionally. Instead, I went to Corinth, where this teacher had gone next. I was baptized in the waters of the gulf."

"Why, Linus," she exclaimed with relief, "you've become a Christian!"

"For some time now, although only recently have I admitted to the world. The deception was for my father's sake." The young man lowered his eyes for a moment. "Now, Corinna, I must ask *you* something."

"Yes, of course."

"Why is your friend peeking at me from behind that grist mill?"

His expression sheepish, Caleb gave up his concealment. "It was not my idea."

"Good," Linus said quietly, "because it is for you I came this morning."

Caleb raised an eyebrow but said nothing.

"We Christians try to help one another. When I stayed in Corinth, some of these believers took me in and fed me. They had once lived in Rome. Now they have returned to the city. After one of our worship services, I learned that they are mutual friends of ours."

Caleb glanced out the window at the smoke again. "Is this the one now lurking out there in the trees?"

"Yes."

"If he is such a friend, why does he hide? Why doesn't he knock on our door as you did?"

"It is difficult for a Jew to travel these days. They are more conspicuous out here in the country than in the city, where there are many races thrown together."

Caleb nodded. "That's true."

"Will you come with me, then? Both of you?"

Caleb had an inkling of who Linus' companion might be, but he was also wary of a trap. Following the patrician across the fields, he did not let Linus get too far ahead of them, thus clearing the way for hidden archers. Any number of people wanted to see him dead, Corinna's father most of all.

But one glimpse at the figure huddled over the smudgy fire convinced Caleb that he had nothing to fear. Laughing, he cried in Hebrew, "I haven't seen another good Jewish face in ages!"

"Are you counting your own as one?" Aquila answered. "I must remind Corinna to loan you one of her metal mirrors."

Caleb embraced the old man. "I never thought I'd see you in Italy again."

"Nor had I imagined that Priscilla and I would ever return. Lady Corinna, you are beautiful as ever."

"Thank you, Aquila. How is your wife?"

"Fine . . . a little weary after all our travels. We've set up our place again on the Street of Ten Shops."

"Then you've seen Sarah and Valerius?"

The old man's eyes moistened as he stared out across the

snow-garnished limbs of the trees. "No . . . despite how much we've wanted to. We decided it would be unwise to draw notice to Sarah with our presence."

"Nonsense—they will be furious," Caleb said. "Even we stole into the city to see my niece."

Aquila's face brightened. "Your niece?"

"Yes, Ruth, named after my sister. Come warm yourself at our hearth."

Inside again, Caleb uncapped an amphora of local wine and poured freely. Yet, Aquila became increasingly quiet until it became apparent to Caleb and Corinna that the tentmaker had something weighty on his mind. He simpered when he realized what effect his reticence was having on his hosts. "You must pardon me my mood; so much is happening in my heart at this time. We had hoped to arrive before dark last night, but the storm caught us on the *Via Flaminia*. We started again before daybreak, and Linus made sure you were alone before I presented myself. You see, I am rather well known these days as a Christian."

"When did you finally decide to become one?" Caleb asked.

"I was one all along, only I was too thick to realize it." Aquila rested his hand on Caleb's shoulder. "I owe you the complete truth: Priscilla and I came back to prepare the way for another. He will be here one day soon, we pray."

"This is the same teacher Linus speaks of?"

"Yes . . . and our beloved Paul sends you his personal greetings."

Caleb's eyes widened. "Does this man know me?"

"So he said when I mentioned my gladiator friend in Rome, a certain Caleb of Jerusalem."

"Is this Paul from Judea?"

"Not originally, but he studied at the Temple. In those days, he was called Saul of Tarsus."

"So it *is* the same fellow," Caleb said. "I was sure people had confused him with another. Saul hated Nazarenes."

"And now, in the gentile provinces, he serves as their shepherd." Aquila began picking at his beard with his dye-stained fingers. "Linus, here, Priscilla, I—all the others in Italy— would value your strength in preparing for the day Paul lands on this shore. There is so much to be done."

Caleb chuckled uneasily. "Oh, no, my old friend, I am not ready to lay down my sword—not with our homeland still under the whip. And if I recall something of this man from Tarsus, he won't need my help to accomplish whatever he sets out to do. He was the most driven man in Jerusalem. It is too bad he did not become a Zealot."

Aquila could not hide his disappointment. "Will Priscilla and I see you in Rome?"

Caleb looked askance at Corinna. "Sooner than you may think."

Caleb crouched with his hands on his knees so he could scrutinize every movement of the two fighters. The scuffling of their greave-clad legs sprayed dust into his eyes, but he did not look away. He circled in the same direction as they did, always keeping the clash of their wooden swords in sight. Twice, he frowned briefly, yet overcame his displeasure. But finally it was too much for him. He stood upright and bellowed, "I cannot believe this! You are putrid. With that kind of swordsmanship you need not worry about any gladiator. Oh, no. You will have to keep an eye out for vestal virgins. They will be leaping down into the arena, armed with brooms, when they see what weak-kneed lilies Serpenius has delivered to the games!"

"We are sorry, Master Metellus."

"Sorry?" Caleb looked bemused for a moment, then asked with disarming gentleness, "So you are sorry?"

Both helmets nodded.

"Well, in that event, I will give you both three days in the stocks."

Caleb was striding away when one of the novices said, "Master, a question, if you will?"

"Speak."

"If we had not been contrite, what would our punishment have been?"

"Three days in the stocks."

"But what is the point, then?"

"This—being sorry has no value in this trade. Report yourselves into the guardroom."

"You missed your calling," a familiar voice said from the portico. "You would have made a grand centurion."

Caleb smirked at his brother-in-law. "I thought I smelled some of that disgusting imperial perfume. You really must get out of Nero's palace more often."

"Agreed, and that's why I'm here." Valerius offered his hand and then pulled Caleb up onto the porch. "I'm off to Judea."

Caleb's eyes became suspicious. "Why? Is there wind of a new revolt?"

"If there were, you'd be the last man in the Empire I'd tell. No, I'm to sail with the new procurator, Porcius Festus. I'll be serving as his adjutant for one year."

"What recommends this Festus to be lord of the Jews?"

"I don't know exactly," Valerius said carefully, a habit acquired by his years on the Palatine. "But he seems a decent enough sort. If it is any consolation, Felix has been recalled to answer for the brutalities he has visited on your people."

"It is not consolation that all these Roman governors leave Judea under a cloud. When will you Romans learn that it is your presence there that is the disgrace?" Caleb exhaled wearily. "That stone Caligula tried to put in the Temple had more sense than any of these procurators. Isn't that true?"

"I cannot answer."

Caleb glanced at Valerius' thoughtful face, then softened his tone. "And do not answer, for the sake of Sarah and my little Ruth. *Survive*, Valerius Licinius. Those dearest to me rely on you."

"I shall try."

"What does my sister think of returning to Judea?"

"She isn't going."

Caleb grasped Valerius' cloak to make him halt. "What are you telling me? Are there problems between you and my sister?"

"No. I mean yes, but it does not affect our love. She refuses to go with me."

"But why? We still have friends in Jerusalem. She could worship at the Temple."

"She says she never wants to see Judea again."

"That is not her heart speaking."

"I know that," Valerius said. "So does she. The truth is that if she went, maybe she would never come back. And I would be compelled to stay there forever . . . her prisoner, as sometimes I feel she is mine." Gently, he undid Caleb's clutch on his cloak. "I am asking you to protect my family in my absence."

"Why ask? You should have simply trusted that I would."

"Thank you, Metellus."

Caleb absently frowned at the use of his Roman name. "But there is something you can help me with."

"Just ask, please."

"What do you know of a woman called Poppaea Sabina?"

"Not much, really. A modest wealth. Very pretty. She's married to a noble called Otho—a crony of Nero's." Valerius winked at his brother-in-law. "Trouble with Corinna?"

"Do not speak foolishly." Caleb lowered his voice. "Poppaea enrolled a Spanish slave of hers in our school, and comes once or twice a week to check on him. Someone must have whispered in her ear that I am a Jew. I mean, she is quite nice, but keeps asking me questions about the Nazarenes—as if I know. I am not sure why . . . it bothers me, Valerius."

"If it is any comfort, Poppaea has no reputation for viciousness."

"For a Roman, that's a pity. It's like a tigress being born without claws." Caleb shouted at a retiarius to mind his wrist action as he practiced flinging his net. Then the sub-*lanista* asked his brother-in-law, "When do you sail?"

"Within the week, if I am fortunate enough to survive until tomorrow's dawn."

"What happens tonight?"

"I am required to attend another artistic performance by the emperor Nero."

IV

DAYLIGHT was still streaming down through the opening in the vaulted ceiling when Valerius took his post at the rear of the great hall. A file of musicians timidly squeezed through the ring of praetorians, which was three ranks deep. Hoisting their instruments over their heads, they made their way to the foot of a facsimile of Troy's wall.

Valerius noticed that a venerable senator was already dozing. "Noble Blandus," he whispered to the aged man, who startled.

"What . . . what is it?"

"Trust me: This is neither the time nor place for a catnap."

"Are you threatening me, Centurion?"

"No, I'm trying to save your life." Valerius melted back into the throng of guards.

A young patrician, his hair as fastidiously arranged as a matron's, then announced in Greek: "We are gathered here to celebrate together with our Emperor the beginning of this month once called April, now Neroneus. . . ." Gaius Petronius had been granted the title of Arbiter Elegantiae, and it was his responsibility to assure the Emperor that there were no violations of good taste in his court. Nothing was considered to be refined unless Petronius first said so. "An extraordinary treat is being provided for us: the performance of a new dramatic representation of *The Burning of Troy*, composed by the poet Nero Caesar with the cooperation of the equally immortal Virgil. In no way will this delight be abbreviated; you shall enjoy it in its entirety. Friends, to the greater glory of the arts and of Rome—*The Burning of Troy*!"

Valerius glanced around the palace hall at the faces: It looked as if these senators and knights had just been ordered to march to Parthia in their bare feet. To the last man, they were either clenching their teeth or furrowing their brows. One magistrate was staring up at the aperture. He was apparently trying to will his body up through the round opening and into the free, blue sky.

Then flutes warbled and sistrums jangled. The crowd sighed as if saying *Well, here it must begin*. A figure in a glowering mask strode down a staircase from Troy's battlements and recited in a voice that was remarkably inferior to the Emperor's own:

> "I have been called to tell you once again
>   How the Greek warriors did level the splendor
>   Of ancient Troy, for which we mourn and weep..."

Sentry duty during eternal African nights had given Valerius a skill he now found useful in Nero's service: He could stand still for hours on end without becoming hopelessly bored or agitated. The trick, he had discovered, was not to seize any one thought and ride it to its conclusion. He would let fragments of cognition, pieces of daydreams, gallop past, unharnessed. And, all at once, he would realize that an hour, two hours—even more, sometimes—had elapsed and his mouth was very dry.

So it was now when he peered up and was gratified to see a night sky through the aperture in the ceiling. The Emperor himself had emerged in a tragic mask, and the lulling quality of his voice was torturing the audience with drowsiness, dangling a sweet, delicious fruit before them no one was allowed to taste.

> "See how the citizens, screaming and scurrying,
>   Scamper like wood lice from logs freshly thrown
>   on the fire—"

Nero abruptly stopped. Fear rippled back from the foremost benches to where Valerius stood.

"Oh, God," the centurion whispered to himself, "some fool went and *yawned*."

Nero dropped his mask. "I not only demand attention, I demand appreciation as well." He snapped his fingers to catch the eye of a praetorian colonel. "Take that man out, and I don't want to see him again."

That meant *ever* again, Valerius realized.

"And that one there!" Nero pointed at a flabbergasted knight.

"He's been maliciously distracting me by blowing bubbles from his spit." The Emperor then addressed everyone: "Don't think me harsh, my friends. I was quite lenient about the rash of nose-picking in my scene with Cassandra. Now, where were we . . . ?" He massaged his neck muscles before donning his mask again. "Let's see . . . 'Roaring like lions and howling like wolves of the wood lice' . . . no, no—'of the wood.'" Gasping, Nero threw his hands up in exasperation. "Oh, we've forfeited the mood! We'll have to start all over. Musicians!"

Frozen in place by these words, Valerius listened to the same preamble of flutes and sistrums he had heard two or three centuries before. He resisted the overpowering urge to scream and break his sword in half over the nearest bald head.

Less lively now, the chorus plodded down from Troy's ramparts:

> "I have been called to tell you once again
> How the Greek warriors did level the splendor
> Of ancient Troy, for which we mourn and weep . . ."

Valerius was at sea, the needle-sharp spray dashing against his face, the wind roaring in his ears, when he was roused from the pleasant fantasy by movement on the curved bench directly below him. An old man with only a thin streak of purple on his toga was doubled over, his mouth puckered by some intestinal agony. Valerius hesitated but then crept up to the sufferer and whispered in the quietest voice possible, "You must be still."

"I cannot." His eyes were watery, and his skin feverish. "I've had this ailment."

"You *must*—at all costs."

Then the man was racked by a spasm that nearly jerked him off the bench. "I simply cannot," he panted.

Valerius' gaze flickered toward Nero and back again to the lesser noble, who would die if he attracted the Emperor's attention. Quickly, he leaned into the man's ear and rattled off a string of instructions. The noble nodded and, despite his pain, sat up, only to pitch forward a few moments later. His body lay lifeless on the floor.

> "Ancient Anchises, caught sleeping, awakening
> Now to the flames that devour his ancestral abode,
> Calls to his son, young Aeneas, to rescue him—"

Nero paused, glaring down at this fresh disturbance.

Valerius scooped up the "corpse" and made certain Nero could clearly see the gaping eyes and mouth, the arms that dangled limply.

Nero shrugged indifferently and continued:

> "Pious Aeneas, our father, the builder of Rome,
>   Bore on his shoulders, so handsome and muscular,
>   His father, the father of all the fathers of
>   Rome..."

Two praetorians unbarred the doors to let the centurion take his burden outside.

The night was cool. Valerius set the man on his feet and called for a litter.

"You have saved my life, my son."

"I'm sure Fortune would've stepped in, had I not. At Neapolis she shut down his performance with an earthquake, although he sang through to the end, despite an empty hall."

The man ventured a wan grin, although still clutching his abdomen. "We are mad to go on like this."

"No... simply frightened."

His nudity was pocked by large boils, but the young woman appeared not to notice, perhaps because her own skin was coarse to the touch. Using the tip of her little finger, she wiped a residual streak of makeup out of one of the folds beside his mouth. "You were glorious this evening," she murmured. "I found myself praying to the gods that it might go on forever." Then she smiled demurely. "Just think: me, a humble freedwoman, here—with *you*."

"And why not?" Nero asked, reaching across the covers for his wine cup. "Isn't the Emperor's bed the very place for the most beautiful woman in the Empire."

"I'm not beautiful," she said quietly, her eyes downcast. "But I know how to gratify you, don't I? And I care for you. I will always have these feelings."

He gave her a brief kiss. "There is more peace of mind for me in what you have just said than all the wisdom of Seneca."

"Who's he?"

"My mentor... tormentor. He thinks he knows everything. And perhaps he does—everything but pleasure."

She giggled. "*I* taught you that."

"Oh, yes—indeed, Acte. You have taught me everything a man could desire to know." He was reaching for her when there was an insistent knocking at the door.

"Where's your wife?" Acte was already reaching for her *tunica*, which lay crumpled on the marble floor.

"Octavia is in her own bed . . . with those cold hands of hers tucked between her thighs."

"Nero?" Agrippina's muffled voice came through the door.

"A moment, Mother." Nero shunted the freedwoman toward another door. This one opened onto a back corridor, an access for the Emperor's personal slaves. "Come tomorrow the same hour. Do you still have the ring?"

"Of course, my love."

"Just show it to the guards. Farewell." Throwing a gown over his pustulated body, Nero hurried to the door.

Agrippina barged into the chamber. She sniffed the air and appeared to find something unsavory about it. "You are slow to learn, my son," she said with as much hurt as disgust in her voice.

"About what, Mother?"

"The entire household knows. Our slaves make wagers on who is next. If you must satisfy these sordid appetites, do it outside the palace—away from the city, better yet."

"As you and Lord Pallas do?"

Her eyes became furious. She was close to striking him when he traipsed back to his bed and reclined. "You will never speak to me that way again."

"The Emperor will speak to anyone in any way he wishes. The Emperor will do what he pleases, despite the stultifying advice of Burrus and Seneca. To begin with, I think I shall send Pallas away. He's a bad influence on you. After all, the mother of the Emperor should conduct herself like a respectable matron."

Agrippina glared at him. "Don't play your little-boy games with me—"

"I have tired of any kind of game with you, Mother." Nero reached under his bed and brought out a lyre. He gave her a sassy smile and began strumming the instrument.

"Put that thing down!" she demanded.

When he refused, she batted it out of his hands and kicked it across the floor in her fury. The strings made a moaning noise that died away in slow reverberation. "Oh, listen," Nero pouted. "That's the sound Cupid would make if you cut his throat."

"*You* listen." She dug her fingernails into his forearm until he cried out. "This latest one, the ex-slave Acte, is not so stupid as she looks. Nor is she as enamored of you as you think she is. She'll drag you into compromising situations where your title and status won't help you. Know this: Acte is in the pay of Britannicus."

"Oh, rubbish, Mother. You're making that up. Britannicus has accepted the situation."

"Perhaps, but he has friends who will never accept it. Britannicus was publicly named his father's successor. Rome has only my word and Pallas' that Claudius nominated you. These times are more perilous to you than—"

"I'm young. I'm entitled to live my life."

"You will have no life if your rule is a failure. Nero, do not forget: There is another candidate waiting to sit on Augustus' throne. Your adulterous promiscuity makes Britannicus look better each day. Part of your claim to the purple rests on your marriage to Octavia. Humiliate her, and Britannicus might finally take action. Honor your wife."

"Oh, she's such a frump, Mother. I look down, and it's exactly like making love to Claudius."

Agrippina appeared to recall something unpleasant for a moment. "Then you have some inkling of what I went through to make you Emperor." She bared her gritted teeth at her son. "And, more and more, I think I was wrong to make you the most powerful man in the world. You are not worthy."

"Mother?" For the first time, Nero looked as if he had been stung by one of her remarks.

"What?" She had started to leave.

"Please don't go."

Agrippina turned and saw that he was holding out his hand to her.

"Please stay, Mother."

"Why?"

"You know why."

V

"THEY are predaceous," the Procurator Porcius Festus muttered from the saddle.

Valerius was so heat-worn after two days of dusty Judean roads that it took a moment for him to rouse himself from his own stupor. "In what regard, sir?" he asked through flaking lips.

"Predaceous when it comes to their religious law. Come now, you're married to a Jewess: Tell me the essential difference between a Roman and a Jew."

"I had hoped there was none . . . that, in our deepest selves, we are all the same . . ." Valerius squinted up at the afternoon sun. ". . . brothers to one another."

"A lovely notion—but, sadly enough, not true. We Romans can imagine a secular world. We've gone and built one, now, haven't we? But these Jews, they fancy that their god wants to meddle in every little thing they do. It's just not a responsible attitude, and that's what keeps them so juvenile, so vehement." Gingerly, Festus touched his reddened pate, then sighed and slumped down in his saddle again.

Obviously, the procurator was still mulling over the result of his meeting with the Sanhedrin two days before in Jerusalem. Festus had been disappointed that, of all the difficulties facing Judea, the priests and elders of this council had wanted only to discuss a minor criminal case Felix had failed to adjudicate before being recalled to Rome. Festus admitted to Valerius that he did not understand what this Roman citizen named Paul had done wrong. "But whether this fellow is guilty or innocent," Festus pointed out, "it behooves a new governor to ingratiate himself with his subjects."

For some reason, Valerius had found Jerusalem to be much less than what he had expected. Perhaps he had imagined that it would be more like Rome, but on a much smaller scale, of course. And he had gathered from countless conversations with Sarah that it was some kind of golden, mystical place where a man could feel God's breath on his skin. Instead, the centurion had arrived in a squalid Oriental city made all the more insufferable by early summer heat. There were too many flies and not enough houses for the ragged population. The vaunted Temple of Herod would have been relegated to obscurity had it been erected in the forum and not this oversized village of mud and wattle. Yet, he determined to lie to Sarah on that future day when she would ask him his impression of her Jerusalem. "It was splendid," he would say.

"Ah . . . at last!" Festus cried, shading his eyes against the setting sun.

They had crested a long, gentle slope and could finally overlook Caesarea. "It's nice to see a Roman-style city again," Valerius confessed. It pleased him to view the straight lines of the aqueduct and the symmetrical arrangement of the public buildings around the forum. Jerusalem had seemed so jumbled and cluttered to him, a city built without forethought.

Festus motioned for the decurion who commanded the cavalry escort to step up the gait to a canter. It was a needless order: The horses had smelled home on the breeze and were hurrying on their own accord. "Ah, Valerius," he said, "after the baths we'll all feel ten times more like Romans."

Yet, later that evening, as they lingered in the *natatus,* the swimming pool at the substantial Caesarean baths, Festus seemed grave and distracted. He suddenly asked Valerius, "You must be fairly familiar with this supreme Sanhedrin of theirs, having been to Jerusalem before."

"But this was my first trip to the city, Procurator."

"I thought the Emperor said you'd been to Judea."

"Only as far as Caesarea. I carried the dispatch that gave Herod Agrippa the Second his tetrarchies. But I returned on the same ship that had brought me."

"Oh, I see." Festus was glumly silent for a few moments, then smiled hopefully. "Well, you're certainly bright and capable enough to head my board of judicial advisers."

"You're speaking of this Paul case?"

"Yes. When I conferred with their high priest—Ananias, I'm sure his name was—the beggar said I should hand over the Christian to their authority. I don't rightly know if I can do that. This fellow is a Roman, after all."

"What do you want me to do, Procurator?"

Festus must have sensed Valerius' uneasiness at the prospect of performing clandestine duties. "Don't be alarmed: It will involve nothing underhanded. Magistral advisement is an honorable tradition. Quite frankly, I need more information about the accused. And yes, I would be pleased if it could be established that Paul is a Zealot or some other threat to the peace."

"But if he isn't, sir?"

"Then I still have two choices. One is to punish the man without cause and thereby win the favor of these lawless Jews." Festus became pensive again.

"And the second choice, Procurator?"

"Release him because he is innocent. In that way, I prove the validity of Roman law—our very civilization—but will certainly enrage the very people I have come to pacify."

"Surely, there must be another option."

Festus squeezed a sponge over his head. The cool water trickled down his face. "I hope so, Valerius. I would appreciate it if you could find one."

The centurion had a light supper in his quarters at the former palace of Herod. The servant, an Egyptian, remarked that to dine alone and then eat so little in the evening was more Jewish than Roman in custom. Valerius ignored the man's criticism and called for his toga, which was a snowy white but with no traces of the purple that marked a citizen as a noble. He had decided not to go about the procurator's business in a mere tunic: That was the uniform of thieves and assassins. Nor would he conduct his inquiry while in his military garb. He was not going to make war on the Nazarenes. His toga affirmed that he was indeed a *togatus,* or member of the imperial race. But it also suggested that he was more interested in civility and justice than in retribution.

He began his walk to the praetorium by following the quay. This was the most direct path to the forum, but looking westward over the twilit sea made him so homesick, he quickly turned up a side street and continued toward the heart of Caesarea on the colonnaded avenue that joined the amphitheatre to the Temple of Augustus. Within minutes, he was standing before the monumental shrine to a god he had glimpsed once when he was a little boy. It had been in the forum, and Valerius' father had held him above the heads of the throng so he could see Augustus Caesar pass on his litter, accompanied by all the soldiers and slaves in the whole world. Augustus had not looked like a god. He had looked old and tired. Never once had he smiled. Surely, gods smiled and showed affection for the mortals who adored them.

His temple was empty of supplicants. Of course, any Romans of consequence were now dining. But even had the torches within been lit, the building would have still seemed vacant, lifeless, forsaken. The entire forum, which from a distance had been so imposing and handsome, was now revealed to be a shell, a splendidly fashioned repository for shadows and silence. And if there were gods who haunted this place, they had no need of men.

At the praetorium, Valerius was directed to a wing of lightly guarded cells by the warder, an affable man despite his gruffness, who when asked what he thought of his charge, Paul, replied, "Oh, I've got nothing personal against the Cilician. He's harmless, if you ask me. But the crowd he draws is a bit of a bother. You know, sir—locking them in while he preaches, and then letting all the rabble free when he's run out of wind for the day."

"You mean to say this prisoner is allowed to have audiences?"

"Aye, Centurion. The procurator Felix said it was all right. Nobody since has countermanded the order." He halted Valerius at an iron door. "You want to go inside?"

"No, just crack it a few inches so I can hear what is said."

"Very well. Call if they give you trouble. But I doubt you'll have any. This lot has more reason to fear their own kind than us Romans." The warder ambled down the corridor, lightly tapping his *flagellum* against the side of his leg as he went.

Briefly, Valerius peered inside the cell. He was unable to see the speaker from this vantage. But he could view the faces of several of the Christians who were gazing at Paul. Curiously, the expressions of these people filled Valerius with envy. He was not sure why. Leaning against the wall, he began listening to the accused Roman citizen from Tarsus:

"...If I speak in the tongues of men or even angels, but have no love, I am a noisy gong or a clanging cymbal. And if I can see the future, understand all mysteries and all knowledge, and if I have the faith to remove mountains but still have no love, I am nothing. I can give what I have to the poor. I can submit to executions, burning, martyrdom. But without love, this means nothing."

"What precisely is *love*?" a young Greek asked. Valerius could see him scribbling on a wax tablet.

"It is patient and kind. Love is never jealous or boastful, arrogant or rude. It doesn't insist on its own way. Nor is it irritable or resentful. It doesn't rejoice at wrong, but gladdens at what is right. Love bears all things, believes all things, hopes all things, endures all things."

"Then are we to believe that speaking in tongues, or making prophesies, or attaining knowledge, have no value?" the same astute-looking Greek asked.

"We are to understand that these things will pass away, Luke. But love never ends. Knowledge and prophesy are imperfect. When the perfect comes, the imperfect will pass away. When I was a child, I spoke as a child. I thought as a child. I reasoned as a child. When I became a man, I gave up my childish ways. Now we see by a mirror, darkly. But someday we will see all these things face-to-face and know them in fullness. But for now, understand this: There are three things that last: faith, hope and love. But the greatest of these is love."

The speaker fell silent as footfalls retreated down the corridor, almost at a run.

At first, Paul did not know what to think when the centurion commanding the escort of legionaries wriggled a tightly rolled slip of papyrus into his manacled hands. The Roman was careful to avert Paul's surprised gaze, and from this the Cilician had an inkling that the man might be trying to help him.

They entered the hall crowded with Jews and Romans. After more than a year to prepare for this day, Tertullus, the orator retained by the Sanhedrin, had no new evidence or arguments for the latest procurator, so Paul took the opportunity to unravel the tiny scroll. It was written in an inexpert Greek, although some of the words had been set down in big, square Aramaic characters, as if for emphasis:

> DANGER! Pressure on Festus to hand over you to SANHEDRIN. Plot at highest Jewish levels to kill you. Don't go JERUSALEM. As Roman citizen, invoke *provocatio*. SHALOM.
>
> A Noisy Gong

Paul swiveled around on his curule chair and nodded at the centurion, who remained expressionless.

". . . And so to conclude," Tertullus' voice welled up, "most illustrious Porcius Festus, the man Paul not only persists in teaching dangerous doctrines to the scandal of all pious men in this country, but also he has made no amends or apologies for the profanation of the sacred Temple of your worthiest subjects."

Festus waited as if hoping to hear a more substantial allegation, but Tertullus mopped his brow with a swatch of linen and looked for approval from Ananias and the other priests in attendance. "Is *that* the extent of the charges you make against this man?" the procurator asked.

"It is, noble Festus. What others could be more repugnant to the law?"

"Which law? This is an internal Jewish matter and does not concern Rome."

"But Paul's acts and words were to the detriment of public order and tranquillity, and those are the very reasons for the existence of the Empire."

Absently, Festus traced over his lips with a forefinger. "What does the accused say?"

Paul stood. "I have done nothing improper against the Temple or the law of Moses. Nor have I offended Caesar by violating his laws."

Festus had risen and appeared to be on the verge of adjourning the council when he became aware that Ananias was glaring at him. He sat again and addressed Paul almost congenially: "This entire matter has dragged on far too long. Your confinement is no more pleasing to us than it is you." Festus even went so far as to smile now. "Will you go to Jerusalem and be judged there—before me, naturally—regarding these things of which you are accused?"

Paul pressed his lips together to keep from smirking, then shrugged helplessly. His mysterious Roman friend had been right: Paul had to escape from Judea, and *provocatio* might be his only means of accomplishing that. It guaranteed the right of a Roman citizen to appeal—directly to the Emperor—against a magistrate's handling of his case. "I am already standing before an imperial tribunal, where I ought to be tried. To the Sanhedrin I have done no wrong, as the procurator knows very well. If I have committed some crime for which I deserve to die, I am not seeking to escape death. But if there is nothing to their charges, no one will give me up to them." Paul stared at Ananias as he said: "I appeal to Caesar."

The high priest blanched.

Festus gestured for the centurion to approach him and then he whispered in the man's ear.

"Yes," the officer said softly but loud enough so that Paul could hear, "his citizenship is confirmed by the records in Tarsus."

VI

CALEB put aside his annoyed expression long enough to take Ruth in his arms and kiss her. "Are you ready now for Aunt Corinna and me to see you up to the Janiculum?"

The little girl yawned.

Sarah stepped between Aquila and Priscilla, linking her arms through theirs. "I have been invited to spend the night here. It is too lonely at home without Valerius."

"Please yourself." Caleb handed his niece back to her mother. "We must rise earlier than usual tomorrow."

"Yes," Corinna said, "the school has taken on droves of Britannian slaves. Their masters found them useless for other work, so they handed them over to us."

Sarah's eyes became dolorous. "Rome is so large, so terrifying, to a slave at first."

"These Britons are too stupid to be frightened." Caleb helped Corinna wrap her *palla* around her head and shoulders. "They are the most primitive barbarians Serpenius has ever asked me to train. Only one in a hundred has any promise of becoming a decent gladiator. But I suppose they serve their purpose."

"Which is, my friend . . . ?" Aquila asked, unconsciously tidying up the scraps of canvas on his cutting table.

"If you'd ever find the stomach to attend the games, you would see for yourself. Scores of these northern fools hack at each other as they will. The people love it. I admit it that the spectacle can be amusing. But this should never be confused with serious combat undertaken by trained fighters. *That* has dignity. What these Britons do is buffoonery."

"How *Roman* you can sound, my Brother," Sarah said offhandedly.

Caleb turned and glowered at her. "Let me return to Judea and you will hear from Valerius, no doubt, how fond of Romans I am, especially their blood."

"Please, my friends," Aquila said. "All this talk of blood—"

"But you Christians drink blood. And eat flesh."

"You know better, Caleb," Priscilla said. "We eat bread and drink wine in memory of his last supper, when he revealed that he would give up his life for us . . . his flesh and blood."

"It must be the times that make us so quarrelsome." Aquila leaned out the front door and checked the darkened street. "Our frolicsome Emperor has set a miserable example for the young men of this city. Two of the awnings on this very shop, ripped down during the night for no good reason. And this is just in the last three months. A friend, a moneylender, was beaten senseless and left for dead by one of these roving bands."

"Why are you so appalled?" Caleb said with the same sarcastic tone that had colored his words all evening. "What we are witnessing is only the true Roman character revealing itself."

Corinna sighed wearily and pulled him by the hand toward the portal. "Let us be on our way before you include me in your tireless campaign against the forces of Rome. Farewell, all," she said over her shoulder.

"Good night!" Aquila called out to them. "The Lord protect both of you!"

The couple marched briskly, but out of step and in silence. Except for an occasional vegetable cart that rattled past, the streets were empty. They were skirting around the base of the Palatine Hill when Caleb reached across the space separating them and took her hand. "I would never do *that*," he declared.

"Do what?"

"Make war on you as I do your Empire."

She freed herself from his gentle clutch. "This must end, Caleb."

"I do not understand." He attempted to drape his arm around her, but she batted it down again. *"What?"* he asked.

"Your irritation of late. This impatience with me, your sister—even poor Aquila."

Caleb kept quiet.

"I have held my tongue too long for fear of a quarrel. But it was through fighting that I first earned my freedom. So I will now fight with you if I must."

"Short swords or tridents?"

"*Words*, Caleb. You have begun to punish those who love you."

He chuckled under his breath. "No one is more loyal to his wife, his family. Why would you even think of such a thing?"

"You blame us because you are not in Judea, slitting throats. That is not fair."

"Then who should I blame? Myself? Very well, I admit that I have been seduced by Rome."

"Seduced, nothing!" she snapped. "You are here by your own choosing. If not, go back to Judea. You have had enough money for weeks now."

They whisked past noisy *insulae*, each identical to the one the block before, each wreathed in the pungent smoke of charcoal fires. He counted twenty of the tenements before he spoke again. "If I go, what will you . . . ?" He could not finish.

"What will I do, Caleb?" She sighed once again. "Have you forgotten so soon?"

"Forgotten?"

"'*Where you are, Gaius, I, Gaia, will be.*'"

"Oh, yes," he said quietly.

"'*Oh, yes,*' you say, as if I had told you the Tiber flows down to the sea. I will not allow you to suffer my presence." She quickened her pace and moved out in front of him.

Caleb broke into a jog and caught one of her wildly swinging wrists. He drew her to a halt. "I have never suffered your presence. That is because I love you. And I have no wish to go to Judea alone. The pleasure will be in showing you my country . . . making it your home as well as mine." He could not see her eyes because of the darkness, and not knowing their expression made him anxious. "I will strive to put myself in a better humor."

She refused to say a word. The silhouette of her profile was completely still as she peered down the street.

"Perhaps it is true of me what I overheard at the school. A novice retiarius called me 'the old man' behind my back. My age, all those fights, must be catching up with me."

At last, she turned her face back toward him.

Caleb grinned. "And you lied to me. I had Serpenius check the spot in the back. My hair is thinning, as I suspected."

"Oh, stop this drivel," she said softly. "We will never get home at this rate. And I need your love tonight."

"I know a shortcut across this hill."

"You know Rome better than a Roman?"

"Sometimes . . . in some ways."

Grasping hands after a moment of fumbling in the blackness, they hurried up a narrow passageway of stairs that twisted across the face of the slope in a series of doglegs—and collided with a swarm of bodies rushing in the opposite direction. There were cries and grunts from young voices. Caleb and Corinna backed down the steps and stood in wide stances, waiting for his mass of limbs and hot breaths to advance on them again.

"Who are you there?" someone asked—a patrician, most likely, because of his disdainful tone. The small band also reeked of musk and loud perfumes. "Announce yourselves!"

Caleb and Corinna did not answer.

"Morosus!" the same imperious voice cried. "Where is that damned slave? I told him to hang back a bit, but not all the way to the Palatine. Morosus! Run fleet or you are dead!"

A glow of wavering orange light glanced around a bend in the passageway. A moment later, a torchbearer came panting into sight, and with this the silhouettes of the young men sprang up in sharp definition. The three youths who formed the vanguard of the party rushed down and assaulted the couple with more vociferousness than skill. Caleb hurled two of them against the tufa-stone wall, and Corinna fended off the third by using her hands as she would a short sword. She finally clouted her attacker in the tender place where shoulder joins neck, and the youth sank to the stairs, groaning.

Then Caleb's heart sank as he watched two men, not boys, stride down from the rear of the throng. They each bore a sword. Corinna and he had only their daggers with them.

"Hold, my dear praetorians," the young man who had first cried out said. "I recognize good training when I see it." He cautiously approached the couple, flanked by his guards and preceded by the distressed-looking torchbearer. "Do you know who I am?"

Despite the fact that he was masquerading tonight as a female prostitute, wearing a bright red wig and makeup as thick as plaster, Caleb and Corinna nodded. The man's famous sidewhiskers had betrayed him.

"Who taught you your art?" he inquired respectfully.

Corinna answered, for the emperor Nero had been staring at her as he spoke. "The *lanista* Serpenius and my husband, here, Metellus, a gladiator and a trainer of gladiators."

"Ah, also a champion of some renown. And you, then—
you are the noblewoman who took up with a circumcised retiarius"—Nero turned to his friends—"who resheathed himself
in a Roman name. Do you speak for yourself on occasion,
Metellus?"

"I do," Caleb said quietly but ominously.

"What does noble Metellus think of his wife slashing and
grunting in the arena?"

"It is the life she has chosen."

"Said with great liberality of spirit, yet also with a dispassion
that Seneca would admire." The rouged lips smiled at Corinna
again. "It would give me enormous pleasure to see you fight
in the circus, noble lady. Once more, who is your *lanista*?"

"Serpenius."

"Consider it arranged. Now, the hour is early and there is
much to be accomplished." Nero crawled up onto the back of
one of his fellows and spurred the youth forward as if he were
a horse. His band of revelers followed, abandoning their
wounded.

They ravaged shop after shop in the Subura ward of the
city: yanking down awnings, overturning stalls, smashing the
jars slung from poles that advertised the myriad wineshops.
Eventually, they made their way to the great portico of the
fishmongers. The catch had just been freighted up from Ostia,
and the youths fell upon it with glee, flinging the fishes out
into the street, wagering who could spin one the farthest. The
mongers appealed in vain to a *vigil*, who stood idly by, watching the carnival unfold after he had blown out his tallow lantern
so as not to draw attention to himself. He knew better than to
keep the Emperor from his fun.

The small forum was soon ankle-deep in silvery carcasses.
Yet, one shop owner was not wringing his hands. In fact, they
were planted on his hips as he surveyed the madcap scene and
chortled to himself. His curly black hair glistened in the torchlight. "Hail Caesar!" he cried out as the redheaded harlot whisked
past, giving a drunk boy a ride on a torn awning.

Nero halted and dropped the canvas. "How do you know
who I am?"

"No darkness can dampen the imperial light." The fishmonger was grinning hugely, his big teeth reflecting the torches.

"Now Neptune and I make a gift to the ruling divinity of Rome. Enter my humble shop. You must be famished after such vigorous sport. I offer you fresh sea bass—already in the pan with garlic, sweet butter, cloves and olives."

"You dare to invite your Emperor to supper?"

"That, Caesar, is the beauty of pleasure: It makes us daring. Have you ever known a do-gooder to be audacious?"

"Never." Nero sniffed the air and smiled at the delicious odors despite himself. He trailed the imposing monger inside the dimly lit shop. "What other pleasures in addition to bass do you offer?"

"There are boys and girls for hire in this neighborhood. It could delight me to treat you to them, Caesar."

"So there is money to be made in fish?"

"Oh, yes. To be spent too. I hate hoarding. It denies the flow of life. The magnificent juices of life—blood and semen—should never be dammed up. They were meant to rampage across our days."

Nero drew close to the man. "Your Emperor is graciously pleased to consider you a man after his own heart. What is your name?"

"Ofonius Tigellinus, at your service." He jiggled a heavy skillet over the charcoals with one of his powerful hands. "A euphonious name, would Your Holiness not agree? Euphonious Ofonius."

"Yes . . . the sound of it pleases me already."

Nero glared at each of them as they reclined on their dining couches: Acte, who as usual had nothing to say, and Octavia, who was outraged because Acte was present, and Britannicus, whose habitual expression of self-pity had solidified into a mask, and Seneca, who ate like a glutton despite his hypocritical ranting about moderation, and finally Tigellinus, the only one present who gave the Emperor pleasure. The former fishmonger offered him a conspiratorial wink.

"Do you have any idea who you are?" Nero asked him.

"No, Caesar, I have never thought to ask myself."

Seneca winced, then filled his mouth with roe.

"You, my beloved Ofonius, are my Glaucus."

Acte held up her cup, and a slave dashed to her side with the wine pitcher. "Who's he?"

"Oh, woman, your lack of good breeding appalls me . . .

but your attempts to breed delight me!" Nero, joined by Tigellinus, laughed uproariously, then sobered himself and dried his eyes on his blaze-red tunic. "*Glaucus*, my dear woman, was a humble Greek fisherman transformed by Poseidon into a demigod—a triton."

"What's a triton?"

"Oh, Jupiter." Nero rolled his eyes. "It is a perfectly divine creature that is half human in form—and half fish."

"And Tigellinus is one of those?"

"Well, Acte, I can assure you he's quite fishy from the waist down, if that's what you're asking."

Again, the two men guffawed until tears came to their eyes. Then Nero glared at Britannicus for his refusal to add his mirth to theirs. "You must drink some wine, my Stepbrother. It will give you cheer."

"Thank you, I prefer water."

"Oh, I see," Nero said prissily, and began eating olives one by one, squinting as if something were not quite right about their taste.

"What does Caesar see?" Britannicus asked after a moment's hesitation.

"You are afraid your Emperor is going to poison you. I find that terribly insulting, especially after going out of my way to have a special hot mulled wine prepared for you. Well, I think you need a drop to lift your spirits." Nero turned to Tigellinus. "He forgets that his father, the unforgettable Claudius, appointed me to be his tutor, his mentor, his friend in all enterprises great and small."

"Noble Britannicus," Tigellinus said, "your merriment would add so much to our own. Why not drink? Life is too brief to be spent so down at the mouth."

"Yes, too brief," Britannicus murmured.

"Very well. I will swallow the insult and call for my taster." Nero waved for a timid figure standing in the vestibule to come forth. "Pour this idiot a cup. Then we can all hold our breaths and see if he drops."

The slave brought the cup to his lips with tremulous hands. But he could not force himself to take a sip until Nero bellowed at him, "Drink or die!" The taster downed the warm wine as if it were quicksilver. Then he wiped his mouth and waited, his eyes frantic as he listened to every swish and gurgle of his belly. One minute elapsed—and the slave was still on his feet.

"See?" Nero announced. "Harmless and wholesome. But perhaps my stepbrother would prefer to wait awhile longer. Some poisons, like some men, are slow to anger."

"I am not angry, Caesar," Britannicus said.

"Then what are you?"

The young man's chin sank down into his couch rugs. "Weary of this life."

Nero suppressed a grin and looked askance at Tigellinus, who had even less self-control and had to clamp his teeth together to keep from giggling.

"Don't let them bait you in this way," Octavia suddenly said to her brother.

"You have no right to say anything in my presence! You are an adulteress!"

Octavia was speechless for a moment. "I beg the Emperor's pardon?"

"Oh, aye, do beg it—not that you'll get it. Do you think I'm blind and don't know what you're doing when you're closeted with Seneca, here, pretending to study philosophy?"

"This joke is in very bad taste, Caesar," Seneca said.

Octavia had taken hold of Britannicus by the shoulder fold of his toga. "At least have the courage to defend my honor!"

"Oh, but that would be dangerous, wouldn't it?" Nero sneered. "That might offend the Emperor. The good and kind Emperor who has prepared mulled wine for his winsome stepbrother. Drink, Britannicus. This taster will outlive us all. Drink!"

Britannicus finally took the half-empty cup from the slave. He found the liquid surprisingly hot and nearly gagged.

"Oh, what a shirker you are," Nero whined. "Cool it with some water, there."

Reflexively, Britannicus reached for the pitcher on the table beside him. Only after he had diluted the wine and taken three hefty draughts did he begin to wonder if it was the same urn of water that had been there all evening, or a fresh one.

"I admire a trusting nature," Tigellinus said. "For is it not said, 'If your son asked you for a fish, would you hand him a serpent?'"

"That's lovely. Who's it from—Aristophanes?"

"No, Caesar—the unkillable slave Christus, around whom a cannibalistic cult now centers. I have heard this and other stories from a Christian who abandoned the cult when he was asked to eat human flesh. They eat each other, you know, and not just necrophagously, if you catch my meaning. They fondle each other with no concern for incest. Sister with brother, mother with son, father with daughter—"

"That, I'm afraid, is a slander. I know differently."

"Oh, damn you, Seneca!" Nero raged. "Whenever a thing sounds the least bit interesting, as this Christus business does, you have to throw cold water on it!" These words seemed to remind the Emperor of something. He glanced at Britannicus. "My dear Stepbrother, are you well?"

Britannicus had been gazing at the floor. With difficulty, he raised his wavering head and tried to answer, but could not form the words with his quivering lips. Nor could he apparently focus his eyes on Nero's face, for the young man was squinting.

"Britannicus? *Britannicus?*"

Slowly, he turned toward Octavia and then tumbled off his couch onto the hard tiles with a smacking sound.

"No one touch him!" Nero ordered. "He often has these seizures and always come right out of them with no ill effect. Just ignore him until he finds the good manners to rejoin our excellent company."

VII

Its square sail billowing, the coastal merchant galley was running north before a brisk wind, and the Ionian Greek captain assured Valerius that they would reach the harbor at Sidon by nightfall. The centurion unfettered his prisoner and let the man stroll up and down the cramped aisles between baskets of Judean dates, bales of Egyptian cotton and crated glazing from the workshops of Alexandria. After his long confinement, Paul obviously reveled in the cool air and amber sunlight of autumn. But, perhaps more than anything else, the sensation of motion was delighting the Christian.

It had cheered Valerius as well to watch the seawall at Caesarea grow smaller and smaller, then vanish behind a headland. He was eager to go home, although he had spent less than a month in Judea.

Festus had tasked Valerius and three legionaries to escort the prisoner to Rome. The procurator had been willing to part with his adjutant only because he hoped that the centurion, who was married to a Jewess and therefore would have an insight into these strange people, might be able to explain this ineffable case to the emperor Nero. Festus was so confused by the affair, he had sent no letter with Valerius and instead entrusted the man "to make our position clear to those who might care." Then, betraying his eagerness to be rid of Paul, the procurator ordered Valerius to sail at once, although no ship in Caesarea was bound directly for Italy.

At the time of his departure, Valerius believed that he had a solid grasp of the facts that were pertinent to Paul's case, but Festus would have not been pleased had he known the conclusions his adjutant had reached.

Shortly after he invoked his right of *provocatio*, Paul had been visited by Herod Agrippa II and his sister, Berenice, whose suspected incestuous relationship had been confirmed

when the tetrarch, in an absentminded moment while listening
to the Christian teacher, had begun stroking her thigh with his
jeweled fingers. Yet, despite such unsavory displays, the meeting had given Valerius the chance to hear Paul tell his own
story from his early days in Tarsus and Jerusalem as a Pharisee,
through that watershed day on the road to Damascus, and up
to his present difficulties with the Sanhedrin. Young Agrippa's
only remark after this testimony, which had deeply moved
Valerius, was: "Why, you could have been set free if you had
not appealed to Caesar." Hearing this, Paul had smiled at the
centurion: His own followers had corroborated the existence
of a fanatical plot against his life. Valerius had decided that,
whatever the cost to himself, he would let no harm befall the
Cilician. He had begun to equate the prisoner with his own
silent hopes.

Hands clasped behind his back, the centurion now approached Paul where he sat in the bow spray, smiling like a
child at each stinging wash that flew over the prow. "I think
this voyage begins quite nicely," he said.

"And later on?" Valerius asked, sitting beside him.

"That is in the Lord's hands, Centurion. But I have no fear."

"Nor I."

Paul nodded, then looked westward out to sea. "I tire of
calling you Centurion—someone to whom I owe so much. Do
you mind . . . ?"

"No, of course not. My name is Julius Valerius Licinius."

"May I call you Julius?"

"No one else does. But then, again, you are like no one I
have ever known. Please do: It makes me feel like a new man."

"I suspect that you are very close to becoming one. You
seem to understand my situation much better than the procurator
you serve. I am delighted . . . but puzzled, Julius."

"Well, I have a certain advantage over Festus. My wife is
Jewish."

"Ah, splendid. Where from?"

"Jerusalem."

"What family?"

Valerius looked sheepish for a moment. "I'm not sure. Her
mother was named Leah. And her brother is Caleb. He's a
gladiator in Rome, but goes by a Roman name."

"Amazing," Paul said. "This is the second instance in which
I have heard of my old friend from *Rabban* Gamaliel's school.

Then you must know Aquila and Priscilla as well."

"Yes," Valerius laughed. "But how . . . ?"

"In Corinth, I stayed with them. But none of this is as incredible as it first seems. I must know every Jewish Christian in the world. It is the gentile converts who have become too numerous to recall by name. Well, in Rome I will enjoy a number of reunions, won't I?"

"Yes, and I want Caleb to hear your teachings."

"He is still the firebrand?"

Valerius nodded, smiling.

"There is the matter of a more immediate reunion, Julius. It would mean a great deal to me if I might go ashore tonight at Sidon. Long ago, I persecuted the Greek Jews of Jerusalem. Some of them fled to Sidon and founded a church there. In a sense, I suppose I founded that church, if you will pardon the backhanded compliment I give myself. But nevertheless, before I go on to Rome it would hearten me to visit these brothers of mine."

"On one condition, Paul."

"Yes?"

"That I go with you."

"As my guard; I understand completely."

"No," Valerius said, "*not* as your guard."

The ship remained in Sidon not one night but three while cargo was unloaded and loaded, more sand brought aboard to give the vessel enough ballast for its rougher voyages of late fall, and *urinatoris* hired to dive to the bottom of the harbor to recover two amphorae of expensive wine from Damascus that had fallen overboard. Valerius took Paul ashore on each of these evenings and stood at the rear of the courtyard of the Christian house like any other follower who had come to hear the Cilician. "Take heed unto yourselves," Paul said that last meeting before they sailed again, "and to all the flock, of which the Holy Spirit has made you shepherd, to feed the church of the Lord which he bought with his own blood. Wolves will come among you, not sparing the flock. Men will arise among you, speaking perverse things, trying to draw away disciples to follow them and not the Lord. Be watchful. And, in your labors, remember always to help the weak, for Jesus said: 'It is more blessed to give than receive.'"

They were sailing under the lee of Cyprus, taking advantage of the breeze that blew off the island at night, when Valerius decided to ask Paul about the words he had spoken in Sidon. "You mentioned that it's better to give than take in this world."

Paul was staring up, engrossed by a starry sky. "Yes, Julius. What did you think of that?"

Valerius was silent for a few seconds. "Is it necessary that Christians give up all that they own?"

"When it interferes with their following Jesus in the single-minded way he demanded of us. What do you possess that is more dear to you than your soul?"

Valerius met the star-flecked eyes of the man. "Nothing."

When the ship docked in Myra, a Lycian port on the coast of Asia Minor, Valerius made inquiries along the quay to locate a faster vessel, preferably one rigged to run against the wind and not just before it. An Egyptian grain ship from Alexandria was departing for Italy the next morning, so the centurion transferred his charge and settled him in a dank, cramped cabin. The galley was heavily loaded with sacks of corn, plus nearly three hundred passengers, so Valerius' legionaries were forced to find sleeping space on the exposed decks.

As they skirted the isle of Rhodes, tacking against a stiff, chilly wind that whipped out of the northeast, Paul noticed Valerius' distracted expression. "What makes my friend Julius look so somber?"

"I was remembering Tiberius; he once exiled himself to Rhodes."

"Did you actually know him?"

"Oh, yes. I was on detached service to the palace guard for years. I have known them all: Tiberius, Caligula, Claudius and now Nero."

"What is your impression of our most recent emperor?"

Valerius checked over his shoulder before saying, "What is true of him can be said of all of them: They behaved decently long enough to raise our hopes that here, at last, was an honorable Caesar. Then they abandoned all pretense. If they did right, it was always for the wrong reasons. And when they were wrong, it was purely for the evil pleasure of it."

"Do you honestly believe that most Romans put stock in the divinity of emperors?"

Valerius shrugged. "I don't know. I can only speak for myself."

"And what does Julius say?"

"A good emperor can represent the dignity of the state. But

he can never be God." Then Valerius smiled to himself. "Yet, a bad emperor is every bit a demon, isn't he?"

Paul smoothed his unruly beard and laughed.

For days on end, the wind continued to rail against the ship. Finally, the captain gave up trying to make any progress along the northern shore of Crete—the usual trade route for Egyptian grain ships—and instead steered along the southern coast of the island. He convened a council in his quarters, which included Valerius' presence because the centurion was on imperial business and the captain undoubtedly wanted to remain in the good graces of the Judean governor. Valerius, as a matter of habit, had Paul accompany him; he ignored the glares the officers of the ship gave the Cilician Jew.

"Well, this is how I see it," the captain began. "We've been sailing two days on the protected side of Crete, and are still having a hard push of it. I might as well put these bloody islands astern of us and cross the open sea as soon as possible. Tonight, we'll anchor in the bay at Fair Havens, but only as long as it takes for this gale to slacken. We're too close to the *cessation* for my liking, so I insist: no dawdling in Fair Havens."

"Forgive a landsman," Valerius asked, "but what is the *cessation*?"

"It's this way, Centurion: Right now we're in danger enough as is. But, from the ides of November to the ides of March, Neptune is almost certain to punish anyone who plies his waves."

"I quite agree, Captain," Paul said without being asked.

All eyes in the cabin turned toward him.

Unsure of the prisoner's status, the captain decided to remain civil. "Do you, now?"

"This is the Jewish month of *Tishri*—October to us Romans. I mention it only because there is a saying about a holiday called *Sukkoth* that falls in this month: 'From the time you bind your palm branches, keep your legs bound.' We would do well to keep safe harbor. Winter at Fair Havens is my advice."

Before the captain could rebuff the outspoken prisoner, Valerius asked, "Is there another harbor on this side of the island?"

"Yes, Phoenix. But we're days away from that anchorage with the wind dead against us like this. I'll be satisfied if we make Fair Havens today."

"We shall," Paul said quietly. "But too soon."

His words created an uneasy silence in the cabin.

And, aided by a breeze that blew out of the south and was deceptively balmy for the lateness of the season, the ship reached the bay by early afternoon. But the weather seemed so favorable that the captain decided to push on toward Phoenix. The crew gave thanks for this mild change in the wind, when it unexpectedly shifted once again. *"Euraquilo!"* a sailor cried from the uppermost rigging, pointing toward the mountains of Crete down which a dusty gale was roaring. This northeaster rocked and buffeted the ship, and the timbers of the ponderous vessel began groaning so loudly that the captain gave the order to undergird. A half dozen seamen who had diving experience stripped down to their loincloths and, over the next hour, secured four hawsers under and then completely around the hull. These ropes, one deckhand explained to Valerius and Paul, would prevent the weight of the vessel from breaking its own back. "But we still could be blown into the Syrtis," the man said.

"What is that?" Valerius asked.

"The shoals off the coast of Africa."

"Aren't we still hundreds of miles north of there?"

"Aye, Centurion, but it will take no time for us to fly south when swept along by the hand of Neptune."

An attempt was made to lower the sea anchor, but the crew watched in horror as the line, which was as thick as a man's wrist, suddenly unraveled in a frenzy of mist and snapped. After this, the ship was scurried helplessly along before the growing tempest. Squalls overtook it and drenched the deck with cold rain. So much water was cresting over the parapet that rimmed the main deck, the scuppers could not leak the excess back into the sea. Valerius and Paul found themselves knee-deep in foam.

"We will not die, will we?" Valerius shouted in the man's ear.

Paul smiled back at him, and the centurion shrugged to show that he was unafraid.

"Lend a hand here!" a seaman cried to them. Together, they hoisted a sack of wet sand over the side.

"Why are we doing this?"

"Got to lighten the ship! We're being swamped!"

Within a few hours, it appeared that the jettisoning of the

ballast had not been enough. The crew cut free the mainsail,
which had already been lashed to its spar, and—assisted by
Valerius, Paul and any other passengers who were not too sick
to stand—lowered the drenched canvas into the huge swells.

The centurion and his prisoner huddled with the ship's officers under the faint glow of a gimballed oil lamp. Paul looked
amused when the captain asked him in a croak, "What do you
think will happen?" Prior to this, the man had not revealed his
despair in any way.

"I don't wish to say, Captain, that you ought to have listened
to my words back at Crete before it became necessary for you
to dump all your valuable cargo over the side."

"Wish or not, you've said it."

"I want everyone to take heart."

"Why?" one of the officers demanded.

"We will survive this storm, but the ship will not."

"How do you know this?" It was Valerius now who could
not resist asking.

"It has been shown to me that I will stand before Caesar."

At dawn, the most grizzled-looking sailor of the lot remarked to Valerius, "I can smell land."

"Where are we, then?"

"Only the gods know, but we're near something, believe
me."

"Could it be the Syrtis?"

The sailor dipped his head once, gravely.

Paul then rested his hand on Valerius' forearm. "We should
go below and eat something."

"I'm not hungry."

"Even so, we show our faith in the outcome of this by eating.
And we will need our strength."

After nightfall, the wind abated enough for the crew to begin
taking soundings. Clouds flitted across a wan moon, and the
captain's voice drifted across the deck to the men posted on
the prow. "How deep is it now?"

"Fifteen, sir . . ." And a moment later: ". . . Fourteen!"

"Then drop sea anchors on a rising bottom—all four of
them."

One of the crew groused, "This had better be it. These are
the only anchors we've got left, and if the blow rises again,
we'll lose them."

"We will have no further need of them," Paul said.

Valerius stood closer to the Cilician. "I envy you your certainty, Paul."

"It is yours as well—for the asking."

"But you have *seen* his power."

"And you have not, Julius?"

At first light, which came with agonizing slowness through a gray sky, Valerius' senior legionary sidled up to him and whispered, "Centurion . . . if this truly is a landfall, we'll have to kill him."

"Kill . . . ?"

"The prisoner. He might escape in the confusion."

"What sort of man are you?"

"One who doesn't fancy falling on his sword because a Jew strolled out of his custody."

"Land!" a sailor cried, pointing at a white streak between the lead-colored sky and sea that Valerius realized was the froth from combers that were breaking onto a shrouded beach.

"Cast off anchors!" the captain ordered. "Loosen the rudder bands! Foresail up to the wind!"

Valerius called out to the man: "Your intentions, sir?"

"I'm going to run her aground, Centurion."

VIII

THE Emperor glanced up from the gladiatorial combat at the young couple entering the gallery beside his, but his eyes did not immediately dart back to the clash in the arena.

Tigellinus, sprawling on the couch closest to Nero's, began to chuckle under his breath.

"What?" Nero asked in mock anger.

"I know what Caesar is thinking."

"Do you, now? Then tell him before he tosses you down onto the sands and lets one of these otherwise useless Britons chop you to pieces."

Tigellinus lifted his chin in the direction of the handsome woman who was now sharing a bench with her husband. "My beloved Emperor is thinking that Poppaea Sabina is much too pretty and feminine for the likes of his friend, Otho."

Nero burst into laughter. "You can unravel me like a scroll, you rake."

Octavia, who had buried her face in her couch rugs because of the bloody spectacles on the sands below, now opened an eye on the Emperor.

Nero impatiently waved for Burrus, his praetorian prefect, to approach him. "Ask noble Poppaea to come here." While the commander of the guard hurried off on his errand, the Emperor said, half giggling, to the elegant patrician who always introduced Nero at his public performances, "Dear Petronius, I'm relying on you to entertain her husband while I look into *other* matters."

"My pleasure, Caesar. You have come to the right man with your request. I find young Otho . . . stimulating."

"So do I," Octavia said defiantly. And as Poppaea's husband sauntered into the imperial gallery she eagerly gestured for him to join her on her wide couch. "Here, noble Otho."

Ignoring the fact that his wife had been herded by the praetorian prefect into Nero's embrace, Otho smiled at the Empress. "Thank you, Octavia . . . such a favor. I am honored."

"Oh, you deserve this and more. You have always been such a valued friend of Caesar. Hasn't he, Nero?"

Briefly, the Emperor took his hand off Poppaea's womanly hip, reluctantly disengaged himself from her eyes and muttered, "Oh, I do agree . . . yes, certainly. How would you care for the proconsulship of Syria?"

Otho's mouth was gaping. "Caesar, you stun me with this honor. Syria, one of the most prominent of your domains—"

"Oh, wait. . . ." Nero frowned and conferred with Burrus and Tigellinus for several seconds. "We already have somebody worthy there. How would you like Lusitania?"

Otho was far less ebullient than before. "Caesar, I don't know what to say."

"Well, do you want to be governor of Lusitania or not?"

"How soon does Caesar want me to take over the administration of—"

"Immediately, my friend." Resting his cheek against Poppaea's shoulder, Nero caught Burrus' eye. "Draft my decree, Prefect, and see Otho to Ostia at once. Lusitania can ill afford to be without him."

"But what of a ship to convey him?"

"Commandeer a grain barge for all I care; just make certain my new governor arrives there in time."

"In time for what, Caesar?" Otho asked meekly.

"Just *in time!*" Nero exploded. Then, to demonstrate that he was not about to be disconcerted by the shocked expressions of everyone in his gallery, Nero extended his spindly arm toward the arena below. "What is going on down there?" He sighed loudly as Charon, the mythical ferryman for the dead, struck a prostrate Briton on the head with a maul to make certain the vanquished gladiator was not feigning death, then attached hooks to the corpse and dragged it away. "Yes, yes," Nero groaned, "I've seen dozens of Britons butchered today, but not one of them was dispatched with style. Have their *lanista* show himself."

A few moments later, a Numidian was standing serenely before the Emperor's gallery.

"Who are you?" Nero asked.

"Serpenius, Caesar."

The Emperor's eyes widened. "Oh, yes. Don't you have a special treat for me today?"

"I do."

"Then let's get on with it. Pit a *real* Roman against the best fighter of these outlanders."

Serpenius could not suppress a thin smirk. "As Caesar desires."

There was a fanfare of trumpets, and Corinna promenaded out onto the red-soaked sands, her helmet tucked under her arm and her flaxen hair tumbling down over the back of her cuirass. A moment later, a Britannian youth marched to her side. Heatwaves shimmered up off the sun-warmed blood as the gladiators saluted Nero with their weapons and shouted, "Hail Caesar! Those who are about to die salute you!"

The Emperor chortled at the determined visage of the female Thracian. He raised his wine cup in her honor. This gesture silenced the few outcries being made against her appearance, and he sprawled again, burrowing his face in Poppaea's throat to deliver a kiss there. She suffered his affection without a word, although her eyes kept gravitating toward Octavia's stricken features. Nero looked up again with the first sounds of crashing iron.

The Briton exhibited courage and energy as he charged around the arena, wielding his trident and net. Still, his nimble advances were invariably checked by Corinna, who benefited from greater experience.

Then, seconds into the combat, a decisive instant came and went, with no blood being drawn. The Briton had just hurled his net, missing his prey at the same time the tips of his trident touched the ground. The youth immediately realized his error. His mouth could be seen grimacing in the shade of his helmet: He was anticipating the fall of her short sword. He was defenseless.

Yet, Corinna backed off, returning his life to him with this slight withdrawal.

The Briton said nothing, for they were within earshot of the Emperor, but his gratitude shone from his face. Only the most astute spectators understood what had transpired in the blinking of an eye, and they appreciated the noble gesture for what it was.

"Lady Corinna!" Nero's sarcastic voice wafted down to her. "Strike the wild man dead for my dear father!" By this, the

Emperor meant that she should commemorate Claudius' conquest of Britannia. Resolutely, she kept her gaze on the young *retiarius*. She had learned to let nothing distract her—not even the gore that littered the arena. It was not difficult for her to disregard the wine-bloated face that was leering down at her from the imperial box.

Then, with curious detachment, she watched as the net flowed out from the hand of the Briton. It did not flash at her, but instead slowly mushroomed over her head until the sky was nothing but a dark mesh descending to entrap her. *Those who are about to die,* a voice within her whispered.

But suddenly, incredibly, the sky was once again its washed-out blue. The retiarius had snapped his wrist backward at the last possible instant before ensnaring her. He fended off her swift counterblow with the handle of his trident—and winked.

Yet, with his mounting weariness, the Briton grew more careless. It became impossible for her not to take advantage of his recklessness. If the crowd had any suspicion that they were shamming, it would be death for both fighters, regardless of their previous aggressiveness.

Then the young man made a clumsy jab with his trident, leaving himself open to attack. Corinna struck him alongside the head with the flat of her sword, and the Briton collapsed to the sands, moaning.

The crowd was riotous with approval: It had been the first decent struggle of the day.

She pressed her sandal against the fallen man's chest and hoisted her sword high in the air. Then she peered up at the imperial gallery, but during the combat the sun had crept over the edge of the huge awning, and Nero's hand signal was lost in the glare.

The crowd, which had been chanting "Spare him . . . spare him!" now burst into wild applause, which gradually died away.

Nero's cackle came down to her. "Well, it would appear the good lady *wants* to taste the wild man's blood."

She then realized that the Emperor had given a thumbs-up. "No, Caesar, let my worthy opponent live."

"So be it." Audibly, Nero took a deep breath so he could project his next words to those in the highest benches. "The courage of this woman has made me all the more eager to honor the virtues of another woman—my beloved mother. Later this month I will venture to Baiae for the Festival of Minerva, which

Agrippina and I shall celebrate as one supplicant. May I tell the great matron I bear love from you, the people of Rome?"

The respectful cheer came mostly from the patricians nearest the Emperor.

Corinna strode from the arena to much louder applause. Caleb waited to embrace her.

"I can do nothing meaningful as long as she lives," Nero said within the privacy of the drawn curtains. Then, his face pensive, he listened to the wheels of his sumptuous carriage clatter over the uneven stones of the road. "I thought it was Acte I wanted. And now Poppaea Sabina seems so desirable to me. But whichever I finally choose, my mother will stand in the way and insist that I remain married to Octavia. It is not enough that I have forced the she-wolf into seclusion: My mother continues to snarl at me from her den at Antium."

Tigellinus groaned pleasurably as he stretched on his couch. "Then what does Caesar have in store for noble Agrippina—a drop of poison?"

"No, that's out of the question. It would be greeted with suspicion—especially after Britannicus died at my table. And I know for a fact that she has fortified herself against it by taking small doses over many years. The woman *is* poison, my dear friend."

"This begins to sound like a considerable challenge."

"Oh, it is. But I shall meet it." His own cup dry, Nero borrowed Tigellinus' and drank thoughtfully. "You have some fair acquaintance with the construction of boats, don't you?"

"Some," the former fishmonger said.

"Good. While I'm entertaining my mother, I'd like you to supervise some work I have already commissioned. You may consider this to be the first task of your new office."

"What office, Caesar?"

"Burrus has grown quite tiresome, don't you think?"

"Naturally."

"So I would like you to command the praetorian guard. Just don't wear the poor boys out... if you know what I mean."

"I will make a point of it, my Emperor."

Nero burst into laughter and was quickly joined by Tigellinus.

• • •

When the evening was done and even the more lively revelers had retired to their couches, Nero escorted Agrippina down the long flight of stairs to the quay, where she expected to board her boat and be rowed back up the coast to Antium. Her eyes glistened as she studied her son: He had not been more affectionate toward her in years. She had almost come to believe that the rift that had formed between them would never be bridged again. Still, she had not regretted placing him on the Throne of Augustus. Long ago, she had asked a diviner about her son's prospects, and he had foretold that Nero would become Emperor—but would also kill his mother. Without a moment's hesitation, Agrippina had said, "Let him kill me, as long as he becomes Emperor!" Now, it was doubly sweet that Nero was rewarding her self-sacrifice with kindness.

"Beloved Mother, it was a joy to have you here at this, my favorite villa. Rome makes me so irritable. And no one makes me more so than that hypocrite Seneca, condemning wealth, and all the while he holds the deeds to more estates than we do. I am relieved he has gone into retirement."

"Why, this is not my boat," Agrippina said.

"No, and I insist that you take one of my own. It was suggested to me that yours is old and not seaworthy." He embraced her before she could protest. "Baiae is a lovely place to relax, isn't it? We must meet here again soon. But next time I don't want this gang of swillers and gorgers pestering us. Just mother and son. Alone." He kissed her amorously.

"You *do* love me, don't you?"

Briefly, his eyes were sad. But then they became cold again. Not even the amber light of the torches could make them seem warm. "That goes without saying."

Agrippina was assisted down into the boat. She refused the offer of a couch and instead stood beside the steersman. "Farewell, my son." She watched Nero's silhouette grow smaller and smaller until the quay was swallowed by darkness.

There was faint starshine, and beneath it the sea shone black and smooth. Whenever the oars were lifted out of the water, thousands of pearls trickled off the paddles and danced against the surface. Sighing contentedly, Agrippina wrapped herself in her arms. Then, quite distinctly, she heard her long-dead brother, Caligula, whisper her name. She spun on the steersman. "Did you dare to call me by my name?"

His hands froze on the tiller. "No, my lady, I said nothing."

She glared at her slaves and attendants. "Which of you just spoke?"

There followed a dozen denials from the shadows.

"I will not be lied to! Now, which of you tricksters—"

Agrippina was hurled to the deck. She rolled over onto her back and shouted at the steersman, "You fool! You've run us up on a reef!"

Incredibly, the sailor said, "No, you great pampered bitch, I've run *you* up on a reef." Then he kicked off his sandals and dived over the shoreward gunwale, his splash raining back over Agrippina. Looking forward, she saw that the bow had split open like a walnut shell. The boat, she realized, had not struck anything: It had been rigged to fall apart.

"Help the Emperor's mother!" one of her slaves was screaming. "Help *me*!"

Agrippina understood the fullness of her son's treachery when one of the sailors, obviously mistaking the slave for herself in the confusion and darkness, brought down his oar on the girl's head, silencing her.

"I've done her!" he cried to his confederates. "Let's swim for it, lads!"

Agrippina rose to a crouch. Water was now lapping around the hem of her *stola*. She wrestled out of the weighty outer garments and, clad only in her light *tunica*, slipped over the side.

A moment later, she glanced back to watch the two halves of the hull capsize outward, then vanish beneath the surface. Most of her retinue could not swim and were crying pathetically for help. She ignored the cries and began pulling for the nearby shore.

There were no waves that night, and she walked up onto the shingly beach without having to struggle against the surf. Nevertheless, her exhaustion forced her to lie down at the waterline, where she remained, vomiting salt water, until distant male voices convinced her that Nero's praetorians were combing the shore for her body. She hurried in the opposite direction, past a small fishing village that had been alerted to the disaster and was flecked with numerous torches, and finally out onto the marshy tidelands, where no lights shone.

Agrippina knew she would have to hide until Nero came to believe that the sea had claimed his mother's corpse forever.

After that, her difficulty lay in finding a way to contact Burrus. When Pallas had fallen from grace, she had been left with the praetorian prefect as her only ally. And she did not entirely trust him. She trusted no one now.

The air flowing in off the sea was clammy and made her shiver. But she refused to weep. Her rage would not let her admit such weakness.

After wading through knee-deep water for some time, she was surprised to smell wood smoke. Following this comforting scent, she came to a speck of dry land on which stood a small, round hut. The smoke was rising out of an opening in its thatched roof.

Agrippina could not decide whether or not to make her presence known. But a clamorous dog tethered to a stake at the portal convinced her not to linger outside. She crept up to the hut and called for someone to silence the animal.

A friendly voice cried out in greeting.

The old fisherman within wrapped her in a dirty blanket and gave her hot wine that was half turned to vinegar. " . . . Why, it's a question of workmanship, lady. Things nowadays aren't made as well as they were in the time of Augustus. When it's light, I'd like to show you my boat."

"I want no one to know I'm here."

"Of course. I am sorry I can't give you better hospitality. But you see how things are. A poor man is not used to receiving visits from the nobility."

"You'll get your reward."

The fisherman's dog began barking again.

Agrippina stiffened. "Who can it be?"

"Perhaps no one. My Rusticus is getting old. He was once a good watchdog, truly. But now his own senses can trick him. And he often barks at nothing—ghosts . . . mice in the dry reeds at night."

"Agrippina!" a voice cried outside. "If you are inside, come out—unless you want it reported that you had to be dragged by the hair to your death!"

"Oh, good Jupiter!" the fisherman moaned, gently touching her shoulder with his trembling hand. "Who would speak such words?"

"Assassins sent by my son." She smiled defiantly, then rose from the fire and strolled past the yowling dog into the midst of a dozen torches. She located the centurion and leveled her eyes on his. "I know my son is not responsible. He would never order his own mother's death."

This had been one last attempt to save herself. She was hoping that, if she showed enough nerve, the officer might lose his and decide instead to escort her back to Nero's presence. She believed that she could convince her son to spare her.

But the centurion remained tight-lipped.

"Very well." She then framed her hands around the place over her womb. "Strike here."

IX

In the last light of day, Paul carried his bundle of brushwood back toward the beach. The sands were dotted orange with fires, around which huddled those fortunate enough to have survived the swim that morning across the turbulent shallows. Offshore, the ship lay athwart a hidden shoal, its back broken by the waves.

The captain had courted tears each time he gazed out at the derelict that had once been his proud merchant ship. "We are fortunate to have reached Malta. The people of this island are known for their compassion." And, true to his words, the natives had soon appeared bearing food, drink, smoldering embers from their hearths and kindly spoken words, although only the ship's officers understood their Phoenician dialect.

Two Maltese were jabbering to the captain when Paul arrived back at the fire with his fresh supply of ebony-colored sticks. Valerius nodded his thanks to the Cilician for not betraying his trust and running off into the wilds. Laying down his burden, Paul saw that one branch was still clinging to his tunic sleeve. He was reaching over to pick it off when the faggot stirred to life and wiggled farther up his arm.

Stumbling backward, the Maltese began screeching in horror.

"Viper!" the captain cried. "They say it's deadly!"

Slowly Paul lowered his arm to the level of the ground, and the serpent slithered away.

The Maltese addressed Paul in reverent tones.

"What are they saying?" the Cilician asked the captain.

"At first they thought you were a murderer, because you are being attended by a centurion. But now they see that you are a god and the centurion is charged with protecting you."

"Please tell them that I am not a god. But if I am able to

311

spend any time on their hospitable island, I will make the one
true God known to them."

The captain exchanged several long phrases with the grinning Maltese, then said to Paul, "They think it would be an
honor to worship you, the one god who vipers will not bite."

Shaking his head, Paul turned to Valerius. "Do you see
what a blessing the Empire is to the spreading of the gospel,
Julius?"

The centurion was taken aback. "I don't quite understand."

"What if every people in the Empire were like these and
spoke only their own language instead of Latin and Greek? It
would take forever to make the news known."

That evening, the plight of the survivors on the windswept
northeast coast of the island was reported to the Roman governor. At daybreak, Publius Caprasius dispatched a handful of
soldiers to guide them back to his praetorium. A round-bellied
man with an infectious laugh, he feted the shipwrecked officers
in his sparse private quarters. He accepted Paul as one of their
number without giving Valerius, who had brought him along,
so much as a sideward glance.

"You're all in luck," Caprasius said. "Another ship was
stranded here during the navigation *cessation*. It will sail for
Puteoli shortly before the ides of March."

"I hope it's in better shape than mine." The captain raised
his cup for it to be filled the third time. "What figurehead does
it bear?"

"The *Twin Brothers*."

"Castor and Pollux," the captain said forlornly, "of the con-
stellation Gemini—good fortune against bad weather. I should
have named my ship that."

Valerius tried to brighten the mood in the chamber. "You
seem to be at home here with the Maltese, Publius Caprasius."

"Oh, yes. Pleasures are few and simple on the island, but
adequate. The only drawback is what we Romans call Malta
fever."

"What are its symptoms, Governor?" Paul asked quietly.

"Fever and great loss of bodily fluids. I would show you,
but I do not wish to spoil your appetite. My father is so afflicted
at this time."

"Please do show me, especially if your father has as kind
a heart as you do."

Caprasius smiled in embarrassment under the intense stare of the Cilician, then rose from his couch. "If you wish."

Valerius followed them up to a second-story bedchamber overlooking a windswept courtyard and then waited at the threshold as Caprasius whispered to his father, who lay on a pallet rather than the Roman-style bed the centurion had expected to see. The old man tried to lift his head but could not. And his voice was so weak and breathy, his son had to place his right ear up to the purplish lips.

Caprasius then looked to Paul. "My father begs to know if you are a physician."

"I am not."

"Then he would ask why you want to see him."

"Tell him I come in the name of the Lord Jesus, the savior of whom we Christians preach."

Caprasius bent low to listen to the old man once again. "My father says he has been curious about your sect for a long time. If he were feeling better, he would have many questions for you."

Paul smiled as he knelt. "Then he has been sick long enough." He placed his hands on the skull-like head and began praying.

Valerius withdrew.

The next morning, the old man came down the stairs on his son's arm, smiling wanly. "His first time on his feet in two months," Caprasius announced to the small throng of officers. "And Paul of Tarsus, I intend to give you a public ovation for this miraculous deed."

"Please do not."

"But why?"

"I do not seek attention for these things. They are not my doing."

Caprasius was flabbergasted. "But I *saw* your hands—"

"This man and I would like to chat now," the elder Caprasius interrupted in his wisp of a voice.

Paul assisted him into the atrium, where they closeted themselves for two hours—as long as the old man could endure in his weakened condition.

Paul emerged from this discussion looking disappointed.

Valerius drew him aside. "Was he convinced?"

"No, Julius, not this time. He still has doubts."

"Even after you healed him?"

Paul shrugged. "Perhaps because I *did* heal him. There is

often something within a man that makes him think it was his own powers that made him well. But I must be wary of my own pride: I had rather expected to make him a convert today—the first on the isle of Malta."

"But you did."

"Who here has let the Lord into—?" Then Paul fell silent. He seized Valerius' hands. "*You*, Julius?"

"Yes, I didn't sleep last night, thinking about what I must do. But now I'm ready."

"Was it the healing that persuaded you?"

"No. I'm not sure what it was. Perhaps it was the sight of your hands on the old man's head. I don't know."

"I praise God that you don't know but still believe. Quickly, now, to the shore . . . if you don't mind salt water twice in the same week.

Only when the ship with the figurehead of the *Twin Brothers* was tied up to the quay at the Italian port of Puteoli did Paul ask Valerius what would be done with him. "You see," the Cilician explained, "I try not to look too far ahead, especially when entering a new place. But now it is time to ask, Julius."

"I have thought of little else since we left Malta." Valerius led him down an aisle between two towering piles of wheat sacks. The three legionaries followed at a distance, their red cloaks faded by seawater. "I believe the matter will be quietly dropped after a while."

"How can that be so?"

"As far as I know, there will be no members of the Sanhedrin in Rome to bring their charges against you. My procurator, Festus, has in effect made no recommendation one way or another, leaving his official communication up to me. And even if you're tried, you'll certainly be acquitted. The forum is a long way from the Temple. Frankly, the Emperor's magistrates won't have a notion what all the fuss is about."

"Unless the synagogues here in Italy move against me," Paul said.

"Then you must speak to the Jews in the capital as soon as possible."

"But when will I see the emperor Nero?" Paul asked.

"Why, I doubt you ever will."

Paul was quiet for a long moment, then said, "A pity."

Arrived in Rome, they were striding up the Street of the

Silversmiths when a middle-aged Jew in a leather apron begged a word with Paul. Valerius nodded his approval, but the legionaries groused among themselves: They were eager to deliver their prisoner and hurry off to their favorite wineshop. "I will have no problems," Valerius told them. "Go on to the *castra praetoria* and secure billets for yourselves."

The soldiers lost no time in marching off toward the praetorian headquarters.

"Are you the one called Paul of Tarsus?" the silversmith asked.

"I am. And you, my friend?"

"Job." The man eyed Valerius with suspicion. "A Roman citizen."

Paul chuckled. "You have no reason to be uneasy about my brother Julius, here."

Job raised an eyebrow. "You are a follower of Jesus?"

"Since Malta," Valerius said.

Vigorously, the silversmith grasped the centurion's hand in the Roman way. "Since Alexandria," he said, indicating the place of his own conversion. He turned back to Paul. "We heard rumors from Puteoli that you were coming soon. But I did not expect to see you in chains, like a slave."

"I am a slave, good Job—to our Lord. And in him, I found my freedom. How are things here for our brethren?"

"Oh, we're tolerated. But the Romans don't care much for us. Maybe that's because we're a faith of the poor. And there are the wild stories that we are cannibals, that we eat human flesh and drink blood; I am asked this thrice daily."

"But does the church here grow?" Paul probed.

"Yes," Job said with a satisfied expression. "Despite our hardships, more and more believers come to us."

"And what of the local *sanhedrin*?"

"The council of elders in Rome has come to no decision about us. They ignore us, I suppose."

"Why?" Paul asked.

"Everyone is afraid of another expulsion. Both sides don't want to give the Emperor cause to punish us."

"We must be on our way," Valerius said to Paul.

"Of course."

Job delayed them a moment longer. "Please, Paul, where may I find you?"

Paul looked to Valerius for the answer.

"Do you know Aquila the tentmaker?" the centurion asked the silversmith.

"Certainly—a dear friend." Then Job's eyes widened. "Ah, you must be the Roman who is married to the lovely Sarah."

"I am."

"Do not let me keep you from her. Peace to both of you." He embraced Paul and was on the verge of doing the same to Valerius when the sight of the uniform made him hesitate, then withdraw back inside his shop with an embarrassed smile.

As they were admitted into the praetorian fortress, Paul glanced back through the *porta praetoria* at the heart of the city. For a moment, he was only a provincial tourist, overwhelmed by the magnificence of the imperial capital. Valerius grinned and said, "Come along, please—and close your mouth before you catch flies."

A thousand guardsmen stood at attention in the compound of the *castra praetoria*. They constituted the cohort—four hundred stronger than the legionary force of the same name—that was about to march off to the Palatine for a month's tour of safeguarding the Emperor's person. Their officers were inspecting them, and here and there a centurion was flying into a histrionic rage over some minor infraction or speck of tarnish.

"You are seeing the severest discipline in the world," Valerius said.

"I thought ours was, Julius."

They were working their way through the labyrinth of corridors inside the brick fortress toward the chambers of the *princeps castorum,* the officer to whom prisoners from the provinces were delivered, when a colonel intercepted them. "Centurion Julius Valerius Licinius?"

"Present, sir. Hail Caesar."

"Hail Caesar. Welcome home. I have been instructed to relieve you of the accused."

"I would like the accused present while I make my report to the *princeps,* sir."

"That would be quite irregular, wouldn't it?"

"Well, yes, Colonel, but—"

"I have my orders, Centurion. And you have yours."

Helplessly, Valerius watched as Paul was led away. Then he hurried toward the subordinate to the praetorian prefect who could order the Cilician's release. He knew it was possible, as long as the prisoner was not violently disposed toward the state, for the accused to enjoy a limited freedom in the city. He could choose lodgings of his own choice and roam the streets at will—escorted by a responsible Roman soldier, of course. Valerius intended to secure this kind of house arrest for Paul.

At first meeting, the *princeps castorum* seemed to be a reasonable man. "Yes, yes, Centurion, from what you tell me it appears that these Jewish holy men don't have much of a case. But much has happened in Rome while you've been away . . . much that might affect this Christian sect."

"Such as, sir . . . ?"

"Well, what have you heard since your return?"

Valerius had come to despise this little game spawned by the endless intrigues on the Palatine: *Tell me what you know before I tell you what I know.* As always, otherwise fearless officers were terrified of making a slip of the tongue. "When our ship docked in Syracuse, I heard that noble Burrus resigned as prefect." In truth, he had heard that Burrus had been sacked. But Valerius was not about to throw caution to the winds this late in his career. "Is that so, sir?"

"It is."

"But I heard nothing about a new prefect."

"It has not been . . ." The *princeps* groped for the correct word. ". . . *disseminated.*"

"Then someone has been designated?"

"Yes. Are you bound for the palace today?"

"After I see my family."

"Then you may as well know that noble Tigellinus is the new commander of the guard."

Valerius made certain he betrayed no consternation. In his face could be read that it was perfectly all right with him that a fishmonger had been made prefect. "Very well, sir. Now, if we might address the matter of the prisoner Paul being placed in my custody . . ."

"I have no objection to the accused living outside the fortress until his case is resolved, Centurion."

"Thank you. May I take custody of him now?"

"No."

"I beg your pardon, sir?"

"I have received information that you may have lost your objective sense in this matter, Valerius Licinius."

The centurion struggled not to groan out loud: He should never have allowed the legionaries to arrive at the fortress ahead

of him. Apparently, they had told the *princeps* of Valerius'
friendship with Paul: Perhaps one of them had witnessed his
baptism in the sea at Malta. "Am I to understand that the citizen
Paul is to remain here in the *castra praetoria*?"

"No, I will appoint another guard to watch over him, provided this Jew has the coin to pay for his own lodgings." The
officer picked up a scroll and began perusing it as a signal that
the meeting was concluded.

"I'm sure he can find accommodations somewhere in the
city."

The *princeps* glanced up, his eyes hard. "Just make certain
they are not in your house, Centurion. You're a trusted member
of the imperial household. You have served four emperors—
and are still breathing. A remarkable feat. So it is no time to
start behaving like a fool. Now, go home and have a talk with
your wife. Tell her you've had enough of her Jewish drivel."
The man offered a comradely smile. "I put my wife in her
place every once in a while. She respects me for doing it,
believe me." He rose from his curule chair and escorted Valerius toward the portal. "As far as this Judean affair, I'll say
this much: No accusation has been forwarded to Rome. If after
one more month nothing arrives, we'll put in a writ of liber-
ation. So this is nothing to get excited about—for a Roman,
at least."

His westward progress toward his house on the Janiculum
Hill was impeded by the praetorian cohort that had departed
from the fortress and was now marching to the Palatine. The
ranks filled the Vicus Patricius from side to side, and the walkways were already teeming with pedestrians who had halted to
view the parade. Valerius saw no choice but to fall in behind
them, adding his *caligae* to the thousand other pairs stamping
out an unvarying tempo. Yet, when they turned off toward the
palace and he continued on, alone, toward the Tiber and the
Janiculum beyond, Valerius was made giddy by a great sense
of release. He broke the lockstep pace, skipped half a block
and began running for his home.

"Why didn't you write to me?" Sarah cried, throwing her
arms around his neck.

Valerius released his wife long enough to sweep up his little
girl and include her in the embrace. "I would have beaten any
courier in Malta to Rome."

"Malta?" She looked dazed. "Why were you going to Malta?"

"I wasn't. A storm blew our ship there."

"But how were you able to leave Judea so soon?"

"Tonight, my love, I will tell you everything. But now you must go directly to Aquila."

"Aquila?" she echoed.

"Tell him Paul of Tarsus is at the *castra praetoria*. He and the praetorian guarding him will require lodgings—until our Lord delivers him. Aquila must not delay. Tell him to hurry before the *princeps castorum* changes his mind about letting Paul out of the fortress."

"But Ruth—"

"I will watch her." He bussed the rosy cheek. "Oh, dear God, how I have hungered to watch her!"

Absently, Sarah took her shawl off her shoulders and wrapped it around her hair. "What did you think of Jerusalem?"

"Now I understand why it's called the golden city. I will give you all my impressions later."

"Were they favorable?"

"Yes, of course. . . . Please, my love, hurry. This blessed man's freedom is at stake."

Sarah was halfway to the portal when she halted with her back to Valerius. She stood completely motionless for several seconds, then slowly spun to face her husband. Her eyes were incredulous. "You have become a Nazarene, haven't you?"

"Yes," he said simply.

She considered this a moment longer, expressionless. Then she quickly walked out of the house.

Valerius carried Ruth out into the courtyard, which seemed like paradise to the centurion after his absence of several months. The little girl quickly became drowsy in the warm sunlight of spring, and he decided to lay her down in her chamber. She awoke, whimpering and then crying when she glanced up at the not completely familiar face. Gently, he rested her in her *lectulus* and began singing softly:

> "When you hear the wolf howl,
> Feel no fear.
> Romulus and Remus
> Dropped no tear
> When they heard the wolf howl . . ."

Valerius could not finish. He clutched his child with frantic love.

Sarah returned at dusk, exhausted, and collapsed onto her couch. "I would like some wine."

"Is he free?"

"He is at Aquila's, under guard, if that is what you mean."

"Thank the Lord." Valerius paced aimlessly around the atrium until he remembered her wine; then he strode for the sideboard. "What is the praetorian like?"

"Roman," she answered with her eyes closed.

"I am Roman . . . so was Caligula. What are you saying?"

"He is quite official. His first words to Priscilla were that he wants no Jewish cooking. He insists on preparing his own rations." Sarah looked out toward the courtyard. "Where is Ruth?"

"Having a nap."

"This late? She will be awake half the night now."

Valerius reclined beside his wife on the couch. "So shall we."

"You will not think yourself so clever when your daughter is screaming for us." Following a sad moment in which she studied his face, Sarah kissed him. "I have missed you, Valerius Licinius."

"And I'm glad it wasn't a full year in Judea. I was already mad with loneliness. It is not good to be lonely in a strange country: The pangs are twice as sharp."

"Yes," she whispered.

"Then Paul is settled in and relaxing?"

"Settled in, yes. Relaxing, no. The elders from the synagogues met with him this afternoon."

"Were you there?"

"Of course," she said irritably. "Where do you think I have been?"

Valerius sat up. "What will they do in regards to the charges made by the Sanhedrin in Jerusalem?"

"They were not aware of any charges. . . ." Then, in a weary voice, Sarah told him how Paul had defended his reasons for appealing to the Emperor. The Jewish elders then surprised the Cilician by admitting that they had heard nothing of this affair and did not wish to come to a conclusion about it on the basis of what the accused himself had to say. Paul had thought this fair enough and simply asked that, if an accusation did ultimately arrive from the Sanhedrin, he be given the opportunity to answer it before the Jews of Rome. The elders had agreed.

"But what was their *feeling* toward him?" Valerius persisted.

"Their words neither favored nor opposed him. But the sight of a brother Jew tied to a Roman with a long chain—that softened their hearts, I think."

"How did you feel about Paul?"

"Like the elders: I have no opinion."

"Surely, you must have had thoughts as you listened to him."

"Yes." Her eyes moistened. "And I told your Paul one of them after the council had departed. I asked this man who knows everything, 'If God forgives all, who then forgives God?'"

"Sarah—"

"A worthy God would not have allowed what happened to my mother and sister." She was now sobbing against his shoulder.

"Sarah . . . my Sarah."

"And he said, 'You are not forgotten in your sorrow.' What kind of answer is that, Valerius Licinius? Tell me, please."

"The only one possible, my love."

Valerius sidled up to the praetorian who was standing on a landing above the Tiber. A thin chain was fastened to his wrist; connected to its other end twenty feet distant was a man who was wading in the shallows of the river. His tunic soaked to the level of his chest, he seized a young Roman and plunged him under the waters, muttering some alien tongue at the same time.

"What gives here?" Valerius asked the praetorian.

The guardsman stopped watching the scene long enough to salute. "Hail Nero! Baptisms, Centurion."

"What are baptisms? Some kind of enforced bathing?"

The praetorian almost snorted with laughter before remembering himself. "No, sir. This lad here is being cleansed of what he's done wrong in his time."

Valerius shrugged. "I bathe every day, and yet I still bear within me every offense I ever committed."

"Well, it's not quite like that, sir. You got to be around these folk awhile to really understand what it's about."

Valerius sighed. "I suppose. Who's the fellow with the forehead as big as a spade?"

"That's my charge—Paul."

"How long have you been tending him?"

"Thirty days tomorrow, sir. But I imagine he'll be set free

soon. It was just a squabble among Jews, you know."

Passersby on the Sublician bridge shouted down at the figures in the Tiber: "Christians, there's a better place over by the outlet of the main sewer!" and "That's it! Wash off the filth before you eat each other!"

The praetorian cried authoritatively, "That is enough, there! This is an imperial escort! *Interfere with them and you interfere with me, got it?*"

The deriders moved on.

"Then it's back to the *castra praetoria* for you?" Valerius asked.

"No, sir. My cohort's shipping out for the provinces."

"Why is that?"

"Well—between you, me and the Tiber, sir—Nero's having fits with his legion commanders outside Italy. We're to see to it that everybody keeps smiling, if you catch my drift."

Valerius nodded. "To which province are you bound?"

"Spain, sir, which is fine with me. Plenty of sun. No snow, except in the mountains. Women are a bit too Punic for my taste, but that can be overlooked in a pinch." The praetorian gestured down at Paul, who was baptizing a young patrician woman. "Might even run into my friend again over there."

"*Paul* is going to Spain?" Valerius asked anxiously.

"That's what he told me, Centurion."

Paul had baptized the last Roman in the small group he had brought to the river. Turning back toward his praetorian keeper, he suddenly smiled in recognition of Valerius.

The centurion prevented the man from crying out by pressing a finger to his lips. Then Valerius strolled away.

Their farewell meeting was three months later, although during that period Valerius had twice concealed his features in a hooded cloak and heard Paul speak. Saying their farewells at Aquila's shop was out of the question: Valerius was certain the place was being watched by special praetorians Nero had tasked with spying on Christians. They arranged to meet at the new construction site between the Palatine and Esquiline hills. Here they melted into the crowd of gawkers who, all day long, watched an imperial horde of slaves raze every structure that stood in the way of an enormous palace Nero planned to build there.

"Why Spain?" Valerius asked, looking only at the work.

"I have always wanted to go. It has been revealed to me that I should go now—before it is too late."

"But what of the Roman church?"

"Another teacher will arrive soon."

"You have received a message from Judea?"

"In a manner of speaking, yes."

Valerius tried to keep his voice free of sentiment, although his eyes had already clouded. "You have given me the peace I was afraid I might never find."

"Good . . . and now you must offer the same to your brother-in-law."

"You spoke to Caleb?"

"Last night." Briefly, Paul caught the centurion's eye. "He has not changed since those days we sat together at *Rabban* Gamaliel's feet in the Temple; that is unfortunate. Well, I must be going. It is a considerable walk to Puteoli." He had begun ambling away, a thin smile on his lips, when he stopped and stared back at Valerius. "Of all those I have brought to the light, you, my Julius, have given me the greatest satisfaction and hope. For you are the goodness of Rome. And through you, I have glimpsed what the Empire can become. I will miss you more than I care to describe." He hurried on through the crowd.

X

THE two figures shuffled out the portal of the brothel and stood briefly on the steps, stretching their backs and gazing up into the gray dawn. A small troop of praetorians materialized out of the mists and was quick-marching toward the men when Nero hissed, "Fools, keep out of sight! Do you want all of Rome to know who I am?"

Tigellinus chuckled in his sultry way. "It's no secret, nor should it be. If you feel contempt for your people, exhibit it." He motioned for the guards to withdraw out of sight.

Nero made a rumbling noise in his throat, then spat. "Look at this miserable city. A hodgepodge of wooden tenements, all leaning into the streets. Most of the stone is this soft tufa. There's not enough marble in the forum to make a decent sarcophagus. I don't even know where to begin."

"From the ground up, my Caesar." Tigellinus linked his arm in Nero's and led him back toward the Palatine. "Lest you forget, today you address the Senate in regards to funding for your magnificent new city . . . Neropolis."

"Neropolis." The Emperor savored the feel of the word on his tongue. "Damn the grape—I've forgotten the means of raising money we came up with last night."

"Well, there's the gold lying unused in many of the temples."

"Oh, yes, and that old idea of Messalina's was inspired: selling citizenship to foreign rabble. I rather liked my aunt Messalina. . . . Too bad she ran afoul of my mother," Nero said wistfully.

"And finally, we discussed a tax on nuisance sects—like the Christians."

"We'd better include the Jews under the same decree. The Christians don't own a thing. Poppaea has confirmed that for me."

Tigellinus paused for a moment. "How is it that your new wife knows so much about them?"

"Religious matters interest her."

"I hear that various things interest her."

Nero looked askance at his praetorian prefect. "What is that supposed to mean?"

"Oh . . . whatever." Tigellinus yawned.

"She *adores* me."

"But does she adore what we do together? The visits like tonight's across the river? The boys as succulent as lambs? The perfumed eunuchs? Our adventures give her cause for spite."

"She knows nothing of these things. A wise Empress knows when to keep her eyes closed—unlike Octavia, who was far too observant for a barren woman."

"But Octavia was not as beautiful, as amorous in disposition, as your present Empress."

Nero brooded in silence over the distance of several blocks. Then he encompassed the dingy buildings in an angry sweep of his arm. "All this must go. I don't know how to convince the bloody Senate, but it must be demolished."

"There are ways to circumvent the Senate, Caesar. But in order to do that, one must appeal to the elemental forces of the universe."

"What are you talking about?" Nero asked crossly.

"You cannot create unless you first destroy. Neropolis cannot arise unless Rome is leveled."

"Speaking of leveling something . . ." Nero said with sudden enthusiasm. An old man, an outlander of some barbarian territory, was slowly walking toward them. "Shall we?"

"I don't see why not." Tigellinus rolled up the sleeves of his woolen robe. "He will bruise nicely."

Yet, although they split company and outflanked the old man on both sides, the pair did not approach and pummel him with their fists. The barbarian continued on his way, unharmed. Tigellinus shrugged, "He was too old and frail to offer us any sport."

"Oh, nothing will be fun for me until my Neropolis is built!"

Peter waited until he could scarcely hear the footfalls of the two ruffians, then glanced over his shoulder to make sure the men had not changed their minds and decided to beset him after all. He had fully expected them to beat him and now murmured thanks for his deliverance.

He was seeking a warm place in the sun where he might sit. In the last few minutes, a breeze had begun to pull apart the low clouds, allowing bright rays to shoot over the rooftops. But this comforting light had not yet reached the streets, where shadow still predominated, reminding him of the cold night he had just spent in a passageway near the Circus Maximus.

He shuffled along a portico of nothing but fish stalls. Slowing his pace, he inspected yesterday's catch with a keen professional interest. "What do you call this fish here?" he inquired of one of the mongers.

"*Acipenser*. Do you want it?"

"No, no—I used to be in the business."

"What do you do now, old man?"

"I am a fisher of men." Peter chuckled affably.

"You don't look fleet enough to be a slave-hunter."

Peter looked appalled at the notion. "Why, no—I hate the practice of slavery."

The fishmonger shook his head knowingly. "You must be a freedman."

Peter moved on. Eventually, he was prevented by the Tiber from going any farther. But there he spied what he had been looking for: a small forum awash in sunlight. He eased down onto the benchlike plinth of a shrine and luxuriated in the warmth. Soon he was asleep.

He awoke midmorning, saddened by a dream in which he had overtaken Jesus on a shaded road and asked, "Where are you going, my Lord?" His face wrenched by agony, Christ had then whispered, "To Rome . . . to be crucified once again."

Peter realized that the voices of children had roused him. They were musical, sweet—in startling counterpoint to the sorrow that had just visited his sleep. "You live in simple things, don't you? Things so easy to overlook."

The youngsters began creeping up to him, giggling as they came. Soon they were swarming over the monument, listening to his grandfatherly voice with complete attention despite their inability to sit still for even a moment. ". . . And he loved little children such as you. Some people said it was wrong for God's son to spend so much time with children. But he said that we are all like young sons and daughters to God."

"But you said Jesus had a beard," a small girl objected.

"Yes, I did."

"Then how could he be a child if he had a beard?"

"When I knew Jesus, he was a grown man. But he still had a beautiful heart like a child. He wanted all of us to remain like children in our simple love for God."

A boy announced, "My father says this Jesus was a slave."

"No, that is not true. Our Lord was born to a family of kings. He could have been a king himself—if he had wanted. But he loved us more than he loved any throne." Then Peter turned toward a new juvenile voice:

"Jesus was too a slave. He was crucified with Spartacus. All bad slaves get tied to a cross. My uncle is a *vigil*. He catches slaves all the time."

"Rubbish," a lad of perhaps twelve announced. "Spartacus died a long, long time ago. Chrestus died when Tiberius was our emperor. He was killed by the procurator Pontius Pilate. I know. My father was a legionary in Syria when this happened."

"There you go: That's quite correct." When Peter tried to pat the boy's arm, he withdrew a step, shyly.

"Why did Pilate hate Jesus?" another child asked.

"Oh, he didn't know any better," Peter said. "His heart was closed to our Lord. Many people are like this, but it is not the same as hate."

"Did he ever find out that Jesus came back to life?"

"He must have heard, but perhaps he didn't want to believe it. I don't know." Peter shrugged at the novelty of this question. "It's a shame Pilate never saw Jesus shining with new life, as I did."

"How come we can't see him?"

"Because Pilate got exiled," the same authoritative boy answered.

"No, I mean Jesus. If he's alive, where is he?"

"Yes," yet another child chimed in, "have *you* seen him here in Rome?"

"I have indeed," Peter said, sadly recalling the dream he had just had.

"Can you call him now?"

Peter nodded yes.

There was a ghostly kind of silence as the children considered the possibility. Then the oldest boy said, "Do it."

"I can try." Then the old man whispered with closed eyelids: *"Maranatha!"*

"What does it mean?"
"It means in my language 'Our Lord, come!'"
A few of the youngsters began looking over their shoulders.
Peter smiled.

XI

⌐‾‾‾‾⌐

AFTER the evening meal, Caleb hurried from their house on the Viminal Hill, hoping to walk off his restlessness before trying to retire for the night.

A few young boys, fencing with wooden swords on the stepping-stones, recognized him to be the gladiator Metellus, but their friendly shouts gave him no pleasure.

He had just quarreled with Corinna once again.

It occurred to him that, over the past months, he had argued with everyone close to him. He had accused Sarah of failing to instruct Ruth properly in Jewish religion and traditions: The child was becoming as Roman as a vestal virgin. Valerius' father had died suddenly of a heart ailment in June, and Caleb had then asked the centurion what excuse he had now for serving an Empire he detested. Valerius had not answered, his eyes troubled. Caleb had even had words with Paul before he departed for Spain. On the strength of their old acquaintance-ship, the Christian had begged Caleb to forget his plan of returning to Jerusalem with a sword in his hand. "Go home if you must," Paul had said with that fervent expression of his, "but be worthy of Gamaliel, our great teacher: Bear love as your only weapon. It will strike down injustice more surely than any other." Caleb had laughed in the man's weathered face.

Caleb now reached the summit of the Viminal. There, the wind was no longer shunted by the tall houses. It blew its dry warmth across his skin. He felt sure this was a desert breeze, perhaps coming all the way from North Africa. It made him ache in remembrance of Jerusalem.

Then Caleb noticed something that caused him to shade his eyes against the declining sun. Between the Palatine and the Caelian hills, near the Circus Maximus, a column of white smoke was slanting up over the city, casting a dingy shadow as far north as the Campus Martius. During the few minutes in which he paused at the balustraded overlook and peered below, orange flames began to flicker up through the base of the column.

Shrugging indifferently, he gave his back to the smoldering heart of Rome and strolled back down toward his house.

Corinna opened the door for him with tears in her eyes. But then she gasped, "What is *that*?"

Caleb had been so deeply engrossed in his own cares, he had no idea what she meant until he turned and looked over the rooftops at an immense glow in the twilit sky. "There was a fire near the circus," he said matter-of-factly. "It must have grown."

She darted back inside and emerged a few seconds later with a shawl snugged around her head. "We must see: There has never been anything like this."

"I am weary . . . ready for bed."

"Please, Caleb." Her tears caught the pulsing light.

He smiled in apology for his harsh words earlier that evening, and took her hand. "All right."

They joined the stream of neighbors rushing toward the top of the hill.

Caleb could see the flames glistening on the faces of the spectators before he actually glimpsed the fire once again. Corinna was visibly stunned by the size of the conflagration: It had raced out of the bowl formed by the Palatine and Caelian hills and was now flaring on a broad front toward the Capitoline shrines.

An old man approached the couple and began prattling as if he were an eminent authority of such catastrophes: "It has reached those shops near the Altar of Hercules that sell oil for lamps. You will see." And then, as if he had made some arrangement with his gods to fulfill his prophesies, a ball of fire roiled up out of the distant quarter and exploded into a cloud of sparks. "See? *See?*" He nodded smugly. "Soon there will be the grain and hay at the cattle market to worry about. Oh, this will be considerable, I tell you, before it runs its course. And we must not be unmindful that this is the nineteenth of July."

"What does that matter?" Caleb asked.

"Why, where were you schooled, my man? This is the anniversary of that sad day long ago when the Senonian Gauls sacked and burned our glorious city."

"An admirable people, those Gauls of then."

The old man glared at him, then tramped off to another part of the crowd.

The squad of men came clattering over the Via Sacra in their hobnailed sandals, a wall of flame rearing up behind them. Five of them had, almost involuntarily, fallen into step with one another, although they wore nothing more military than cream-colored tunics that were now streaked with soot. The sixth member was apparently their leader: He promenaded at their van and indicated which way for them to go with smart flicks of his hand. He moved with the buoyancy of a child who is having delicious fun and never wants these moments to end.

Chuckling, he found a bucket that evidently had been dropped by one of the *vigiles* who were frantically trying to arrest the progress of the fire. Holding it up so his comrades could see, the man smashed his powerful fist through the wooden bottom and flung it aside. "That, my lads, is what I think of these repressive efforts!"

Rounding the next corner, they nearly collided with a pair of these firemen-watchmen, who were restraining a praetorian between them. The guardsman was thrashing to be free when he suddenly stopped struggling and instead stared after the small group that had just passed him by. He hesitated but then realized that there was no mistaking that self-satisfied countenance, especially under a sky that was blazing like noon. "Prefect Tigellinus!" he cried desperately.

The leader of the squad refused to slow his pace or even glance back at the caller.

"Why, I believe that *was* Ofonius Tigellinus," one *vigil* declared to the other. "I must speak to him about this."

Still jostling their prisoner between them, they gave chase until they caught up with the unperturbed figure, who asked out of the corner of his mouth as he continued striding, "Why do you stare?"

"Are you not the praetorian prefect?"

Tigellinus kept silent.

The watchman interpreted this as agreement. "We have detained one of your guards. While he may not have started this fire, he most certainly was working to spread its domain."

"Noble Tigellinus, keep faith with me!" The praetorian's voice then broke. "There have already been many deaths.... The prefect of the watch will behead me!"

"Shut up!" Tigellinus had finally halted. Smirking, he met the watchman's eyes and then scrutinized them carefully. "Yes..." he muttered to himself: Here was a pathetically honorable plebeian sort—pathetic because that overweening sense of honor was about to cost him his life. The *vigil* had surmised that the praetorians were responsible for the rapid spread of the fire in the wooden slums, and he probably suspected that the praetorian prefect might be behind all this. And these were dangerous things for a powerless man to believe.

Tigellinus realized that he had no choice in what he himself must do. But pleasure could be drawn from every moment, and he was not about to squander this one. "Yes, I'm afraid you're too clever for the likes of humble guardsmen."

The *vigil*'s jaw dropped at the enormity of this admission. "Does the prefect realize what he's saying?"

"Quite. We are burning Rome to the ground tonight," he said baldly.

"But—but—" the man sputtered, "—that's madness!"

"Oh, no. It only appears to be so because you are not privy to the grand design."

"It's still madness!"

"Well, suit yourself," Tigellinus sighed. "I was only trying to give you the comfort of some meaning for *this*."

"For what?"

Tigellinus drew his dagger and planted it to the hilt in the *vigil*'s chest. Two of the prefect's companions sprang forward with their own blades and felled the second watchman.

The guardsman, finding himself suddenly liberated, laughed with relief. He kicked at the prostrate forms with the toe of his military sandal. "I thank the noble Tigellinus with all my heart!"

"Yes, this must be quite sweet for you." The prefect's eyes were alive with orange flickerings from the Altar of Hercules, which was being consumed. "We take care of our own in the guard, don't we, my brave lad?"

"I really only followed my orders, Lord Tigellinus," the man said modestly.

"Not precisely."

"Good sir?"

"Tell me this: When were you instructed to reveal my identity to the *vigiles*?"

"Well, never—" These were the only words to escape the praetorian's throat before Tigellinus slashed it. The prefect had marched away with his most trusted squad before the man's knees struck the paving stones.

Valerius hitched his cloak back on after once again using it to beat down the flames. He could not recall how many days and nights he had been choking on smoke and ashes, but it now seemed as if Rome had always been ablaze. The same futile effort was repeated again and again: He and a mixed assortment of legionaries, *vigiles* and citizen volunteers would abandon one block of tenements and retreat to the next in the fire's path. There, they would argue with the tenants that their few possessions were not worth their lives. Then, as the walls of the dwelling began to smolder from the suddenly intense heat, the exhausted centurion would have to give the order that the occupants be forcibly removed. They usually went kicking and screaming, and it was astounding how many were more concerned with an old bronze lamp or the wax *imago* of a dead relative than they were their own children. For this reason, Valerius made it a practice to race up the stairs and check each of the landings in a building before the first flames darted along the roof or whooshed out of a doorway with a crackling roar.

So far, his own neighborhood on the east side of the Tiber had been spared. Yet, he had heard a rumor that morning that a spindle of smoke had been spotted at the base of the Janiculum Hill, supposedly in the vicinity of one of Tigellinus' estates. As soon as he could, Valerius wanted to confirm whether or not this report of a second fire was true. His mother had been out of the city for two weeks, visiting her brother in Fidenae. Valerius was thankful for her absence. Yesterday, or perhaps the day before, he had evacuated the Julia Victoria and then watched it crumble in on itself.

Now, at some nameless tenement, he bounded up the stairs in his final sweep of the place. Rats had begun to skitter out of the chambers onto the balconies. They roved back and forth across the footworn boards, crawling over one another in search of escape. Valerius had come to recognize this as a forewarning that the flames were only seconds away. He spun on his heels and started down the stairs.

Then, somewhere on the uppermost floor, a child wailed. Valerius halted and scanned all four segments of railing: He saw nothing.

"Centurion!" a legionary hollered from the courtyard below. "The outer wall's afire!"

Reaching the fifth landing, Valerius bellowed for the child to show himself. Nothing moved—except a shroud of smoke that gusted down past his eyes. It occurred to him that the raw urgency in his voice, which sounded so much like anger, was frightening the child into silence. Gnashing his teeth together to keep from calling out again, the centurion ran from room to room. The wooden walls were hot to the touch, and the air had begun to sear his nostrils. But even after two complete tours of the floor, he discovered no one. He stumbled outside and clutched the railing with both fists, frantic, distrustful of his own fatigued senses.

Then, not budging for a moment because the sight was too incredible to believe, Valerius gaped at a tiny boy in linen loincloth who, two flights below, was stooping a catch a rat on a balcony that was already burning.

Seconds later, the panting centurion swept the child up in his arms and flew downward. The boy shrieked in protest of his hunt being interrupted.

They descended into a blinding, acrid fog. Valerius had learned that there was no defense against it. A man could hoard a deep breath, but the demon stuff would claw down his throat and snatch it away from him. Over his own gasping, Valerius could hear the child hacking and gurgling.

Yet, mercifully, there was an end to it: Valerius located a patch of clear air by walking in a crouch the last steps across the courtyard and into the protection of the tunnellike portal. The legionary waiting there took the boy from him. "We'd given up on you, sir."

"Is everyone out?"

"I believe so, Centurion. But there was so much confusion—"

"Damn." Valerius wiped his eyes on his ruined cloak. When the courtyard was momentarily swept clean to the sky by a freak gust, Valerius decided to take advantage of it. He ventured all the way out to the scummy waters of the fountain, then craned his neck to shout upward, "Is anyone—?"

At that instant, he was overwhelmed by the stench of charred wood. Blackness swiftly followed.

Nero watched the sixth evening of the conflagration from the Tower of Maecenas on the Esquiline Hill. His eyes became liquid. "I had no idea on my way up from Antium that this would be so vivid ... so *plaintive,* my dear Tigellinus."

"At least it will make it plain to the Senate that we must rebuild now."

"Oh, that Troy died this magnificently!"

"I have informed the president of the Senate that you have offered to remove the corpses and the rubble at your own expense."

"Look there!" The Emperor pointed below at an entire family streaming through the Maecenas Gardens, carrying their possessions with them. A youth was bearing his little sister on his back, and this sight appeared to be the cause of Nero's sudden rapture. "Young Aeneas! Vergil would have been pleased to see how faithful our rendition of the sacking of Troy is!"

"Certainly, my Emperor. I have also discussed a fire relief fund with certain provincials who have begged to help their mother city in some way. In truth, it's an excellent way to raise money for the building of Neropolis."

But Nero was not listening. His voice suddenly boomed out over the gardens:

"See how the citizens, screaming and scurrying,
  Scamper like woodlice from logs freshly thrown on the fire.
  Ancient Anchises, caught sleeping, awakening
  Now to the flames that devour his ancestral abode,
  Calls to his son, young Aeneas, to rescue him—
  Pious Aeneas, our father, the builder of Rome,
  Bore on his shoulders, so handsome and muscular,
  His father, the father of all the fathers of Rome..."

Two refugees peered up at the singer. In the wavering light of the fire, their faces shone with hatred.

When soldiers began going from house to house on the Janiculum Hill, Sarah felt certain they had been sent by Valerius. *"Optio!"* she hailed a subcenturion. He stood against the huge cloud of smoke, his cuirass reflecting the hazy, amber sunshine.

"Where is your husband, woman?" the officer shouted back at her. "We are in need of more volunteers!"

"He is already fighting the fire. He's a legionary, like you." She shifted Ruth's body to her other hip. "Please, a question—I beg you."

Frowning, he trotted up to her threshold. "Very well, what is it?"

"Do you know the centurion Julius Valerius Licinius?"

"I don't think so. What legion and cohort?"

"Third Augusta. . . . He was on detached service to the palace."

"Sorry . . . see, I'm with the Fourth Scythians on the Danube. I was home on leave when this mess began."

Sarah paused, her face grave, before asking, "Where are the injured being taken?"

"Some are being carried to the Campus Martius. Others to various temples around the city."

"Then I must start now, if there are so many places."

"Good luck to you, woman."

Sarah carried a hot, irritable Ruth down off the Janiculum to the Tiber. The river was choked with blackened pieces of wood and, here and there, the corpses of citizens who, faced with a choice between the flames and the water, had elected to drown. She turned Ruth's face away from this carnage.

Before seeking Valerius at the Campus Martius, she decided to go to the palace, where he had been on the evening the fire had started. With all the familiar landmarks now erased, this was more difficult than she had imagined. She crisscrossed several intersecting thoroughfares that had been reduced to footpaths skirting the rubble, searching for the Altar of Hercules, which had always served as her guidepost to the Palatine. Finally, in exasperation, she asked a *vigil* who was slumped in exhaustion on a toppled obelisk.

"Why, dear woman"—he gestured at a scorched ruin, its blackened columns like the bones of a carcass, on the hill above them—"*that* was the Palatine."

"But the soldiers who served there . . . ?"

"Scattered throughout the city. Is your man a guard?"

"No, a centurion of the Third Legion."

"Pity. The praetorians are being rested in shifts up at the *castra praetoria*. I have no idea where the legionaries are being billeted. Most of them are just sleeping in their cloaks."

"Thank you."

"The gods protect you and the child, woman."

Sarah then resolved to hurry to the praetorian fortress—despite Valerius' warning that she never go there. With the exception of Cassius Chaerea, he had never completely trusted any of the officers of the guard—nor had the years since the emperor Claudius' expulsion edict lessened Valerius' fear that her Jewishness might one day be used against her. He had told her of a nightmare that had wracked his sleep more than once: She wandered through the *porta praetoria* and never emerged again.

"Sarah!" A male voice jarred her out of these thoughts. "You're Sarah, aren't you? Valerius' wife?"

"I am. I'm sorry, I should recall your name...."

"Linus."

"Of course. Forgive me."

Valerius had brought the Christian home for dinner some months before. The young patrician from Etruria had been agreeable enough company, but she had tired of Valerius' and his interminable conversation about the Nazarene sect.

"How is my friend, the centurion?" Linus asked.

Her voice quavered despite her efforts to control it. "I can't find him... I haven't seen him for days."

Linus' expression sobered. "I understand." Then he took hold of her by the arm. "We Christians have been keeping track of one another. Perhaps someone will have seen him."

"Do you think so?" she asked, brightening.

"There's only one way to find out. Will you come with me to a place off the *Via Appia*?"

"Oh, please... thank you, Linus."

"Here, let me relieve you of your little burden."

Where her cheek had perspired against Sarah's arm, Ruth had tracings like the veins on a leaf. She began whining.

For the first time, Sarah realized that Linus' cloak had been shortened to the length of a tunic, almost exposing his loincloth. "What has happened to your robe?"

The man chuckled at himself. "I've been ripping off a swatch now and again to bandage the wounded. One or two more patients, and I will be forced to compromise my decency."

The Roman became increasingly furtive as they hastened along a portion of the *Via Appia* whose tile-roofed shops had been spared by the vagaries of the wind. He glanced over his shoulder at every opportunity. And when two praetorian guards burst from a goldsmith's establishment they had just looted, Linus startled Sarah by suddenly halting and resting his face on her shoulder. He wept inconsolably—or at least pretended to. At last, she understood: He was reenacting the tableau of grief she had seen all over the city.

The guardsmen continued on their spree without pausing, although they had to slip around the despairing couple.

Waiting until the praetorians were out of sight, having smashed into another shop, Linus then led Sarah up a passageway that was no wider than his shoulders. She wondered if he had somehow forgotten the way when the corridor abruptly ended in a stone facing. But the Roman turned aside and knelt at an iron grate from which issued gusts of musty air and, she thought for a moment, faint voices.

"What is this place?" she whispered, frightened suddenly.

"Please wait: I will explain all." His nervous eyes kept darting toward the entrance to the passageway on the street.

The grate finally came free in his hands. Impatiently, he gestured for Sarah to crawl into the darkened space. Once he himself had wriggled inside, he handed her the child so he could replace the grill in its stone mounting.

"Keep moving!" he cried under his breath, taking Ruth from her again.

Scraping her knees across the stones, Sarah was urged forward by a dim glow. The cramped adit twisted downward at a gentle angle and eventually opened onto a long passage that, incredibly, was lit by a string of lamps and filled with people. The women and older children were preparing meals, the men conversing among themselves in hushed tones. There were galleries along the walls that had been cleared of their dead or funerary urns and were now occupied by wounded Christians.

"The Nazarene quarter of Rome," Linus explained.

"Do the *vigiles* know that you live in these tombs?"

"Perhaps, but so far they have done nothing."

Two men helped Sarah and Ruth down into the subterranean corridor. Immediately, she began inquiring if anyone knew her husband.

"Is he the follower of Jesus who is a centurion?" one man asked.

"Yes!"

"I saw him four days ago. He and his legionaries removed my mother from where she lives."

"But have you seen him since?"

"No, sister."

Sarah continued along the passageway at a frantic clip, leaving Linus behind. "Does anyone here know Julius Valerius

Licinius?" Everyone gave her a slight shrug or smiled in commiseration. After what seemed to have been a mile of habitation, she came to the last lamp and entered a deep purple murkiness where the deceased still held sway. There was no one to ask after this point. Tears welling in her eyes, she turned back toward the Christian abode.

She found Linus again in a large alcove. He and a score of others were listening to an old man with weary eyes who, she slowly realized out of her distraction, was speaking Latin with an Aramaic accent.

"There is word that the fire has died out at last. So be it. For now it has been revealed to the many what the few have known all along: Even a city of stone cannot endure forever. But the city of God is everlasting." The elderly Judean motioned with his knobby fingers for Linus to approach. "To those who don't already know this brother, I would like to present Linus. Young as he is, he will soon be the father of all Christians in Rome—your shepherd."

"But what of you, Peter?" a worried voice asked.

"My time is short. But I don't quibble with this. I have lived gloriously for a man who thought he'd spend all his days hauling fish out of the Sea of Galilee. *Gloriously*," he repeated, his eyes shining. "The future of the faith is now with the young. Most of us who lived and broke bread with our Lord have now rejoined him. There is even a rumor that Thomas, who crossed the Indus River into the land of the elephants, was martyred years ago." The eyes that had seemed so bright the moment before suddenly misted. "But these misfortunes are only signs that, one by one, we have finished what our Lord asked us to do. We must rejoice in the triumph of our mission."

Angrily, Sarah walked away from the threshold of this alcove. She had had enough of Nazarenes and their talk of faith. Valerius had even begun to prattle in an annoying fashion, speaking of being tested by a loving God. She felt that he was revealing his ignorance with these words: A loving God would not want to test his followers.

"Are you the woman married to Valerius?" a young man asked. "I know where he is, if you are the one looking for him."

Sarah was too stunned to speak for a moment. She gawked at him, his wife, their little girl, who was Ruth's age. "Please . . . *where*?"

"Inside the Temple of Saturn; hundreds of wounded have been rested on its floors."

"Wounded?"

The man hesitated. "I have been going there each day, to help with the injured and bury the dead. I recognized your husband from our worship here. He has not awakened since he was struck with falling debris."

"I must go there," she said desperately, becoming aware of Ruth sleeping in her arms at the same instant.

The woman must have read her thoughts, for she said, "Let us care for your child, sister. She will be a fine playmate for our Claudia."

"Thank you." Kissing Ruth, she handed her daughter over to the Christian woman. "I will hurry back as soon as I can."

"No, no, take as much time as you need to nurse our brother Valerius."

XII

The Emperor alighted from his litter and, smiling, strolled back
to the less ornate *lectica* that carried his pregnant wife. He took
one of her hands in his as he addressed the crowd that had
gathered outside the Curia. "My poor, distressed citizens, while
I attend to urgent matters with the Senate, my beloved Empress
will pay the imperial respects to the vestal virgins. She does
this willingly, although she is heavy with child, so that the
gods may see for themselves how dire a calamity we have
suffered."

"Yes!" an anonymous voice rang out. "The prospect of
another Nero!"

The Emperor glared at the colonel who commanded his
immediate guard, and the officer waved for a squad of praetorians to filter through the silent assembly in search of the
suspect. Nero was beginning to move away from Poppaea in
order to greet Tigellinus, who had arrived with a reinforcement
of guards, when the Empress refused to let go of his hand.
"Please, Nero, do not persecute those who mean you no real
harm."

"What? And let this insulting fool get away with such a
remark?"

"I mean the Christians, my dear husband. I beg you, don't
denounce them before the Senate."

His expression softened. "Is that what you really want?"

"With all my heart. I know for a fact that their teachers
counsel acceptance of our Roman order."

"Then I will not accuse this sect of the recent mischief."
Patting her hand, Nero freed himself from her tense grasp and
finally made his way toward the praetorian prefect. "Tigellinus
will do it for me," he muttered to himself with a smirk.

"What will I do for you, Caesar?" the prefect asked.

"Most anything, I would imagine."

"Once again, my Emperor is absolutely correct. Shall we go in and cow the patrician scum?"

"That would give me extreme delight this morning."

Inside the Curia, Nero immediately sensed the rebellious mood of the Senate. The "Hail Caesar!" given him was less than resounding. Moments later, the *princeps senatus,* or president of the Senate, attempted to assert the authority of the ancient body in a roundabout way: He had a water clock set on its stand to the rear of the Emperor, reminding him that no one desired a performance that would last well into the night. Still smiling, Nero decided that there was no time like the present in which to quash a fledgling mutiny. He sauntered over to the stand and overturned it with a flick of his toe. The clock crashed against the floor, leaving a puddle of unused time on the marble.

"How dare you!" Nero screamed. HIs praetorians could be heard rustling at the rear of the hall, eagerly awaiting the order to sack the Curia. "How unforgivably insolent to treat an heir to the god Augustus as if he were some petitioner from the provinces, trembling before you! Well, I do not tremble!" He turned to his guardsmen. "Strike your shields!" The senators flinched. "But look!" Nero howled with glee. "See who sweats the seconds now!" Then he lowered his voice to a growl: "You will listen to Prefect Ofonius Tigellinus. He will tell you what has happened and what must be done." The Emperor flopped onto a curule chair, appearing to be immensely satisfied with himself.

Hands on his hips, Tigellinus faced the senators. "Caesar, noble Conscript Fathers, I am here to report on the findings of an imperial commission charged with looking into the causes of this disastrous fire. Documents, letters, depositions—all of which the Senate is invited to examine—lead to one inescapable conclusion: This outrage was perpetrated by a group of dissidents whose enmity toward the Empire has heretofore been grossly underestimated. Unfortunately, it has taken the destruction of ten of Rome's fourteen wards to convince us of the depravity of this Judean sect." A few senators began shaking their heads. "Now, I am not accusing the Jews as a whole. Most of them in this city are guiltless and have been quick to contribute lavishly to the Neropolis Reconstruction Fund. No, I am not speaking solely of those known to us as Christians— those cannibalistic, incestuous arsonists who at this moment hide like rats in the rubble they have created from our once-great city. Quite rightly, they cower in anticipation of the wrath of the Roman people. . . ." Tigellinus frowned severely: A senator had stood to speak. "Yes, yes, what is it, Flavius Sabinus?"

"I know a number of men and women of the Christian sect. What you have just said misrepresents them and should not go uncensured. These people are honest and peaceable. Many of us could learn much from them."

"Perhaps many of you already have," Tigellinus said with an accusatory stare. He was about to continue his tirade when he saw that a second patrician had found the courage to speak.

"I am Calpurnius Piso, for the benefit of the praetorian scribe I see who is diligently preserving our comments in wax. I am flattered by the attention. After years of speaking in this chamber, I had grown fearful no one wanted to listen to me anymore."

There were a few chortles from the benches.

"What does noble Calpurnius wish to say?" Tigellinus asked.

"Only that I marvel at the speed with which Caesar implemented his measures to relieve the misery of Rome. Laborers are already building temporary shelters for the homeless. Emergency supplies of grain began arriving on barges from Ostia fully *five* days ago. It almost seems as if our Emperor was forewarned by the gods of this calamity."

Applause broke out and was quickly organized into a hard, rhythmic clapping by Sabinus and Piso—who, obdurately, had remained on their feet. Tigellinus and Nero exchanged glances; they were not sure what to make of this.

But then the Emperor decided that, even if it was some kind of protest, he would harness the gesture and make it behave as a compliment. "Why, I thank my dear friend Piso," Nero said amicably. "But my recent actions should be no mystery to you. We have both been molded by the teachings of Annaeus Seneca, have we not?"

"Caesar?" The senator motioned for the others to stop clapping.

"Well, doesn't my mentor say: 'Lives that have been ruined, lives that are on the way to ruin, are appealing for some help: It is to you that they look for hope and assistance'?"

"I . . . believe so." Piso blinked at the weak blue eyes that were boring right through him. The senator was uncertain what he was committing himself to.

"You mean you haven't visited Seneca in his retirement?"

"A few times, Caesar."

"Recently?"

"A few months ago; we met unexpectedly in Thurii."

"Unexpectedly, my friend?"

Piso did not answer.

Nero sighed. "Then I leave this thought with you, Calpurnius Piso. It, too, is from our beloved Seneca: 'At whatever point you leave life, if you leave it in the right way, it is a whole.'"

The senator slumped to his bench. He wrapped his left hand in his toga.

"And now," Nero said with a jaunty lilt to his voice, "let us look forward. Rome must shake off its gloom. I intend to convene games this very afternoon." He ignored the few surprised gasps. "Surely, it was for this end that the gods spared my circus on the Vatican Hill. And I invite every one of you to share my gallery with me. It will demonstrate our unity to the people."

The young *vigil* wondered what kind of assignment the ordinarily aloof praetorian guard could have for his comrades and him. The centurion from the *castra praetoria* relieved the *vigiles* of their firefighting poles but had left them their short swords. Even more puzzling to the watchman was the tone of voice used by the imperial officer to the men of a municipal force he heretofore had addressed only with contempt: "We thank the noble prefect of the watch for the loan of your able services. Now, if you will please follow us to a district just off of the *Via Appia*. . . ."

The *vigiles* fell in behind a century of splendidly attired guardsmen, and the watchman was beginning to feel quite dashing himself, despite his rather plain tunic—until he noticed that the tallest of his contingent was still a head shorter than the least of the praetorians. And despite their miserable condition, people along the ruined streets had begun to snigger at the parade of giants followed at a half-trot by a gaggle of dwarves. The watchman began to suspect that his lack of stature had something to do with his having been chosen for this detail. His cousin, also a *vigil* but slightly taller than most in the city cohort, had been dismissed from the ranks by the praetorian centurion. Whatever the watchmen were about to do, it was something the guradsmen could not do themselves.

They arrived in a small square one street distant from the *Via Appia* and the *vigiles* were divvied up into three-man squads, each commanded by a praetorian. The young watchman scurried behind his guardsman to a passageway that was so narrow, the praetorian's thick arms brushed the stone walls, although the *vigiles* he led had no difficulty negotiating the corridor to its end.

They halted and waited.

"Sir," the watchman whispered to the praetorian, although the man was no more an officer than he was, "can you tell us what this is about now?"

"High treason. We guards will batter through the doors in the cemetery. You boys will keep the mice from scampering out."

"I see." The young *vigil* could not help but grin: For the first time he was genuinely at the thick of things. *High treason*, the guardsman had said. Suddenly, he ached to be a praetorian himself. The guard did exactly what had to be done, and damn the public outcry. Hadn't they brought Octavia's head back from the isle of Pandateria, even though the people had rioted in the former empress' behalf? It was different with the *vigiles*. The prefect of the watch was frightened of his own shadow, not to mention the magistrates who freed wanton offenders on the least pretext.

A trumpet sounded over the rooftops. Quickly, the guardsman removed a grate that had previously sealed off some kind of crawlway. "Get in there! Stop short of the main tunnel and let no one past you!" he cried.

The watchman's face fell. He understood at last that he was being charged with no glorious assignment. Like a dog, he was being sent into a burrow to deny the rabbits within one of their escape routes. This was the only reason the praetorian guard had brought him along, and all that flattering talk from their centurion had been nothing more than a little scratching behind the ears. The *vigil* hesitated before the dark opening.

Then he was dealt a sharp kick by the guardsman.

Scrambling forward in anger and humiliation, the young watchman vowed to distinguish himself in some way. When his two comrades branched off into the side crawlways, he continued on toward the glow. "Who do those bloody praetorians think they are?" he muttered to himself. He kept advancing toward the lighted passageway and then, instead of halting as ordered, leaped down into it, flashing his sword before him. He parted a thick cluster of people, and the women began screaming. "*Shut up!* You are all prisoners of the Emperor!" That made him smile: He liked the sound of his own words. Keeping everyone at bay, he sidestepped down to an alcove and peered inside.

An old man was speaking to a dozen or more small children: ". . . and a terrible storm blew up on the sea of Galilee. Let me tell you, I was frightened. So were my friends." He closed his eyes. "I still see it all. Our open boat bobbing on waves as tall as you are. Lightning snapping at the mountains all around the sea. And then, when we were beyond hope, a figure out in the darkness, shining—"

"Hold your treasonable tongue!" the *vigil* shouted at him.

The old man stared at him, then shook his head sadly.

Screaming at the far end of the passageway announced the entry of the main force of praetorians, who immediately began seizing prisoners. They used the flats of their swords to beat those who dared to question them.

Working his way past the stunned Christians, the centurion was surprised to see the young *vigil* standing at attention and saluting with his sword. "What are you doing here?"

"Taking prisoners, sir."

"Oh."

The watchman was disappointed that the officer was not more pleased with the initiative he had shown. "I have also separated the children from their elders." This was not entirely true, as he had come upon the youngsters already gathered together. But it would appear to be true, and that, he reminded himself, was all that mattered.

Nodding with vague approval, the centurion glanced inside the alcove. He asked the old man, "Who are you?"

"I am called Peter."

The officer's eyes widened. "With those words, you condemn yourself."

"Is that all there is to your famous Roman law?"

"In this case, yes."

"Then in all cases." The old man hefted himself to his feet.

The centurion turned to the watchman. "Seize him."

"*That* worn-out fellow, sir?"

The officer smirked. "Yes, it's hard to believe that he's their ringleader, isn't it? Manacle him—guard him as if your own lives were at stake."

"And the children, Centurion?"

The man was pensive for a moment. "All of these prisoners are to be marched to the Emperor's circus. My orders did not specify that the children are to be handled any differently than their parents. Perhaps some sort of school has been set up for them there, to dissuade them from following the path their parents have blundered down."

"But, sir, there are no schools on the Vatican Hill," the *vigil* said.

"And you were doing so well . . . for a watchman." The centurion spun on his heels and strolled deeper into the tombs.

His cheeks searing, the *vigil* waded through the children, who had begun to sense danger and were now whimpering, to the old man. "Do you have any weapons on your person?" he demanded.

"No, I do not believe in their usefulness."

"You will before this day is done, grandfather." The *vigil* felt a tug on the hem of his tunic. He looked down into the face of a small girl. "Yes, what is it?"

"Do you know my father? He's a soldier too."

The watchman glanced toward the passageway to make sure no praetorians were in earshot. Then he asked, "No, my love, what's his name?"

"Julius Valerius."

"Is he a brave praetorian?"

"No, a centurion."

"Do you know which legion, my pretty one?"

She nodded and held up three tiny fingers.

The *vigil* rolled his tongue between his teeth. Uncovering a legionary officer who was secretly a Christian—that was certainly good for a commendation. But after the snubs and insults the praetorians had heaped on him today, the watchman had no intention of sharing this information with a guardsman. At the circus, he would take some legionary aside and seal the fate of this Julius Valerius.

The old man touched his arm, startling the *vigil* out of his deliberation. "My good man—"

"What do you want?"

"Don't bring any suffering to these little children."

"You're a fine one to say that, after dragging the small beggars into this mess."

Valerius struggled to unstick his eyelids. He was terrified to imagine that they were permanently closed, but then one eye snapped open. His first watery sight was of the god Saturn. The stone countenance glared down at him, accusing him of betraying the gods of his father. Valerius rolled onto his side and immediately groaned: The blood had slopped from one half of his swollen brain to the other, blinding him again with a torrent of pain.

Gradually, he became aware of others around him. They were moaning weakly, calling for loved ones or demanding water.

"Valerius?"

Gingerly, so as not to ignite another fiery ache, he turned his head. He sighed without moving his lips. "Sarah?" The cool touch of her fingertips convinced him that she had actually come to him.

"Rest . . . do not speak. Squeeze my hand if you want something to drink."

He grasped her hand as hard as he could.

"I'll be back in a moment. . . . Lie still."

Later, he could not recall having tasted the water he had so eagerly awaited. While counting the seconds before Sarah returned, he experienced what seemed to be a brief spell of blackness, deep and deathlike. Then his gaze focused on his wife's face. The ache was still trapped inside his skull, but it was no longer excruciating. His thirst obsessed him, and he asked, "Where is my water?"

She brought a bowl up into view. "Right here—since yesterday."

Valerius seized the lip of the wooden vessel with his teeth and drank noisily. "More."

"Wait awhile. I have seen that those who drink too much throw it up again. After that, they can keep nothing down."

"Am I . . . burned?"

"No. You were struck on the head by pieces of wood."

"Where's Ruth?"

"She's safe with your Nazarene friends in those underground tombs."

"How did you . . . ?" He appeared to lose his own thought.

"Linus and I crossed paths. I went there searching for you."

"What about . . . fire?"

"It has finally burned itself out."

"Our house . . . the city?" he asked.

"The Janiculum was never touched, but much of Rome is destroyed."

His eyes glassy, he said nothing for a long while. "I must sleep . . . now . . . a short . . ."

It was the worst of all possible nightmares. Sarah was clutching herself in her arms, rocking back and forth as she crouched on her knees. Somehow, inexplicably, Ruth had been taken from her, and Sarah—with her writhing silence—was blaming Valerius for the loss of their child. Her stricken face was full of loathing for him, and he had never felt more lonely. "The Lord will safeguard her," he heard his own voice croak. He watched his hand slowly drift outward for hers. "He will not abandon us in the hour of our need—"

"Stop it!" she hissed. "Stop this Nazarene idiocy!"

This agonized cry shocked him into full wakefulness. "My God, what has happened?"

"They've been taken—and Ruth with them!"

"Who?"

"All the Christians hiding in the tombs."

Valerius touched his fingers to his forehead. "How do you know this?"

"Aquila ran here. He had gone to the tombs—and found them empty."

"Where is he now?"

"Gone to the Emperor's circus on the Vatican Hill."

Valerius grimaced in the midst of his confusion. "I don't understand. Sarah, *who* took them?"

"Soldiers."

"But on whose orders?"

"Tigellinus'—Aquila heard this from the same man who told him we were here." Sarah pressed her lips together to keep them from quivering.

Valerius slowly sat up. He tested his equilibrium before completely rising.

"What are you doing?" Sarah asked.

"I'm going to get our daughter."

• • •

"What are those for?" Caleb thrust out his lower jaw at the six upright timbers that had just been erected in the arena.

Corinna glanced up from adjusting the leg straps on one of her greaves. "I don't know. But whatever they're for, hold your tongue." Her eyes darted toward the imperial gallery, which was only a few paces away. From there, the emperor Nero and his henchman, Tigellinus, were presiding over the somberest games she had ever attended. The clothes of the Romans packed into the circus still reeked of smoke, although Nero was radiant in a snow-white toga.

"Those two are dammed jolly, aren't they?" Caleb said under his breath. "Of course, they're the only ones here with no singed hair."

A troop of praetorians escorted six female captives across the sands to the timbers. The women tried to kneel and pray, but the guardsmen yanked them up out of genuflection and tethered them to iron rings mounted on the posts.

Caleb had begun to scrape his short sword up and down in its scabbard.

"Please don't do that," Corinna said.

"What manner of nonsense is this?" he sighed. "And what kind of serious fighting could this possibly involve?"

"I don't know."

"Who are they?"

"Christians, I would imagine. And I suspect they will not be expected to fight . . . only die."

Nero had risen to cursory applause, punctuated by a smattering of boos that put the praetorians on edge. "Citizens of Rome!" He paused, and the rage of the crowd was palpable in the silence that followed—to everyone but Nero, who breezily continued, "The Christian sect, which is craven in most every aspect, has nevertheless found the audacity to do what even inveterate Roman-haters such as Spartacus and Hannibal could never do: They have leveled our sacred capital! They have left us the proprietors of a heap of ashes! They have transformed our dearest antiquities into so much charred junk! Well, what do you say to these indignities the Christians have inflicted on you?"

There was a loud outcry, a floodlike outpouring of infuriation. But Caleb and Corinna glanced at each other: They could not be certain if it was directed at Nero or the pathetic figures in the arena.

"It gives me great pleasure to announce the arrest of the chief agitator of this sect!" Nero went on, grinning hugely. "But his demise will entertain us on another day." He then gestured at the women. "It is said these Christians will not fight. But I am open-minded enough to reserve judgment until I see for myself. Now, let us settle this question. . . ."

On a signal of trumpets, the praetorians marched in six men who bore the marks of scourging. These Christians blanched so severely at the sight of the bound women, it was immediately apparent that they were their husbands. Each man approached his wife and offered her some words of comfort. Then all began muttering some prayer in unison.

The file of praetorians wheeled around the timbers and trampled off the sands, leaving the Christians with no inkling of what awaited them.

An iron door in the barrier wall slid open and a brace of leopards streaked out into the arena and made a circuit of the parapet in search of escape. Finding no way out, they turned back over their own tracks, halting and crouching once when the crowd roared at them to spring to the attack.

The Christians did not dare to blink. Their faces glistening with sweat, they waited as the wild cats pranced back and forth in front of the imperial gallery, making hideous soughing noises that amused the Emperor and Tigellinus. Caleb leaned over the top of the wall and sneered at the leopards. "This is not a worthy way to draw blood."

"Quiet," Corinna whispered.

Then one of the Christian women could no longer bear the anticipation. She lowered her head and closed her eyes. This slight movement attracted the attention of one of the cats.

A cheer went up from the benches as the animal charged the Christians. It tussled with one of the men for only a few seconds, then dragged the body away in its jaws. Instinctively, the five surviving men ducked behind the posts, earning the derision of the crowd. But then the men found their courage once again and stepped out in front of their wives.

Caleb turned away as the second leopard began closing in to make its effortless kill. "This is an insult to the dignity of the games!"

Corinna's eyes shifted toward the imperial box to make sure that no one had overheard Caleb's outburst. Then, holding a breath to keep down her anger, she said, "If you think this kind of recklessness means anything, you're a fool."

He ignored her, and they walked without passing a sound between them except for the strumming of their sandals over the crossbars of the iron grates that formed the walkways behind the parapet. All at once, he halted and peered down through the mesh into a bay that ordinarily caged wild animals until they were required in the arena. Not quite believing his eyes, he crouched to get a closer look. "There are children being penned here!" he cried. They stared up at him, their faces checkered by the light filtering through the grate. Each child was garbed in a lambskin tunic, and a man dressed as an Etruscan shepherd was jabbing them with his crooked staff to make them baa, which only a few did with any enthusiasm.

"What is this about?" Caleb demanded.

The shepherd glanced up, then barked, "Move along, there."

Caleb turned to Corinna. "What could possibly be amusing about this—even to Romans?"

She did not know what to say.

Caleb stood up again, scowling. "Stay here until I return. I will see the gamesmaster for an answer to this."

Silently, she knelt on her greaves, then enfolded herself in her arms and closed her eyes. "Go . . . quickly."

Caleb had traversed over the latticed tops of three more of these bays—all filled with large cats or bears—when the fourth made him pause. It contained a pack of sleek Egyptian hunting dogs. Obviously, they had been denied food and water in order to give them a savage disposition for the games: Each took his turn leaping up and snapping at the two men protected by the grate who were standing ready to raise the door. Caleb peered back down the walkway at Corinna, who had been joined by a pair of men who were now preparing to release the children onto the sands. "Lord God of Israel," he whispered.

"Metellus!" someone shouted frantically from a tier higher up in the circus.

His gaze darting back and forth across the throng, Caleb finally picked out Aquila's face, which could not have looked more excruciated had he been suffering death by fire. *Yes, friend! What is it?*

Aquila shouted in reply, but his words were drowned out by the *hydraulis;* at that moment the water organ loosed the lilting notes of some pastoral song Corinna sometimes sang to herself. It seemed offensive now.

Aquila waved for Caleb to approach him, and the gladiator bounded over a railing and fought his way through a dense phalanx of spectators.

"Ruth!" Aquila hollered before Caleb had reached him. "They have taken Ruth!"

Caleb froze. Then he tipped back his head and groaned. Those he had jostled aside now taunted him with nudges and pokes. He flailed at the Romans as he spun around and fought his way over heads, shoulders and arms back down to the grates over the bays, landing on all fours to the clatter of his scabbard. He was rising and stumbling forward in the same instant when a cheer erupted around him.

"No!" he screamed. "Corinna—stop the bastards!" But he was unable to snag her attention. She was leaning over the parapet, sadly watching a file of tiny figures in lambskins parade out to the center of the arena. Their shepherd had already abandoned them and was running for safety. The younger ones, who had no inkling of danger, were laughing and baaing, unaware of the grisly human debris that Charon and his helpers were finishing clearing away from the timbers. The older children had slowed their pace to a shuffle. They sensed the violence awaiting them. One or two had begun to cry.

Changing direction once again, Caleb sprinted for the men who had been posted at the door that held back the dogs, but then he saw that they had already wheeled it up. "Ruth, my Ruth!" he cried in rage and helplessness. The pack was lunging toward the children. Small screams could be heard through the clamoring of the crowd.

Caleb hurled himself over the barrier wall and assaulted the melee with his sword flashing over his head. His first blow was so ferocious it cleaved the hound in two. He determined to kill as many of them as he could as swiftly as possible; there was no way to tell which little girl was Ruth in the confusion.

It encouraged him a moment later when he saw that Corinna had joined him in the fight. But another sideward glance told him that she was as hard put by the pack as he was; they were being forced to fend off bared teeth on every side. Unlike bears and other beasts of the games, the hounds were working in concert with each other. Three or four of the dogs would keep after the gladiators while another would continue to attack the children.

"Stand back to back!" Caleb cried to Corinna. In this way,

they no longer had to protect themselves full circle and could
once again concentrate on thinning the pack. Caleb ignored the
shrill screams and plaints of the children, the roar of a crowd
delighted by the spectacle of two famous gladiators rescuing
the small figures from certain slaughter; he thought only of
hacking the dogs to pieces.

"Caleb!"

He had struck down a hound that had been springing toward
him. In a blind fury, he chopped at the carcass again and again
with his sword.

"Caleb! It is done! You have killed the last of them!"

He looked up at her as if she were a stranger.

Nero had stood and was glowering from the imperial box.
Placing his hands on his hips, he surveyed the scene in the
arena for a long moment: the bloodied dogs, the clutch of
surviving children, the fighters awaiting his decision after they
had interrupted the progress of the games without his permission. "I had not expected to see Metellus and Lady Corinna
on the sands today," he said gravely.

Caleb was too devastated to speak: Ruth was not among the
children still on their feet.

"We had not been certain Caesar desired our services,"
Corinna finally said.

"Nevertheless, I received them."

Tigellinus approached the Emperor and whispered in his
ear. Nero suddenly regarded the crowd with suspicion. A dis-
contented murmur had arisen, especially in the plebeian benches.
He turned back to the gladiators. "Well, Metellus, I thought
you preferred life as a retiarius."

"Metellus is a master with both the trident and the sword,
Caesar," Corinna answered for him.

"So I have seen." Nero held his fist out in front of him,
thumb projected to the side. Then, grinning, he gave a thumbs-
up. There was a din of approval; but, when the cry tapered
down, catcalls directed at the Emperor could be heard at the
heart of the cheer.

Corinna saw that Caleb had been transfixed by the sight of
the tiny bodies littered across the sands. Lightly, she touched
his arm. "We must think of the living and get these Christian
children out of here."

Caleb nodded, then said in a dry croak, "I will be along in
a moment."

Corinna led the children away at a run. She grasped the hands of two of them, but others held out theirs, begging to be comforted. Caleb began going from corpse to corpse. When Charon pranced out to drag them away, Caleb warded the robed figure off with the point of his sword.

Valerius clung on to Sarah as he stumbled along the passageway toward the arena. If he attempted to walk any faster, he risked fainting, as he nearly had twice on their hurried way from the Temple of Saturn.

Bored by the games or simply weary after the travails of the week-long fire, people had begun to stream out of the circus across the lush imperial gardens of the Vatican Hill toward their shelters pitched on the Campus Martius—their only homes now.

Valerius felt Sarah's arm jerk away from him. "Aquila!" she cried, waving.

The old man halted. Yet, instead of greeting his friends, he blanched and turned around, revealing Corinna, who stood behind him. She, too, became ashen-faced as soon as she glimpsed Sarah and Valerius.

The centurion seized his wife's hand in both of his. He sensed that he was about to receive the worst news of his life, but tried to repudiate it with a stony calmness.

Surrounding Corinna were six young children whose woolly tunics were flecked with blood. Looking bewildered, they huddled around her legs and refused to budge. Valerius took stock of each little face: None gave him the delicious jolt of recognition he craved so much. Then it was his turn to keep Sarah from collapsing. "What hap—" His voice winked out, and in that instant the brightness vacated his eyes. He seemed middle-aged, defeated.

Aquila steeled himself and embraced the couple. Then he burst into sobs.

His eyes glassy, Valerius stared over the man's shoulder. Then, without warning, he rudely pushed Aquila away. He made a sound like a gasp or a choke and took several unsteady paces down the passageway.

Caleb was striding toward him. He held Ruth in his arms.

"Metellus!" the more boisterous plebeians had kept shouting at him, wondering out loud why the gladiator had fended off

Charon and was inspecting the face of each dead child with agonized care.

Eventually, Caleb turned away and strode out of the arena. He entered the passageway that led to the baths and armory of the gladiators. His expression fixed by some deadly resolve, he told himself that, with a little luck, a skilled retiarius had a fair chance of breaching the ring of guards that surrounded the Emperor and planting a trident in the imperial torso. The key to success lay in the net: It could be flung over the heads of two or three praetorians, clearing the way long enough for the fatal blow to be delivered. Of course, there was no doubt that the assassin would be felled by other guardsmen in the imperial gallery, but a Zealot accepted the inevitability of his death on the same day he dedicated himself to the freedom of his people . . . and the destruction of Rome.

Caleb had not found Ruth's body on the sands. He now assumed that she had died by some other means or was slated for some special entertainment Nero would enjoy later in his special quarters.

There were footfalls behind him in the tunnel—the distinctive clicking sounds of military sandals. He had known right away that the impertinence he had shown Nero in the arena would not go unpunished. *So be it,* he thought as he halted and faced the onrushing figure, a legionary who slowed and carefully regarded Caleb's defensive stance and short sword. "Does the Emperor send you for my head?" Caleb spat at him.

"What?" the man asked, sounding confused by the question.

"Never mind. What do you want?"

"Are you the fighter known as Metellus?"

"What of it?"

"I am glad."

"Why should you be? Who are you?" Caleb demanded.

"I am Gavius—Third Legion Augusta . . . Palatine service." The man paused as if he expected Caleb to say something. "I must ask you something important to both of us."

"Ask."

"Why did you search among the slain children?"

Caleb studied him in the torchlight, then decided to hide nothing. The fact that a palace legionary was no match for him further emboldened him. "I was looking for my niece. If any harm has come to her, all of Rome shall pay—I promise you."

Astonishingly, the soldier nodded as if he understood and

even sympathized. "Does the name Valerius Licinius mean anything to you?"

Caleb hesitated for Valerius' sake, then decided that nothing remained to be lost. Besides, he would kill the legionary if need be. "He is my brother-in-law." He waited for the Roman to draw his short sword first. Even then, it would be no contest.

"I thank our Lord," the legionary sighed.

Caleb gaped at him. "*What* did you say?"

"I prayed for some way to steal his daughter out of the circus. Now I have been shown it. Come, please: We must not delay."

Talking in short bursts as they ran, the legionary explained that he had served under Valerius at the palace before it had been destroyed by the fire. In fact, the centurion had persuaded Gavius to convert. "He is the best man," the legionary said, "in a very bad place."

"This is true," Caleb conceded.

That morning, Gavius had been perplexed when one of the *vigiles* herding the Christian children into the circus had drawn him aside and whispered that he expected a reward for ferreting out a "spy of Chrestus" lurking in the Emperor's own retinue. The legionary had presented the watchman with an *aureus*—a lucky piece he had been carrying for years—and promised much more as long as the *vigil* kept quiet "until we can find out who this Valerius has for confederates." Then, as soon as the opportunity had presented itself, Gavius whisked Ruth away to the only hiding place he could think of—the gladiatorial baths—and had entrusted her safety to a slave, also a Christian, whose chore it was to regulate the flow of hot water into the pools of the *caldarius*.

Caleb now followed the legionary through this steamy chamber, where a young Thracian was blissfully soaking in a porphyry tank. "Ah, Master Metellus!" he cried with admiration. "Today's games—what a travesty, yes? I was made to fence with a tailless ape from the hills of Mauretania!"

"What a surprise not to see the monkey in that tub instead of you," Caleb muttered, quickly stepping down a flight of stairs into a service corridor. It was flanked by huge boilers whose charcoal fires had been freshly banked. At the end of this torrid passage, the legionary stooped under one of the pipes that channeled hot air into the various chambers of the baths. He rapped softly on a half-size wooden door under which lamplight was leaking. "It is Gavius . . . and a friend we can trust," he whispered.

"Come," a high, almost feminine voice said from within.

Gavius gestured for Caleb to enter first.

Ruth was being jiggled on the eunuch's knee. She was dressed in two swatches of canvas that had been stitched together with strands of a *retiarius'* net. Eyes wide, she yanked her thumb out of her smiling mouth and, obviously thinking herself quite clever, mimicked the urchins of the Subura ward whenever they espied her famous uncle: "Hail Metellus! How many have you won now?"

Caleb then did something he had not done since an evening long ago on the heights above the Essene village of Mesad Hasidim: He wept. And he had no sooner dried his eyes on Ruth's coarse garment than another spate escaped him and he clutched the fragile body with renewed desperation.

"You must get her out of here as quickly as possible," Gavius said softly. "We burned the sheepskin they made her wear, and I'm sure no one noticed me take her, but still . . ."

"Yes, yes, I will go directly," Caleb said gruffly, choking down a sob before it crested. "But is there a way other than through the baths?"

"Indeed," the eunuch volunteered, "follow me if you will."

Caleb delayed the Christians briefly by seizing their forearms. "I thank you for my sister, her husband . . . but for myself as well."

Minutes and a labyrinth of crawlways later, the slave unbolted an iron door, and Caleb carried Ruth into the corridor that emptied into the gardens of the Vatican Hill.

Yet, before reaching the end of the tunnel, he glimpsed Valerius, who was being consoled by Aquila. Then Sarah came into view: She had withdrawn into the deepest part of herself, leaving a pallid and lifeless exterior for the world to see. Realizing that they had made the same assumption about Ruth's fate as he had, Caleb hefted the little girl over his head. She giggled, but neither of her parents noticed. Caleb lowered her and lengthened his stride, rushing to cut short this needless torment as quickly as possible.

Finally, Valerius trained his listless gaze on them. He looked vexed, frightened—perhaps wondering if his grief had lit upon some monstrous way to torture him, to dangle an apparition of his daughter before him. Blinking, he tried to banish the vision; but when he opened his eyes, it was still there. He pushed

Aquila aside and, with the word Ruth forming on his lips, staggered forward to greet them. His knees caved in before he had gone ten paces, and he sank to the flagstones, his hands clasped before him.

Sarah made a soft wailing sound that ended in tears of laughter.

"We have no time for weeping," Caleb said with a collected tone of voice, returning Ruth to her mother.

"Where . . . ?" she gasped.

"I will tell all, but first we must leave this place." Caleb turned to Corinna. "Help these children out of their lambskins. It must not be known that they are Christians." Then he helped Valerius to his feet. "Where have you been this past week?"

The centurion stared at him, dazed. "Why, fighting the fire."

"Fine job you did: My house is ashes."

"I see," Valerius said ineffably. Caleb had to nudge him to start him walking.

But as the small party trudged up the Janiculum and neared his house, Valerius halted. After having listened expressionless as Corinna and Aquila described the horrors that had passed for games in the arena that day, he seemed like himself for the first time since leaving the Emperor's circus. He glanced up at the orphaned children who had gone ahead a short distance with Sarah while he learned how their parents had died. "No more," he said.

"No more what?" Caleb asked.

Valerius unhitched his cloak and let it drop into the gutter. Motioning for Caleb to help him, he shucked off his cuirass and pitched it aside. The clattering sound made Sarah turn, her eyes quizzical. Next, he drew his *gladius* and broke the blade in two over a stepping-stone. Then he repeated: "No more."

"The Lord be praised," Aquila whispered.

"But what will you do now?" Caleb asked, suppressing a grin.

"We will get by." The former centurion again studied the children: The terrors of the day had been etched into their faces; he wondered if it would always be there, a visible memory no amount of time could erase. "But all of us will get by."

Sarah set down Ruth among the other children, who had nothing more than loincloths to wear. Then, wiping her eyes, she walked back down the street to her husband and embraced him. "I love you, Valerius Licinius."

XIII

THE kiln slaves had stamped the Emperor's name on each brick, so the mason, when he had the time, made it his habit to deface the mark of Nero with a surreptitious scrape of his trowel before scooping up another dollop of mortar. Then he would smile to himself, praying that whenever this wall was eventually demolished there would remain no symbol glorifying a Caesar who slew children for entertainment.

Like most of the buildings in Rome, the tenement he was helping finish for his uncle, the master *structor* on this project, was largely made from a durable concrete. Brick was added only as a veneer on the surfaces facing the street; it was too expensive to use as the sole material for all but the grandest mansions. Marble and travertine were impossible to find in the stone markets: Nero had appropriated the supplies for the erection of his Golden House, the centerpiece for his Neropolis, which would arise from the ashes of the old capital.

The mason's uncle, Celsus Victorinus, now rested his lime-bleached hands on his hips and inspected his nephew's work. "A good job, Valerius," he said in his robust way, "and done faster than I expected of you. I'm pleased that being a soldier so long did not ruin you for honest labor."

"No, Uncle, but it came close." Valerius tapped another brick into place with the butt of his trowel handle. "Although there are certain adjustments I've had to make."

"Such as . . . ?"

"Ignoring the way the *vigiles* keep looking at me."

"How is that, my boy?"

"They eye me as if I'm a slave with running away on his mind."

Celsus spat. "That's what is wrong with these city-bred Latins—no offense to the memory of your poor dead father. I did like him, and I always said so. But, you see, your mother and I are different, being from the country. We know there's no shame in work. The only shame is on them what leave their labor to shiftless slaves. And what a way for a decent man to spend his day, doling out coins to his clients in the morning and wallowing on a dining couch all evening." He shook his fist against the azure sky. "Look at your most noble Romans: They all had dirt under their fingernails. Take old Cincinnatus, may the gods honor him as we do. Why, he let go of his plow, wiped his sweaty hands on his tunic, donned the toga he'd hung on a branch and then thrashed your bloody Aequian army like the no-nonsense workingman he was." He offered Valerius his wineskin and chuckled when his nephew took a long draught. "That's the way. Well, after these past months, can you say that you like the trade, my boy?"

"Yes, Uncle, it gives me peace . . . and quiet hours in which to pray."

Celsus raised an eyebrow. "What? Oh, I see." He glanced around the building site. "Where's your soldier friend this afternoon?"

"He'll be along shortly, I expect."

"Why does he keep coming like this?"

"He wants to quit soldiering as I did. He just doesn't know how to yet."

"Well, unless there's a rebellion or you got the likes of the Carthaginians knocking on your gate, I don't see the need for a bloody army. It's no more than a nursery for lazy men. . . ." Celsus finally realized that Valerius was impatient to get back to his work. "But it's time I let you finish this facing." He took a few paces, then halted and asked, "But you're sure you like what you're doing?"

"Yes, Uncle."

Satisfied, the man moved on in search of another laborer he could lecture.

Valerius settled back into the meditative rhythm of building one row of bricks atop another. Yet, surprisingly, after a morning of nothing but the most pleasant musings, he found himself recounting the string of imperial outrages Gavius had told him about.

Shortly after Valerius had resigned his *officium* and gone to work for his uncle, the legionary had begun to show up at whichever new building his former centurion was disguising to look like a brick structure. Preoccupied with the excesses of the Emperor and his retinue, Gavius seemed compelled to make these visits. He talked incessantly, eyes feverish, about this or that scandal Valerius would rather have not heard about, but endured for the sake of the man who had saved Ruth's life and perhaps his own.

"I wish I had your courage, Valerius, just to walk away from your pension—everything," Gavius had whined. "What am I doing? What do I want?"

"The same thing I held out for all these years: the hope that someday my Christian and Roman duties might be combined under one just banner."

"Yes, that's it!" Gavius said fervently. "Precisely!"

"But I do not believe that will happen within our lifetimes, dear friend. Nevertheless, it is the goal we are working toward. Despite our present misfortunes—the new persecution, the imprisonment of Peter in the Mamertine—our Lord and not Nero will be the one to forge a Rome of renewed vigor."

"Ah, without your encouragement I would go mad, Valerius Licinius." The legionary sighed. "They've elevated me to *optio,* you know."

"Congratulations," Valerius said earnestly.

"It's only until a new Third Legion centurion is shipped from North Africa to replace you."

"But be wary, Gavius. A palace promotion sometimes means that they want you to do some dirty work for them."

"In the name of God, I pray not."

Yet, Valerius' warning had been justified by the events that followed. Within a week, Gavius had appeared again, thoroughly beside himself. "Damn, but you were right." His eyes were red-rimmed and his lips thinned by anger. "I haven't slept a wink in two nights now."

"Why not?"

"A plot against Nero has been uncovered."

"Who's behind it—if you can say?"

"Dozens, maybe hundreds: It's widespread. Surely, these must be the Emperor's last days. But Calpurnius Piso has been implicated . . . and Annaeus Seneca."

"Seneca?" Valerius noticed that the other laborers were gawking at the agitated young *optio.* Wiping the mortar off his fingers onto his tunic, he led the legionary aside by the elbow. "What will happen to them?"

"You mean, what *has* happened to them," Gavius said,

fighting to keep his voice level. His words then came out of his mouth wrapped in a long sigh: "Our Lord forgive me, but I carried Nero's order to Seneca that he take his own life."

Valerius was silent for a moment. "How did he die?"

"Like a Roman. Piso, the poet Lucan, even Gaius Petronius—nearly all of the accused went with dignity and courage. More than I would have."

Valerius clasped the *optio* by the arms. "Listen to me, Gavius, I think it's past time you leave this service. It's beginning to harm your spirit. Do you understand what I say?"

The man nodded, his face a scowling mask. "You're quite right. I will give it serious consideration—believe me."

But Gavius remained with the palace guard, and several weeks later he interrupted Valerius as he was building a garden wall for a mansion being restored on the Caelian Hill. The *optio* was giddy and seemed drunk, although he did not smell of wine. "Last night," he said with an ineffable little giggle, "Nero accused the empress Poppaea of adultery. He knocked her to the floor and then kicked her to death. She was with child, you know. The birth was imminent, but the baby was destroyed as well. He was rehearsing her funeral oration when I left. . . ."

"My dear God." Valerius closed his eyes. "In time, Poppaea might have been converted. She was always curious about us."

"And this morning, Seneca's brother, Gallio, was denounced as a public enemy by Tigellinus and arrested by the guard."

"Gallio's a fair man. As proconsul of Achaia, he freed our brother Paul when the Corinthian sanhedrin brought false charges against him." Valerius shook his head. "I thought the Emperor said he was finished with the executions."

"That's right—he declared a general amnesty. Now, the Senate intends to hold him to it in Gallio's case. The man's innocent."

"At last, the Conscript Fathers show some spine."

Gavius rubbed the dark hollows under his eyes. "Perhaps, but Nero and Tigellinus will answer their boldness by murdering a few of them. The rest will quickly get the message."

Valerius studied the *optio* for a moment. "You really need to remove yourself from the capital."

"Yes, yes, I intend to. I'll take some leave soon, go to Campania . . . walk in the fields."

"How does Nero regard Peter after all this time? I mean, isn't it clear to him that pagan Romans and not Christians are perpetrating these plots against him?"

"Peter has been forgotten in the present chaos, but that makes him no closer to being a free man," Gavius had said. "I don't much hope he'll be released. Perhaps my faith has started to weaken. It is difficult to believe in a loving God when one spends his days in the company of Nero and Tigellinus."

Valerius now finished setting the last brick in a row and cleaned off his trowel in a bucket of water. Sensing that he was being watched, he slowly craned his neck and glimpsed Gavius, whom he had not seen in nearly a month, standing off at a distance. Furtively, the *optio* motioned for Valerius to approach.

"Gavius, my brother, how are you?" Valerius asked, sidling up to him.

The man did not immediately answer. There was a peculiar lack of expression to his facial movements, and he failed to grasp Valerius' right hand when it was offered. "About an hour ago," he finally said, "I led a detail of legionaries, praetorians and *vigiles* up to the gardens on the Vatican Hill." He smirked humorlessly. "The Emperor trusted no one unit enough to send it without the other two. He believes that we Christians are everywhere. He also probably believes that we are braver than we really are." His voice broke, but then he recovered himself and assumed the same withdrawn manner.

"Why were you sent there?" Valerius asked, although he already guessed the reason.

"To crucify Peter . . . the rock on which our Lord builds his church." Gavius' eyes narrowed as if what he had just said mystified him for some reason. "We're talking about *Peter* . . . the *rock*."

Valerius began fighting tears—and rage. "Is he still alive?"

"When I left, yes, barely. He asked me to crucify him upside down. He said he wasn't worthy to die in the same way as Jesus did." Gavius stared down at his sandals. "I didn't say a word when Tigellinus gave the order. They must know about me. Yes, that's it—I'm sure. And Peter . . . I know he's seen me at the meetings. But he never betrayed me. In fact, as he carried his cross past the Circus of Nero, he whispered, those sad eyes trained on me, 'Courage, brother.'"

Valerius overcame his momentary revulsion for the man and embraced him. "I'm going to the Vatican Hill. Do you want to accompany me?"

"I don't think so. I have other business now."

"Gavius . . . ?"

He looked up out of some torturous distraction. "Yes?"

"You must always remember that Peter himself denied our Lord. He was letting you know that he understood."

Hope lit the *optio*'s eyes. "Do you really think so?"

"Yes."

"There are others too," Gavius then said, as if volunteering some dark secret. "Twelve in all."

"Are they being crucified as well?"

The *optio* nodded. "So be careful, Valerius Licinius." Without another word, his eyes gliding over the top of Valerius' head as if he could not bear to lock gazes once again, he did an about-face and hurried off, changing direction twice without apparent reason.

Valerius was not the only Christian to have heard. Others he had seen at gatherings were now sifting through the dusky imperial gardens under a stripe of faded purple like that on an old toga. They kept to the cypresses, well below the crosses erected on the slope of the Vatican Hill. There was not much to be seen: Twilight had reduced everything at a distance to silhouette, although Valerius found it jarring to espy the figure inverted on a timber, his arms outstretched across a beam set low to the ground. Roman troops were milling around the man: The soldiers were not leaning on their spears, and there was an air of expectation about them, as if death was close at hand for their victim and they were eager to return to barracks.

"Hail, Valerius. . . ."

He spun around and beheld Linus, whose features were waxy and grave in the last light.

Together, they turned back to witness the crucifixions that easily could have been their own. "Forgive me," Valerius finally whispered, "but I keep wishing I had my short sword . . . so I might go down there and free him . . . our brothers."

"Peter would not have you forfeit your soul to win his release."

"I know."

"Of course you do, my dear friend." Linus rested his hand on Valerius' shoulder.

"Now we inherit the burden."

"We?"

"The Romans," Valerius said.

"But Paul still lives. Hopefully, he will soon join us from Spain."

"When I said Romans, I was thinking of him. The Empire is not roads, aqueducts, procurators; it's a foretaste of one world at peace, united. Paul, more than anyone else, has known and used this. It has taken a Jew from Cilicia to show us what our ancient Latin League shall eventually become. . . ."

Linus clutched Valerius' upper arm in warning: Praetorians, distinguished from the legionaries by the tall Attic crests on their helmets, had begun to approach the onlookers, asking them what business they had on the hill, and compelling some of them to denounce the Christian god before being permitted to go on their way. "We must leave—quickly," Linus said, his eyes gliding across an advancing line of guardsmen to fall on Peter's cross one last time. "He was a mirror held up to our Lord's comforting light. And this is a terrible pity, for that light had not yet stopped shining of its own accord. Hail and be well, Valerius."

"And peace to you, Linus."

Valerius skirted around the circus, windswept, darkened now but for a few torches sputtering in the arched niches that framed statuary of the Emperor. Caesar's various faces, imperious with resolution by daylight, were benighted, suggested some mindless ambition the former centurion thought appropriate.

Despite his weariness and sorrow, Valerius felt as he once had on the eve of a military campaign in North Africa: restless and apprehensive, yet secretly glad to have been part of events larger than himself. In truth, there was no place he would rather be than Rome, despite the perils of the hour. For the first time in years, he had no doubt he was worthy of his own life. The dangers served only to magnify that worth.

He was climbing the main street of his Janiculum neighborhood when a large figure stepped out from an alleyway, blocking his path. "Valerius?"

He sighed: It was Celsus. "You rather gave me a fright, Uncle."

The man chuckled. "A soldier-boy like you? Scared of an old mortar-slinger like me?"

"What are you doing out here? Come inside for a drop of hot wine."

Celsus lowered his voice. "Some other night, lad." He hesitated. "I bring sad news for your ears, and didn't want to upset your pretty Sarah."

"Dear God, is it Mother? Has something happened . . . ?"

"No, no, she's fine. She'll outlive the lot of us. It's your friend, the legionary. . . ."

"Gavius?"

"Well, whatever the poor boy's name was. After you quit for the day, he came back to the site, kicking about, head up in the clouds. He didn't explain himself, so we figured he was waiting on you. I lost track of him—until I made a sweep of the *insula* as I always do at day's end. Tools are a big expense, and the lads never stow them proper—"

"What has happened to Gavius?"

His uncle snuffled loudly: He was readily moved by misfortune, and Valerius now knew that there was no hope that his friend was alive. "He used his sword . . . opened his wrists," Celsus said.

Valerius' silence became unbearable for the man. "Say something, Julius Valerius."

Valerius roused himself with a shudder. "I'm sorry . . . I was standing here wishing I could say this is a shock to me."

"It isn't?"

"No, I knew this would happen. And I ignored its coming."

"Ah, there's no wisdom in blaming yourself. The shame is on luck's head."

"The shame belongs to the palace. And it's not just because of the intrigues, the poisonings. Those can be uncovered in the best of realms. It's the meaninglessness of all that cruelty. Bad men can exist on their pleasures, but Gavius needed a vision . . . the one that slowly withered inside him." Valerius' eyes had begun to burn. "I could've helped him find other work. I could've—"

"The choice was his. And you should give thanks to the gods, lad."

"Thanks?"

"That might've been you this afternoon, bleeding away in an empty tenement."

Valerius held his uncle's stare, then slowly nodded. "Yes . . ." He did not add that this had been his first thought upon hearing of the legionary's death. It had given him a surge of relief that had tainted his sorrow. He now felt enormously selfish. "Well, Sarah will be wondering where I am. Will you dine with us, Uncle?"

Celsus waved off the invitation. "I must be home to my own couch. Just one more thing, lad . . ."

"Yes?"

"Things are bound to get rougher for folks of your persuasion. I have a friend in Florentia—another builder. He's doing a bridge and could probably use one more mason. There's not the high feeling against Christians in that city that there is in Rome."

"Thank you, Uncle, but I belong here."

"Are you sure? Think of Sarah, your child."

"I am. The Lord is no less caring for our safety in Rome than He would be in Florentia. Besides, this is my city. I was born here."

"As you please, Nephew, but I can prevail upon my friend to give you work."

"I'd prefer a world in which we prevail upon no one," Valerius said with a smile.

"Now, what kind of Empire would that attitude leave us, boy?"

Laughing weakly, Valerius hugged his uncle, then ambled on toward his house. He lingered in the portal for a few moments, praying, giving thanks for the sense of purpose that was allaying his terror, which was palpable only in the form of his tightened throat. Then he asked for clemency in Gavius' behalf. In his distress and confusion, the *optio* had fallen back on what Romans held to be an honorable retreat from hopelessness. So his only transgression had been this: He had failed to value himself, the need Linus had for him in preserving the fledgling church in the imperial capital. ". . . And I thank you, Lord, for making it plain to me that no man can serve that which he detests—not without destroying himself," Valerius concluded in a hush. "Amen."

The atrium was deserted, but he heard voices from the dining chamber. The house was barren of much of its furniture; Valerius, with Sarah's approval, had sold the couches, ornate lamps and curule chairs—all to help feed the numerous orphans left by Nero's atrocities. Her only comment had been that she had never thought Roman furniture very comfortable.

In the small dining chamber, Valerius found his wife and daughter joined by Caleb and Corinna, who was holding an infant of only a few months. "What is this?" he asked.

"A baby," Caleb said, ripping off a hunk of bread from the loaf.

Corinna was beaming. "Aquila begged us to take him. His parents died that day in Nero's circus. He is really quite good. He seldom cries."

Caleb looked askance at her.

"Well," she quickly amended, "when he does cry, it is always for a reason."

Valerius smirked at his brother-in-law. "Excellent Roman stock."

"Jewish," Caleb insisted. "Well, half Jewish."

"His mother was a Jewess, his father an Etrurian. They were both slaves before..." Corinna did not finish; her eyes grew sad.

"But that is why Aquila thought it fitting we should take him." Caleb tweaked the baby's foot to awaken him, earning a glare from Corinna.

"What have you named him?" Valerius asked.

"Joshua." When the Roman said nothing after several seconds, Caleb muttered, "Is something wrong with that?"

"No... our Lord was called by that name. But have you given thought to a Latin praenomen as well? It will make things easier for him in the city."

"You mean something like *Metellus*?"

"Yes."

Caleb chuckled. "A first name like Quintus or Marcus will not make things easier for him in Jerusalem."

"Jerusalem?" The effect of this single word rippled across Valerius' face like a stone dropped in a pool. Stiffly, he turned into Sarah and saw for the first time that she had recently recovered from crying.

"Tomorrow they sail," she said, "from Ostia."

"First to Puteoli, and then by another ship to Caesarea. Corinna shall see Judea in the springtime." Of the foursome,

only Caleb seemed to be of buoyant spirits. He helped himself
to more bread. "You, Brother-in-law, are finally doing what
you want. It has made you a better man." Then his eyes shifted
toward Corinna. "No longer must I put off this voyage. When
it is finished and we are standing on Judean soil, I, too, will
be a better man."

"What do you think of this, Corinna?" Unconsciously, Valerius had taken Sarah's hand under the table.

"It will be an adventure. I am looking forward to it."

"But you will be leaving Rome . . . perhaps forever."

Her eyes were wistful but also slightly amused. "There is
no way to leave Rome, Valerius Licinius. It is part of each of
us, even if we hate the Empire. There was a time I would've
gladly fled because I despised the Caesars. But now I go for
a better reason: I want to share a new life with my husband."

Caleb was looking at his sister: "You might think about
going home."

"Me?" As if wanting to change the subject, Sarah lifted
Ruth onto her lap and pried the child's thumb out of her mouth.

"Yes, both of you. Valerius is the least offensive Roman I
have ever known. I'm sure he can find something to do in
Jerusalem."

Valerius was watching Sarah too intently to respond to Caleb's backhanded compliment. Her face began to burn under
the confluence of inquisitive gazes. But then she composed
herself and said firmly, "I have grown fond of this house. It
was in the next room that Ruth was born. I believe we shall
stay."

Valerius squeezed her hand, hard.

"Then it is time," Caleb said. "We have hired a carriage
that is waiting at a stable on the Via Ostiensis." He rose and
relieved Corinna of the baby, who languidly opened a dark
blue eye on him, then closed it again.

Valerius suggested that Sarah, Ruth and he accompany them
to Ostia, returning to Rome on the same carriage in the morning. The night was clear and vividly starlit, but his plan was
quietly put aside after a brief enthusiasm for it. Sarah argued
that the trip would leave Ruth cranky for days, although Valerius guessed her real objection from the liquidity of her eyes:
She saw no wisdom in prolonging this moment of heartache.

Holding her bottom lip between her teeth, she first embraced
Corinna and then her brother as best she could without awak-

ening the infant. "I'm frightened I'll never see you again," she whispered in Aramaic.

"You mustn't think that. It will make the distance seem greater than it is. I will never be separate from you. Mother and our sister Ruth will never be apart from you. That is because we are a *people*—something these empire-builders will never understand." He turned to Valerius and said in Latin, "Be careful for the sake of my loved ones. You could not have chosen a more foolish time to become a Nazarene."

"And you as well, in returning to the life of a Zealot. Honor the peace, my brother."

"If possible."

"And may the Lord watch over you."

Caleb shrugged. "It has always been so. Come, Corinna." He was outside the portal when he suddenly halted, handed young Joshua to his wife and strode back over the threshold. He clutched Ruth for the dozenth time that evening. Then he grasped Valerius' hand—in the Roman fashion.

XIV

As soon as he saw the centurion and his host of praetorians waiting on the quay at Puteoli, Paul knew that it was finished. He had received no assurance at the outset of this trip that all would pass without harm. For years, he had anticipated such a sign. He did not find his sense of relief at this moment strange—not after his myriad flights from the executioner, the encounters with brigands along countless mountain trails, the stormy sea crossings.

It was time, and his heart was not heavy. His greatest fear, even in his days at *Rabban* Gamaliel's school, had been the humiliation of failure. Now it could be said that he had not failed: Churches were thriving in many cities of the Empire.

"Paul of Tarsus," the centurion announced, "by order of Lord Tigellinus, prefect of the praetorian guard, you are to be conveyed to the Mamertine Prison."

"I understand." Paul suspected that a member of the crew had betrayed his identity to a garrison at one of the ports the ship had visited after leaving Spain, but he did not turn to accuse the seamen with a stare. Quietly, he allowed himself to be escorted to Rome.

There, a week passed and no imperial functionary appeared to confront him with charges. He began to fear that he would be forgotten in his cell—denied his right, as a citizen, to defend his cause. But then one morning, the bolt was slid back, and a centurion of the Seventh Legion marched through the door and dismissed the warder who had admitted him into Paul's chamber.

The Cilician stared at him a long moment before crying in a hush, "Blessed Lord—it is Julius!"

Valerius seized the man's hands. "I have little time."

"But as a *centurion,* a trusted officer—"

"This is all pretense. I'm wearing my father's old uniform."

"I don't understand, Julius."

"I quit my service some months ago. The warders have seen me here before on palace business. I lied and told them I had a message from the Emperor for you. It worked . . . but one of them may know about me and send a courier to the Golden House."

"Yes, yes." Paul gripped Valerius' hands until his own were white with trembling. "They have forbidden me to write. I must get a letter to our brethren in—"

"A moment." Valerius turned his ear toward the corridor, listened for footfalls, then whispered, "This is why I have come: You must delay them. Use whatever means you must. The Empire is in terrible confusion, and finally it appears that Nero's days are numbered. The legions in the provinces may have already revolted. The praetorian guard is even reported to be grumbling about this bad actor they have for a master. So make them hold off a decision in your case. Meanwhile, we shall pray for a new and more honorable emperor."

Paul smiled warmly. "It will not come soon enough."

"You must hope."

"Oh, I do, dear Julius. But my body can't be preserved forever, even if I'm freed from this place. So all my hopes ride on the eternal life my spirit shall enjoy." He let go of Valerius. "Now, is our brother Timothy here in Rome?"

"Yes."

"Excellent—while in Spain, I received a missive from him telling of his intention to join me here. What I now say is for him to put in a letter that will assure our brethren." Paul wiped his large brow, gathering his thoughts. "Tell him that the Lord has not granted us a spirit of fear but one of strength and love. Although we are persecuted like criminals, we should not be ashamed to be a witness to his love. The time has come for me to join him. I am filled with happiness—yes, make certain that it is known, Julius. I have kept the faith—"

Their gazes glided to the door: A warder was looming there, his expression confused. "Centurion, a praetorian runner has just arrived from the *castra praetoria*. He says that he comes in advance of an execution detail for this prisoner. Is that why you are here?"

"This . . . this man is a Roman!" Valerius sputtered.

"That has been taken into account, sir. He will be beheaded rather than crucified."

"No . . . no, that is wrong."

"Would you care to speak to the guardsman yourself?"

"I would. Tell him I am on my way."

The warder hurried down the corridor.

Paul spoke tersely under his breath. "Ignore this praetorian and leave immediately."

Valerius shook his head no. "If I do that, it is the same as denying you."

"If you go now, you can live to proclaim the truth I die for. Don't you see? Staying is the same as denying all I have struggled for. Go, Julius, I beg you in behalf of the living God."

"But how can we continue without you? Our abilities in these matters are too meager. We know so little. We are so simple, Paul, and the issues are so great."

"You will have the sincerity of God to sustain you. And it pleases him that you are artless, lacking in guile—"

"Centurion!" the warder's voice bawled from down the passageway.

Paul lowered his head, then closed his eyes. "Go."

A moment later, Valerius' sandals could be heard scraping over the flagstones.

The Cilician smiled.

Epilogue

"I must walk," Caleb said to Corinna on the quay at Puteoli.

She nodded in agreement from the midst of her own irritation: Young Joshua had not been eating, and she sat on a sack of wheat with him, coaxing the infant to take a dollop of moistened breadcrumbs off her fingertips. He refused and cried desolately. She sighed.

Growling under his breath, Caleb strode away. Only this morning—after a delay of two weeks due to a storm—had their ship arrived from Malta. The *Twin Brothers* was secured to the stone landing, but the captain would allow no passengers to board until his cargo was off-loaded.

Yesterday at dawn the earth had trembled alarmingly for a few seconds and the night fog had reeked of sulphur — an omen, surely. Gazing now across the bay at the temples and grandiose villas of Baiae, Caleb murmured to himself, "Your time is at hand."

"What was that?" An authoritative voice intruded on his thoughts.

Caleb turned and met the narrowed eyes of a praetorian guard. He resisted the urge to glance down the quay to check on Corinna's safety—that would only betray her to the Romans. "I said nothing," he finally answered.

"What is your name?"

"Metellus."

The praetorian's eyes widened a bit. "The famous *retiarius*?"

"Yes."

Suddenly, the Roman became quite affable. "*You*, certainly, are no Christian."

Caleb glared in reply.

"We are seeking a member of this sect who is attempting to flee Italy with seditious correspondence." The praetorian winked conspiratorily. "We'd like to question him about this message of love. Do you, by any chance, know of a Christian named Timothy?"

Caleb shook his head no.

"Then be on your way."

But Caleb had taken only a few paces when the guardsman barked at him to halt. "Yes?" he asked over his shoulder.

"I look forward to seeing you fight one day soon, Metellus." Caleb smiled, tightly. "You shall, my friend—I promise."

The spray over the figurehead of Castor and Pollux was relentless. Corinna had taken refuge from the darts of saltwater by crouching behind the canvas weather cloth. She nested the baby in her lap and was murmuring to him. Caleb, who was standing squarely against the wind, turned his head and smiled at her.

"Does he sleep?"

She brought her finger to her lips.

Caleb knelt and stroked the baby's fine dark brown hair. "Joshua—"

"Shhh!" Corinna protested.

"Joshua . . . Jesus. Velerius was right: They mean the same. So much of our story as a people in those names. A patriot for whom God stopped the sun and the moon until our nation could take vengeance on its enemies." Caleb ran his sword-calloused fingers along the baby's tender cheek. "And a prophet of love who died on a cross . . . but continues to trouble Rome, for reasons I don't understand."

Joshua began whining, and Corinna brought her mouth close to his ear and softly sung:

> "When you hear the wolf howl,
>   Feel no fear.
> Romulus and Remus
>   Dropped no tear
> When they heard the wolf howl
>   Near and near;
> Mama is coming,
>   Mama is near . . ."

Caleb rose again to watch the decline of the sun over the isle of Capri, the outlines of the villa Jovis—Tiberius's old mansion—obliterated by the brilliance and sheen of the light. "May the praetorians be blind to your escape, Timothy— whoever you are."

Bestsellers you've been hearing about—and want to read

More Bestsellers from Berkley
The books you've been hearing about and want to read